A Murderous Tangle

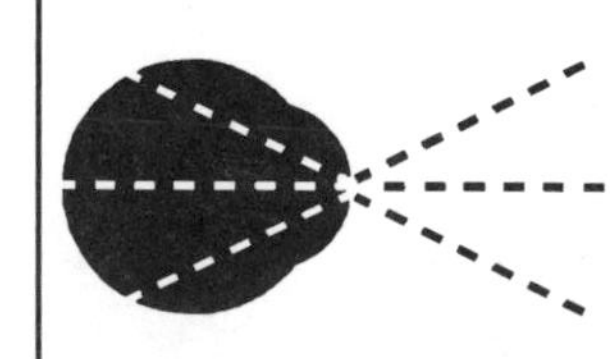

This Large Print Book carries the
Seal of Approval of N.A.V.H.

A Murderous Tangle

Sally Goldenbaum

WHEELER PUBLISHING
A part of Gale, a Cengage Company

Wheeler Publishing Large Print Cozy Mystery.
The text of this Large Print edition is unabridged.
Other aspects of the book may vary from the original edition.
Set in 16 pt. Plantin.

LIBRARY OF CONGRESS CIP DATA ON FILE.
CATALOGUING IN PUBLICATION FOR THIS BOOK
IS AVAILABLE FROM THE LIBRARY OF CONGRESS

ISBN-13: 978-1-4328-7171-0 (softcover alk. paper)

Published in 2019 by arrangement with Kensington Books, an imprint of Kensington Publishing Corp.

Printed in the United States of America
1 2 3 4 5 6 7 23 22 21 20 19

For Sister Rosemary Flanigan,
Mentor and dear friend

A MURDEROUS TANGLE CAST

The Seaside Knitters

Birdie (Bernadette) Favazza: Sea Harbor's wealthy, wise octogenarian

Cass Halloran (Catherine Mary Theresa): Co-owner of Halloran Lobster Company; married to Danny Brandley

Izzy (Chambers) Perry: Former attorney, owner of the Seaside Knitting Studio; married to Sam, an award-winning photographer; toddler daughter, Abby

Nell Endicott: Retired nonprofit director, married to Ben Endicott, retired lawyer and family business owner

Friends and Townsfolk

Annabelle Palazola: owner of the Sweet Petunia Restaurant

Archie and Harriet Brandley: owners of the Sea Harbor Bookstore and Danny Brandley's parents

Bobby Abbott: owner of the Harbor Club

bar; Robert Abbott's son

Clark and Penny Turner: veterinarian and his receptionist wife

Ella and Harold Sampson: Birdie's housekeeper and groundskeeper/driver

Elizabeth Hartley: headmistress of Community Day School

Esther Gibson: police dispatcher

The Fractured Fish band: Andy Risso, Pete Halloran, and Merry Jackson

Gabby Marietti (Gabrielle): Birdie Favazza's granddaughter

Gus McGlucken: owner of McGlucken Hardware Store

Gracie Santos: owner of the Lazy Lobster and Soup Café

Harry and Margaret Garozzo: owners of Garozzo's Deli

Helen Getty: Bobby Abbott's wife

Jake Risso: owner of the Gull Tavern

Jane and Ham Brewster: former California hippies; founders of the Canary Cove Art Colony

Jerry Thompson: police chief

Laura Danvers: mother and philanthropic leader; daughter Daisy

Liz Santos: manager of Sea Harbor Yacht Club

Lucky Bianchi: friend of Cass and Pete Halloran

Mae Anderson: yarn shop manager
Mary Pisano: newspaper columnist; owner of Ravenswood B and B
M.J. Arcado: salon owner, married to Fire Chief Alex
Merry Jackson: owner of the Artist's Palate Bar & Grill; singer in band
Pete Halloran: Cass's brother; co-owner of Halloran Lobster Company
Tess Bean: staff at veterinary clinic and part-time environmental science teacher
Tommy Porter: police detective

CHAPTER 1

It would be days later, after the December days took on a new kind of chill, that Gabrielle Marietti would look back on the episode in the cove with a clarity — and a fear — that would startle her.

But on that day — a chilly December afternoon — she felt no alarm or fear or foreboding. Instead, what she experienced was a powerful sense of nature: of deep blue-black water, the salty taste of the air, and the shiver of the cold breeze as it lifted the dark hair on the back of her neck. She'd felt the sun coming through the pine trees and the voices that traveled across the cove. The power of nature.

And then another kind of power. *Girl power.* That's what Gabby had thought that day.

But in hindsight, the colors and sounds would change. The breeze turned sinister, the wintry chill a warning. And the memory would make Gabby close her eyes and will it all to disappear.

It was a school day, but her grandmother knew she liked to loosen her legs, wander a bit after being cooped up for too many hours in a classroom. Some days Gabby would wander around the docks, where Cass Halloran's lobster crews kept their traps and boats, and colorful fishermen wandered around. She loved their stories and jokes and how they welcomed her as if she were ageless, like so many of them.

Other days she and her friend Daisy would head over to Izzy's yarn shop to help unpack boxes of yarn or watch customers' kids in the shop's playroom — the Magic Room, they called it. But the outdoors was Gabby's natural habitat. That was where she felt truly free. And that was where, one day after school, she'd discovered the private cove that she soon claimed as her own.

Her *nonna* Birdie said that when she was young, she was that way, too — needing space and time for being alone with her thoughts and feelings. Her *nonna* liked stretching her arms out wide and shouting into the wind. Something they both agreed didn't play well in the middle of Harbor

Road. But sitting in the cove all by herself, Gabby's shouts were embraced fully by nature, sometimes with nature whistling or crooning right back at her. And she loved imagining her *nonna* doing the same thing.

It was through a different lens that Ella Sampson, Birdie Favazza's housekeeper, saw twelve-year-old Gabby's need to wander. "Your grandmother worries, Gabrielle Marietti. You keep in touch with her. Always. Always let her know your whereabouts."

The housekeeper's words echoed in her head as Gabby checked the time on her cell phone, then tapped in a message: Biking and writing — not at the same time. Heading home soon. What's for dinner?

Gabby was never sure if the texts were for Ella or for her grandmother. Birdie had told Gabby often that she didn't worry. Not really, she said. Or at least she tried not to. *Pretended not to* was Ella's take. But Birdie was quick to coat both Ella's comments and her own expressions with the fact that she trusted her granddaughter fully. She knew Gabby had common sense. She knew right from wrong. Gabby agreed.

But Ella had made Gabby swear on a Bible, anyway, promising to keep all worry away from her grandmother. Then Ella had hugged Gabby tightly and told her she loved her like her own child, but she loved her employer more. And if Gabby didn't do as Ella said, she might be responsible for Birdie having a heart attack, painting the awful possibility vividly enough to give Gabby nightmares two nights in a row.

She loved her grandmother more than almost anyone alive, other than maybe her father. Killing her *nonna* was a seriously horrendous thought. But for a twelve-year-old who had mostly grown up in a New York penthouse with a globe-traveling father, no mother, and more freedom than God afforded birds (as the cook often told her), reporting in took great effort. But she did it. For her *nonna.*

And to escape Ella's wrath.

She slipped her phone into a pocket of her backpack and pulled her knees up to her chest. The old dock rocked beneath the movement, the waves choppy as they hit the shore. Gabby shivered. Winter was in the air. The holidays beginning. She hugged her heavy jacket close.

"Wear this one, my darling," Birdie had called out that morning, catching Gabby a second before she raced down the long circle drive to catch the school bus. She'd tossed the puffy down garment to her.

Gabby liked the cold — but was happy

for the jacket. Her nose and cheeks were turning red and her black hair flew wild and damp from the windy spray.

She loved this hidden cove — her special place. The abandoned dock, beaten by winds into a wobbly plank. The paths, tangled and overgrown with shadbush and greenbrier that challenged her as she lugged her bike through the undergrowth and down to the water's edge. She imagined what it would be like soon, covered in white, the trees bending beneath winter's weight. Quiet. Amazing.

She looked out over the perfect half-moon of water, the curve of land dotted with bushes and trees tangled from decades of ocean winds and tucked into the granite boulders that formed a hill rising above the water. This was her place. *Her* earth, as Tess Bean would say to her and the rest of the class. *Their* earth, one they had to protect and care for.

A gust of wind swept across the water, sending shallow waves lapping against the old pier. Gabby tightened her hold on her long legs — deer legs, people said. Too long. Gabby thought it was a good description of her whole body. It was *too* everything. Her freckles were too dark and too many. Eyebrows too thick. And her baseball cap only pretended to contain the mass of dark, too-thick waves now damp with sea air. She didn't much care, not usually, not often. The legs won track meets, and her *nonna* loved the freckles.

The harsh squawk of gulls broke the silence and pulled Gabby's attention to the opposite side of the cove. At first, her eyes were drawn to the tide, darkening the boulders at the shore's edge. And then, as if the rising tide had been but a harbinger, the sounds of foliage and birds scattering from danger drew her eyes halfway up the rocky incline, where a figure emerged from a stand of trees and tangle of sumac and bearberry.

She rarely saw people on that side, especially when the sea air grew heavy and the spray stung and colored cheeks. Gabby liked that — an isolated spot.

She leaned forward now, squinting to bring the intruder into focus. Another followed, emerging from the trees and following the other. Smaller. The first was clearly a man, tall and nondescript with a mud-colored hoody covering him like a monk. He seemed to be laughing at what the woman was saying behind him.

The woman's head was bare and a heavy sweatshirt covered her whole body, disguising her shape.

Just then, a billowing cloud shadowing the cove moved on its way, allowing a ray of afternoon sunshine to light the woman from behind, her shaggy yellow-white hair shimmering like an angel's halo.

Gabby's mouth dropped open. And then she grinned.

It was Tess. Amazing Tess.

There was no mistaking her now. She had walked onto the smooth plane of a boulder close to the water. Her stance was familiar, resolute and strong, and it made her seem even taller than Gabby's gangly height, even though Tess was shorter. The haircut was unmistakable. The same one that every seventh-grade girl at Sea Harbor Community Day School coveted: thick white and gold strands that looked like they'd been shaped by Ella's pinking shears. A careless look — hair escaping from whatever she'd used to control it — hairpins, bands, a baseball hat. Gabby and her friends coveted its cool, exotic messiness, one they all wished they could mimic and that was made even more dramatic by the rumors that said Tess cut her own hair. She was most definitely the best part-time teacher the school had ever hired.

She stood just a foot or two beyond the man, talking, her small hands gesturing in sync with her words. Passionate words, Gabby guessed. Tess was a passionate woman. An occasional word broke free of a sentence and floated across the water to where Gabby sat.

Garbage. Killing fish. Spoiled. Always. Always.

Gabby frowned, not sure of what was happening. She started to get up, to wave at the woman whose convictions and wise words about clean water and wasted food and global warming were still rattling around in Gabby's head — words she had heard earlier that day in science class. Words she had minutes before recorded on her tablet, along with other things Tess had taught them and her thoughts about it all.

The man seemed unperturbed by Tess's tirade, uninterested in whatever the woman was saying to him. Maybe not even listening. Or laughing away the message. *Cocky.*

He took a step closer to the water's edge, where the rising tide rose nearly up to his sneakers. He leaned over, picking up a handful of small rocks from the sliver of shore. Then, one by one, he tossed them into the water as if unaware of the woman standing a few steps away. Ignoring her in a way that seemed practiced. As if she weren't there. Or didn't matter.

But he did know she was there. Of course he did. Finally he lifted his head and stood up, looking over at her and raising his own hand. He spoke loudly, his words carried on the breeze.

"A tree-hugging babe," he said. "Bean-babe. Geesh, trees? Plastic?"

His laughter followed his words, rolling across the cove like a bowling ball. Gabby tensed up. The man laughed again and took a step in Tess's direction, his hood falling around his neck as he moved.

The scene was surreal. Gabby bit down on her bottom lip and willed herself still.

But Tess didn't look frightened at all. She took a step closer to him and cut his words off sharply, slicing the air with her hand like a machete.

The man didn't look deterred, his words muffled now. His back was straight and his shoulders broad, nearly blocking Tess from sight. He took a step toward her.

The wind picked up and Gabby felt something building deep inside herself, even more powerful than the beating of her heart. She pulled herself upright and stepped to the end of the old dock.

She stared intently across the water. But before she could frame her emotions sensibly, before she could yell out for Tess to do something — to run or hide — before she could do a single thing, Tess took over. She shouted at the man, a sound that reached Gabby's ears like an animal sound. Angry and loud. The man didn't move, not even when Tess took the next step — a long one that brought her inches away from the man facing her.

Tess wasn't afraid. Not at all. Gabby could see that clearly now, even from her distant post. Just mad. She'd seen it before, how she could stand up to people who were refusing to correct their ways. Fearless. Bold.

Gabby grinned and shielded her eyes from the late-afternoon sun, peering intently at the drama being played out across the cove. A drama, for sure. She wondered what act this one was? And what would the last act be?

She watched as Tess raised her hands out in front of her, and with a strength that betrayed her size, she placed her palms flat on the chest of the man in front of her. And then she pushed.

At first, the man teetered like a wobbly set of dominoes, arms and legs not connecting to his body. Seconds later, he arched backward, arms flailing, and his long body flying into the shallow, freezing water of the cove.

A spray of water rose up to where Tess, still watching silently, stood. Her words were loud, intended to reach the flailing man. "That's my thanks. For nothing."

Gabby's breath came out in a whoosh. She snapped her mouth closed and squinted so hard her eyes hurt, forcing the scene into focus. The man's hoodie billowed like a balloon around him as he lay on the shallow rocky bottom. Tess leaned forward, her hands on her knees, watching while the man grabbed an outcropping of weeds and began to pull himself safely from the frigid water.

Gabby waited, her breath caught in her chest, her eyes moving from the creature rising from the sea, spraying water wildly, to the woman pulling herself upright, still watching as the man regained his footing.

A stream of profanity floated up as the man tugged at strands of seaweed caught in his sodden jeans and sweatshirt.

But Tess didn't move. Just looked, watching while the man regained his balance.

Then one word traveled down to the man, and across the water to where Gabby stood, listening, watching, waiting for the next act.

"Payback," Tess said. And then she calmly turned and climbed back up the rocky incline, through the scrub bushes until the evergreens at the top seemed to part for her, then close gently behind as she disappeared into the fading day.

Gabby stood frozen on the dock, processing the scene that had played out in front of her.

She watched the man strip off his soaking sweatshirt and stare into the trees after her, making no move to follow. He was shaking his head, as if in wonder. Or terrible anger. She couldn't be sure.

Had he looked the other way, he might have seen Gabby standing there on the dock, her face registering awe and amazement and pleasure at what one heroic woman had done.

"Girl power," Gabby whispered, a smile filling her whole face.

Chapter 2

Birdie Favazza brushed a speck of dirt from her wool pants and wrapped her fingers around the door handle of the Lincoln Town Car, hushing her driver's desire to race around and open the door for her. Her age didn't equate to feeble, she had told him more times than she could count. And the fact that Harold Sampson, her grounds-keeper, chauffeur, and a multitude of other things, might still be adequate behind the wheel of her Lincoln, he himself was slightly more stooped than Birdie, and no spring chicken.

"It's cold out there, dear," she said, patting Harold's arm. "I certainly have enough strength in this seasoned body to open a car door."

And then she paused for a brief moment, taking a moment to breathe in the familiar scent that lingered in the car.

Even after all these years, the grand old

car still smelled of Sonny Favazza, dead for decades but leaving behind the sweet scent of cherry pipe tobacco. It was still there, hiding in the creases of the aged leather seats. Right alongside a passel of memories and emotions that fueled Birdie's soul.

Although other men had shared Birdie's life after Sonny's early death, he was her complete love, the one who filled her heart fully and remained there always. It was Sonny who walked through life with her. The one she talked to first when she needed advice or a listening ear. The one she whispered a Godspeed to before closing her eyes every night of her life. And the one she awoke to each morning, as if Sonny had been beside her all night long, holding her close beneath the down comforter. Sharing her life, her day.

Like she had done that morning — and again, now on the ride to Izzy's yarn shop. Harold sat in the front, humming along to an old tune on the radio and leaving Birdie with quiet time.

Sonny hadn't been much help that morning, though, but she couldn't blame him. He was surely as confused as she was at being the grandparent of a twelve-year-old child. Burgeoning on young womanhood, really, but still a child in so many ways.

"It's a challenge, my dear love," she whispered. "Help me to listen, to guide, to be as wise as you . . ."

Harold had pulled over and double-parked in front of the yarn shop, waiting patiently. Finally Birdie opened the door and stepped out into a bracing wind, but she held on to the car door for another minute — and on to the thoughts of Gabrielle Marietti.

When Gabby had come into Birdie's life unexpectedly a few years before, Birdie's heart had soared. The skeleton in her closet, some townsfolk had affectionately teased. Birdie ignored them. Her last husband had died without knowing he was a grandfather. And Birdie a step-grandparent, though the *step* had never entered into her relationship with Gabby. Not once. And it never would.

But what was more unexpected than Gabby's surprising appearance in Sea Harbor those years ago was the love that had swallowed Birdie whole, jarring her with its intensity. Filling her up like a balloon.

The love between the two of them had grown into a force that Birdie thought would keep her alive forever. And the bond seemed to grow deeper and more profound as Gabby grew.

But this year Birdie had sensed something different about Gabriella Francesca Marietti. Her granddaughter had made the choice to come back to Sea Harbor and to attend Sea Harbor Community Day School rather than a school in Italy while her father built a new factory there.

Gabby was taller than she had been the summer before. That was to be expected, of course. Birdie's chin required an upward tilt now when she talked to her granddaughter. And the whites of her eyes were still very clear, the irises bachelor button blue. Arresting eyes.

But changes were there, subtle differences. Gabby's long black braid still hung down between her shoulder blades, wisps escaping as if the braid was well-worn, like a frayed knit sweater. But these days it was streaked with a lovely band of pink.

"For breast cancer awareness," Gabby had explained to Birdie.

And as for breasts, Gabby had the beginning of those, too. The small buds of a year ago were no longer invisible, hiding beneath worn T-shirts. Now they changed the contour of sweet Gabby's body beneath her cotton shirts. And even the T-shirts were different, especially the ones her granddaughter favored — the ones her school environmental club was silk-screening, emblazoned with messages like *Think Green,*

I Speak for Trees, and *Save Our Ocean.* Gabby had even made one for Birdie. It featured three happy little yellow bees with their message: *If we die, we're taking you with us.*

Gabby. Her Gabby. This wonderful little person who had changed her life. Now if only Birdie's decades-old mind and body could keep up with this gift she'd been given.

Behind her, Harold's voice and a honking horn caused Birdie to jump. Only then did she realize she was standing still beside the car. In the street. In the cold. With Sonny's mighty Lincoln blocking traffic.

"You all right, Miz Birdie?" Harold had rolled down the window and was leaning out the window, concern deepening the hollows in his long face.

Birdie shook her small head. "Of course I'm all right, Harold. Why wouldn't I be? Now off with you," she said, waving her small hand in a queenly way. "I am fit as a fiddle." For emphasis she straightened her small back, rising to her full five feet and stepped briskly away from the car and up the curb.

She waved at Father Northcutt, the local priest, who was coming out of the bookstore next door, a bright red scarf flapping about his chins, his jowled face filled with a kindly smile. Then she turned and walked toward the bright blue door of Izzy Perry's yarn shop, wrapped in ropes of greens and tiny white lights.

Birdie paused briefly at the door, images of Gabby still spinning about her. *My granddaughter.* Imagine that. A sudden rush of cold wind ruffled her short white bob as she pressed a thin blue-veined hand against her heart. She looked down as her hand moved slightly with the beat. In and out. In and out.

Goodness, she thought. *Who ever thought one's heart could grow so large?*

Izzy Perry knew she'd be late getting back to her knitting shop, but having Mae Anderson, the world's finest manager on duty, eased her worry. If Mae were in charge of the whole world, it would run more efficiently. Or so the gray-haired, bossy Mae often reminded her much younger boss. Izzy's bigger concern was that the Thursday-night knitting group might go rogue. Her very good friend Cass Halloran in particular.

Cass, who co-owned the Halloran Lobster Company, had been far more familiar with pearls found in oysters than a kind of knitting stitch when she joined the four-woman knitting group those years earlier. But when she walked past Izzy's yarn shop one evening, and an aromatic wave of garlic and butter and wine were pouring out the door, she was pulled directly into the knitting shop's back room. Forever more, Thursday-night knitting was a sacred part of her week. Although she had finally learned how to knit caps for her lobster crew, Cass came mainly for Nell Endicott's savory soups and casseroles.

And although the dark-haired lobsterwoman was a trim and fit forty-year-old, she always ate enough for two. Izzy knew if she didn't get back to the shop soon, she'd be scraping the bottom of the casserole, and the wine bottles could quite possibly be empty. She felt a definite need for the wine tonight.

It's been one of those days, she'd texted to her husband, Sam Perry. Please wait up for me.

Sam had texted an image back to her: the cover of one of their daughter Abby's favorite books: *Alexander and the Terrible, Horrible, No Good, Very Bad Day.*

It had made Izzy smile and decide that maybe the day hadn't been quite *that* bad. Or at the least, it would get better. Especially after Sam followed his first text up with an image of their little Abby's magnificent smile hidden behind a piece of chocolate cake.

She glanced over at the passenger in her car. He was her "first child." Wonderful Red. He'd come into her and Sam's life before little Abby was ever born. A dog stranded after his elderly owner had died. Old even then, Red was now a collection of achy joints. And Izzy wanted desperately to make every single one of them feel better.

She drove into the small parking lot and found a space near the front door, right beneath the freshly painted sign: TURNER ANIMAL CLINIC AND KENNELS. The clinic lights inside were on, and outside, the building eaves dripped with lit icicles.

Red looked up at her with soulful eyes.

"I know — it's cold out there," she whispered, "but you'll feel better soon." Izzy switched off the engine and circled around to the passenger door. She pulled it open and slid one arm beneath the sixty-five-pound dog, ready to ease him off the seat.

"Hey, wait. Let me help."

The voice came from behind Izzy's shoulder, and before she could turn completely around, a small body was wedging itself between Izzy and the dog.

"Hey, wait —"

"No, it's okay. I'm used to this. It's his hips that hurt, right? Goldens have problems with that. But you'd better move out of the way before we both freeze our butts off, not to mention the poor dog's."

Before Izzy could protest, the younger and shorter woman had elbowed her completely out of the way. In seconds she'd wedged her arms beneath Red and carefully scooped him up, all the while murmuring indecipherable words into the dog's ear.

Red seemed to be listening.

"Get the door," she said to Izzy. And then, a muffled afterthought: "Please?"

Red didn't seem to be objecting to the stranger, who was almost invisible now behind his bulk.

Izzy bit back the urge to grab her sweet dog from the arms of the bossy interloper. Izzy might be ten years older than this woman, but she was strong and fit and ran miles whenever she could fit it in. But she could see that the young woman knew where to hold Red comfortably. And she obviously had the muscles required to keep Red intact.

Once inside, the woman carried Red over to a nook on the far side of the waiting room. Here and there a poinsettia acknowledged the season, along with a contemporary version of "Jingle Bells" coming through corner speakers. Izzy remembered a magazine stand once filling the small alcove in the corner, but today, a round dog bed and a pile of soft blankets covered the floor area. The woman crouched down, settling Red on the pile.

Izzy looked at the woman's strong back. Streaked blond hair was pulled back and secured with a rubber band, but the cut was irregular and short, and strands escaped, messy and haphazard. She wore jeans and a nubby green sweatshirt with some kind of symbol on the back, sleeves rolled up now as she began to massage Red on the top of his head, the pads of her fingers circling lightly. Red seemed to be answering back, his body relaxing beneath her touch.

Izzy recognized something familiar about the messy hair and the glimpse of the profile, but before she could put the image together in a meaningful way, the receptionist called to her from across the room.

"Mrs. Perry, yoo-hoo. Over here." A young woman waved at her from behind the desk. "You're here to see Dr. Turner. Here's where you check in."

Izzy walked over to the desk. Maybe it was the worry about Red's joint pain that robbed her of patience today — or the troubling, long day in the store — or that she had asked Clark Turner's very young wife to call her Izzy, not "Mrs.," every time she came in. She held back a retort and softened her words.

"Hi, Penny. Mae Anderson called the clinic earlier for me and you nicely agreed to squeeze Red in. Thank you."

Penny scanned the computer screen, as if it were an important point. Her long red fingernails tapped the keys. "Yes, Mae Anderson called. This is about the dog, right? Not that cat you have?"

Izzy glanced across the room at Red. His mouth was slightly open, his tongue out and his eyes relaxed as fingers moved down his back, circling through his coat, kneading lightly.

"Yes. He has aches and pains. Arthritis. I need something to make him more comfortable." She realized she was explaining too much to Penny. Penny didn't deal well with details. Clark Turner had surprised all his clients a while back when he married her, a woman nearly half his age. And they were even more surprised when Clark had allowed her to work in the clinic. While tales of Penny's upstate Hooters career had followed her to Sea Harbor — that was about all they knew of her professional experience.

Moreover, most of the clinic's clientele realized quickly after meeting Penny Turner that she didn't like animals very much. Maybe not at all. Or so it seemed.

Penny sneezed, then wiped her nose, tossing the Kleenex into the wastebasket. "Dr. Turner will take care of that in a jiffy. He's really amazing." Penny straightened up on her high heels and beamed at her own mention of her husband's name. "But where is the dog — did you forget him?" She looked beyond Izzy and spotted Red, now stretched out in the cushioned alcove.

Penny frowned, her lips tightening. "Oh geesh!" She glared at the woman crouched over Red and released a torrent of words beneath her breath.

But all that Izzy heard were the soft murmurings coming from the corner. And what she saw was a completely relaxed Red and a woman crouched down next to him, whispering in his ear as she worked her fingers through Red's coat, kneading gently, then circling slowly, around and around, down his back toward the painful muscles near the dog's hips.

Izzy turned away from Penny and walked across the room, stopping a short distance from Red. She watched in amazement as the woman patted and rubbed his coat, kneading gently, then applying slight pressure, then gently again. All the while the woman's eyes were on Red, her soft words caressing him to the rhythm of her fingers.

Izzy was entranced.

"Miz Perry?" Penny called again, loud enough to turn the heads of two other pet owners in the room. She tapped her nails on the polished desktop. "It's your turn. And you can bring the dog. My husband will see you now. He'll make him feel like new. Hurry now."

Izzy hesitated, then hunkered down and looked at the woman hovering over Red, her face just inches from the woman's. "What is it that you're doing to Red?"

"*Effleurage.* Massage. It soothes the joints and muscles and makes it easier and less painful for him to get around. Getting up and down is the hardest. This helps, but you have to do it slowly, letting the dog guide the pressure."

Izzy's eyes were on her contented Red. He looked like he was about to fall asleep.

"Hey, sweet Red," she said softly.

The tail flopped back and forth. Finally Red lifted his head, then his body, his back legs seeking traction.

"He hasn't been able to do that easily —"

Izzy started to reach out to help him.

"Yeah. Dogs in pain have a hard time using their back legs to get up. But he's doing it on his own now, so he must be feeling a little better. Not a hundred percent, sure — but better." She leaned over again and kneaded his ear. "Good boy, Red," she murmured, a hint of pride in her voice. But mostly affection for the big old dog that was already feeling better.

Izzy watched them — both dog and woman, communing in a way that made her feel briefly like an outsider. Finally she looked at the younger woman, not sure what to say.

"Thank you," she began. She wanted to say more; but just then, Red moved over to her side, wobbly but on all four legs, and better than he'd been all day. The dog was smiling. Izzy would swear to it.

"I've seen you walking your dog along the shore," the woman said. "Well, full disclosure, it was Red I saw. I love goldens." She held out a hand. "I'm Tess Bean."

Izzy's mouth dropped open, then closed. She looked more directly at the woman. "Tess. Sure. I'm sorry for not recognizing you. I own the yarn shop that hands out the posters you left in our shop. And I've seen you around everywhere. Not to mention that Gabby Marietti has elevated you to the status of saint."

"You know Gabby?"

"Oh yes. And I love her. You probably know that Gabby's grandmother is one of Sea Harbor's most amazing residents. She's . . . well, she's wise and wonderful. And she has become one of my dearest friends."

Tess's brows lifted.

"I know," Izzy said, noting the look on Tess's face. "Birdie Favazza's probably forty-plus years older than I am. Things like age don't matter much around here. Anyway, when Birdie discovered she had a granddaughter she'd never met, we all — Birdie's friends — adopted Gabby as if she were one of our own. My aunt Nell, my friend Cass Halloran, and me. We knit together, we mess in each other's lives together, but mostly we are dear friends together. And all of that means Gabby not only has a grandmother but three other women who love her, too."

When Izzy stopped for air, she noticed that Tess was listening carefully, almost wistfully.

Tess offered a half smile. "Well, Gabby's great. Her friend Daisy, too. And smart. Those kids listen. They think. They really get it. They're our future."

Izzy was about to delve into what exactly it was that the preteens were "getting," but before she could ask, a petulant Penny cut into the conversation with an even louder voice.

"So you and your dog might lose your appointment spot if you don't hurry, Miz Perry. I'm really sorry, but Dr. Turner is a seriously busy man." She looked at Tess and glared at her, as if she were contaminating the waiting room. "And you, missy, you really shouldn't be messing with the doctor's patients. You might hurt them. That's not your job. You need to mind the messes."

Tess completely ignored her, turned her back, and whispered to Izzy, "Just FYI, I'm not sure Red needs the drugs Clark will probably prescribe. Maybe a low-dose NSAID now and then, but the massage will help. Just watch and see."

Before Izzy could question her further, Tess opened the front door, letting in an icy breeze that caused Penny to race to retrieve the papers flying off her desk. And then the door closed, bringing calm back to the room.

Izzy walked over to the window and watched Tess round the side of the clinic and head toward the kennels out back.

She was embarrassed she hadn't spoken up sooner. She'd seen Tess often, usually riding her bike. But she'd also seen her walking the downtown area, talking to people on the street, pinning flyers to the bulletin board in Coffee's or the library. Questioning some teenage smokers about their habit and the awful effects it had on them and the environment. And she'd been in the knitting shop a couple times. Mae liked her. A definite plus.

Gabby thought Tess hung the moon. Izzy knew that. She loved the environmental-science class Tess taught at the Sea Harbor Community Day School, and she and her friend Daisy zealously followed Tess's dictates about saving the earth and the sea. Birdie worried a little about the girls' crush on the inspiring teacher. But Izzy, who was decades younger than Birdie, remembered having dynamic teachers and lecturers who had changed her view of the world. It was part of growing up. From everything she saw, Gabby may have picked a fine role model.

Izzy looked down at Red, walking over to sniff at the Yorkie. He was still hobbling, but barely. And he looked happy.

No matter who Tess was, right now, right this minute, she was a dog whisperer. And

that was enough for Izzy.
Almost.

CHAPTER 3

Birdie Favazza pushed the yarn shop door closed against the sudden gust of wind that came in with her, the cold smell surrounding her like a bubble. She shook it off and looked over at the checkout counter.

Mae Anderson barely looked up from the checkout counter. Her glasses had slipped to the end of her long nose as she peered at the computer screen, scrolling through the day's receipts. "I lit a fire for you, Birdie. Get yourself down to the knitting room and warm your bones."

"A fire? Wonderful. Thank you, Mae." Birdie rubbed her small hands together, bringing color back into them. She looked around the quiet, nearly empty shop. The closed sign was already hanging on the door, and through the archway on the far side of the room, she could see flames in the old fireplace dancing against the brick. But there was no music, no voices coming up the three wide steps. "Am I early, Mae?"

Before Mae could answer, the door opened again, the gust more forceful this time, riffling a cardboard display of bamboo needles near the wall.

Nell Endicott and Cass Halloran hurried in. Nell was carrying a round dish sealed with foil, a knitting bag looped around her arm. Her high cheekbones were flushed, her salt-and-pepper hair blown wild around her head.

Nell set the dish on Mae's desk and shook free of her heavy parka. "It's crazy out there, Mae," she said.

The yarn shop manager ignored the weather comment and eyed the foil-wrapped dish. "Are you trying to drive me insane, putting this right here in front of me?" Mae pressed one hand against her abdomen, then reached over and peeled back a corner of the wrap. The smell of outdoor air was snuffed out, replaced by a blend of lemon, rosemary, and garlic. "I've died and gone to heaven," Mae said, closing her eyes and breathing in the enticing smells.

Nell laughed. "We wouldn't forget you, Mae." She handed her a smaller container with *Garozzo's Deli* printed on the side in large, swirly letters. "Harry Garozzo dished up a special portion for you to take home."

"Our dinner is from Garozzo's?" Cass's words lifted in exaggerated amazement. She moved closer to the food, dipping her head to breathe in the tantalizing odors.

"I had seven zillion things to do today Cass. Retirement is a misnomer, I'm afraid. And besides, I know you love Harry's deli food as much as mine, though I'm happy you'll never admit it."

The tantalizing odors continued to circle around the shop, quieting Cass.

"Was Margaret there?" Mae asked, tucking her dinner into her large tote bag.

"Was Margaret where?" Nell asked.

"At the deli."

"Margaret Garozzo?" Cass asked.

"Yes, of course, Margaret Garozzo," Mae said. "Was she at the deli that she and her husband run? Who else are we talking about?" Her narrow face was pinched and she spoke slowly, as if those in front of her were not understanding her language.

"Of course she was there. That's an odd question," Nell said. "In fact, one of the waitstaff was giving her a hard time. Or maybe vice versa, though Margaret is too nice for that kind of thing. She had a few choice words for her husband, too. Harry may have messed up one of her recipes. Why do you ask?"

"Well, Harry came in here a couple hours ago. Huffing and puffing. He said Margaret walked out on him. Took her deli apron off and threw it at him. He thought maybe she was hiding out over here, spending the deli's good money on yarn." Mae shook her head, then went on.

"The thing was, he was sort of right. Margaret had been in earlier. It was odd because she's always at the deli midday, so I was surprised to see her. She walked on through the shop and went down and joined the afternoon knitting group. A short while later, she left. Said she had to get back to work or the restaurant would have to close its doors. But I guess she made a detour before going back to the deli because Harry came in shortly after looking for her. Something is not quite right there."

"You need to stop worrying about the whole town, Mae," Nell said. "Harry's turning into an old worrywart. Margaret has spoiled him, always reporting in and out. We all need our secrets. Ben and I ran into Margaret a couple weeks ago in Beech Tree Woods with Figlio, their silly old basset. Margaret loves the woods, just like we do. She told me it was her secret place, where she regains her balance, and she asked us not to share it with Harry. This was *her* place, he could find his own. So maybe that's where she went. But all's well that ends well, right? And the scampi smells delicious, so *someone* was in the kitchen. My money is on Margaret."

Mae nodded. "All right, then," she said, abruptly changing the topic. She pointed out a display of yarn in the corner. "You've all missed our newest masterpiece."

They all looked to the far wall where a shoal of colorful fish was swimming up to the ceiling.

"That's beautiful," Birdie said, walking closer and noticing what the fish were made of — skeins of colorful yarn tied in strategic places to form the swimming school of fish.

"It's that new yarn Izzy ordered," Mae said. "Coolest display we've had in a long time. The yarn is flying out of here."

"So now everyone is knitting fish?" Cass asked.

Mae laughed. "Customers may not be knitting 'em, but people are sure trying to save 'em," she said. "Saving the fish is a big cry these days. This display is a part of the effort. I'm loving it."

Birdie turned and looked over at Mae. "Is my granddaughter involved in the campaign?"

"Sure is," Mae said. "An artist over in

Canary Cove designed the display, but the young'uns came in after school and helped put it together. It's to bring people's attention to saving our sea, Gabby told me. She and her buddy Daisy were all over it. Talked nonstop about the fish and the ocean and pollution and you name it. Gabby took a bunch of photos of the display and rushed out to make a poster warning people about dumping trash in the home of these beautiful aquatic animals."

Birdie reached up and touched a fish with the tip of her finger. "She's all about saving our earth these days. I'm glad she's helpful to you when she comes in, Mae. And I'm glad she found a warm place to be, instead of riding her bike down near the water. Gabby has difficulty acknowledging the change in seasons."

The shop manager laughed. "Speaking of cold, she was telling me about her environmental-science teacher, the gal who lives in a cottage around here without heat. Heated by pebbles or some god-awful thing."

Birdie's face registered concern. "Her teacher doesn't have heat?"

Mae waved away the look on Birdie's face. "Nah, nothing to worry about. They said something about using pellets for heat instead of gas or what have you. Better for the environment. Gabby seemed to think it was a great idea. She's something else, that granddaughter of yours. In spite of some of the crazy ideas she has, she lights up this whole place. Customers love her. She's gonna be like one of those wicked famous singers who only needs one name."

Nell watched the exchange, seeing the worry cloud Birdie's face. "It's nothing to worry about, Birdie," she began.

Mae stepped in, shaking her head. Strands of thin hair fell loose from a makeshift bun. "Hey, I get it, Birdie. I worried about my nieces at that age. It's what we do. Worry. But they don't need it. Smart whippersnappers that they are. Gotta let them fly."

Nell wandered off as Mae went on about her twin nieces and their latest boy friends.

A small table held an enormous wooden bowl piled high with balls of angora and soft wool in holiday colors, begging to be touched. Nell picked one up, listening to the conversation. She thought of her niece Izzy's daughter, her own great-niece Abigail. The toddler was still at an age when worries were contained and controlled. Was her cough too raspy? Were her teeth coming in on time? Did her vocabulary have the right number of words for a three-year-old?

But she could read her dear friend Birdie's mind: It was the independence that caused the concern. Not knowing all Gabby's thoughts and needs.

Let her fly, Mae had said. But to where?

Cass had taken Harry's scampi down to the knitting room and came back up, taking the three steps in one long movement. "Hey, where's Izzy? I thought she'd be down there getting out plates?"

"I'll tell you if you promise not to uncork the wine until she gets back." Mae looked stern.

"Back from where?" Cass said, ignoring the wine issue.

"It's Red, poor pup. Izzy took him over to Clark Turner's clinic for something to help the old guy's aches and pains. He was moving slower than I was today."

Nell shook her head. "Getting old can be difficult."

"I'll second that," Mae said. "So, anywho, that's where she is. She left orders to go on down and be comfortable, but she was pretty emphatic about leaving some wine. And I'd second it. Give our girl some hugs, too, while you're at it."

"Bad day?" Nell asked.

Mae shrugged and turned off her computer. "Oh, you know. Some days are like that."

But Nell didn't know. What she knew was that her niece rarely let work impose itself on her "other life," as she called it. And Thursday-night knitting was definitely a part of her other life. "She's doing too much," she said out loud, glancing at the poster near the front door: SEASIDE KNITTING STUDIO'S FIRST HOLIDAY HYGGE.

"Izzy does a lot, that's the truth." Mae looked at the poster over the top of her glasses. "But customers came in this week to sign up for the first gathering or whatever the heck you call it, and they are lovin' the idea. I expect there will be more folks as the word gets around." Her words clipped, Mae read the rest of the words on the colorful invitation: " 'Come one, come all. Bring knitting or crocheting supplies, wear comfortable sweats or PJs, and warm yourself with friends and a blazing fire. Hot spiced cider and homemade cookies provided.'

"I mean, who can turn that down? I finally figured out how to pronounce the darn thing. *Hoo-gah,* Izzy says."

Cass looked at the poster. "I think it means *hugfest,*" she said. "And that's something I sure as heck don't need. That's why I married Danny Brandley, to take care of all that. And he does a good job of it, thank you very much."

The others laughed and refrained from reminding Cass that the four seaside knitters — of which she was one — had been holding their own Thursday-night version of the *hygge* lifestyle for years, long before they became aware of either the word or the Danish concept.

Mae pulled a heavy parka off a hook and wrapped herself in it, then picked up her bag and headed for the door. "Well, ladies, I'm headed out. *Law and Order* reruns and this deli doggie bag wait for no woman."

Izzy walked through the archway and down into the cozy knitting room a short while later and tossed her jacket on a chair. She sank into the old leather chair near the corner fireplace and glanced at the serving platter that just a short time earlier had held scampi in a rich buttery wine sauce. She looked over at Cass. "Fine friend you are."

"Would I do that?" Cass asked. "Fat chance. Your dear aunt Nell beat me with her stick when I tried to finish it off. Your portion is heating in the toaster oven." She leaned over and pushed an ottoman over to Izzy's chair. "You're freezing. Put your feet up to the fire. Is the weather that bad?"

"Not so bad, not really," Izzy said. She took the glass of wine Birdie handed her and kicked off her boots, lifting her feet up. "I'm just tired, that's all. And cranky. Thanks for saving me food. I shall never again doubt you, Cass."

Nell set a plate down in front of Izzy. The tension in her niece's face was beginning to ease away, the crackling flames adding a glow to her cheeks. "How's Red?" she asked.

"Better, thanks Aunt Nell. I dropped him off at home, and Abby and Sam are treating him to steak and fries."

"What drugs did Doc Turner prescribe?" Birdie asked, considering herself somewhat of an expert on soothing creaky joints with nonsteroidal anti-inflammation drugs.

"Well, that's the thing," Izzy said. "No NSAIDs, no nothing. In fact, I left the clinic without even seeing Clark. It was a different kind of medicine that helped Red. Here's what happened." Izzy briefly explained Tess's intervention and how she had soothed not only Red's sore joints but her own spirit, too.

"Tess Bean?" Nell asked.

Izzy nodded.

"Tess is a dog whisperer?" Cass said. "That's cool."

"So Tess works for Clark Turner? What

does she do?" Nell asked. "Besides whispering, I mean."

"No, really Aunt Nell. She was working miracles. Officially she works in the kennel part. Penny described her job as cleaning poop, but her tone of voice said more about her opinion of Tess than the job. She thinks Tess has too much influence over Clark and is trying to take over the whole clinic."

"By giving dogs massages?" Cass refilled Izzy's glass.

"Well, whatever. Red sure didn't object to Tess." Izzy rested her head back against the chair, her eyes half-closed. "Maybe she's just trying to protect her hubby."

"From what?" Cass asked. "Penny is the only woman I've ever seen him talk to. He has money, sure, but pet owners aren't the kind of folks who try to snatch people's money away."

Nell listened without comment. Clark Turner was quiet and a good veterinarian, in her mind. Her husband, Ben, played pick-up basketball with him at the YMCA and Ben said it seemed to be Clark's main social activity until he married Penny.

"Well, no matter what Penny thinks," Izzy said, "Clark is my hero for letting Tess do her magic in a corner of his waiting room."

Nell looked over at Birdie. She had arranged herself in an overstuffed chair on the other side of the fireplace, a crocheted throw covering her dangling legs that didn't quite touch the floor. In the middle of her lap, Purl, the shop's cat, formed a perfect circle. "You're awfully quiet, Birdie. What are you thinking?"

It took a moment for Birdie to answer. She sat still, rubbing Purl's cheeks methodically. Finally she smiled, just a little, and said, "I didn't know Tess was an animal lover. Gabby has told me many things about the young woman, but she missed that." She paused, concentrating on Purl, then went on. "The real fact of the matter is that I know facts about Tess, but I don't *know* her. Except that Gabby thinks she is a pretty amazing person."

"You don't like Tess," Izzy said.

"I didn't say that, now, did I?"

Nell picked up a carafe and filled four mugs with strong coffee. This was all new to her dear friend. Birdie who had never had to deal with an impressionable preteen, especially not one she loved so deeply. Nell and Ben hadn't had children either, but she had been a part of her niece Izzy's life from the time she was born. When she and Ben married, Izzy was a constant houseguest in the Boston brownstone. And it didn't end when Nell retired from directing a large Boston nonprofit and Ben from his family business. Izzy eventually followed them to Sea Harbor. Nell had been privy to all phases of Izzy's life, all the difficult decisions. But this was new to Birdie. She looked over at her now, sensing her worry, wanting to help. "Birdie, I think Tess is a decent person. Ben and I have both talked with her. She brought a petition around to our neighborhood, collecting signatures. It had something to do with that Harbor Club tavern out on the pier. I can't remember what the issue was, but we both thought she was bright and knowledgeable."

Birdie nodded. "That's good." Her eyes were focused on her coffee.

"And I heard the headmistress of Sea Harbor Community Day School praising her, too. She said Tess is waking the kids up to things they should be aware of — to their world."

"I'm happy Gabby is engaged," Birdie said, "and it does sound like a good thing. But she's at such an impressionable age, and I barely know this teacher who has such influence over her." She looked at Izzy over the rim of her coffee mug. "But I'm happy to hear about the dog-whispering encounter.

Having her love dogs comforts me somehow."

"Well, she definitely had a magic touch with Red. But you're right, Birdie. Girls, especially, are impressionable at that age. Kind of idealistic. You want to be able to . . ."

Izzy let the sentence drop off, unsure of what might follow.

The truth was, none of them knew Tess Bean well enough.

But they all knew and loved Gabby inside and out.

For a moment there was quiet; the only sounds the popping of the fire and a recording of Adele singing "When We Were Young" in the background. The lyrics seeped into their thoughts, turning them back in time to their own youths. When they were young: impressionable, exploring new ideas, experimenting. Sometimes in ways that expanded them and helped them grow.

Sometimes not.

Finally Birdie put down her coffee. "Enough about me and my grandparenting craziness." She reached down for her knitting bag and pulled out the bright orange beginnings of a sweater. "This is going to be beautiful. Don't we all agree?"

The mood switched almost by magic as

colorful skeins of yarn and patterns and a basket of bamboo needles so often did. The few rows of knit and purl in Birdie's hands would end up being a Christmas gift for Gabby, designed by Izzy, and lovingly stitched by Birdie, her bent fingers still adept at slipping yarn onto needles and creating something beautiful.

The written pattern lay flat on the coffee table, Izzy's pencil sketch uncannily lifelike. They could already visualize Gabby, her long legs in tights and the soft sweater falling nearly to her knees. Big pockets and a row of cables defined the front, and a hood would fall gently in back. And by the time it was boxed and wrapped and put under the tree, none of them had any doubt that it also would be accompanied by mittens and socks and a long, loopy scarf.

They all happily moved away from worry and on to other things — to the expectations for the first *hygge* gathering, to newsy gossip about pregnancies and retirements and December parties being planned all around Cape Ann.

Later, as the last embers of the fire disappeared, the music turned off and they were buttoning up their coats, Birdie remembered her knitting needles. "I nearly forgot," she said to Izzy. "Mae called the other day and left a message that those fancy bamboo needles I ordered had come in."

Izzy looked pained. "Yes," she said.

Birdie's brows lifted.

Izzy sighed. "Yes, they came in early in the week. But somehow they disappeared."

"Disappeared?"

"Mae had set the set behind the counter to give to you, but today when she checked, it was gone. It disappeared. I'm so sorry Birdie. We seem to be missing some things."

"Things?" Nell asked.

"Yes. An odd assortment. Harriet Brandley's umbrella, Laura Danvers's car keys, Mae's lobster roll lunch. Birdie's needles. Among others."

"Missing?" Cass asked. "As in *misplaced*?"

Izzy sighed. "As in stolen."

Chapter 4

December in Sea Harbor was fickle. On Friday, bright sunshine took the edge off the cold that had settled on the town. It was the kind of day Nell liked best — "walking weather," she called it. And today it was paired with an almost-empty calendar — just a trip to the market and the usual Friday-night dinner with friends. A soup night. With something grilled tossed into it to allow Ben his time on the deck with friends, sipping a very dry martini and solving the world's problems.

But first she needed a cup of coffee, and then the early-morning walk. She needed some grounding today — although if forced to put reason to the feeling, she'd be at a loss to explain it. But no matter the cause, walking along the harbor would work its magic.

She sent Ben off into a busy day of council meetings with a reminder to bring home cheese and wine for the evening gathering.

But sometimes even Nell's early-morning plans got slightly skewed. And many times those changes came about with a text from her niece. Like today.

Aunt Nell, I took the day off to be with Abby, but something came up. Any chance you want to hang with her for a few hours? P.S.: Abby says "Please, Nini."

Nell smiled at her phone, half expecting it to smile back. Izzy knew very well that she would never say no to having time with Abby. She had been known to cancel dentist appointments, library board meetings, and once, although Izzy only found out by accident, canceled accepting the mayor's monthly Citizens' Award at city hall. All to be with Abigail Kathleen Perry, a three-year-old who had changed all their lives.

Nell texted her reply, then refilled her mug while she waited for Abby to be dropped off. Thursday night's knitting had ended with an unsettling feeling. Not the usual warmth that knitting and being with dear friends brought. Maybe it was just the recent cold. Perhaps they weren't at all ready for winter.

But no matter — sweet Abby would change all that in an instant.

And she'd still get her walk along the

wharf, a place Abby loved with a toddler's passion: a place to run, boats and captains to wave to, dogs to pet, not to mention a stop at Gracie's café for her favorite hot dog. A desecration perhaps — hot dogs at a lobster shack? But Gracie Santos, the owner, loved Abby Perry, too, and a fat hot dog on a bun, no ketchup, would be served up with great flair.

She wondered briefly about Izzy's unexpected appointment. Something important enough that she'd give up part of her coveted time with her daughter. And then she shrugged it off, concentrating instead on the fact that whatever the reason, it was responsible for giving her a few hours with her grand niece. And that was a lovely thing.

An hour later, Nell, Abby, and an empty stroller walked through the quiet Sandswept Lane neighborhood toward a bustling Harbor Road.

"Just one stop at McGlucken's Hardware Store for some batteries Ben needs," she explained to Abby. "Then on to the wharf."

Abby pronounced it *woof* and clapped her small hands as she ran a few steps ahead of Nell, curls escaping from beneath her stocking cap and her tiny pink UGG boots slapping the sidewalk.

Nell held the door and Abby rushed in. She knew what kind of treat she could expect in each store surrounding her mother's yarn shop. McGlucken's offered lollipops and fresh popcorn.

Nell looked around for the batteries and the storeowner and old friend, Gus McGlucken, all the while keeping one eye on Abby. She was standing in front of the large red popcorn cart, happily watching the kernels transform into tiny white puffs.

Nell spotted the battery display and pulled off two packages. She smiled at Billy Ohde, a teenager she knew from the neighborhood. "Did Gus take the day off? It's a rare day he isn't either standing outside the front door or behind that counter."

Billy laughed. "Yeah. For sure. Gus is a talker. He's here if you want to see him —" He cocked his head, indicating a small room behind the checkout counter.

Through the glass door Nell spotted Gus, sitting at an old round table, leaning back in his chair, arms across his chest. He seemed to be listening intently to someone out of her vision. She turned back to Billy. "No, he looks busy. I was only going to say hi."

"I usually help him stock, but today he asked me to take the desk." Billy handed

Nell the batteries and picked up the credit card from the counter. "A meeting or something."

While Billy processed the card, Nell looked beyond him, trying to see through the smudged glass door. Gus had tilted back his chair, his hands clasped behind his head. Another face came into view, this one leaning in toward Gus, elbows on the table. Archie Brandley, Harbor Road's bookshop owner. The two men were old friends, and seeing the two of them gabbing on the sidewalk would have been normal, but meeting in a back room on a Friday seemed out of place somehow. Unless there was a morning poker game going on that no one knew about?

"So, Mrs. Endicott, if you'd please sign right here?" Billy pulled her attention back to the desk. He pointed to the strip of paper.

Nell scribbled her name and handed it back.

"Hey, that's Izzy Perry's little girl, right?" Billy said, pointing at Abby. She was standing quietly, still mesmerized by the cavorting popcorn.

Nell smiled and nodded.

"Did she come in to see her mom?" He nodded again toward the back room.

"Izzy's in there?" Nell looked behind him,

but now she could only see Gus, his hands waving in the air, his face serious. She wondered who else was there — and why Izzy gave up precious hours with her daughter to spend it with people she saw every day. Were they all shop owners? But why? The merchant's association held its monthly meetings at the Sea Harbor Yacht Club — not a dusty back room on a busy Friday morning. Something wasn't right.

A tug on the edge of her parka drew her attention down to a smile so full and innocent her heart melted into a puddle, and thoughts of covert meetings of shop owners evaporated. Abby clutched a huge red lollipop. Behind her, a trail of fallen white puffs dotted the floor.

Billy saw it, too. "No problem, Mrs. Endicott. I got this." He grabbed a broom.

But before he could walk around the counter, Abby squealed, dropped her lollipop, and ran toward the front door, pressing her hands and nose against the glass.

On the other side of the door, Gabby Marietti crouched down to Abby's height and grinned back, running her fingers against the outline of Abby's.

Nell pulled Abby away and pushed open the door, releasing her great niece to tumble into Gabby's waiting arms.

■ ■ ■ ■

Abby skipped along between Nell and Gabby, laughing and clutching Gabby's hand as Nell pushed the stroller. They headed down the wide-planked wharf, its remodeled look highlighted in the sunlight, the rails smooth as glass. Several schooners, which were moored at the side, bobbed in the harbor waters, readying for late-morning sightseers. Their captains returned Abby's waves. The new wharf seemed to go on forever, with benches, brass plaques, and viewing telescopes anchored along the sides.

Nell looked over Abby's head. "Gabby, tell me you're not playing hooky today, or I'll be in serious trouble with one of my dearest friends."

Gabby laughed. "Nope. Teachers' meetings or something. I had a sleepover at Daisy Danvers's house and was headed to nowhere special when I spotted Abby at the popcorn machine. Who can pass up the cutest kid in Sea Harbor?" She tickled the tiny hand and Abby squealed, then pulled away and ran ahead.

Gabby pulled off her slouchy beanie and tossed it in the stroller. Strands of thick black hair poofed out around her head and shoulders. One pink plait fell across her cheek.

"You barely need a warm hat with all that hair. Relish it, Gabby."

"I've been thinking of cutting it all off. Tess Bean says they need human hair to make wigs for people who lose their hair."

"A good cause. Maybe wait until spring when you don't need it for warmth."

Gabby laughed.

"So tell me about Tess. Are you enjoying her class?"

Gabby stopped walking for a minute and looked directly at Nell, her eyes huge and her voice rising with unfettered enthusiasm, as if Nell had just tapped into words eager to get out. "She's awesome, Nell. Ridiculously great. I mean" — she started to walk again, her spinning arms emphasizing her words. "We're learning like . . . like so much. Tess — and she lets us call her by her first name — has opened me up to lots of things and made all of us so aware of our world and the ocean and the land we live on. Of things we do to mess up that world without even realizing it. It all makes sense to me. It's about stewardship, Nell."

Stewardship? That wasn't a word she'd heard come out of Gabby's mouth often. Or maybe ever.

Gabby went on. "I'm even thinking I might want to become an environmental marine biologist," she said.

Nell's brows lifted into a wave of graying brown hair. "That's interesting. I don't know much about that."

"Maybe I made it up. If there aren't any degrees in it, well, then, I'll be the first."

Nell smiled. That was a definite possibility — and she'd be very good at it. Whatever the "it" was.

"Daisy and I are in this cool new club at school that Tess started. We're planning awesome ways to give people ideas on how to help take care of the ocean and our earth. Trying to change bad habits, like using plastic. They've already banned single-use plastic bags over in Gloucester. We need to catch up. And we're encouraging people to help us clean up the beach. It's exciting, Nell."

Nell nodded, listening and watching Abby as she ran ahead. The toddler stopped at a new climbing toy in the middle of the wharf built by several fishermen. The structure was like a geodesic dome, but in the shape of a huge lobster trap. Abby's bright curls bobbed along with the rest of her tiny body as she grinned out at them from between the red wire squares.

Gabby let the discussion drop and raced after Abby, crouching down beside the lobster gym. Environmental biologists forgotten for a moment as the child in her took over.

Nell leaned against a nearby railing and watched the two of them, Gabby making funny faces that caused Abby to shriek in laughter. Across from them a crowd of tourists looked over at the little girl in the pink parka, her laughter making them laugh, too.

Nell slipped on her sunglasses and looked out toward the harbor waters. The ocean shimmered with sunlight, rippling gently.

"Abby says we're starving, Nell," Gabby shouted above the ocean sounds. The two abandoned the lobster trap and ran toward Nell, Abby's tiny feet rotating like bicycle pedals.

"Of course you are. Me too."

"Hot dog," Abby cried gleefully.

A pinging tone came from Gabby's cell phone. She pulled it out as they walked back down the wharf, checking messages with a flick of her thumb in a way that baffled Nell. Her own thumbs inevitably hit three keys at once.

Gabby typed in a message, then slipped her phone back in her pocket. Her smile was bright. "I need to meet Daisy."

"Oh?"

"A meeting. Big-time. But I have time to eat. And I truly am starving." She grinned and picked up her pace.

At the land-end of the wharf, several eateries held prime real estate. One of them was Gracie Santos's Lazy Lobster & Soup Café, a favorite among locals. Casual and rustic, with a deck that hung right over the water.

Once the only place to eat on the wharf, it now huddled between a souvenir shop and a recently remodeled bar named the Harbor Club, a name some thought a bit pretentious for a sports bar.

Abby had picked up speed and Nell leaned down and stretched out her arms to catch her. But the tiny body flew right by her, racing toward the café, where she knew hot dogs and hot chocolate waited for her.

"Hey, Abby!" Gabby's yell competed with the shrill squalling of a seagull colony flying overhead. "Wait up, kiddo."

But before her words caught up with the flying toddler, a dark-haired man walked out of the Harbor Club, the sound of loud country-western music following him. He stuck one hand in his jacket and pulled out a pack of cigarettes, then began strolling away from the bar and directly into the path of a flying pink tornado.

At first, the only sound was a dull thud as the law of inertia took over and Abby Perry landed smack into the back of the man's knees, nearly buckling them. A split second later, a string of curse words spewed forth, mixed with a very loud and plaintive little girl's howl. The cigarettes dropped to the ground and the man stared down at Abby through nearly black eyes. He rubbed a shadow of a beard, his face dark and frowning.

Abby was sitting flat on the wharf now, legs stuck out in front of her. Tears streamed down her round cheeks.

Gabby reached her in a split second, scooping her up and stepping away from the man, her eyes examining Abby for damage. Nell huffed up a second later and took Abby into her arms, cuddling and wiping away the tears.

Gabby turned back toward the man, a flush climbing up her neck and turning her cheeks bright red.

Nell walked closer to apologize for the unintended collision, but Gabby's look stopped her. She couldn't quite read the expression clouding her face. Anger? Or something else, maybe? The man seemed to be muttering something that might have passed for an apology — or maybe not.

He looked familiar to Nell, but she couldn't put a name to him. That wasn't at all unusual. The harbor area was busy and bustling with fishermen from the surrounding areas in and out. But this man was noticeable. He was handsome in a dark, rough sort of way. Longish hair, a short beard — the kind that looked like it grew there almost by accident. A cowboy look, she thought, although she couldn't have defined it further.

"Gabby, let's go. Abby is fine," she said.

The man leaned over and picked up a bright green pack of cigarettes that were dropped in the scuffle. Then he looked at Abby, still cuddled in Nell's arms. A thick strand of hair fell over one eye and he brushed it back. "Maybe you need to keep the little squirt leashed," he said, offering a discomforting smile. "Didn't see the kid coming, is all. Come on in for a beer or lemonade on the house, if it'll make y'all feel better."

Nell smiled politely, and the man walked away, back toward the bar. With Abby held tightly in her arms, she bent over and picked up the discarded cigarette pack he'd dropped on the ground.

"Flag," Abby said, poking a finger at the

Canadian flag emblazoned on the bright green cellophane wrapping.

Nell smiled and tossed the package in a nearby trashcan, then began walking away with Abby still in her arms. She glanced back at Gabby and motioned for her to come.

Gabby grabbed the abandoned stroller and caught up with Nell and a now-cheerful Abby.

"Are you all right?" Nell asked. "He wasn't really at fault, sweetie. It was an accident. Abby's fine. All's well."

Gabby nodded, then glanced back at the man. He was still standing outside the bar, a cigarette hanging from one side of his mouth, and his eyes following the threesome as they walked away. She jerked her head back and focused on the stone lobster outside Gracie's Lazy Lobster & Soup Café, welcoming them.

"I don't think I know that fellow," Nell was saying beside her.

Gabby was silent. She didn't know him, either. But she had seen him before. She didn't remember at first, not until he laughed. The laugh was the same.

The laugh that had floated across the private cove, invading her private space on the rickety dock.

Just minutes before Tess Bean had sent him flailing into the freezing cold water.

CHAPTER 5

"So you think this is serious? That there's some kind of organized theft going on in the Harbor Road shops?" Nell had been wrong about the surprise meeting in Gus McGlucken's back room that morning. The shop owners weren't there to discuss minor merchants' complaints or simple things like holiday store hours. They were there to talk about theft.

She handed Cass a circle of brie to arrange on a plate, then went back to the six-burner stove, stirring the kettle of soup. Steamy spirals rose into the heated air, filling the kitchen with the smells of garlic and onions and wine.

"I don't know how serious it is," Izzy said, chewing on a piece of celery. "Mae and I noticed things missing, here and there, but we've been known to misplace things. But when Gus and Archie Brandley noticed missing merchandise in their stores, Gus thought we should talk about it." Izzy sat at the end of the island in the Endicott kitchen, the hub of Friday dinners.

Next to her, perched on a stool with her legs just reaching the footrest, Birdie lifted her head. "I was in the hardware store this afternoon and Gus McGlucken told me about his concerns. He was blaming the thefts on the weather."

"The weather?" Danny Brandley stepped over to the island, the martini shaker in one hand, a seltzer in the other.

"I suppose that's what we do in December," Birdie said, smiling up at Cass's husband. "All ills can be blamed on the demise of autumn."

The butcher block island was oversized, but crowded now with signs that dinner was close: a stack of plates and bowls, glasses lined up, a basket of rolls, and a huge wooden salad filled with arugula and escarole, toasted pecans, olives, and pomegranate seeds. Tiny squares of roasted sweet potatoes rested on top. Izzy opened a package of sourdough croutons and feta cheese and sprinkled them on top.

Nell never knew what side dishes would show up in the hands of her friends, or even how many friends or family would be there. It was always different. But it was always the perfect amount — both of friends and food. Just as it was tonight. She smiled, looking around. On the other side of the kitchen her husband Ben moved quietly around, joking here or there, making sure everyone had a drink or a seltzer. That everyone was comfortable. She and Ben were a good match, she thought — moving in a finely choreographed dance.

Birdie sipped her icy martini, explaining Gus's weather predictions. "Gus says cold days bring kids inside the store to get warm after school. It's the popcorn smell, he says."

"It gets me in there every time," Cass said.

"So he's thinking these freezing kids steal nails when they come in?" Danny stood next to his wife, smearing a hunk of warm Brie on a cracker. His brown brows lifted above his glasses. "I guess it's better than stealing those outboard motors or water skies Gus sells."

Cass poked him in the side, then looked back at Izzy. "But this isn't a joke, right? It's just so weird. Someone is stealing nails and yarn?"

"Don't forget Mae's lunch," Birdie added. "It was probably a few days old."

"You're right," Izzy said. "It doesn't make sense. But it's more than just our end of Harbor Road. The cheese-and-wine store is missing things, too — corkscrews and some fancy silver toothpicks. And Lulu's Sweet Shoppe was missing a silver box of chocolate kisses. And Danny, your dad and mom have had a couple of books stolen from their store. A box of Christmas cards and a new book of Billy Collins poetry. Did they tell you?"

"Yeah, Mom mentioned it. But you know my mom. If she thought she was introducing someone to her favorite poet, she'd have given him the book and a couple others. But, hey, I don't mean to make light of it. I'm not convinced it's kids, though. Having been one once, I don't think it's yarn or nails I'd go after. Books? Well, maybe. But the thefts could be isolated cases. Different people. Holidays can be hard on retailers — but it's also hard on people without any money for gifts."

That silenced the group briefly. Cass looked at her husband and smiled. "You're a nice man, Danny Brandley. I'd marry you again if I could."

"Wisdom for the season from our favorite mystery writer," Birdie said with a smile.

Ben grabbed his grilling tools from beneath the counter. "If the merchants think this is serious, why haven't you brought the police in on it, Iz? Chief Thompson could have assigned extra people to patrol Harbor Road."

"As wonderful as your buddy Jerry Thompson is, I'm wondering how he'd react to a report of nails and knitting needles and toothpicks disappearing. It might not be time yet to bring in the cavalry."

Ben laughed. "Right. Maybe everyone just needs to be a little more vigilant. At least for a few days."

"Well, as long as the stores aren't hurt in a serious way, and no one attempts to steal Purl from Izzy's shop, then Ben's advice sounds wise," Birdie said. "You know what my Sonny always said — if someone steals your jacket because they're cold, try to find them a scarf and mittens to go with it."

"Sonny said that?" Nell asked. Birdie's first husband had died much too young, but his spirit was alive and well in the love he had left behind.

Birdie thought for a minute. "Well, no, maybe it was me who said it, or I read it somewhere."

Nell smiled. Birdie's message wasn't as muddled as the memory. Her thoughts matched Danny's. What if someone *needs* that yarn or the needles to knit mittens for an old sick grandmother, or a poor young fellow is desperate to read a book? Who would want to disrupt that, much less punish someone? Nell wasn't sure what kind of spin Birdie would put on the nails taken from Gus's shop, but she had no doubt there was one.

"Oh, one more thing about our thief," Izzy said. "Apparently some of the things have been returned. A silver corkscrew showed up in an envelope left on the wine shop counter one day."

"A repentant thief," Sam laughed. He stood behind his wife, gently rubbing Izzy's back.

"And somehow that brings us to food," Ben said. "All hands on deck. Or at least your hands, Sam." Ben handed him a long handled brush and pulled on a jacket. He took a plate of prime boneless fillets from Nell and the two headed out to the deck.

"Endicott steak soup," Nell said, although everyone already knew what was coming. Every year Nell welcomed in the beginning of winter with *her* steak soup. Grilling steak fillets kept Ben's Friday-grilling duty intact, while Nell worked on the other ingredients. And in Nell's opinion, floating juicy, perfectly grilled slivers of steak on top of a smooth perfectly seasoned base was the only way to make steak soup.

The salad was tossed, hunks of sourdough bread warmed and returned to the basket, and wine bottles uncorked.

By the time Ben and Sam returned, Nell had filled each bowl with the broth, smooth and thick, with small chunks of orange, green, and red vegetables swimming to the surface. Ben sliced the grilled fillets into precise slivers and added them to the bowls while everyone gathered around the island.

Candlelight reflected off the raised glasses as everyone turned toward Birdie in a ritual as old as friendships and Friday dinners at the Endicott home.

"To friends, to family," she said, her soft voice prayerful. "And to life. *L'chaim.*"

Glasses clinked and immediately the room came alive. Scurrying around the island, they formed a ragged line, piling plates high with salad, rolls and butter, and scoopfuls of black olives, gherkins, and shredded Gruyère.

Izzy and Cass sank into one of the couches, legs tucked up beneath them, while Birdie claimed the rocking chair next to the fireplace, the only chair in which her feet could touch the floor. For a while conversation gave way to the voice of Norah Jones in the background, the crackling fire, and the gentle slurping sound of disappearing soup.

When the group was small, like tonight, Cass or Izzy often directed the conversation with stories of the Halloran lobster crews or yarn shop gossip or town events.

But tonight Ben raised his hand to the side of his head as if pulling out a forgotten thought. He looked over at Birdie, then the others. A smile softened his jaw.

"I learned something new today. Did any of you know that if things go as planned, we will all be underwater in one hundred years?"

Birdie sat up straight in the rocking chair and put her glasses in place as if that would bring Ben's words into clear focus. And then she said, "I'm willing to wager you've been spending time with my granddaughter, Ben. She's shared some of that wisdom with us at home. Ella questioned whether it meant she should be taking swimming lessons."

"We may laugh, Birdie, but Gabby knows her stuff. She's growing into quite the young woman. Impressive as hell."

"Thank you, Ben," Birdie said. "I agree that Gabby is a wonderful, amazing girl. Not quite a woman, yet. I am holding on to every second of her girlhood."

"I get that, Birdie. Womanhood is rushing things. I'm having a hard time with Abby growing up too fast. Seems she was born just days ago."

"But semantics aside, when were you and Gabby discussing the fate of the world?" Birdie asked.

"She and her friend Daisy Danvers showed up at our city council meeting this afternoon."

Birdie's eyes widened. "Gabby?" Her voice caught in her throat.

"Well, the kids weren't on the schedule — they were observers. They came to support a woman who had asked to be on the agenda. You probably know her. Tess —"

"— Bean," Birdie said softly.

Ben nodded. "Right. Tess Bean. Daisy and Gabby were there to support her. Tess — wisely, I thought — had the kids answer some of the council members' questions. And they were impressive." He looked over at Birdie. "Gabby stood there like she did it every day of her life. Daisy was a little more hesitant — she's not as outgoing — but she's also smart as a whip and answered questions very intelligently."

"So Tess asked them to come to the meeting?" Birdie asked.

It was clear to all of them that Birdie had no idea her granddaughter had plans to attend a city council meeting. But it wasn't hurt or disappointment that she didn't know her granddaughter's plans that registered on her small, lined face. It was worry.

And that was the look that made Nell remember the text Gabby had received while walking along the wharf. "I think showing up at the meeting was a spur-of-the-moment thing. Gabby got a text from Daisy while we were heading to Gracie's for lunch. Gabby said it was about a meeting Daisy suggested they go to that afternoon. I assumed it was a school thing."

Birdie seemed relieved somehow.

"That would explain it," Ben said. "Daisy's mom, Laura, is on the council committee, so that's how they knew Tess would be at the meeting. Tess seemed surprised to see them. But she was happy about it and had them come up front and sit right next to her." Ben stopped and hesitated a minute, as if not sure what details to cover. Finally he went on.

"Tess was petitioning the council to get behind a project she's putting together." Ben got up and placed another log on the fire, then sat back down next to Nell. He leaned forward, his elbows on his knees.

"What kind of project?" Izzy asked.

"It's interesting. And the young woman presented it intelligently. She wants people in the community to become more eco-savvy. But not only that, she wants them to work."

"To save our earth," Nell said.

"Well, Sea Harbor, anyway," Ben said. "One campaign would be cleaning up beaches, collecting all the trash before the tides take it to sea. And another is to petition restaurants to stop some of their bad habits, and to help them understand why they're harmful. It goes along with the class Tess is teaching at the Sea Harbor Community Day School."

"Gabby seems excited about what they're learning," Nell said. "Tess has lit a fire beneath the girls."

"So the girls were simply there to support their teacher," Birdie said, as if to herself, circling back to a comfortable fact. She settled back in the rocking chair and suggested Sam refill her wineglass.

"Whatever they were there for, experiences like that can't hurt them," Ben said. "The girls saw up front how projects begin, how citizens get involved in cleaning up parks and playgrounds. How everyone who lives in Sea Harbor has a voice and a responsibility. And as Tess's showed them directly, how to lobby the council to support good works. Who knows? Maybe Gabby or Daisy will be our mayor someday."

"How did the council receive the proposal?" Sam asked. He uncorked another bottle of wine and filled Birdie's glass.

Ben hesitated again. He frowned, then said carefully, "Some liked what she said. It's things we should be doing. They're doing these things over in Gloucester. We need to get on board with some of this. A campaign to get rid of using Styrofoam, straws, plastic. Most of us already know that's a good thing to do. Of course some people won't like it."

"That's right," Cass said. "It'll cost money. The straw thing, for example. Every restaurant in town uses plastic straws. All our customers do. Heck, even hospitals use them."

"But it will save fish. Straws can kill them," Izzy said. She looked over at Birdie. "I have to admit, I'm becoming a Tess fan, Birdie. We're looking into things at the shop, the bags we use, the kind of needles we sell — that kind of thing."

"It will cost restaurants some money, but they can ease into it. Gracie is getting on board," Nell said. She looked over at Izzy and laughed. "Even little Abby may be. Gracie showed us her new compost bins, which Tess helped her build. They're in that wide area between her restaurant and the

Harbor Club bar next door. They're nice-looking. Gracie let Abby dump her leftover hot dog bun into the bin, then a corncob. Abby was really into it. She tried to toss her mittens in, but we stopped her in time."

"*Compost?* Is that what she was chatting about tonight, Sam?" Izzy laughed. "We thought she was asking for *hot toast.* So Sam made her some for dinner."

Birdie was quiet, listening, her eyes focused on the flames dancing off the blackened sides of the old fireplace. Her expression unreadable.

Soon the conversation moved on to other things: to the yarn shop's *hygge*-inspired Sunday session, to a casual fund-raiser for something or other at Gracie's lobster café planned for that weekend, to plans for a holiday party at the old movie theater on Harbor Road.

Thoughts of Tess Bean and saving the world drifted into the background.

Nell watched Birdie as she rested her head back against the chair cushion. Now and then she'd add a word or two to the conversation, but mostly, Nell thought, she's thinking about the things she had shared with Nell before the others arrived that evening.

It was the unknown that bothered her, she'd said. And the niggling, uncomfortable feeling that had settled deep down inside her, one she couldn't begin to understand.

Just days earlier Gabby had come home from school flushed with emotion, reciting the doomsday announcement Ben had repeated tonight: *If we don't do something, Nonna, Sea Harbor will be underwater in a hundred years.*

And then she had added: *We have to do something. Think of my children.*

And then Gabby had disappeared, off to the kitchen for a snack, and then to track practice.

"Birdie?" Izzy said, touching her arm lightly.

Birdie's eyelids blinked open, then shut, and then opened wider as she pulled herself forward, the rocker creaking on the wide plank floor.

"Goodness," Birdie said, slowly moving back into the moment, the music, the talk, the heat of the fire beside her. And the fragrant smell of strong coffee as Ben placed a mug in front of her. She smiled to no one in particular. "Daydreaming, I guess."

But the others didn't seem to have noticed, and Nell had already headed back to the kitchen. She was back in minutes with warm apple crisp — scooped into bowls and topped with a salted caramel sauce Birdie's housekeeper Ella had made. Ben poured more coffee and conversation drifted to the weekend ahead.

But Nell could see that Birdie's thoughts were separate, her mind still filled with images of a beautiful, vibrant twelve-year-old taking on the challenges of the world.

A world in which, she prayed, she could keep her granddaughter safe.

CHAPTER 6

Izzy leaned over and patted the smooth head of the oversized ceramic lobster beside the restaurant's door. "Jane's lobster always makes me feel safe," she said. "He's so faithful-looking or something." Jane Brewster had made the art piece for Gracie when she opened the Lazy Lobster & Soup Café several years before, and the clay crustacean had stood as a stalwart bodyguard over the restaurant ever since. Loved — and rubbed — by many.

Cass looked down at the lobster and laughed. She shoved her car keys into her pocket and rubbed her hands together, fighting off the cold. "I wish I had known you when you defended people in court, Iz. I just can't see a crusty or mean side to you. You're such a pushover. *Faithful-looking,* what's that even mean?"

Izzy pulled open the door and gave Cass a nudge into the restaurant's warmth. The wind whipped the door closed behind them.

They wriggled out of their jackets and looked around the room. The small restaurant was crowded, two-deep at the bar, and the chairs around the cheery fire were all taken. The long rectangular space was filled with tables and chairs, some round or square, others with benches and long enough for a hungry family. Servers wound their way around the tables, balancing trays filled with whole lobsters, lobster tails, lobster rolls. And lots of things in between.

At the far end of the room glass doors opened out to a deck that looked down on the harbor waters. Tonight Gracie had lit towering heat lamps across the deck and a scattering of folks in warm jackets, drinks in hand, had made their way outside, huddling beneath the lamps. Old Beatles music filtered inside through ceiling speakers.

"Who's playing? Is that Pete's band?" Izzy asked Cass. "Playing outside in this weather? Your brother is a crazy man."

"Those three goofs are the only band crazy enough to play outside, right on the water, in this weather. The Fractured Fish are fractured in the head."

"Gracie probably offered them free beer," Izzy said.

"Free beer and those scary heat lamps,"

Gracie Santos said, coming up from behind and hugging her two friends. "I'm just hoping no one catches fire out there. Why're you guys so late?"

"Babysitter problems for me, lobster crew problems for Cass," Izzy said. "Same ol' same ol'."

"I'm glad you made it. Welcome to a full house. I'm psyched. The Backyard Growers, my volunteer gig over in Gloucester, is getting a percentage of our take tonight. That's why Nell made you come, by the way. She's going to volunteer with me over there. They teach kids to grow vegetables — and to like them — and other things too."

"Vegetables?" Cass groaned.

"Oh, get lost, Halloran," Gracie said, tugging Cass's long black ponytail. As she talked, her eyes scanned around the room — checking the crowd, the servers, the bartender, waiting for a glass to topple or a lobster to slide off a plate or a bartender to flag her for help. Gracie had miraculously turned a tumbledown fishing shack into a thriving restaurant. An amazing feat. And if she was asked how she did it, she would say it had taken a village.

Izzy and Cass and others who had burned the midnight oil painting, decorating, cleaning, and telling everyone they knew about the amazing food at the Lazy Lobster & Soup Café would heartily agree.

"You're looking good, Gracie," Cass said, taking a step back and surveying her friend. "Working forty-eight-hour days agrees with you."

Gracie laughed. Although the same age as Cass, Gracie was still sometimes carded in bars, much to her chagrin. Tonight her straight blond hair was pulled back and secured with a wide clip, her jeans were clean, her crisp white blouse wrinkle free, and her smile the kind that made diners feel at home and want to come back again. Then many more times. And she always gave her good friends equal credit for her success — especially Cass, who had been her friend for years.

"Thanks," Gracie said, waving at a waiter, then pointing to an empty table with dirty dishes on it. "A little worse for wear these days, but that's the nature of the beast."

Izzy and Cass looked at her. "Oh?" Cass said.

"It's nothing. Just the beast next door."

"The Harbor Club?"

She nodded. "They'd like me gone. And they don't hesitate to let me know it."

But the words were barely out before Gracie seemed to regret them, brushing them away with a wave to people coming through the door. She looked at Izzy. "And speaking of being gone, your aunt's been asking about you two. She wondered if you came and went without her seeing you."

Izzy laughed. "Fat chance. So are they all here?"

"Yep. Ben, Danny, and Sam grabbed some drinks and went out on the deck with the band. Nell had better sense and has been catching up with friends. I swear that woman knows everyone, and she's not even a native. Every time I look over, someone new is sitting down to chat."

"Queen Nell," Cass said.

Gracie laughed and pointed toward a table not far from the deck door, then swiveled and waved at Harry and Margaret Garozzo, coming through the front door. "Oops, I have to give my sweet Garozzos hugs. Go join Nell. Eat — I see that lean and hungry look in your eyes, Cass. I'm off to act like a grown-up who owns a restaurant." She wrinkled her nose at them and disappeared into the throng of diners, hugging the Garozzo deli owners, meeting and greeting, her smile in place, her eyes ever vigilant.

Nell noticed Izzy and Cass at the same time they spotted her. She stood and waved them over.

It was only when they got close that they noticed who Nell's most recent friend was. She was sitting next to Nell, her fingers playing with the small lobster salt and pepper shakers that adorned each table in the restaurant. They matched the lazy lobster outside and had been given to Gracie by her many friends.

"Tess," Izzy said happily. "Hey, just the person I want to see."

Tess looked up. "Me?"

"It gives me a chance to thank you again for helping Red."

"Oh, no problem," Tess said, looking relieved. She set the tiny ceramic lobster down. "How's Red doing?"

"Better. But I'm wondering if I can talk you into a home visit to teach me how to do the massage? Red was like a puddle of melted butter when you got through with him that night. I'd like to know how you do it."

"Sure. It's maybe a good idea because Clark is starting to make noises about my 'witchlike antics,' as his wife calls them. Or does she call it 'voodoo'? Maybe both."

They laughed. Tess wore the same outfit she'd worn when massaging Red — the jeans and green sweatshirt with an image of leaves or plants or something on it. A symbol for something, Izzy figured, although she wasn't sure what. And somehow her hair, messy and looking like it'd been cut with pinking shears, was attractive.

"Penny is a case," Izzy said.

"That's not exactly how I'd word it," Tess said. "You're nicer than I am." She looked across the table at Cass. "That's your brother's band playing on the deck, right? They're good. I'm about to become a groupie."

"Might be a lonely place to be." Cass laughed. "Can you be a groupie of one?"

"That's absolutely not true," Nell interrupted. "Cass loves that band, and her brother — we all do."

"I'll give him credit for having good taste in places to play," Cass said. "Gracie's is the best."

"They definitely have the best lobster rolls in the universe," Tess agreed. "You're all friends of Gracie's."

"We are," Nell said. "Izzy and I more recently, but Cass and Gracie have been friends forever."

Izzy threw a scolding look at her aunt for opening the door for Cass to repeat a story they had heard more times than they could count.

"Not really *forever* forever," Cass said,

ignoring Izzy's groan. "Gracie and I have only been friends since First Communion at Our Lady of Safe Seas Church."

It made their friends laugh because it was hard to imagine Cass in a little white dress with a veil on her head — not to mention looking prayerful — but Cass insisted it was true.

Tess listened politely, and Cass went on.

"Gracie was the blond-haired angel who got to wear wings and lead us all into church. And I was the dark-haired kid at the back of the line, poking the dumb kid in front of me to stop picking his nose."

The story rang true enough that people believed it.

Tess laughed.

"How did you discover Gracie's place?" Nell asked.

"I helped her make compost bins and she pays me with food. I got the better end of the deal, for sure."

"Gracie showed the bins to Abby and me yesterday," Nell said. "At first Abby thought they were sandboxes and she wanted to climb into them, but Gracie was very good at explaining composting to a toddler."

"And now Abby and I are going to talk you into helping us make one," Izzy said.

Tess smiled, clearly pleased.

A waitress interrupted with a basket of calamari and tray of lobster rolls. A pitcher of beer followed, even though they hadn't ordered any. Nell caught Gracie's eye across the room and waved her thanks.

Shadows fell over the table as Ben and Sam appeared, surrounding the table with the smell of cold, wet sea air.

Ben noticed Tess and smiled a hello. "I saw you out on that freezing deck, but couldn't get close enough to talk. I wanted to say what a good job you did at the council meeting. Hope we didn't scare you off."

Tess was partly standing, ready to leave the table. She met Ben's greeting, her smile polite. "No," she said. "I don't scare easily."

Ben poked a toothpick into a piece of calamari and offered it to Tess along with a compliment. "I was at a meeting at the yacht club the other day and the information you and the students dropped off is being taken seriously. Until we saw the photos the kids took, we weren't aware of how bad it was. Bottles and food wrappings bobbing in the tide are attention getting, and the board is serious about efforts to curtail it. Thanks for bringing it to our attention."

Tess looked surprised. "They were terrific photos," she said. "The girls are amazing.

They understand that this is their town, their ocean, and they truly care. Sometimes more than adults." She bit into the calamari awkwardly.

Nell watched Tess's body shift, her posture change when she stopped speaking. Was it Sam and Ben?

Clearly, they weren't the kind of men any woman would be wary of, but Tess had stiffened when they walked up, almost as if she were now in enemy territory. Ben's compliment was heard, but Nell suspected it was only half believed.

While the others changed the topic to Gracie's crowded fund-raising night, Tess finished the piece of calamari and slipped off the bench. She looked at Cass and Izzy. "Hey, if you guys want to see the bins, it'd take two minutes? Give you an idea of what we can do at your house, Izzy."

Izzy and Cass immediately agreed. Cass had recently talked Danny into chickens and a coop at their home out on Canary Cove. A compost bin was next. "Anything to keep up with the Perrys," she told Tess as they moved through the crowd.

Tess led them through the kitchen to the side delivery door and pushed it open. They stepped outside, adjusting their eyes to the dimly lit area separating Gracie's restaurant from the Harbor Club next door.

Several wooden bins were lined up, complete with slated sides for air to circulate. Izzy stepped over to one and rubbed her hand along the smooth wood. "Good job, Tess."

On the other side of the bins and down several yards was the bar's side door, propped open slightly. The pulsing sound of electric guitars poured through the building's seams.

Cass looked over, wrapping her arms around herself to keep warm. "That place is hopping."

"Always," Tess said. "At least that's what Gracie says."

"Do they share the bins with Gracie?" Izzy asked.

At first, Tess didn't answer. She stared over at the Harbor Club, as if daring it to answer Izzy's question. Finally she said, "No. They throw their waste off their deck. Much easier."

Izzy looked at her, startled at the tone in Tess's voice. She looked down the easement toward the ocean. It was high tide, and waves pummeled the shore directly beneath Gracie's small deck and the much larger one recently added to the back of the bar next door.

"Into the ocean?" But before Izzy could ask Tess to clarify, two figures walked out of the bar's side door. The men were lit from behind — one tall and gangly, the other short and fat. Aprons covered their shirts and jeans and sounds of Garth Brooks poured out the door behind them.

"Abbot and Costello," Cass said.

"Dishwashers, I guess," Tess said.

The three women watched as the men walked toward the compost bin closest to their door and leaned against the edge, their backs to them, their beer cans balanced on the side of the bin. One struck a match, lighting two cigarettes and handing one over to the other man.

The men were unaware of the three women standing a short distance away and traded rough jokes while enjoying their break. Finally one of the men stood up and, before the women could react, turned and relieved himself into the compost bin.

"Eww," Cass said, her face contorted.

Aware of the women for the first time, he laughed loudly, tossed his beer can and cigarette into the compost bin, and followed his friend back into the Harbor Club. The door slammed shut, muting the sounds from within.

"Jerks," Tess said, but the mundane word

didn't begin to reflect the anger that filled her face. She clenched her fist, a gesture so forceful, the other two women heard her knuckles crack. She walked quickly toward the bin and leaned over, carefully picking out the cigarette butts and beer can. Then she headed toward the bar door and dropped the debris into a garbage can against the building.

Izzy and Cass yelled after her, urging her out of the cold and back inside Gracie's, where the warmth of the kitchen was waiting for them.

But Tess didn't hear them. Or didn't care. She tugged on the metal door handle to the bar. When she realized it was locked from within, she turned in the opposite direction and walked away, toward the sea, until the night swallowed her from sight.

When Izzy and Cass returned to their table, Ben and Nell were reaching for coats.

"So early?" Izzy asked.

"So sensible," Nell answered, and gave her niece a hug. "But I'll see you both tomorrow."

"Tomorrow?" Cass asked.

"The afternoon *hygge* in Izzy's shop," Nell said.

"You'd better come, Halloran," Izzy threatened. "I need you all to set the mood."

"Comfort and harmony, that's me," Cass said. "But sure. I'll come. Cider and cookies will get me every time."

Ben helped Nell into her heavy coat and they went off in search of Gracie to settle their tab.

Danny had joined the group and pushed the nearly empty basket of calamari across to Cass and Izzy, along with the last partially eaten lobster roll.

"My man is a giver," Cass said.

Not to be outdone, Sam offered Izzy the rest of his beer. "Okay, don't scold. I have a proposal you ladies can't refuse."

Izzy pushed her hair over one shoulder, looking up at her husband with what she intended to be a beguiling look. She lifted her brows. "Oh? Tell us . . ."

"Free cocktails and what some claim are the best buffalo wings on the North Shore."

"Where?" Izzy asked.

"Next door. I took some photos of the Harbor Club a couple weeks ago and the owner gave me an open invitation. Food and drinks on the house, he said."

"We don't have to stay long," Danny said. "But the place is worth seeing. At least once. And the wings are supposed to be great." Danny looked at Cass, assuming the mention of food would have an effect.

It did. "I'm in," she said. "Wings and I have a long history."

They bundled back into their coats and stepped outside, assaulted by a sharp wind coming in off the water. But the walk to the Harbor Club took less time than to put on their coats, and in seconds they were walking into the bar next door.

A tiled, heated entry kept the weather from going inside with them. And when they walked through the second door, Izzy's skepticism began to wear away.

A wooden bar shaped like the winding Cape Ann coastline dominated one side of the room. It was polished to a high sheen and tall leather stools circled it. Gigantic televisions hung from the ceiling at strategic angles.

The crowd had thinned out, and Cass and Izzy walked around groupings of small couches and leather sling chairs, and over to a huge stone fireplace centering the room. Curved leather booths lined one wall and, farther back, a wall of windows looked out onto the deck. The blinking at the top of a distant lighthouse was the only light in the black sky.

They found two couches not far from the fireplace. "A perfect spot for people-watching," Izzy said, sinking into the cushioned love seat. From here they could see the bar, the fireplace, and the deck, ringed with gaslights. The stage in the far corner was empty, the band either on break or had called it a night.

"Wow," Cass said. "I peeked in here one day, but it didn't look like much, with ladders and paint cans everywhere."

"It was interesting to photograph. Bobby is hoping to get a feature in a Boston events magazine. I said I'd put in a good word with those I've done work for." Although Sam's photography was the kind that won awards in art shows and featured in galleries, he still enjoyed what he called his "humble beginnings," and often honored friends' requests to shoot events.

"Who's Bobby?" Cass said, then answered herself. "Oh yeah. Bobby Abbott, the owner. The guys on the dock talk about him. Why don't we know him?"

"Probably because he's spent the last year trying to make this place amazing. Or could be it's because you don't hang out much in sports bars. Danny and I know the guy. Ben's been in with us a couple times, too, mostly for games. I think maybe Pete and the Fractured Fish played here a couple times this summer."

"So it's like a men's club?" Cass asked.

Sam laughed. "Not so you'd notice." He pointed over to the bar.

They looked over to the packed area. Sam was right. It wasn't just a men's bar. A bevy of women crowded the curving bar.

"Oh geesh," Izzy said suddenly, staring at the bar. She stood up to look more closely. "Look who's here."

Penny Turner sat on one of the cushioned bar stools, her stiletto heels hooked on the metal rung. But it was the red dress that captured their complete attention, sparkly and tight, with a plunging neckline that allowed her breasts more freedom than dresses normally did. Her lashes were thick and long, her blond hair piled high on her head and fastened with shiny combs. She held up a glass, her manicured nails bright marks against the clear drink.

"Who's that?" Danny asked, adjusting his glasses slightly.

"Who's who?" Cass said. "That guy with the Fu Manchu mustache and tattoos on his neck? Cute, huh?"

Danny chuckled. Penny had shifted on the stool, crossing her legs. One shapely leg swung back and forth. "Ian Fleming," he said.

"No, I'm pretty sure it's a she," Cass said.

"She looks like nearly every James Bond

book cover. I always wondered why my publishers didn't go that route. Do you know her?"

"Of course. You do, too. That's a dolled-up Penny. She's married to our chickens' doctor."

Danny's head jerked back. He stared at his wife. "Our *what*?"

"Chickens. The ones in the coop you built in our backyard. Well, actually, the doc has only seen one chicken, Hortense. She's the chief hen and she didn't look very good the other day, so I took her in to see Doc Turner."

Izzy chimed in. "You know him, too, Sam. He plays pickup basketball with you and Ben and those other old guys at the Y. He's probably responsible for at least one of your basketball injuries."

"Okay, sure. Quiet guy. Big hands — makes a lot of baskets."

"But back to Hortense?" Danny said, pushing up his glasses.

"Clark checked her out. He was very sweet and suggested I keep the chicken coop a little warmer. So I did. It was very good fowl advice."

Sam and Izzy laughed, wondering what else Cass would throw into her chicken adventure. Danny clearly didn't have the same devotion to Hortense and her friends as his wife.

"Okay, again," Danny said. "You did what?"

"I heated the coop. It worked and Hortense is feeling much better."

"Whew, that's a relief," Danny said, rolling his eyes and not wanting to hear what else Cass had added to their household.

"And that sexy James Bond book cover model is his new, much younger wife, Penny."

When they looked over again, Penny was hidden from sight by a couple of men standing behind her. *Close* behind her, Izzy noted. She wondered where Clark was.

As Sam started to get up to get drinks, a shadow fell across the group and a low voice greeted them. "Hey, so you guys made it."

"We did," Sam said, standing up and shaking the man's hand. He introduced the bar owner to Izzy and Cass.

Bobby Abbott offered his hand. "I've seen you both around town. Glad you finally came in."

Izzy and Cass recognized Bobby, too. He was noticeable. Young. Self-assured.

"We were right next door," Izzy said. "Sam suggested we come over to see the place."

"Next door?" He shook his head, frowned. "Gracie's dying dive? I don't think it's long for this world."

"Hey, she's a very good friend," Izzy said. Bobby's tone irritated her. Who did he think he was, anyway? She felt the need to talk more about Gracie, about what a great restaurant she had. So she did, cutting him off and expounding on the Lazy Lobster's amazing lobster rolls. And how Gracie Santos worked diligently to make her restaurant eco-friendly.

She stopped just short of asking him why he threw trash over the deck railing.

But Bobby Abbott seemed to have lost attention after the first sentence. He was looking across his own restaurant, as if looking at Gracie's through the wall, but his words were aimed at Izzy. "No biggie. Nothing lasts forever, right?" The words were muffled by laughter coming from the next table.

Izzy wasn't sure she was hearing him right, but before she could pursue it, Bobby had caught a waitress by the elbow. He had her take drink orders for the group, his eyes canvassing the room as he talked.

Cass had been looking around the room, too, waving at people she knew. "This place used to be a dump," she said. "You've done a decent job."

Bobby laughed. "Faint praise. Whattaya mean? This place is great. Have you been around here long?"

"Born and raised," Cass said.

Izzy sat back and watched him talking with Cass about the bar and the town. He seemed to skirt the issue when Danny pushed on how he got the coveted land, changing the subject and talking about how he'd probably expand, maybe open another one in Gloucester. Make this one bigger. He was good-looking, she supposed, but with an edge — his hair a little too long, his voice gravelly. A "three-day stubble beard," as Sam called them. And his dark eyes held something else that Izzy couldn't define. But they made her uncomfortable. She didn't like Bobby Abbott. And her guess was Gracie Santos didn't, either.

Bobby surveyed the room once more, then took a step away. "Hey, I gotta check on a few things. Everybody needs me. It's tough being big man on campus." He laughed. "But Bobby's *fantastico* buffalo wings are on their way over."

Izzy watched him circle the fireplace, his eyes on the bar, his boots loud on the hardwood floor and his swagger in tight black jeans drawing glances from a group of women sitting in a booth. He stopped, said a few words, and responded generously when one of them stood up and kissed him.

Next he headed to the bar, walking behind the crowd looking up at the final minutes of a football game. Izzy watched the cocky smile he gave to some, a joke to others. Not far down the bar, Penny Turner was looking at him, too. She had swiveled on her stool, the martini glass still held in her hand, her ruby red lips together.

Bobby slowed, his eyes moving up and down Penny's body. He ran a finger down her outstretched arm, whispered something in her ear. She stiffened, and he whispered again, pointing to his watch. Grinning. Then he moved on, toward the kitchen, and Penny slipped off the stool, following through the swinging door. In minutes she was back out, climbing back on the stool. Her face was contorted, angry, but in minutes the anger was gone and a smile slipped back into place. Controlled. In charge.

She turned to the blond-haired man next to her, a comfortable smile on her face. She laughed at something the man had said.

The man looked familiar and Izzy squinted, trying to see his full face.

Finally he turned and Izzy smiled. mostly because one of Lucky Bianchi's gifts was making people smile. And it made sense he was sitting up there at the bar. Lucky was everyone's friend. He loved bars, not for the alcohol, but because there were so many people to talk to.

She poked Cass and whispered, "Look who's here. Your buddy."

Lucky sometimes helped Pete and Cass and other fishermen out when they needed extra crew. As best as any of them could figure out, Lucky didn't do much in the way of work — a fact Pete Halloran confirmed. But no matter how unhelpful he might be, people liked having him around.

Cass laughed. "I should have known he'd be here. Pete says he's become especially attached to this bar. Pete comes with him sometimes, along with other guys on the crew. Crazy thing is, Lucky doesn't drink that much, but he likes hanging out. Especially here."

"Well, I guess the place can't be all that bad if Lucky likes it."

"I think everyone likes it. I'm thinking it's the boss man you don't like, Iz. I get it. But he's all talk. There's no way Gracie will let a guy like him get the best of her. He has no idea the power of the Lazy Lobster." She grinned, then turned away to greet a new guy she'd just hired to do some work for the Halloran Lobster Co.

Izzy went back to people watching. She zeroed in on Penny again, then looked around for Clark. The bar area was thick with people, and Penny seemed to know most of them, greeting and chatting. She was certainly more at home in the bar than in the Turner Animal Clinic and Kennels.

Then she spotted Clark, making his way through a break in the crowd. At least she *thought* it was Clark. Yes, it was, but without his buttoned-up shirt and starched white clinic jacket, he was barely recognizable. She poked Cass to look.

He carried a bottle of beer in one hand, but it was the outfit that had Izzy and Cass starring. The tight jeans looked slightly unnatural on his body. His plaid shirt, open at the neck, was adorned with a bolo tie.

"A bolo tie," Cass whispered loudly, and several heads turned their way.

"It's beautiful," Izzy said. The black silver-tipped cord was held together with a gleaming silver oval that caught the bar lights. An embedded turquoise stone sparkled as Clark moved, shining all the way across the room. "Pricey."

"Are you sure that's our Clark?" Cass said. Once the bolo tie surprise faded, they noticed his hair — slicked back in a swoosh.

"I think his hair is darker," Izzy whispered, although she supposed it could be the thick gel that held it in place. The beginnings of gray she had seen at his temples — distinguished-looking, she had always thought — were mysteriously gone tonight. This wasn't the same veterinarian who had taken care of Red, who had treated Purl's infection.

Nor the man who looked out for Cass's chicken.

Izzy wondered if Penny had seen Clark. She had an irrational urge to distract him, to protect him from the flirtatious scene he was walking toward.

But there was no need to protect Clark Abbott. As he approached, Penny turned, her face lighting up. She held out one arm, tossing her head back, and pulling him close. Clark leaned low, kissing her full on her lips. A kiss that kept on going.

Ugh, Izzy thought. *Too much PDA.* She quickly looked away, but Cass kept looking.

"Who knew a chicken doctor had that in him?" she said.

Clark finally pulled away and stood back, fiddling with the bolo tie around his neck as if he'd like to tear it off. He pulled something out of his pocket and lifted one of Penny's hands, his eyes focused on her face.

"Poor Clark," Izzy whispered, feeling instant empathy for her veterinarian. "Penny must have dressed him."

"And rehearsed him?"

Cass was right. Clark did look a little like someone who'd been pulled out of the audience and made to perform onstage.

But it was clear he adored his wife. And unless Izzy was losing her ability to read people, Penny loved him right back. She realized suddenly she was analyzing him, as if she were back in the courtroom. Watching his gestures, expressions, as if she needed to understand the man better. But this wasn't her business. Cass's either. They were being intrusive.

She looked away. But Cass poked her to keep looking.

Lucky Bianchi had gotten off his stool, clearly enjoying Penny and Clark's interaction, too. He slapped Clark soundly on the back. A good-natured, congratulatory gesture.

Clark smiled back at Lucky, a glimmer of pride in the expression. Then Penny held up her arm and showed off a new gold bracelet dangling from her wrist.

"Hey, that's touching," Cass said. "I'm seeing my chicken doctor in a whole different light. I think he just gave her a mighty

fancy piece of bling."

Clark leaned low again, whispering something in Penny's ear, one hand resting on her knee.

Penny reached up and touched his cheek with her fingertips, then let it slide off slowly. Her smile so warm, Izzy and Cass could feel it.

"What do you think he's saying?" Cass whispered to Izzy, their heads close together.

But just then, a waitress appeared, blocking their view. She carried a large platter heaped high with buffalo wings and small bowls of sauces. The coffee table between the two couches nearly groaned beneath its weight.

When the waitress had moved away, the two women looked back to the bar. Penny was still there, still smiling, her elbows on the bar. On one side of her, Lucky straddled the stool, his long legs stretching out. And Clark Turner was settling in on the other side, looking tired, but holding his own. Another beer appeared, and his free arm went around Penny's waist, settling comfortably in place.

"Hey, you two, where'd you go? Look at this spread." Danny was already on his second wing, his fingers greasy and his face happy.

The aroma of the garlicky buffalo wings was strong. Cass took a bite. She immediately closed her eyes and smiled full approval, words spinning out as if for a restaurant review: *crispy, light — spicy and peppery, amazing.*

Izzy laughed. With her taste buds, Cass could probably identify nearly every ingredient in the coating, every single spice and herb, even though the most complicated thing she cooked herself were scrambled eggs. And usually she left that to Danny.

Pots of blue-cheese dipping sauce were passed around, along with hunks of artisan bread and a pile of napkins to wipe away the piquant orange sauce dripping from their fingers and lips. Sam refilled heavy mugs of beer.

"I hate to admit it, but my eyes were bigger than my gut," Cass said finally. "But they were good. The guy is right. I'm totally losing interest in how he got this place or why he hires creepy dishwashers who flick cigarettes — and other things — in compost bins. As long as he keeps these wings coming."

"Yeah. Pretty good stuff," Sam said, getting up and looking around for their host. "But it's the first time ever I've seen you leave food on your plate."

Danny agreed as he wiped a smear of sauce from Cass's cheek with his napkin. "But I made up for what Cass didn't eat. If I eat one more, you'll have to carry me home again, Kathleen."

"It's 'I'll Take You Home Again, Kathleen,' " Cass said. "And I'm Catherine, if we're being correct. But it's a good idea. I'm bushed."

Sam reappeared. "Hey, I just saw Red's doc over at the bar. He and his wife are heading out, too."

"What did they say? What are they celebrating? An anniversary?" Izzy asked.

Sam shrugged. "Mostly we talked about our Sunday pickup game at the Y."

"I feel old," Izzy said, pulling on her coat and looking around the room. The band had packed their instruments away, but music was now pouring out of speakers around the room. Loud music — Led Zeppelin, Kiss, and Gallows-type songs. And a twenty-something crowd seemed to be moving in and loving it. Dancing bodies were filling up the area where the band had once been, even pouring onto the heated outdoor deck, the air pulsating with bodies and music.

"*Old?* Nah. Never old, Iz. They're just too young. I think this guy is trying to reach all age groups — and our time just ended. I saw some of our lobster crew in here earlier. A nondiscrimination kind of place. You can't blame him for that." They walked out to the heated entry to wait for Sam and Danny.

Izzy wondered. "Do you think he wants to run Gracie out of business?"

"He'd fail, Iz. Gracie's is a totally different kind of place."

Izzy nodded — but only because she wanted to believe Cass was right.

Cass was right about Gracie's restaurant — the two places were as different as two towns on the Cape Ann shore. Each distinctly handsome in its own way. Not to mention that the Lazy Lobster & Soup Café had to stay there forever because her Abby loved it — no matter that all she ever ate there were hot dogs. If Abby had her way, which she almost always did, it would house every birthday party to come.

"Hey, Iz, look." Cass pointed through the side window, toward the easement and the compost bins that separated the bar from Gracie's restaurant, now dark and locked up.

The windowpane was frosting up from the cold winds gusting over the harbor. Izzy rubbed her fingers in a circle, shaving a clean spot.

Two figures were silhouetted in the dim

outdoor lights, the wind blowing them and creating eerie Giacometti-looking shadows across the wooden bins. A tall man towered over a small woman, her green sweatshirt visible through an unbuttoned parka, her heavy boots planted firmly in front of the man.

Her face, caught in the light, was filled with emotion.

Horns honking pulled their attention to Sam and Danny's cars out front, lights on, waiting. Then honking again.

Cass pushed open the atrium door and the two women hurried out, each to her own car, but not before Izzy took one more, last look.

For the second time that night, Tess — she was sure it was Tess — had disappeared.

But a few feet away, his head lowered into the wind, Bobby Abbott was walking toward the front door of his restaurant, his hands shoved into the pockets of an unzipped jacket, his eyes down, and his face unreadable.

CHAPTER 7

It stormed that Saturday night, hours after they had all left the wharf restaurants. But a twist of the currents had turned the air just warm enough that what fell wasn't quite snow, though some would call it that. Instead, raindrops as big as flakes, as fat and heavy as winter water, covered Sea Harbor.

The fierce wind that accompanied it tore at the sand, mangling and rearranging long-ago fallen leaves and the shape of the land itself — and as it did, it turned a murder scene into a wintry mess.

Nell and Ben had gotten up early on Sunday morning, pulled from the warmth of the down comforter by the sound of wind on the large bedroom windows that faced the sea. They'd moved slowly, planning nothing for the gray morning but Birdie coming for breakfast, coffee before a fire. Moving into the day slowly.

But before the coffee had completely perked, Izzy bounded through the front door and across the family room in gloves and hat and a running jacket, her Nikes leaving damp imprints on the pine wood floor. "Hey, what's going on? The wind practically threw me out of bed, so I figured I might as well go for a run. But halfway through, it got the best of me. Strong Endicott coffee sounded better. And maybe one of Uncle Ben's scones?"

Birdie showed up at the Endicotts' slightly later, but while the sky outside was still dark, the early-morning light struggled against the wind and rain for its rightful place.

Nell heard the Lincoln Town Car pull into the driveway and switched on the outside light. Harold held a flapping umbrella over Birdie while he hustled her to the door. He hurried back to the safety of the car with barely a hello.

"I've probably gotten up before any of you," she said, shrugging out of her heavy coat and leaving her boots at the door. "It wasn't an easy night for sleep."

Nell looked at the lines on her dear friend's face. They were lovely lines, a map of Birdie's life. But her usually clear gray eyes lacked the luster usually found there.

"You're worried, Birdie. Is Gabby all right?"

Birdie patted Nell's hand. "Of course everyone's fine. And I am, too. I'm just rattled a bit. I don't know why. I'm thinking it must be this weather."

Ben poured four mugs of coffee as Nell passed the creamer around.

"It *was* wicked," Izzy said, stirring her coffee to a light tan. "Abby woke up and ended in bed with Sam and me. A long night."

"I'm sure I would have slept much better with that sweet bundle of goodness cuddled up next to me," Birdie said. "Instead, I had the wind. It has always unnerved me a bit. And in a thirty-room house with dozens of windows and creaky floors, it can turn the night into a bad symphony of rattles and groans and squeaks."

Nell smiled, but didn't dare suggest Birdie could easily move out of her Ravenswood Road mansion and into one of the new condos on Canary Cove. Birdie lived and would die, surrounded by the walls that held the lingering smells and memories of Sonny Favazza.

"And then there were the sirens," Birdie said.

"Sirens? When?"

"I don't know. An hour or so ago? Time has gotten away from me."

"I thought I heard them, too," Izzy said. "But I figured it was just the wind."

"A fire, I wonder," Nell said.

"Harold turned on the radio on the way over and there was no news of one. He heard the sirens, too. He thought they were headed toward the wharf. For as old as he is, his hearing is spot on."

Nell looked out the kitchen window. With the trees bare, she could see through their wooded backyard to the ocean. The wind was dying down, and the sky was finally a lighter shade of gray. There was no sign of flames, although the harbor was too far away to see from the windows.

"That nor'easter a few months ago pushed some boats up on shore," Ben said. "I hope those near the wharf are okay." He moved to the stove, checking a pan of scones.

"I was thinking of Gracie's place," Birdie said. "Her restaurant hangs right out there like it was about to take a swim."

"I'll check on her. Then you'll feel better." Izzy pulled out her cell phone and sent Gracie a text, then looked happily at her uncle as he put on an oven mitt and pulled his weekend treats from the oven.

Nell glanced at the wall clock. She felt

slightly uprooted, too. That anxious feeling that has no grounding, but refuses to leave. "Has Gracie texted back yet?" she asked Izzy.

"Nope. But we've only given her two seconds. She may still be asleep. I think she'd have called one of us if there was a leak somewhere and she needed her bucket brigade. Gracie's resourceful."

But Birdie didn't look comforted. "If she doesn't call, why don't we take a drive over there in a bit? Just in case. Just to make sure —" Her thin silver brows lifted.

"Sure, Birdie. That's a good idea," Ben said. A small schooner had been bouncing around on the waves when they'd left the night before. One Ben had actually helped the captain build a few years earlier. He suspected it might be in greater danger than Gracie's well-built restaurant, but it wouldn't hurt to check on both.

Nell passed plates and napkins around. "Gracie's place has weathered worse storms. I think she'll be fine, but there's no harm in checking." She cradled a warm coffee mug in her hands, feeling a chill.

"It's just a premonition. Most likely nothing. I seem to have more of those these days. Sometimes I'm not sure what it is that causes the niggling feeling that the world is slightly off its axis. But it's there. And this morning it seems to be very much there."

Nell nodded. She understood the feeling. She had had it many times herself. But she wondered now if Birdie's feelings these days weren't heightened by the responsibility of a preteen living in her home. Gabby was the heart and soul of Birdie's life right now. Her granddaughter's world was young and safe. And Birdie was determined to keeping it that way.

Ben had poured a basil-seasoned bowl of eggs into an oiled pan — its fragrant sizzle somehow comforting.

But when time came to bundle up and pile into the Endicott SUV an hour later, the comfort of scones and eggs and hot coffee had been handily wiped away by the freezing damp day, sliced in half by the sound of sirens.

The large parking lot near the wharf was nearly empty, the weather having kept most people inside.

"I think that's Gracie's green Prius up ahead," Nell said, pointing in the distance to the row closest to the water.

Ben nodded and drove across the lot, pulling near it. The rain had finally stopped completely. They got out of the car and

walked up the paved walkway toward the wharf. Birdie walked in silence beside Nell, one hand pressed to her heart.

As they rounded the small maritime museum, they slowed, then stopped, staring at the edge of the wharf, staring at the scene ahead. It wasn't close to what they had expected, and the damage had not been done by the storm. In the distance they spotted Gracie, standing alone, her back to them, her head held high as if impervious to the cold.

"Gracie!" Ben called out as they began walking toward her. Faster now. She stood between her café and the Harbor Club. And it was only then that they spotted several officers patrolling the area between the lobster café and bar. They were barely recognizable, their thick stocking caps pulled down around their ears and cheeks. Until finally they spotted a tall man, older than the others and hatless, walking between the two buildings, around Gracie's compost bins, until he spotted the small group that had come to Gracie's side. He lifted a hand in greeting and hurried their way.

Chief Jerry Thompson was one of Ben Endicott's closest friends. They sailed together, went to games together, but mostly enjoyed relaxing on the Endicott deck over a chilled

martini, debating issues, solving the world's problems, and trying to understand the capriciousness of human nature — something Jerry often saw up close and personal.

Jerry was shaking his head as he approached the group. His voice was grave. "It's not what we need for the holidays."

Birdie went over and wrapped one arm around the waist of Gracie's puffy jacket, a gesture that brought a sad smile to the younger woman's face. She pressed closer to the comfort of Birdie.

"I'm thinking it's not storm damage we're talking about," Ben said.

"If only," Jerry replied, a weary smile crossing his strong face. "Someone fell off the balcony of the Harbor Club's deck, probably late last night or early morning. He landed on the rocks below. There's only a sliver of beach down there when the tide is out. Nothing much to cushion the fall. A few boulders and the ocean. The man is dead."

Nell looked over at Gracie. Her face was white, her bottom lip caught between her teeth. She wondered if Gracie had discovered the body, and desperately hoped she hadn't.

"A drinking accident?" Ben asked. He looked over at the bar next door.

Nell tried to visualize what Ben was suggesting. A few weeks ago she had stood on Gracie's deck, looking over at the larger, more elaborate one behind the Harbor Club. Unlike Gracie's deck railings, these were curved and low, perfect for holding glasses or to lean against, even to sit on, though not intended for that. But lower than the norm. Nell had thought the height looked dangerous, plus it lacked the glass protection some Sea Harbor decks had to soften the wind. Even with Gracie's higher rail, safe and sturdy, the image of someone falling over was enough to make sure she never took her eyes off Abby when she ran around Gracie's deck devouring a hot dog.

"I don't think it was the drinking," Jerry said. He frowned, as if wanting to make his statement stronger. Instead, he said, "We'll know for sure when we get the autopsy results."

Before they could ask why, or if the man had been identified, Tommy Porter, Jerry's second in command, walked toward them from the back decks. He hugged Ben and Nell like he always did. Tommy was a legend in Sea Harbor, if someone in his thirties could be called that — the sweet neighborhood boy who had grown up and gone off to the police academy, making his parents and the whole town inordinately proud. Especially when he'd returned and woven himself back into their lives, keeping them safe.

Today Tommy looked older than his years.

"I think they're almost through down there, Chief," Tommy said. "Want me to go over to the house?"

"The house," Jerry repeated, thinking. His brow pinched together as if something hurt. He rubbed it absently with two fingers. Then he nodded. "Yes. Thanks, Tom." He tore a piece of paper off a pad in his hand and handed it to him. "It's one of those big ones over near Granite Road. Near Beech Tree Woods."

Nell looked up. She looked over at Birdie — the area wasn't far from her house. Birdie was listening carefully, too.

Gracie had barely said a word.

Tommy said his good-byes to the group and walked off, his boots heavy on the wet wharf. Jerry stuck the pad in his pocket, watching him disappear around the museum.

"Not an easy job. But the lad is damn good at it."

"Job?" Birdie asked.

"Telling the next of kin. Bobby Abbott's wife."

Chapter 8

Bobby Abbott. The name rippled through the room, hurting their ears.

They had gathered around the fire that Gracie had lit in the café's fireplace. She plugged in a pot of coffee and turned up the heat. Still shivering, she stood in front of the fire, rubbing her hands.

Chief Thompson had moved apart from the others. He was standing near the deck doors, making phone calls and drinking the cup of coffee Gracie had handed him.

"I couldn't sleep, so I came in early," Gracie began, staring into the fire. "Just to be sure there was no damage from the storm. I didn't think there would be, but you know, it's like double-checking to be sure your kid is safe in bed, even though you know they are. The police were already here. The morning security guard called it in."

"It doesn't seem real, Gracie. We just

talked to him. We were over there . . ."

Gracie's head went up. "You were over there? When?"

"You were at the Harbor Club?" Nell asked.

"We went over after you and Uncle Ben left last night. Sam wanted to give Bobby a flash drive of photos and Cass and I hadn't seen the inside and were curious. So we all went." Izzy tried to bring back the evening: the noise, the people, the expensive interior. And Bobby Abbott.

The back doors opened, letting in a breeze, as Jerry Thompson walked out, then down the deck staircase.

"Was it crowded over there?" Gracie asked. "I didn't pay attention because we were so busy here. But it's always packed over there on weekends. People seemed to come in groups — the after-work crowd, then the dinner and sports crowd, if there's a game on. Fishermen, millennials. And the late nighters? I know when the younger crowd comes in, it's time for me to close up shop."

"That's a good description of what we saw before we left — a twenty-something group that was pounding the dance floor with more energy than I've had since before Abby was born."

Nell listened to the conversation, her eyes moving from the fire to activity beyond the front windows where she saw a police car drive off, then back to the small group huddling around the fire.

"When does the bar close?" Ben asked.

"The law requires bars to close at two. I think sometimes Abbott does. Sometimes not." She looked over again at the building. "It's kinda surreal, that he'd fall off his own deck like that. And I don't think he even drank. He told me once his dad was an alcoholic. A rich alcoholic. He had said, 'the worst kind.' "

Jerry had come back inside, and he stood a few feet away, texting.

Nell watched his face and realized he was also listening.

"Were you friends with Bobby, Gracie?" Birdie asked.

Gracie didn't answer at first. And when she did, she seemed to regret what she was about to say even before she said it.

"Not really. In the beginning he seemed nice, wanting to be good neighbors. He was . . . suave, I guess. Flirty. He could talk to anyone. But then I saw what he was like with people who disagreed with him. With some of the women staff. Not very nice at all. And then I saw it firsthand."

They listened. Jerry Thompson's head lifted, too.

"Bobby wanted to buy me out. Not because he wanted to run my Lazy Lobster and love it like I do. He wanted to buy it and destroy it. Build another glitzy place." She looked out the front windows, her voice dropping. "And he didn't, not for one minute, even think that I might say no."

A clearing of his throat and shuffling of heavy boots announced that Jerry Thompson was returning to the group. Nell watched their good friend, suspecting his noisy walk was to allow them to stop talking if there was something they didn't want him to hear. A generous and diplomatic gesture, and probably one he didn't use with everyone.

Jerry slipped his phone into his pocket. "This is tough, Gracie." He tried to put a smile into his words. He'd known Gracie since she was a little girl who played with his own daughter. "I'm not sure there's a heap of town folks who knew Abbott, so I will need to talk to you some more. Maybe later today. Or let me know and I'll send Tommy to you. Whatever works best. And, Izzy, you said you were over there last night? You and Sam?"

Izzy looked confused, not sure how her

presence could be relevant to an accident they hadn't witnessed. "We were only there for an hour or so. Danny and Cass were with us. There was still a lot of activity going on when we left. An accident is an accident, right?"

The police chief had pulled his pad out again and scribbled something on it, then looked up with a sigh that didn't indicate he was tired. At least not the kind that required a nap.

"Unless it's not. Bobby Abbott didn't fall off the deck accidentally. There's some initial evidence both from the railing and from the body itself that he was pushed over the railing. And he was pushed hard. Hard enough to kill him."

Nell, with Birdie and Izzy in the back seat, had dropped Ben off at home, then picked up Cass at her cozy home on the ocean side of Canary Cove. They arrived at the yarn shop just as the sky was finally beginning to clear, thin rays of sunlight making their way through the thick gray sky.

They had filled Cass in on the ride over and soon realized how little time it took in the retelling — certainly not nearly as long as news of a murder should take. But there was little to say. A man had been pushed over a railing to his death. A man they knew, however superficially. Someone they had talked to just hours before. And somehow that proximity of time made this death uncomfortably personal.

Nell had suggested to Izzy that they cancel the Sunday knitting *hygge* session, but Izzy had said no. It was exactly what they needed. No one knew how soon the news would be out, but surely some enterprising reporter had followed the early-morning sirens and had been lurking in the shadows of the wharf, taking notes. But even if the news was still confined to a few, there was nothing they could do.

Izzy was right. Nell saw the wisdom of her thinking clearly. The coming days were going to happen around them in whatever way they would. They would have little control. But this day, this moment, they could make their own. Peace before the storm.

Gracie had stayed behind at the Lazy Lobster & Soup Café, insisting she didn't need company. She needed to talk to her staff, to let them know they'd be closed that day — and to try and process it all.

Fortunately, the Harbor Club wasn't open on Sundays anyway — there'd be no chance of people showing up at the door and the police could call the staff in quietly. Although it had stopped raining, the damp cold would keep most strollers and joggers away from the wharf itself.

Ben had asked Jerry Thompson if the whole wharf area would be cordoned off, and he said no, just the bar. He and his crew had been there for several hours, and they had most of what they needed. He'd have extra men around, though, just in case.

Nell wasn't sure what *just in case* meant, but it had caused a shiver up her spine that was still there, and she welcomed the burst of warm air that met them inside Izzy's yarn shop.

"Someone pushed him?" Cass said for the tenth time. She knelt in front of the fireplace in the knitting room, placing crumpled paper and pine logs on the hearth and lighting a match. She sat back on her legs and watched the burst of flames fill the opening. Her face glowed. "How do they even know that?"

None of them knew the answer. Nor if it had happened when the bar was packed and noisy, as it had been when Izzy and Cass were there. Or later.

"If it happened with a packed bar there," Birdie said, "surely someone would have seen it. And once they have a chance to talk to people, it will all be resolved."

But the police chief didn't mention being called to the scene while the bar was open. No 911 calls until the morning security guard called in. Finding the answer soon and easily was wishful thinking.

What was more pressing to them right now, closing in on the small group and soon the whole town, was the reality of a murder. The lives that would be affected, including a woman who had been widowed in a fraction of a second.

"Did any of you know Bobby had a wife?"

"I don't think even Gracie knew," Izzy said. "At least not from the look on her face when the chief sent Tommy to the house."

"That's weird," Cass said.

They all agreed. But some people kept their home life private.

"Or maybe it's like Mr. Rochester's third-floor secret that spooked Jane Eyre," Cass suggested.

Izzy went over and swatted her friend lightly on the back. "I didn't know lobster-women took English lit?"

The note of levity was welcome, and Izzy reminded them that the *hygge* group would be coming in before long.

Birdie unpeeled the wrapping on a plate of sandwiches they'd picked up on their way over. "I still can't get Gracie off my mind.

She looked so little today. Trauma seems to shrink people. Having a murder just a few feet away from her restaurant is a lot to handle."

"Not Gracie. If she looked smaller, it was because she was cold. Gracie Santos is a trooper," Cass said, leaving her perch at the fireplace and reaching for one of the sandwiches. "She's one of the strongest people I know. And it isn't that Bobby was a friend or anything."

"I guess not." But the more Nell tried to put the whole evening in focus, the more little details came to light. The man she and Ben had seen the night before when they left Gracie's place. He'd been greeting people outside the bar. He looked familiar, but it was only now that she realized it was the same man she'd seen the morning before. The man who had walked out of the Harbor Club as if he owned the place. Directly into sweet Abby's path.

Of course. It was Bobby Abbott. Or was her imagination playing tricks on her? Maybe what trauma did was shrink one's memory, not the whole body. Or perhaps the opposite — it exploded it into vivid imagination.

Days ago Bobby Abbott didn't figure in her life in any conceivable way. And suddenly, in death, he was taking up space. Much more than she would have liked.

Chapter 9

The fact that Mae Anderson arrived an hour later with a smile on her long narrow face and a spring in her step told the four of them what they needed to know: the news of Bobby Abbott's murder was still buried beneath the cloak of the cold gray day and the Sea Harbor Police Department. Mae knew nearly everyone in town. If she wasn't aware of the horror on the wharf, even the mayor was probably still in the dark.

But they would know soon. Yellow tape strung in front of a popular bar would not go unnoticed.

"Down here, Mae," Izzy called as she set out candles around the knitting room.

With Nell's help, Mae carried supplies down to the knitting room and the two began plugging in pots for hot chocolate and spiced cider.

Cass busied herself finding music to set

the mood.

"Peaceful," Izzy said. "Cozy. But not too 'churchy.' "

"Got it," Cass said, and in the next minute a virtual *hyggelig* playlist of gentle soul-filling music — a medley of soft jazz, classical guitar, and a few Norah Jones and Adele songs mixed in — floated like a soothing balm over the room.

The room grew warmer with the music, the candles, the crackling fire lighting up dark corners of the room and casting cheerful shadows along the walls. The two Danish rockers Izzy had brought from her den at home furthered the Danish *hyggelig* mood.

"I've died and gone to heaven," Mae declared, her skinny arms lifting into the air. "And to think I thought this was one of the worst ideas on your list of many, Iz."

"Thanks, Mae." Izzy wrinkled her nose at the store manager and threw a bag of large needles at her. "Let's put these out, along with those baskets of super chunky yarn. I think we're nearly set."

A bit of heaven. Exactly what the day called for.

As they all helped Izzy loop soft afghans over the couches and chairs, the room began to fill. The feeling created before the women ever arrived encouraged softer voices and lots of hugs.

Nell looked over at Cass. She'd been right all along. It was a hugfest.

Izzy had suggested people dress in their most comfortable, loose, and cozy clothes — pajamas if they wished. It would be like a grand slumber party — without slumber.

Laura Danvers — Izzy's friend and mother of three young girls — was the poster child for attire, her plaid pajamas thick and warm, and a pair of wooly knit socks coming nearly up to her knees. Laura showed off her outfit, strutting around the room and passing out freshly baked cinnamon donuts she had made that morning.

A dozen people had gathered, some good friends, but all acquaintances, all who moved into the warmth of the music-filled and apple cider–scented room as if it was a tonic they had been waiting for. Plump yarn was pulled from knitting bags, and patterns for easy pillows and blankets, head huggers and inside-out hats for chemo patients, and bulky scarves and sweaters, were passed around.

Thus did Izzy's first *hygge* gathering begin, blocking out a cold and damp day and putting news of a murder at bay, at least for a few more hours.

"This is a wonderful beginning to our holiday season," Beatrice Scaglia, Sea Harbor's mayor, said, walking over to where Nell and Birdie were sitting. She placed one elegant hand on Nell's shoulder as she looked around the room for a chair.

Nell smiled at her. And waited. The hand on her shoulder seemed to portend something, but when she looked into her eyes, she could see that Beatrice was there, just like all the others, for coziness and warm fellowship. Or mostly. Knowing Beatrice, there'd be an ulterior motive, too, but thankfully not news of a murder. The mayor liked to keep her finger on the heartbeat of her town, something she was convinced beat strongest wherever a group of women gathered. And though she eschewed Izzy's invitation to dress comfortably — appearing as always in a tailored and tasteful suit — she'd come and supported the happening.

Nell lifted her knitting off the couch and Beatrice happily sat down in the space.

Birdie greeted her warmly and glanced down at Beatrice's elegant knitting bag, dotted with pearls.

Beatrice caught her look. "Harrods. I bought it on my vacation across the pond," she said happily, offering a rare self-deprecating laugh. "Someday, when I am old and gray and have a nice rocker on the front porch, you two will teach me to knit."

Nell and Birdie chuckled, taking no offense. Everyone in town knew Beatrice couldn't knit or purl if her life depended on it, but as Mae Anderson attested to, she had the largest stock of yarn in town and should they ever have some horrible storm, they'd all head to Beatrice's, where more yarn existed than in the whole of Izzy's Seaside Knitting Studio.

"I'm seeing your lovely granddaughter all over town," Beatrice said to Birdie, changing the subject and rubbing her smooth bamboo needles as she talked. "She's growing up so quickly. Such a sweet, impressionable age."

Birdie lay the soft head hugger she was knitting in her lap. There was something behind Beatrice's words and smile that she couldn't quite read. She waited.

Nell leaned forward a bit, listening, too.

"I thought perhaps she was coming here with you," Beatrice went on.

"To the shop you mean?"

Now Beatrice looked confused. But it wasn't quite genuine. "Well, yes. That was a possibility. I saw her over at Coffee's as I passed by." Then she added, "She was with that young woman who works over at Dr.

Turner's clinic. At the kennels, actually. I board my sweet Henry there when I travel and I met her this summer. She grew up north of here, I've heard. You know whom I mean. She's been teaching part-time over at Sea Harbor Community Day School."

Nell frowned. Beatrice's tone indicated exactly what she thought of Tess Bean. Without conscious thought, Nell found herself defending the young woman.

"Tess is lovely. A smart, interesting woman. As you probably know, she believes strongly in protecting our environment. She even offered to help me build my own compost bin. Perhaps she'd help you with one?"

Beatrice smiled. A mayoral kind of smile. Dismissive. At least of the topic.

Nell glanced at Birdie and read her thoughts. They both waited patiently for what would come next: for the mayor to connect Gabby Marietti to the environmental activist. Nell knew from Birdie that Gabby had spent the night at the Danvers house again, working on a school project about the environment. Gabby had been excited about it, and Birdie was happy she'd be busy. But there was still concern lurking behind it all.

Nell looked across the room to where

Laura Danvers was working on a thick wool scarf for the shop's winter donation project. Laura wasn't concerned. Birdie shouldn't be, either, she thought.

Beatrice followed her look. "Maybe it was Laura who gave them a ride. I believe her daughter was there, too. She looks just like her father, don't you think? Elliott is a handsome man. He and Laura are so generous to our town."

Beatrice rambled on for a bit, extolling the Danverses' contributions and philanthropic endeavors, while Birdie and Nell wondered silently when she'd get to her point. It certainly wasn't reporting that Gabby and her friend were at Coffee's, a place preteens often gathered.

"Did you go inside?" Nell finally asked. But they knew the answer before she'd finished the question.

"Well, just for a second. Just to say hello to some of the regulars who hang out in there. To keep in touch with my constituents. I like to know what's going on."

"Which was?" Birdie asked.

"Not very much. A group of girls were in the back, Daisy and Gabby and others."

"What were they doing?" Birdie asked.

Beatrice was embarrassed now, a light flush to her cheeks. She didn't want to appear like she had been spying on young girls. "Oh, you know. Just girl things. Giggling, being silly. They were working on some kind of project, making something. Gluing things. The tables were a mess, but they weren't bothering anyone. No one. Gabby is such a lovely young girl."

"And Tess?"

Beatrice shrugged. "I didn't pay too much attention to her. She had a serious look about her. A little bossy, maybe. But Randy, he's the new barista at Coffee's, seemed charmed by her, just like the girls are. Even when she suggested to him that the straws he was sticking in the mocha drinks were harmful. 'Killing fish,' she said, which embarrassed him I thought. Or maybe not. Randy seemed okay with what she said. He even said he'd talk to his boss to see what they could do about the straws."

Nell and Birdie watched Beatrice, amused. She seemed to be arguing with herself about Tess, and Tess was coming out ahead. And finally Beatrice rose from the couch and graciously moved on to another group.

Later, as the flames died low, the amber light receding, the room began to thin out. People moved slowly, smiling, their faces showing signs of cinnamon and sugar, their arms carrying nearly finished projects.

Voices faded away as the bell above the door chimed its good-bye and finally the knitting room fell silent.

Nell walked over to the casement windows and looked out to the sea and the sky. Even the day seemed to have lightened, the waves moving in slow motion, the sky opening as the day grew old. The happenings of the last twenty-four hours seemed not to have happened. They didn't fit in this world.

Cass and Birdie were sweeping up the final crumbs; Mae and Izzy were collecting needles and stray skeins of yarn, their faces flushed.

"A *hyggelig* moment. That's what this was," Izzy said, looking over to where her aunt stood.

"It was that." Nell smiled.

"It still is. It lingers," Birdie said. She'd relaxed completely after Laura had whispered in her ear that all was well with "our girls." Working on a project was all. One that got them up at the crack of dawn, she had added. She'd collect them on her way home.

Even Cass admitted she felt like she'd just had a massage. The fire, the cider, the music. "A wet noodle, that's what I am."

Only Mae seemed slightly out of sorts.

"What's up?" Izzy asked.

"It's Margaret. I'm worried about her."

"Margaret Garozzo?" Izzy said. "Was she here? I didn't see her —"

"That's the thing," Mae said. "She came in the shop three times yesterday, making sure she had the right time for the *hygge.* She bought a heap load of the super chunky yarn we got in last week." Mae chuckled a little. "I asked her if she was going to make a Santa suit for Harry out of it. And then I saw her at church today, looking tired, like she really needed the afternoon we had planned. I gave her the time again and it brightened her up a bit. Her good friend Harriet Brandley asked after her, too. She was supposed to meet her here."

"Maybe Harry needed her in the restaurant," Cass suggested.

They offered up other reasons, too, though none of them really knew. Illness. Tiredness. Family plans. It didn't seem that important. People changed their minds. They let the matter go.

It was a short time later, after they had pulled on boots and heavy coats and dimmed the lights, reluctant to leave the mood that hung over, that they heard the commotion outside. Children's laughter at first, and then a few horns honking. Voices.

When Cass opened the heavy front door and they gathered outside on the steps, they realized quickly how wrong they were in their conjured-up excuses for a tired, forgetful Margaret Garozzo.

Across the street, coming toward them from the opposite end of Harbor Road, was a makeshift parade. Nearly a dozen young girls in puffy parkas were carrying colorful signs and wearing an array of plastic hats — some made from plastic straws, some from plastic bags or wrappings, and some from six-pack rings that hold soda bottles together. One colorful sign read: OUR EARTH CAN'T DIGEST PLASTIC.

Small children shopping with their parents waved and laughed at the silly hats and the girls wearing them. The girls complied by entertaining the kids with crazy, impromptu dances, making their giggles soar higher into the icy air and bringing a sidewalk-fair atmosphere to the scene.

And along the walk, at each Harbor Road shop, one person would stray from the group, leaving behind yet another stack of flyers before she was absorbed back into the group.

"Oh my," Birdie said, her gloved hand pointing across the road.

They all looked, and no one had any

doubt at whom Birdie was pointing.

Her height pulled Gabrielle Marietti above the others, and her black hair looked shiny beneath an eccentric-looking plastic hat. Daisy Danvers, Gabby's bespectacled — and much shorter — best friend, walked at her side.

Gabby and Daisy stopped in their tracks, spotting the women across the street. They waved their arms wildly, grinning, and calling out loudly to Izzy, Nell, Birdie, and Cass. Their faces were bright, their youthful bodies lively.

Just behind them, a watchful Tess Bean followed the haphazard group, keeping the girls safely on the sidewalk, urging the stragglers to keep up, and carrying a mountain of flyers in her arms.

But it was the person bringing up the very end of the line, like a giant punctuation mark to the youthful bodies ahead of her, who got the most attention from the four women standing on the step.

Carrying an enormous green sign with SAVE OUR OCEAN painted across it, her head adorned with an elaborate homemade plastic hat that rivaled any royal wedding fascinator, was the knitters' missing *hygge* member, clearly having her own *hyggelig* moment.

Margaret Garozzo looked happier than she'd looked in a long, long time.

Chapter 10

Gabby pushed her plastic hat back in place as she continued to wave vigorously. She had spotted Birdie right away. She could always spot her *nonna,* no matter where they were or how crowded it was. She had decided it was because her *nonna* had a special air about her, kind of like a glow, and it made her stand out. Like it did right now. It had a name, too, although Gabby would never say it out loud at the risk that someone might smudge it somehow. It was *goodness. Nonna* Favazza had it deep inside her. And because she did, she could see it in others, even when Gabby couldn't.

Nonna was standing in the midst of a towering Izzy and tall Nell. Even Cass had a couple of inches on her *nonna.* But there she was, her silvery head practically invisible beneath the thick hat Gabby had knit her for Christmas last year. And she was smiling and waving right back.

Her *nonna* was proud, Gabby thought. She was beginning to get it. At least Gabby hoped she did. She touched the plastic hat she'd made — a combination of plastic six-rings, multiple straws, and bottle caps, things they'd gathered early that morning when they'd joined Tess at the beach, scavenging for plastic trash and finding more than anyone could ever have imagined.

Daisy's mom had insisted on washing the bag of disgusting plastic before they took it to Coffee's to make their creations. They were making things people would notice and remember. At least that was their hope.

It was all about awareness, Tess had told them. And using the plastic that people used every day and sometimes thoughtlessly tossed on the beach, waiting for waves to take it out to sea, might help people make a connection.

The mayor hadn't been overjoyed to see the mess they were making in Coffee's, but sometimes you just had to make a mess to clean one up. And that was the truth.

Tess said not to get discouraged. It took time, she said. Good things did.

Yes, Gabby agreed. She knew for sure that was true. Good things took time. It had taken her over half her life to meet her *nonna.* And that had been a great thing in her life. Better than good. But other things took time, too. She was just beginning to realize that. And that she didn't know everything right off the bat, even though sometimes she thought she saw things more clearly than adults did. Maybe it was because she had less baggage.

She glanced back at Tess. She was walking slowly to keep Margaret with the group. Tess had been different today. Distracted. Tired, sort of. They had all gotten up early that morning for the beach cleanup and Tess had come, too — which might be why she looked tired. But it seemed more than that. There was a kind of sadness about her. As if her thoughts were dealing with something else. None of them knew if she had a boyfriend, but maybe that was it. That's what some of the girls thought. Or maybe her thoughts were simply somewhere she didn't want to be. Gabby got that.

"Hey, Gabs, you're falling behind," Daisy said, grabbing her friend's arm and tugging her along. "My mom's meeting us at the gazebo. Pizza at Papa Diego's."

Gabby took in a deep breath and released it slowly through pursed lips, sending puffs into the icy air.

"Onward," she and Daisy said in unison.

■ ■ ■ ■

The women hadn't intended to walk down to the corner park. It had been a long day and they all wanted to get home to a glass of wine and warm fire. But they were finding it difficult to pull their eyes away from the girls in their colorful jackets. Or maybe it was the plastic "baroque" creations that rose high off their heads that lured them.

Or maybe it was Margaret Garozzo, bringing up the rear.

"I wonder if Harry knows Margaret is doing this," Nell said. They were all wondering similar things, including whether Birdie was aware that her granddaughter and her best friend were this involved in Tess's eco movement. But no one said it out loud.

"Gabby spends a lot of time with her best friend, Daisy Danvers. That's what twelve-year-olds do," Birdie said aloud, as if their wonderings had passed from head to head and finally ended up in her own. And needed an explanation. "Gabby and Daisy are both interested in the environment, a good thing, and Daisy's mother, Laura, is a great help in shepherding the girls to these events. Laura is a wonderful mother, and she loves Gabby like one of her own. She's careful and wise, and I trust her . . ."

With my granddaughter went unspoken. But the fact that Birdie couldn't say the same about Tess Bean was noticed by her friends.

They reached the small park on the corner, directly across from the Sea Harbor Museum, and found the girls gathered near the gazebo, where an enterprising vendor had set up a hot chocolate stand for the holiday season and was handing out cups to eager hands. Tess had moved slightly apart from the girls and was sitting on a bench, drinking from her water bottle. A distracted look shadowed her face.

Margaret had leaned her sign against the gazebo and was wandering around the square park, nodding to passersby to make sure they saw her plastic hat. She was handing out flyers while reciting all the damage that plastic did to our earth and to the ocean, especially here in Sea Harbor. Nearly everyone in Sea Harbor knew Margaret from the deli that she and Harry owned — the large, gentle woman who kept Harry in line. The woman who made the most amazing *stracciatella* soup on this continent. So everyone smiled as Margaret approached. And no one refused a flyer.

They spotted Laura Danvers helping the

hot chocolate vendor pass out cups. A basket of donuts sat on the steps and was being emptied rapidly. She spotted the women and hurried down the steps, greeting Birdie with a hug.

"Can you believe our girls, Birdie? Community activists. I'm so proud of them." She then suggested to Birdie that she and Gabby join the Danverses for pizza that night at the girls' favorite place.

Nell saw a smile light up Birdie's face. The earlier worry seemed to fall away as she accepted Laura's invitation. Nell knew that pizza — which Birdie rarely ate — had nothing to do with the look. It was being included in an ordinary family's routine on a Sunday night — families with kids.

Nell walked off with Izzy and Cass, leaving Laura and Birdie to make their plans. They spotted Margaret feeding a donut to a squirrel and began heading her way.

"Hello, ladies," Margaret called to them, her cheeks ruddy from the cold. She held up a small piece of donut. "That squirrel was ferociously hungry."

As Nell approached, she noticed that Margaret looked like she had, in fact, dressed for the *hygge.* She wore heavy sweat pants and a thick Patriots sweatshirt. Comfort clothes.

"We missed you today, Margaret," Izzy said. She smiled and touched a ring of plastic that had come loose and was now tangled in Margaret's loose gray hair.

"You missed me?" Margaret looked confused.

"At the knitting *hygge*?" Izzy said. "Or 'hugfest,' as Cass calls it."

Margaret wrinkled her face in thought, deep grooves forming across her forehead. And then her face relaxed and she raised a palm to her cheek. "Oh, dear Izzy. The knitting *hygge.* Of course. Is that tomorrow?"

"It was today, Margaret. But no problem," Izzy reassured her. "We'll be having a very special one closer to the holidays. And you will be there."

Margaret nodded. Embarrassment and frustration clouded her face.

"But look at what you've done instead, Margaret," Izzy said quickly.

"Marching out here in the cold with these amazing young girls. Helping them. We're so proud of you."

That pleased Margaret and she looked over at the chatting and laughing girls on the gazebo steps. "They are something, aren't they? That's Birdie's granddaughter over there." She pointed a gloved finger in

Gabby's direction. "She helped me with my hat."

A neighbor walked by, giving Margaret's outstretched finger an affectionate squeeze. Margaret responded in kind, a smile filling her face. She handed her a flyer. "There's lots to do," she said, turning back. Her face serious.

Cass looked at the flyers and offered to take some down to the docks. "My guys appreciate people taking notice of the ocean. Keeping it clean."

"As well they should," Margaret said. Her voice rose a little, louder than normal, a touch of anger carrying her words. "Everyone needs to do his or her part, Cass. Especially those who build bars near the water, don't you think? Those people have a duty to care for the ocean, to keep it clean." She pressed a hand to her heart as if the emotion had exerted her.

The mention of a bar seemed to come out of nowhere, but before anyone could pursue it, Margaret took a deep breath and went on. "Harry says I need to watch my blood pressure. I tell him he puts too much salt in the tomato sauce."

Nell tried to cover up her surprise at Margaret's strong statement. At least, strong for Margaret, who was adept at calming babies in the deli. She was usually steady and measured, one of the reasons, they all knew, that Garozzo's Deli ran as smoothly as it did.

Nell glanced over and saw that Tess was watching Margaret, too. She looked concerned. Had Tess recruited Margaret today? Perhaps that's why the *hygge* session had slipped the deli owner's mind. But the older woman seemed energized with what she was doing. Having a purpose was important.

At that moment parents began to drive up, lining the side street with their SUVs and honking to get their daughters' attentions. Izzy and Cass took advantage of the commotion to give their own quick goodbyes, heading to their cars and anxious to get out of the cold and home to a crackling fire.

"Hey, Nell."

Nell looked over to where Laura Danvers stood with Daisy, their car doors open, waiting for Birdie and Gabby to join them.

"You're welcome to join us for pizza," Laura said. "Papa Diego's — karaoke night." She chuckled at Nell's too-quick excuse that Ben was already home, reheating leftover soup.

Still laughing, Laura hustled Birdie and the girls into the car.

Nell turned back and looked over to the park bench for Tess. Her leftover squash soup was certainly a match for Papa Diego's, and maybe Tess would like to come join them, warm her tired and cold bones in front of a fire. She spotted her just beyond the gazebo, climbing on a bike. Nell hustled, nearly running along the crisscross paths of the corner park, calling to Tess to stop for a minute. She was already planning the salad she'd toss together, the wine and cheese Ben would pull out to have in front of the fire while the soup warmed on the stove. But before the thoughts could fully form, Tess was out of earshot and pedaling down Harbor Road. Fast.

Out of breath, Nell gave up, coming to a stop at the edge of the sidewalk. She watched her fleeting figure winding away down the street. She regretted the idea hadn't come sooner. She wanted to get to know Tess, to talk more meaningfully than the chance meetings they'd had recently allowed. A stronger connection with Tess would be good for Birdie, too — something to lessen her anxieties. But her own reasons were simple. She found the young woman interesting. And slightly mysterious. Ben had expressed the same thought last night as they'd gotten ready for bed.

Last night.

The thought jarred her for a minute. How could it have been last night? Last night was a lifetime ago. Nell shoved her cold hands into the pockets of her coat, sobered at the thought of how irrelevant time became in the face of tragedy and death. It no longer had structure. Nor meaning.

She headed down Harbor Road toward her car, parked in front of Gus McGlucken's hardware store. Cars zipped by as if they, too, felt the cold. Horns blared at shoppers crossing the street, scolding them. It was as if the cold was rattling people, dulling the holiday spirit briefly. Gus stood just inside his door, his hands in his jacket pockets, ready to lock up. Nell waved as she reached her car, then rummaged around for the car keys, vowing for the hundredth time to put them on the key fob.

Just as her cold fingers finally wrapped around the metal key chain, a shadow fell over her car.

Nell looked up, ready to tell Gus to get back inside where it was warm. But it wasn't Gus. Margaret Garozzo stood close behind her.

"Oh, Margaret, were you still in the park? I'm so sorry — I would have waited for you." She smiled along with her apology.

But Margaret wasn't smiling. Her face was as solemn as Nell had ever seen it. Even her ready smile and the myriad lines that spread out from her eyes were gone, as if frozen out by the cold. Her plastic hat was missing and strands of graying hair blew across her lined forehead. Brown, watery eyes locked into Nell's.

"What is it, Margaret? What's wrong? Let me drive you down to the deli."

Margaret shook her head and assured Nell that she was fine. She blinked the moisture from her eyes and lay one mittened hand on Nell's coat sleeve. Then she moved her face so close to Nell's that Nell could smell the hot chocolate on her friend's breath.

Her voice was a whisper. "He was a bad man, Nell. Bad. Good ridd—"

A gust of wind seemed to come out of nowhere, blowing the words away. Before Nell could react, Margaret had turned away, weaving her way through the sidewalk crowds.

Nell stood alone on the curb, staring after her.

CHAPTER 11

Nell pulled into the drive and sat in the car for a long minute. The vision of Margaret Garozzo, her head leaning into the wind, was rolling around uncomfortably in her mind. She had almost followed her, stopped her, and asked what she could possibly be talking about. But Margaret had already crossed the street and merged into a crowd of shoppers. In a hurry to get back to the deli, to Harry.

But there was something else, too. The truth was, Nell didn't want to follow her. As Margaret hurried off, she felt herself giving in to an overwhelming weariness, whether from the grim morning or the long day or Margaret's curious words, she wasn't sure. The power of the *hygge* had diminished, no longer keeping the cold at bay. Nell was feeling the suddenness of reality seeping into her bones.

She finally got out of the car and started

walking slowly toward the door. She looked up at the comfortable two-story house, a cheerful wreath hanging on the front door, and light peeking through the drapes, casting shadows on the cold ground. Not elegant or fussy, but clean and airy and light. And welcoming. Always that — always warm and welcoming. Nell took a deep breath and smiled. *Home.*

Her heart lifted a bit and she walked inside.

"Are you sure that's what she said?" Ben sat across from Nell in front of the fire he'd lit a short while before. He leaned forward, firelight playing across the creases in his face.

On the old low coffee table, two trays held bowls of leftover winter squash soup that Ben had found in the freezer and heated up. He'd added a splash of wine to make it taste new, and a dollop of sour cream because Nell hadn't been there to stop him. A glass of wine sat beside each bowl.

Nell took a sip of wine and thought. And thought and thought. She had good hearing, even better than Ben's. But there'd been wind and traffic, and Margaret had spoken in a whisper. The more she thought, the more the words became frayed, as if overused and no longer effective. Margaret's head had been lowered and Nell had been expecting her to say something inconsequential, maybe apologizing for missing the *hygge,* or maybe a good-bye or how they needed to get together soon.

Not what she thought she heard.

"Maybe I misheard. I must have, don't you think?"

Ben swirled the sour cream into his soup, watching it lighten to a golden tan. He took a spoonful. And then another, thinking while he ate. Finally he put his spoon down and took a drink of wine. "Maybe you heard Margaret correctly, but maybe she meant something totally different than what we are digging out of it. Our thoughts are so tuned in to what happened that it colors everything. It's so fresh."

So fresh. *Hours* fresh. And the day hadn't stopped long enough for them to absorb the fact that a man had been pushed off a deck. And was dead. Nell considered Ben's reasoning.

"Where would Margaret have even met Bobby Abbott?" Ben went on. "I can't imagine her and Harry frequenting his bar."

"No, of course not." She moved to another thought. "Margaret and Esther Gibson are good friends. I wonder —"

Ben shook his head. "Esther is a consummate police dispatcher and would never share news before the police chief had released it. But in addition, I saw Richard Gibson at the wine store Friday. He and Esther were going to a distant relative's weekend wedding in Portland. Richard was storing up on beer to get him through it."

Nell played around some more with Margaret's words, wondering how an ordinary man on the street would have interpreted them. *He was a bad man . . .*

Finally she looked up, not comfortable with another possibility, either. But it might fit.

"Harry," she said.

"Harry?" Ben frowned again. He'd nearly finished his soup and was glancing back into the kitchen, playing with the idea of seconds. He turned back. "Harry. Hmm. She could have meant Harry, although I can't imagine why she'd say that about him. They've always been one of the healthiest couples in town. They balance each other out. He's crazy about her, and she keeps him in line — but gently."

"I agree. They're like two old Scrooges with each other sometimes, but it's always with affection."

Nell felt better. Margaret could have been

speaking out of a Scrooge moment, one she rarely had with anyone but Harry. "Well, that has to be it. An argument — maybe over Margaret disappearing and leaving him alone during the deli's busy time. By now, after working together tonight, they've made up and are closing up the restaurant, and now they're heading home to rest their tired feet in front of a fire, probably listening to old Frank Sinatra songs."

Ben laughed. "It's a plausible scenario."

By the time Ben had finished seconds on the soup and the bottle of wine was empty, they felt comfortable with what they had figured out. And even more comfortable with being alone together, their stomachs full and the warmth of the wine and the fire gently massaging their spirits.

Nell took the dishes into the kitchen while Ben stirred the embers in the fireplace, then added a log and sat back on the couch. He looked up when Nell returned. "I stopped by the station this afternoon," he said. "Checked in on Jerry to see if he needed anything."

"And?"

"It was bedlam, as you'd expect —"

But Ben's thought was interrupted by the doorbell, sounding shrill in the quiet of the evening. Few people rang the doorbell at the Endicott house, and whenever someone did, even if it was the mailman, Nell always felt a small twinge close to her heart. A skipped beat. The twinge would come, and then it would disappear when she would answer the door to a friendly face.

Most of the time.

Ben was already at the door and Nell felt the swoosh of cold air as it opened. She listened for the greeting.

"Hey, Tom, come on in."

Tommy Porter walked into the family room and Nell got up and greeted him with a hug.

He grinned. "Hey, Nell, thanks. I needed that. How'd you know?"

"And you also need a beer," Ben said. He headed to the refrigerator as Nell moved the Sunday paper to give Tommy a place near the fire.

"I'm off duty as of a couple minutes ago, so, well, sure. A beer sounds good. But here's why I came — besides the beer and an excuse to see you guys."

Tommy took the beer from Ben and pulled a cell phone from his pocket. He handed it to Ben. "A phone for a beer."

Ben looked at the cell phone, turned it over, then clicked it on to see the home page. "Hmm, this is mine. That's strange.

Where was it?" He looked around the room as if Tommy had picked it up off a chair or table in the family room. Even while he looked, that made no sense and he realized where Tommy had found it. "My mind must have been somewhere else when I was at the station today. That's not like me at all."

That was an understatement, Nell thought. Ben checked his text messages far too often. Not missing his phone for an hour was momentous.

"The chief said the same thing — that it wasn't like you, and that once you discovered it missing, you'd be kind of upset, so he asked me to bring it by. Looks like I got here in time."

Ben laughed and slipped the phone into his pocket. "Speaking of phones, things were humming loudly down there today. You must have been out. There was a reporter out in the hall when I left. I suppose they've gotten a whiff —"

Tommy nodded. "You can't wrap a place in yellow tape and not have it noticed. I was down at the wharf and there was a reporter there, too, although no one was talking to him. We were inside, mostly, going through things at the Harbor Club. Doesn't matter, if we don't give them info, they'll find it somewhere. I have to hand it to them, though — some of those reporters are pretty amazing. The chief expects them to come around, and he'll give them what he can. He's really good with them. Even though they're pests sometimes, that's their job, the Chief always says. At least they'll have good information and the town deserves that."

"What are you looking for in the bar?" Nell asked.

"Anything. We don't know what we're looking for. But even though the deck was the scene of the crime, we need to collect things from the kitchen, the bar, Bobby's office. Ninety-nine percent may prove irrelevant, but that one percent could lead us to whoever was out there with him."

"Jerry says he was probably killed after the bar closed," Ben said.

"We'll know more tomorrow, but that's the thought. We've got all the names of the staff over there. That'll help us figure out who saw him last."

Nell wondered if the police were looking for a needle in a haystack. Izzy had said there was a crowd there when they left. One of those people could have been the last person to see him alive, not a staff person at all. She looked at Tommy's face, seeing tired lines around his eyes.

"Lots to figure out, to take apart and put

back together," Tommy said. "But we'll do it. We'll find the guy."

"How is Bobby's wife?" Nell asked. "It must have been difficult for you to wake someone up with such terrible news."

"Her name is Helen Getty. I may have seen her around town once or twice, but I'd never met her before. Do you know her?"

Nell looked at Ben, but neither registered recognition. "Sometimes we think we know everyone in Sea Harbor. But we don't, and it always surprises me. I'm not even sure where Bobby lived. I thought I heard Jerry mention Granite Road."

"Yep, that's it. One of those gigantic houses that popped up a few years ago. The ones just beyond the woods."

It was an area Nell knew well. "It's lovely over there — the woods are beautiful." The houses were too new for Nell's liking, mostly too big. However, the forested acreage that separated them from the rest of the town was enchanting all seasons of the year. It stretched from Granite Road down to the sea. Over the years the paths in the woods had been worn into hiking trails that began just off the road and wound through the woods, around a small pond, and down to the ocean. Several small weather-beaten cabins dotted the acres. In the spring she and Ben often walked the trails as the wildflowers peeked through copses of birch and cedar.

Years ago a fire, started in a deserted cabin, had eaten away a part of the park. A homeless man trying to keep warm was what most people figured. But today one could barely tell where it had been. Nature had covered it over. Sometimes, when Ben and Nell were walking through that area, they would stop and wonder about the fire. And about what other secrets the woods held.

"Did Bobby have any children?" Nell asked. "We know so little of the man."

"No kids that we know of. Frankly, I was surprised he had a wife. I've been in that bar more than a few times and I'd never guess he had a wife — although I guess that's not a fair judgment to make. It clearly wasn't in Abbott's case."

"But we all do that, don't we, for right or wrong? Impressions," Nell said. She'd done exactly that when she had met Bobby Abbott on the wharf that day.

"How did you find out he was married?" Ben asked.

"A guy in the department knew he was married. The guy's wife does some work for Abbott's wife. Landscaping design, I think.

He didn't think there were kids. His wife never saw signs of any when she was there. Abbott isn't that old, you know. He's about my age — early thirties. I guess he grew up close by, maybe over in Hamilton, but our paths never crossed until he opened the bar. His family had some land around the area and over in Rockport. Maybe a summer home. We're still looking into all that, but apparently there's not really a lot to know about him. Wealthy father. Older wife."

"What about the father?"

"I don't know about the father. He's dead, according to Helen. But Bobby's wife is older than he is, for sure. I don't mean she's *old* old —"

Nell smiled, wondering if *like you two* would follow, but it didn't. She suspected when people have been in your daily life for as long as the Endicotts and Tommy's family have been in each other's, age didn't factor in.

"I'd guess her to be forty-five or so. A career-type woman. Again — just an impression, so who knows how wrong it could be? And I'm awful at guessing ages. I didn't ask her questions like that or where she worked, none of that. Not yet. Delivering that kind of pretty awful news is about all people can handle at first. It needs time to sink in, to be absorbed. They need space. You know?"

Tommy was sounding older than his years, and, yes, they did know that losing someone you love takes time — and laying homicide on top of that must make it nearly impossible. She buried the urge to give him another hug. He had shifted into professional mode, outside the comfort zone for hugs.

Nell asked a few more questions, about relatives, perhaps someone working for the couple that could offer comfort. But Tommy had no answers. The wife had seemed to be alone in the house, he said.

Nell felt an instant empathy for the woman Tommy was describing. She was no longer a total stranger. She wondered what they might do to help, to somehow lighten the burden. Or, at the least, to show support. It came naturally when you knew someone, more difficult for a stranger. But maybe even more necessary.

Beside her, Ben was feeling her thoughts, and he addressed the issue more directly.

"This Mrs. Abbott — or Getty, you said? — might be alone over there," he said. "I'm wondering what we can do to help. How is she doing? An empty question, but does she need a doctor, a priest or minister? How is she taking the news?"

Tommy looked down into his beer, as if the answer was complicated and needed some serious thought. But when he looked up and answered Ben's question, it wasn't complicated at all.

"She took it very calmly," he said. "She said it was bound to happen sometime, and then she closed the door. So I left."

Chapter 12

Gabby woke up early, an unusual thing since Monday mornings were not her favorites. But in spite of a math test, the rest of the day would get better fast.

It was what she and Daisy were doing after school that pulled her from the warm bed to the shower and then her closet to find her warmest jeans and sweater.

A trip to the docks to talk trash with Pete Halloran and maybe other crew members who worked for Cass and Pete. An awesome Monday.

At least that's how she described it when she told Cass what they were doing. Cass had laughed hard in that kind of throaty way she had and said they should, for sure, come hang out. "Talk trash with those guys?" she said. "That's right up their alley."

Actually, it was to talk *plastic, trash, and fish,* while handing out sheets to explain their efforts to clean up the beaches. At least that's how they had presented it to Tess Bean last week. A project for the eco club. Tess had liked the idea. "I may run by and see how you're doing," and she'd tapped it into her phone calendar.

Gabby hung out on the dock whenever she had a chance, though usually when it was warm, hoping she'd get a ride on one of the lobster boats. And sometimes she did. Pete had taken her out on the *Lucky Catch* a couple weeks earlier to untangle some buoy ropes. The crusty old guys told great stories. And sometimes Pete would get out his guitar. One time Gabby and Daisy sang with him. It was some old Irish shanty that had the Italian and Portuguese fishermen stomping and hollering that Pete needed to expand his repertoire. They were funny, like no one she knew in her other life, her "Rapunzel life," as Harold called it, teasing her about living in a penthouse high above Central Park when her dad was in the country. But she'd never been locked in a tower, she told Harold vehemently every time he teased her. And nice Harold knew it was safe teasing because he knew she loved her dad. But she sure loved her Nonna and Sea Harbor, too.

This time she and Daisy had a mission.

And even if there wasn't anyone to talk to, they'd get to hang out with Pete. And Cass always dropped by with snacks.

She had reminded Tess about it yesterday on Harbor Road, but she had looked distracted, and Gabby wasn't even sure she had heard her. Maybe it had been the weather. The wind had been seriously cold. Or perhaps Tess was tired from spending her whole free Sunday afternoon with a bunch of noisy kids. Maybe when Gabby saw Tess in class today, she'd invite her to come along. Maybe she'd be feeling better.

Gabby bounded down to the sunny kitchen, where Ella already had a plateful of pancakes, crisp bacon strips, and a bottle of syrup at her place.

Between bites of pancake she filled Ella in on how they'd cleaned up the beaches the day before, then used the plastic in fanciful ways to get people's attention. She talked about the hot chocolate in the Gazebo park and how her *nonna* had eaten two pieces of pizza that night.

Then she moved on to the day and filled the housekeeper in on the math test and what the school day promised. It was the day Tess was teaching their environmental-science class, getting them excited about all the things they could do and how things like plastic could destroy our harbor, our fish.

She refrained from talking about a trip to the docks after school with Daisy. There was only so much Ella Sampson could handle, and Gabby prided herself on knowing when enough was enough. And her *nonna* knew — they'd talked about it with the Danverses over pizza the night before. All was well. Finally she stopped, just long enough to look at Birdie's empty chair. She frowned.

"Where's my *nonna*?"

"She's on the phone, dearie, up in the den, down in a minute," Ella said, bringing over another slice of bacon.

"Hmm," Gabby said, the frown still on her face. Her *nonna* rarely missed joining her for school day breakfasts, then waiting with her until the school bus came.

"Must be important," Ella said, her words nearly drowned out by the rattling of the back door. "Or maybe Nell's suggesting they go out for breakfast."

"Howdy in there. Y'all decent?" Harold lumbered in, laughing at the greeting he growled out every morning. He pecked Ella on the cheek, then dropped the newspaper on the table for Birdie to read with her coffee. Then he plopped down beside Gabby, his eyes warm as he pressed her about plans for the day. Harold loved all the details, the liveliness, even the gossip. Gabby's entry into the Favazza household had brightened his and Ella's lives nearly as much as it had their employer's. The house was alive again. And even Ella's occasional worry and the rise in the noise level couldn't diminish their pleasure one bit.

Ella put a plate of hash browns and eggs in front of her husband. She started to walk away, then took a step back toward Birdie's empty place and looked down at the newspaper. She frowned, glanced over at Gabby and Harold, then put a hand down to scoop up the paper.

But she was one second too late. Gabby had glanced over, too, and spotted the same thing Ella had seen staring up at her. An inch-tall headline seemed to be screaming at them: SEA HARBOR MAN PUSHED OFF DECK, PLUNGES TO HIS DEATH.

And below the headline, a photo stretched over two columns: a handsome man, longish hair, a too-familiar face. At least to Gabby. Who stared down at the paper as if it were on fire.

The man who had collided with little Abby, causing huge tears to roll down her round cheeks.

The man who had been pushed off another ledge. On another day. In another place.

But this time he didn't pull himself up out of the sea. This time the man was dead.

Gabby felt her world begin to spin around her. She got up from the table and murmured a rushed good-bye to Harold and Ella. Then she fled from the house, her backpack flung over her shoulder, her jacket clutched in one hand, and her phone in the other hand, typing in Daisy Danvers's number.

Birdie did something that morning that she swore she would never do. She called Sea Harbor Community Day School and asked to speak to Dr. Elizabeth Hartley, the headmistress — a kind woman and a friend. Would Elizabeth do her a favor? Would she please check to be sure Gabby was there, in whatever class it might be? Birdie made no excuses, except that she was new at parenting, and hadn't seen her granddaughter get on the bus that morning. It was irrational, she knew.

Elizabeth was happy to check. She paused for a moment, and then she added that in her experience a large part of parenting might seem irrational. But mostly it was simply love playing out in different ways.

Birdie had just missed Gabby that morning. She'd come down to the kitchen as the school bus pulled away, just minutes after talking with Nell. If she hadn't seen the paper, Nell had told her, Bobby Abbott's death was all over it, as well as on Internet news. The police hadn't released many details, but the write-up was clear that it was a homicide, not an accident. Bobby had been pushed. Nell thought Birdie might want to talk with Gabby about it before she left for school, because Gabby had witnessed Bobby and Abby colliding on the wharf last Friday. There was something about the man that had caused a reaction in Gabby. She had seemed alarmed at first, but Nell thought it was simply a reaction to Abby crying. Gabby seemed to blame the man for it. But either way, besides the jarring news of a homicide in their small town, the murdered man's face would be familiar to Gabby. And that might be difficult for a twelve-year-old to process.

But Gabby was already gone when Birdie hurried into the kitchen. She had rushed out with barely a good-bye, Ella had said. And she looked ashen, like she might be coming down with something.

So Birdie had made the call. And Headmistress Elizabeth Hartley had walked down the hall with her cell phone in her hand and looked through the window into the class, smiled at the teacher, and then reported to Birdie that Gabby was indeed at school, and busy taking a test. And probably, she added, getting an A on it, as was her way.

Birdie refrained from asking Elizabeth if Gabby looked ill. But only with great effort. Then she tried to convince herself. *Of course she isn't ill.* Ella said she'd eaten a full plate of bacon and pancakes, just like every day.

But she didn't see photos of a dead man every morning staring at her as she tried to digest them.

All over town, the same edition of the *Sea Harbor Gazette* was being tossed on doorsteps that morning, then picked up off the cold ground and brought inside, spread out near steaming coffee mugs. Newspapers that often were rendered unreadable beneath spilled orange juice or coffee, or looked at briefly for game scores and tossed into recycling bins, would be read today. Bold one-inch headlines did that, especially ones like this.

Murder rarely went unnoticed. Coffee's café was no exception.

■ ■ ■ ■

Cass was settled in her usual corner near Coffee's massive fireplace when Nell and Birdie walked in. The fire was lit, but not roaring today, perhaps a tribute to the sun that had finally graced Sea Harbor with her presence, camouflaging the cold winter air.

Nell waved over at her, happy Cass was still there, even though it was midmorning. Cass usually took Mondays off, leaving the company accountant alone in the office to do her magic and make sure the Halloran Lobster Company stayed in the black. Her first stop was always a triple-shot latte at Coffee's. And sometimes that stretched into a chocolate croissant while she buried herself in the latest Stephen King tome. She was usually alone, but certain friends were always welcome.

"So let the games begin," Cass said as Birdie and Nell settled on either side of her, cradling the oversized mugs in their hands. Around the coffee shop customers passed newspapers back and forth and pointed out comments on their cell phones or tablets. Nods, quizzical looks, questions, as people pointed at the photo, the headline, the photo of the Harbor Club bar.

Birdie sighed. "Not any kind of games we want to be caught up in. More like the gladiator type."

"I didn't mean to make light of it. I'm just trying to make it go away."

"Tommy Porter seems hopeful it'll be solved soon," Nell said.

"I guess we all hope that," Cass said. "Hopefully, it's no one we know. Hopefully, they'll find something. Hopefully, the storm didn't wash away all evidence."

But they all knew that the weather had turned vicious that night, rain and sleet pouring down as if venting wrath on a town in which something wicked had happened. And, in the process, had punished the town, wiping away prints and clues that might have helped make it all go away.

And as for Cass's other hope, it absolutely might be someone they knew.

Birdie leaned forward in her chair, pulling her rimless glasses from a cap of silvery hair and putting them on. She waved her hand, taking in the crowded room. "But it's not exactly what I would have expected. Look around, have you noticed anything?"

They looked around at the milling groups of customers. The clientele was different on Mondays than over the weekend: Some moms, with kids at school, who came over from yoga and sat with their phones or with a friend to rehash the weekend. Business people holding meetings away from the office with a latte or espresso. Some late Boston commuters warming themselves before heading over to the commuter rail station.

"I guess I'm not sure what I'm looking at," Cass said. "It's Monday, remember. My day off, brain included."

But Nell saw what Birdie was talking about. "It isn't chaotic. People have heard the news and they're digesting it. But quietly, in a way, if one can receive homicide news that way. Not rumor mongering, as you might expect. People are disturbed that a man has been pushed to his death — but with confidence in the police, in friends, in neighbors."

Cass wasn't sure she got all that by looking around the coffee shop, but she was willing to let it be. "It helps that the statement in the paper says that the police are working on the premise that whatever and however it happened was limited to the two people involved. A homicide, but maybe not even planned. It could be manslaughter. And it didn't involve anyone else."

"I wonder how they know that," Birdie said.

But none of them were sure. And maybe it was a statement meant to calm the townsfolk, to bring them back quickly to the spirit of the month — to festive parties and holiday cheer, while letting the police do their job — and to forget that a man, whom not too many of them knew well, had fallen to his death.

The coffee shop was thinning out, people heading into the day. The three women lowered their voices, not wanting their words to carry in the quieter café.

They were sitting near the fireplace, their mugs balanced on the raised hearth, with Nell the only one facing out into the coffee shop. She noticed a woman sitting at a table close by, someone she didn't remember seeing in Coffee's before. Or maybe anywhere before. She was attractive and well-toned, wearing a soft green tailored suit with a wide plaid belt, suede boots with heels Nell couldn't begin to walk in, and a certain air about her. Confidence, maybe? Or success?

She was holding her cell phone in one hand, looking at it intently, but not touching it, not flipping through screens or texts. Her fingers were still.

Listening, Nell thought.

The woman's head lifted, as if she knew that she was being watched. Her eyes met

Nell's and held them for a minute.

Nell couldn't explain later how she knew, but somehow she did, and she knew it with a certainty that emboldened her to stand up and walk over to the woman, holding out her hand.

"Helen, I'm Nell Endicott. And I am so terribly sorry for your loss."

CHAPTER 13

Gabby walked out of her math class at Sea Harbor Community Day School, her thoughts messed up. She tried to sort through the confusion in her head. Before the test, her teacher had talked about what they'd learned in class so far, about investigating new relationships, new and efficient ways to solve real-life problems through math. *Geesh. Real-life problems!* The words screamed in Gabby's head. She pressed a hand against a throbbing in her forehead and bumped right into Susie Wilson's back, sending her books flying.

Susie swung around. "What's your problem, Gabby?" She scrambled to pick up her books and hurried to catch up with her friends.

Daisy came up behind her, breathless. "I guess you showed her," she said, coaxing a smile from Gabby. She pushed her glasses up and pulled Gabby over to the side of the hall.

Around them the halls buzzed with voices, happy and loud, students moving to the next class or to early lunch. No one seemed to be worried about anything. Gabby envied them.

"Okay, I've thought of this all morning. Here's what we need to do," Daisy said. Her voice was matter-of-fact.

Gabby waited.

"Nothing."

"Nothing?" Gabby said, thinking. "But I saw Tess push that horrible man into the cove."

"But he didn't die. She didn't kill him, Gabby."

Not then, Gabby thought, but she wouldn't — couldn't — ever put that thought into words.

"And what I mean is, nothing for *now.* Did you ever tell Tess that you were there that day?" Daisy asked.

Gabby shook her head no. "Only you." The truth was, she had felt kind of sneaky about the whole thing — standing there so quietly, inserting herself into a private moment. *Like a voyeur, sort of.* And she'd always connected voyeurs with nasty people.

"I know what you're thinking, Gabs. The

police might want to know about seeing them together, but let's think about that. Analyze it. We know Tess didn't do it. So, what would the police do with that information? And besides, it's only been a couple days. They will probably figure out who did it, before you know it, and we will have saved Tess from some really embarrassing stuff. If you had seen something that might help the police find a murderer, that'd be one thing. Like, if you'd been standing on Gracie Santos's deck and saw it all. But you saw something totally different. And we know Tess Bean is no murderer. We both know that. She gets upset when a fish dies."

That got a slight smile out of Gabby. She knew what her best friend was doing. She was pulling out Gabby's own thoughts and emotions and putting them into words. So she could hear them outside herself. And then she could hold on to them tight or toss them away.

But a plan she figured she could hold tight to was this: "Daisy, how about this? I think it's what you're thinking, too. How about I tell Tess what I saw that day out at the cove? Or we tell her. Maybe I should have told her right away, but it is what it is. We just put it out there, give it to her. And Tess will do the right thing."

Daisy beamed. "Together we're a team, Gabs. The best team." Then Daisy wiggled her nose and grinned in a funny way.

"But you know what else this means?" Gabby said.

"Sure I do. But you say it, Gabs."

"It means we need to be super vigilant. It might take the police a while and we need this all solved really quickly. Tess didn't like this guy, and all of us knew it. All the kids knew. He was really messing with the ocean waters. So we need to push the police in the right direction. They need to find the right person before any suspicion falls on Tess."

A bell rang in the distance and immediately the hallway flooded with some students heading to class and others to lunch or to the study hall.

They started to walk again, toward the cafeteria.

"I say we insist Tess go with us to the docks today," Gabby said. She wasn't sure why that seemed important. But maybe keeping Tess close was as important as keeping any suspicion of her away.

"She's in class right now," Daisy said, pointing ahead. "She's in the eighth-grade science class. Let's peek in —"

They waited a minute until the room filled, then quieted, a voice coming from the front of the room saying something they couldn't hear.

They walked quietly to the back classroom door, standing in the shadow, looking into the room.

What they saw first were the students' disappointed faces.

Next they heard a few whispers and saw notes passing across aisles. Some cell phones snuck out of pockets and pecked quietly. And then they looked toward the front of the room and saw why.

A substitute teacher with a reputation for being a mean drill sergeant was explaining to the class that the teacher they loved, Ms. Bean, was sick today. And she was in charge.

Cass walked down Harbor Road, thinking about the woman in the coffee shop. She hadn't known Bobby Abbott long enough to conjure up an image of a wife for him, but if she had, it would have been about as different from Helen Getty as one could get.

She could tell the woman had little interest in her, and Cass, for her part, wasn't willing to give her free time to a stranger. So when Bobby Abbott's wife suggested to Nell and Birdie that they might talk for a bit, Cass had quickly excused herself and headed out to check off the second item on her day-off list: dropping in at Gracie's Lazy Lobster & Soup Café to make sure her friend was okay. And maybe get a lobster roll while she was there.

She walked past Izzy's shop, dodging several customers who had stopped to admire the festive Christmas tree display of holiday beanies and sweaters in the yarn shop window before walking on inside.

On a sudden whim, Cass turned back and followed them inside. It was surely time for Izzy to have a break. Mondays were her awful days, mostly spent helping customers fix all the mistakes they made over the weekend when they'd been on their own.

A few minutes later, the two friends were walking briskly toward the wharf, scarves wrapped around their necks and collars up, but enjoying the bright sunshine lighting up the garland-wrapped gaslights.

"You're treating me to one of Gracie's lobster rolls, right?" Izzy said.

"And also to a brief but shining impression of Bobby Abbott's wife." She filled Izzy in, along with some editorializing on who this woman might possibly be. "Izzy, I didn't say more than two words to her. So I don't have a clue what she's like. But believe me. You will be surprised."

"I'm surprised he even had a wife. Watching him in the bar that night presented a certain image, I guess that's all I'm saying. But maybe that's not fair. He was working. What we saw was a bar owner keeping his customers happy, his staff in line. I wonder what people would think about Gracie, if all they knew was what they saw when she was on duty."

Cass thought about that as they walked around the maritime museum and down toward the wharf. "You have a point. But you will still be blown away when you see Helen Getty. I didn't stick around to talk with her, though, so what do I know? Maybe Nell and Birdie will have a completely different take on it. Besides, it's probably pretty awful to try to access a person when they are dealing with the loss of a husband. I can't even begin to go there in my own mind."

They had seen Gracie's car in the parking lot, along with several others, a couple of trucks, and bikes.

The wharf itself, although not crowded, had people walking its length for the view of the harbor, the ropes of cedar along the railing, the holiday decorations on houses across the water. One lone harbor taxi boat was moored at the bottom of a flight of steps off the side, ready to take people across to the Canary Cove Art Colony, or for a ride to the Ocean's Edge restaurant at the other end of the harbor, or simply to meander around the loop to view old sea captains' mansions and a town getting ready to welcome in a holiday season. In a short while the taxi would close up shop for the season, but the stalwart captain was on duty for as long as weather permitted.

The yellow tape still girdled the Harbor Club bar, but Izzy and Cass hadn't seen any police cars in the lot.

"It's only been two days," Izzy said. "So strange."

They walked up to the Lazy Lobster & Soup Café. As Izzy leaned over to pet the lobster's head, Cass nudged her. "Look. Isn't that Tess Bean?"

Izzy stood and turned back toward the wharf. "What am I looking at?"

"Over there. Just past that toy lobster trap."

Izzy took a few steps away from the restaurant and looked again, shielding her eyes from the sun.

Leaning against the railing, her elbows on the wood and her hands clasped in front of her, was Tess Bean.

"Oh, Cass." Izzy's breath came slowly, sadly. "She . . . she looks so alone. The way she's standing there. I wonder if we should —"

At that moment Tess turned around, away from the water, and began to walk in their direction. In spite of the wind off the water, she wore only the familiar green sweatshirt and jeans, but her chin was held high and she looked straight ahead, seemingly oblivious to the wind. And oblivious also to the two women standing in front of Gracie's restaurant, watching her walk slowly toward town.

"I wonder why she was out there in the cold, looking like that," Izzy said. She and Cass were perched on bar stools, watching Gracie get ready for the lunch crowd.

"Out on the wharf?" Gracie asked. "It's freezing out there. I hope she comes in. I left her a couple messages, hoping she'd come by. She doesn't really have anyone here in Sea Harbor. I mean, no one close." She handed a stack of folded napkins to one of the waitresses. "I haven't seen her since, well, since Saturday night. How did she look?"

"That's the thing," Izzy said. She took a bite out of a lobster roll Gracie had set down in front of her. Buttery juice dripped from the grilled bun. Gracie insisted on drizzling clarified butter and lemon on top of the hunks of fresh lobster. Izzy swallowed a bite. "I'm not sure. It was as if she were somewhere else. We were only a few steps away when she walked back toward the parking lot, but she didn't even see us. She looked sort of —"

"Lost," Cass said.

"Or sad," Izzy added.

"That's odd," Gracie said. "It's not a look I'd attribute to Tess. We've become friends. Sort of. Tess is not an open book. But I do like her and she's worth turning the pages. There's something special about her. She's lots younger than I am, a dozen years plus, I'd say. But there's an old soul in that body. Like she's lived one life and is now on her second go-round."

"Nice image," Cass said. "I like it."

"Me, too," Gracie said. "Tess has a strength about her, but lately I've caught her looking vulnerable, like whatever that other life was, it might not have been easy. It's made me want to protect her. Crazy, huh?"

Izzy had felt the same way when they'd seen her with the girls in the park. She looked like she'd lost something valuable. "I had that feeling, too, Gracie."

"The kids sure like her," Cass said. "And

they're usually pretty good barometers."

Gracie nodded. "She's doing a great job over at Community Day School. She's hoping there might be a permanent staff position for her eventually."

"So those are good things. But what about her disdain for your friend next door," Cass said.

Gracie glanced behind her as if Bobby were standing there, listening. "He's not my friend. You know that. I didn't like him, but you're right. Tess seemed to have complicated feelings toward him. Severe feelings. Like a deep-seated anger. More than I'd expect she'd have over the Harbor Club's bad habits."

"You mean like peeing in the compost bins?" Cass asked. Cass repeated the compost episode they'd witnessed.

"Ugh." Gracie grimaced.

"She was freaked out over it. Or at least that's how it looked to us."

"That's curious, too," Gracie said. She pulled a tray of clean glasses from beneath the bar.

"Curious?"

"Well, it's gross that Bobby's guys were so crude, but it's actually not bad for the compost. The cigarettes and cans were bad, sure, but the other, well, not so much. It's rich in nitrogen — Tess told me that herself. It can accelerate the effects of composting. Not that we want people to be doing it, but I'm just saying it wouldn't account for fierce anger, if that's what she had."

"Then she must have been mad about something else," Cass said. "She just took off."

"He didn't give a care about things Tess cared about, that was clear. And it bugged her when people wouldn't even take the time to listen, to try to understand. Bobby had about as much interest in the environment and the ocean as a slug. He wasn't a good guy. Tess and I both saw him dump a whole bag of plastic off his deck one day. It was almost as if he wanted us to see him do it. He wasn't the best business neighbor, either. One night a bunch of drunk kids came in here wanting to eat. One of my waitresses had seen them come over from Bobby's place. In itself that's fine, sure. But it was when all the families come in and these guys sat right in the middle of the restaurant and created a real mess, loud and awful. Cussing. A couple of families got up and left. I heard the next day Bobby had given them money and sent them over here to have a good time. And to make sure no one else did. You know how rumors spread around this town. If the café started getting that kind of reputation —"

"Stop, Gracie," Cass said. "We'd never let that happen."

Gracie smiled. "I know you wouldn't. But I started to be on guard, not knowing what he would try next. Anyway, that was Bobby. He could turn on the charm one minute and cuss someone out the next. He seemed to be missing that kindness gene. I don't think Tess liked him, either, and she sure wasn't easy on him. And now he's dead. So maybe that explains the look you saw out there on the wharf."

"You mean she was sad because she gave him a hard time and then he died? Guilt?" Izzy washed down the last of her lobster roll with a drink of water. "I'm trying to put the Tess we just saw on the wharf with the furious one we saw that night and the one you've described. And then there's the amazing Tess who is a dog whisperer with Red. And the one every girl at Sea Harbor Community Day School thinks hung the moon."

Gracie was thoughtful. "The many faces of Tess Bean. Maybe it is the guilt thing. But I don't think so. I don't think that's Tess. She was tough on Bobby, sure. But she seems more evolved, more in touch with life and with herself. The fact that Bobby was murdered is sad, for sure — no one deserves that kind of death." Gracie fiddled with a stack of napkins, sorting through her thoughts. "As for Tess, I'm not sure what is going on with her. There was something between her and Bobby Abbott."

"A relationship? That doesn't seem to fit," Cass said.

"No, not like that. But something. Something deeper than her protesting his disregard for the environment. Her reactions weren't always what you'd expect. Like what you described Saturday night. Throwing a beer can into a bin isn't all that bad. And it wasn't even Bobby who did it. Did she explain what really got to her?"

"Nope," Cass said. "When she couldn't get in the side door to the bar, she didn't come back. She just walked off toward the water without a word."

Another image hit Izzy at the same time Cass was talking. *Tess walked off . . . but she didn't leave. Or if she did leave, she came back . . .*

They'd seen her much later as they were leaving the bar. Standing in the shadowy lane between the two buildings.

With Bobby Abbott.

■ ■ ■ ■

A short while later, the hostess came in and tables were beginning to fill with the noon lunch crowd. The smell of garlic and buttery lobster wafted in from the small kitchen.

"It doesn't look like the problems next door have affected your business at all, Gracie," Izzy said, taking her coat off the hook.

"No. And maybe that irked Bobby more than anything. He hated it that I couldn't just give up and surrender." She tried to laugh off her own harsh words. "I think he was embarrassed about being next door to an eatery with a ceramic lobster out front."

"That's why he wanted to buy you out?" Izzy said.

They were quiet for a moment, the words carrying far more weight than they had intended. Izzy wished she hadn't said them, bringing them to life. They knew Gracie had refused Bobby Abbott's offer, and that she'd never sell her beloved café. But the fact itself — that Bobby had made the offer would mean something completely different to people assigned to solve a murder. To unearth motives. Izzy had noticed the concern on Jerry Thompson's face when Gracie had mentioned it on that dismal morning. Even if he didn't want to, Jerry had to consider it.

"Did your talk with Jerry go okay?" Cass asked to break the silence.

"I met with Tommy, which was easier. I love the chief, but he *is* the chief, after all. Tommy's like a little brother. He asked the questions you'd expect, and I answered them honestly. I explained that I didn't like the guy. I didn't notice anything out of the ordinary the night he was killed. I don't know who might want to kill him. And, yes, he wanted to buy me out and throw my Lazy Lobster into the sea. And I said no." Her smile was sad.

"Did he ask about other people?"

Gracie hesitated, then nodded. "Tess."

"Why?"

"I'm not sure. But the staff over there knew Tess had been protesting the bar. And apparently she'd brought him up at a council meeting recently."

"Uncle Ben mentioned that," Izzy said. "But activists aren't known for killing people who throw garbage in the ocean."

"That's what I said. Tommy didn't comment, just scribbled on his pad."

"Hey, Gracie," a waitress called over from

behind the bar, interrupting the moment. "Where are the rest of our salt and pepper shakers? A couple tables don't have any and it's making that little girl near the window cry. Her mother says getting a hot dog and playing with the lobster salt and pepper shakers are the reasons she insists they come in here every day. Did someone refill them?"

"I put all of them out. Did you count?"

"Yeah. We're short four."

"Oh geesh," Gracie said. She slapped the rag she was holding down on the bar.

"Hey, Gracie, you okay?" Cass pulled on her parka.

"I guess. It's nothing big, except to me, anyway. Those are the salt and pepper shakers the artist in Canary Cove made for the restaurant when we first opened, remember? Lazy Lobster's babies, that's how I think about them."

"I know. They're great. People want to buy them."

"They're pretty special. My mom and uncle had them made. A gift."

"Do you think someone took them?" Izzy asked.

"Yes," Gracie said without hesitation. "It must have been Saturday night, since I wasn't open yesterday. And last week someone took that plaid scarf I hang around the big Lazy Lobster's neck when it gets cold. The one you knit for him, Iz."

They could see Gracie was trying to make light of it, but she looked like she was close to tears.

"That's crappy, Gracie. Too much at once. It's like the Grinch has come early, and he's stealing from all of us," Izzy said. She filled her in on some of the odd thefts from stores around her yarn shop. "We thought it was just those of us on Harbor Road. I guess we need to be more watchful. Though I guess it's difficult to keep an eye on salt and pepper shakers."

Gracie nodded and followed them to the door. They stood for a minute looking out the front window toward the Harbor Club. It was dark and empty.

As they watched, two policemen walked up and began tearing off and rolling up the yellow tape.

"Looks like they're finished looking for whatever it was they were looking for," Cass said.

"Yes," Gracie said. "Tommy stopped in earlier and told me they were trying to get it finished today. I guess the bar is going to reopen soon."

"What?" Cass said. "Open?"

"My reaction, too," Gracie said.

"How can it open without an owner? Who decides that? Who would open it?" Izzy pulled on her gloves and watched the last strip of police tape disappear.

"The other owner," Gracie said.

The two women looked at her.

Gracie sighed. "Rumor has it that Bobby Abbott had a silent partner no one knew about."

Chapter 14

Birdie and Nell suggested to Helen Getty that they talk away from the coffee shop. There was a quiet spot close by, one with comfortable chairs and without an audience: Birdie Favazza's den. It would be private there, Birdie assured Helen, who seemed aware of Coffee's customers looking at her and wondering who the well-dressed woman was, and why she was in their coffee shop on a Monday morning.

"Birdie's home is tucked away," Nell said, "a place where one can see out, but few can see in." She meant it as a note of levity, but Helen remained quiet.

Helen had been the one who suggested they talk. She knew who Nell was, she said, but only because she'd asked the fellow behind the counter earlier. And she knew of Birdie, too.

"One can't live in Sea Harbor for longer than a day without knowing of Bernadette

Favazza." The words came with a smile that seemed practiced, not entirely genuine.

"And have you lived here longer than a day?" Birdie asked. "I don't think we have met before." Birdie's smile was warm, but again Helen was quiet. Her mind seemed to be moving on to other matters as they walked out of Coffee's.

A short while later, the threesome made themselves comfortable in the soft leather den chairs while Ella brought in coffee and an assortment of teas, along with small crumpets she had taken from the freezer and heated up. Sunlight streamed in the bank of windows framing the harbor area of the town. Sonny Favazza's brass telescope was set up on its tripod, ready to bring the scene into closer view: of people or fires or wild summertime parties on the far beaches. The town was in Birdie's hands, or, at the least, in view of her telescope.

Helen crossed her long legs, her wool skirt lifting slightly, and glanced at the assortment of teas Ella presented. "These are lovely," she said, "but would you have Bloody Mary makings available?"

Ella looked at Birdie, and Birdie smiled at Helen. "Certainly. We have a little secret bar up here for just such occasions." Birdie excused an irritated Ella and walked over to the thick rosewood bookcase, dropping down a door and revealing a stocked bar with a small refrigerator below.

"This is comfortable," Helen said, her gaze roaming around the room and settling on the mullioned windows. "You can watch the world go by from here."

For a moment she sounded almost wistful, but when she turned back, her face was controlled, her expression unreadable.

"Yes, you can," Birdie said, her eyes warm as she handed Helen the drink. "But you can't stop it."

Birdie sat back down, and she and Nell waited quietly, sipping tea and wondering what this woman wanted from them. What they would have liked to do was offer condolences, support, perhaps suggest dinner, or bring food to the house. That's what they knew; that's what they did easily, along with offering shoulders to cry on, arms to embrace, and ears to listen.

But Helen's demeanor forbade any of that, so instead they sat quietly, waiting. Unsure of their roles.

The ride to Birdie's house had been silent, too, revealing nothing. Nell drove, with Birdie beside her, and Helen Getty sitting in the back, staring out the window as if seeing the town for the first time.

Finally Helen spoke. "I realize that this must seem odd to you, and awkward perhaps. I don't mean it to be such, it's just the way I am. I'm an uncomfortable woman, or so I've been told."

Birdie shifted in the wide chair, her feet resting on an ottoman. "We're not here to judge, Helen. And especially someone who has just suffered a terrible trauma. Each person handles great loss in her own way."

"I understand. But that isn't relevant here. Bobby and I are not the norm."

"I'm not sure there is a norm in marriage," Nell said.

"Maybe not. But that isn't why I suggested we talk. I'd rather not talk to anyone, frankly. I run a company in New York and what I'd like is to get back to that, to running it. I don't really care about any of this —"

She paused, leaving Nell and Birdie looking at each other in confusion. Neither of them had any idea what Helen didn't care about. Nor what she did care about, which may have been more relevant.

Helen rotated her glass, watching the tomato mixture swirl around the sides. "I was only in Sea Harbor this weekend because I was tired and felt the need to get away for a day or two, to escape the craziness of the city. I have an apartment there." She looked up, a slight smile on her face. "Coming this weekend was clearly not the best decision I've ever made."

"If there's anything we can do —" Nell began, but even the words sounded hollow.

"That's why I suggested we meet. When I spoke with Chief Thompson early this morning, he suggested that I not leave town. *Suggested* is a nice way of putting it, I suppose." She sighed and finished her drink, then looked over at Nell. "Chief Thompson mentioned that you and your husband had offered to help and went so far as to pass along cell numbers. I'm not in the habit of relying on other people and I don't expect to burden you with anything. But since I have to stay here for a few days, he thought I might have questions or need some direction. I'm not sure what he had in mind, but I suspect I will have some things that need taking care of. And perhaps you or he will be able to point me in the right direction."

"Of course. If there are any legal questions, Ben is knowledgeable, though he no longer is practicing law."

"I don't need legal advice, if you're thinking of that in the criminal sense."

"No, of course not. I was just explaining

that any advice Ben gives is as a friend, not official."

"A friend." Helen repeated the word as if the word was foreign to her.

Nell went on. "But Ben is a font of knowledge. And what he doesn't know, he knows where to look. True wisdom, according to some." She smiled. There was something in Helen Getty that might be worth getting to know, although she seemed determined to hide it. "Also, if you'd like Birdie or me to call anyone for you —"

"There is no one," Helen said quickly, ending the issue and standing up. She pulled a laminated business card from her purse and set it down next to her glass. "I'll be in touch." Then she nodded to both women, thanked them for their time, and walked quickly out of the room, tapping something into her phone as she walked.

They listened to the sound of her stilettos echoing on the hardwood floors and down the curving staircase. The door slammed.

And then she was gone.

Nell and Birdie looked at each other. Helen had no car. And it was cold outside, not to mention the shoes she was wearing.

"Well, goodness," Birdie said. "What just happened here?"

Nell looked at the door, thinking Helen

would be coming back. But for what, Nell wasn't sure. Not for kindness, which she and Birdie wanted to give. Not hugs or understanding. The woman's husband was dead. But all she had left them with was the unsettling impression that at the most his death had been an inconvenience.

Birdie looked out the window. "It's mostly up hill to those new houses. And Helen's shoes weren't exactly made for walking."

"And it's cold. You're right, Birdie." Nell stood and grabbed her coat and car keys. She gave Birdie a quick hug and hustled out of the room to catch up with the newly widowed woman, who, Nell suspected, might not welcome the company. But at least she'd be warm.

But as she stood at the end of Birdie's long driveway, looking up and down Ravenswood Road, Helen Getty had already disappeared up Ravenswood Road and out of sight.

Chapter 15

Gabby had almost decided not to go to the dock that afternoon.

Tess had been on her mind all day, to the point that she tried to wish her away, out of her head. Out of her mind. Maybe even out of her life. But she wouldn't leave. Gabby started to ask her language arts teacher about her, then realized how stupid it would sound. What would she ask? People got sick. And then they got better. And maybe she wasn't sick at all and had to work at her other job and just called in sick like kids did when they hadn't finished a project. Or maybe Tess didn't have an excuse.

But that wasn't like Tess, and beneath all her wonderings, Gabby felt a niggling fear. So she had sat through language arts class thinking she would just go on home after school. The one person in her life who could get rid of fear in an instant, just by a hug and a smile, was her *nonna*. Besides, she hadn't seen her that morning and now the thought of snuggling up beside her on the couch near the fire, with popcorn and watching an old movie, would be a pretty cool way to end the day.

But by the time she and Daisy had finished their last class, they decided together that climbing around a Halloran lobster boat might be just the way to get bad thoughts out of their head. And they'd pretty much told other kids in the eco club that they were taking flyers down to the lobstermen, making a dramatic show of how they were going to the ocean itself, to the actual men who fished the sea. *To talk trash.*

Their friends loved it, and since a lot of them were pretty much into the lead singer for the Fractured Fish, Pete Halloran, they'd be hanging on Daisy and Gabby's report. And begging to go along next time.

But the real reason she and Daisy both decided to go was because Tess knew they were going to be there. Who knows? Maybe she'll show up, they figured.

"About time you got here," Pete hollered down the pier as Daisy and Gabby, bundled up in heavy parkas, made their way down to the Halloran slips. The pier was active, with men throwing buckets of water overboard and several boats coming in, their now-empty traps piled high on their boats. Horns blew and rough voices traveled out across the water from boat to boat to shore.

The two girls hollered back to Pete and waved.

As they walked closer, Cass climbed out of the *Lucky Catch,* the Hallorans' newest lobster boat, and headed toward the two girls.

Gabby's smile was wide. "Hey, Cass. I didn't know you'd be here."

"And miss two of my favorite eco activists? What are you, crazy? Besides, it got me out of the office for a while. Here, Daisy, let me help." She took the stack of informational flyers that Daisy was carrying, along with a see-through sack of tangled plastic beach trash. Cass held it up.

"Show-and-tell, smart thinking. That's always good. Especially for these guys. Is Tess coming?" Cass hoped so. Gracie Santos liked her, and in Cass's opinion Gracie could read people in a way not everyone could. And Gracie, for whatever reason, insinuated Tess might need friends supporting her. For what, she wasn't sure.

"Not today," Gabby said. "A sub took her place at school. She was home sick."

"Oh," Cass said. Maybe that was the look

they'd seen. Although Cass seriously doubted that it had been the result of a cold or flu.

Pete stood waiting at the side of *Lucky Catch.* He threw his arms out toward the boat in a welcoming flourish. "Come, ladies. Gabby has seen our new baby, but this is your chance, Daisy." He held out a hand while Daisy balanced, then jumped onto the deck of the blue-roofed boat. The others followed.

"By the way, ladies, just so you know, the real reason Cass came over to chaperone is because she was afraid I'd put you both to work cleaning the boat." He puffed up his chest and suggested they look around. "Check it out. It's all hosed down and beautiful. See" — his arms swept wide — "not a smelly lobster trap in sight. This boat is so clean you can eat off the floor."

"*Eat off the floor?* Ugh, Pete." Daisy wrinkled her nose at him, then stepped over a rope and followed Cass to the side where a plate of gooey peanut butter squares was balanced on top of a cooler. A thermos of hot cider and cups stood beside it.

"You scrubbed this down for us, Pete?" Gabby grinned, brushing strands of windblown hair off her cheek. She pulled her bright orange beanie down tighter. The ocean was not only her favorite place to be, it was a tonic. She loved the sting of the cold air, even the mechanical smells of working boats. She took a deep breath. Even without Tess there, she was already feeling better than she'd felt all day.

"Don't you believe a word that scrawny excuse for a lobsterman says." A new cheerful voice floated up the cabin steps, followed by a tall, lanky man. "I did it all. Cleaned the whole da . . . darn place. That's why they named the boat after me. *Lucky Catch.*"

Cass laughed as the man reached across her and grabbed a peanut butter square off the plate. He bowed slightly to the two girls. "Pete tells me you two are all about clean oceans. Me too. I like them Tide-clean. Tell me everything you know." He leaned against the side of the boat, chewing on the bar, his face open and waiting.

Pete intervened. "Girls, this is Lucky. Lucky, Gabby and Daisy. And don't believe a word he says. You know why he's called 'Lucky'?"

By now, the girls were giggling and intrigued by the awesome guy with the thick black beanie pulled tight, but allowing strands of blond hair to escape.

"He's called 'Lucky' because this long drink of water has never worked a full day in his life. All good things seem to come to Lucky Bianchi. Or Luigi, as he was known in his other life by parents and such. And none of those good things have been deserved."

Lucky punched Pete's heavy slicker sleeve. Then he grinned and said, "Yeah. It's true. But I work really hard at doing nothing." He looked at Pete. "But you, Halloran, you better watch yourself. I may actually be turning over a new leaf."

Pete laughed and reminded the girls that Lucky Bianchi was a lazy galoot, but underneath it all, buried deep, was a decent guy. *Maybe.*

A couple of other fishermen on the pier spotted Cass's peanut butter squares and climbed down into the stern while Cass urged the girls to pass out their information sheets. "They may not look like it," Cass said, nodding toward the men, "but these guys read."

And they listened, too. Gabby and Daisy brightened up, pouring forth with facts and figures and showing them the mounds of plastic they'd picked up off the beach. And how those very things were killing *their* fish and messing up the water in awful ways.

"Yeah," Lucky spoke up. "I saw you little scavengers combing the beach Sunday morning, right? Crack of dawn. And an older lady, too. I worried about her, out there in the cold."

Cass tuned in. "Who?" She was pretty sure Birdie hadn't ventured out with them. But she needed to be sure.

"Margaret," Lucky managed to say around a mouthful of peanut butter. "That's who it was. Deli Margaret."

"Oh sure," Gabby said. "Margaret Garozzo. She's one of us. We love her. She even got down there before us Sunday morning — early enough to see the sun rise. We teased her about sleeping on the beach. She's a great lady. She had a whole bag full of trash when we met up at Paley's Beach."

"That's devotion," Cass said, wondering — and worrying — if Harry knew his wife was combing the beach on a horribly cold morning.

She wandered down to the boat cabin, leaving the girls to their proselytizing, half-listening while she checked some of the electronics, then headed outside again, just as the group was dispersing. The plate of peanut butter squares were gone, and faces were now rosy red from the cold. The girls were standing up on the pier laughing at some story Lucky and Pete were charming them with.

Cass watched the grin on Lucky's face. It was a sweet grin, charming. He was actually kind of a sweet guy.

It was the same flirty grin she saw the other night at the Harbor Club. Only it was more grown-up then, and it was a grown-up woman he had been smiling at. And one who was charming him right back. Pete had told her that Lucky spent a lot of time at the bar. Not drinking heavily, but hanging out. She wondered how well he knew Penny Turner.

Lucky looked up and saw her watching him, then sauntered over as Pete took the girls to look at some new buoys he'd painted.

"So, what's up, Cassandra?" he asked. "Have you heard any news about the Harbor Club mess? I saw you there the other night. You never came over to say howdy. Embarrassed to admit you knew me?"

"You were otherwise engaged, Lucky. What was that about?"

"Ah, it was just fun. That bar has an interesting crowd."

"Like Danny and me, you mean."

Lucky laughed. "That's exactly who I meant."

"Do you hang out there a lot?"

Lucky thought about the question. "I like

bars. They're fun. I meet nice people."

"I meant that particular bar."

"Yeah, that's what I thought you meant. Actually, I do. I like that bar. Do you like it?"

"Well, I didn't think I would. But I did. Good wings. And nice décor. Like Penny Turner," she added with a grin.

"You're funny. But, yes, she's nice décor, all right. Quite the little flirt."

"Is she in there a lot?"

"Penny loves bars, too. She says she doesn't have enough fun people to talk to at the vet clinic. She used to work in a bar and is comfortable in them. So, yeah, she's there a lot, flirting up a storm. But nice. The regulars like her. Though she did tell me Saturday night she might be cutting back a little. We all teased her about it, which, of course, she loved. She was a little pale, so I thought she might be sick, but she said she was fine. And she was kind of glowing."

"She must have an understanding husband," Cass said.

Lucky shrugged. "I guess. She brings him in sometimes, too. But I admit, it's all a little odd."

"Was she friends with Bobby?"

Lucky didn't answer at first. Cass noticed the hesitation. It was one of the things she liked about the guy, that he heard a lot but said little. But this was different. A guy was dead. She asked him again and this time he answered.

"She knew Bobby well. Penny was a tough lady. You might not know it from looking at her, but years working at Hooters probably contributed to it. Black belt in karate, can you believe it?"

Cass laughed, imagining the buxom blonde sparring.

"But I don't mean just physically tough. No one pushed her around, not men or women. That night he died? She chewed Bobby out royally in the kitchen. But she could turn it on or off. Maybe especially with him. If Penny wanted something, she got it. And other women around here knew it."

"What are you saying?"

"I think you know what I'm saying, Cass."

"Okay, then." Cass shifted gears. "Were you friends with Bobby?" she asked.

That answer came more quickly.

"Nope. I didn't like him. But it worked out okay."

"*Worked out?* That's a strange thing to say. Especially since the guy just died."

Lucky looked suddenly embarrassed. "Hey, you're right. Sorry. That was dumb. I just meant that I can like a place without liking the guy who's boss. Right? And even though I like the Harbor Club, I didn't much like Bobby Abbott. In fact, not at all."

It seemed odd to Cass. Everyone liked Lucky Bianchi. And she assumed it was because he liked everyone back. "You were in there often. You must have known him well."

Lucky looked back to the dock where Gabby and Daisy were collecting their gear. He turned back to Cass and shrugged. "Sure, I knew him. Everyone who went in there knew him. Probably for dozens of different reasons and in lots of different ways. Bobby Abbott liked women. There I said it. He liked them a lot. Some people can't go without alcohol. Bobby couldn't go without women."

Then Lucky let it go and managed to bring back the familiar smile. "But, hey, it is what it is. Sometimes good things rise from the dead."

Before Cass could figure out what Lucky meant or figure out the expression on his face, he gave her a high five and loped off toward the parking lot, looking, Cass thought, as if he were trying to escape from her.

■ ■ ■ ■

A few minutes later, Cass found herself back at the side of the *Lucky Catch.* The girls had almost forgotten an important mission: taking selfies with the boat, or so they said. But as Cass watched in disbelief, Pete patiently posed for selfies of himself with Daisy and Gabby. Then with Gabby. Then Daisy. And again with them both. All squeezing a glimpse of the boat in the background.

"It's to prove to *our friends* that *we* really did bring the flyers over," Daisy explained to Cass and Pete with great emphasis.

Cass nodded, holding back a smile and the urge to tell the girls what a homely preteen Pete had been — braces, skinny, BO, and with acne like they wouldn't believe.

Instead, she mouthed irreverent words to Pete behind their backs, then suggested they head to her car. It was getting dark.

Gabby and Daisy waved good-bye to Pete, walking backward on the pier to make sure he saw their happy looks.

"I love it down here," Gabby said. She looked over the water as they walked. "It's as if we're on a different planet. And if you need to escape farther, you just jump in a boat and head out to sea."

Cass laughed. "I guess it might seem that way, Gabs, especially if you don't *have* to jump in a boat and head out to sea — and to spend the next hours untangling buoy ropes, facing harsh winds, and hoisting up traps that could break a lesser man's back."

"Yeah, I see your point. But for me, for right now, it's pretty awesome. I found another place I love, too. Different, but also amazing. There's a small cove not far from *nonna*'s house. A rickety old dock. Rocks and trees and a sliver of beach. The only sound is the wind in the trees, the sound of the water. Another face of the ocean. It's magical. And no one goes there but me."

Before Cass could pursue Gabby's magic cove, Daisy interrupted, stretching her hands out wide like a crossing guard, holding the cars back.

"Wait, wait, stop. Look —" Her voice was hushed and her eyes enormous behind her glasses. They followed her finger and looked toward the first row of cars in the parking lot. Nearly hidden by an oversized SUV was Tess Bean, her back to them, but clearly identified by the green sweatshirt and her size, and the bike propped against her hip. She was leaning against a truck, talking to

Lucky Bianchi.

Lucky stood with his shoulders hunched, lowering his stature to meet Tess's much shorter one. His voice was low, but it carried across the short distance. Serious, yet kind. Friendly.

But it definitely lacked Lucky's infectious humor. Cass could barely make out the sentences, just snatches of words, questioning Tess about something or other.

Cass turned toward Daisy and spoke up, her voice louder than necessary, alerting the couple that they weren't alone. "I think you're right, Daisy. I think it is Tess."

"Tess," Daisy called out, taking a few quick steps ahead and waving.

Tess turned around. Her face was drawn, but she put a smile in place when she saw who it was. "Hey, Daisy. Hi Gabby. I'm so glad I didn't miss you two," she said. She balanced her bike and walked it their way. "How did it go today? I bet you guys were great."

"It was fun," Gabby said. "You'd have loved talking to the guys. And Cass and Pete's boat is seriously amazing."

"I can confirm that they were great," Lucky said. "Terrific, in fact. You wouldn't believe how smart I am because of these two. They invited me to join their club. What do you guys call it? *Echo club?*"

"EEE-CO," the two girls shouted, grinning at Lucky.

Tess's smile relaxed. She thanked Cass for letting the girls bring their flyers by. "I'm sorry I couldn't get here sooner to help. It was one of those days."

"We all have them," Cass said. She glanced at Lucky. "So you know our friend Lucky? I thought Lucky only knew fishermen and people who hung out in bars."

Lucky shrugged. "She's kidding. Well, sort of."

"He hangs around wharfs, too," Tess said. "He happened to be there one day when Gracie and I were lugging lumber over for the compost bins. Gracie shamed him into helping us."

"Are you sure you have the right man?" Cass said. "This Lucky doesn't work. Like ever."

Tess explained that Gracie's lobster rolls had some sort of magic power over Lucky Bianchi. "Crazy, I know. But that and a beer and he worked for three hours."

Tess looked like she'd been doing manual labor for hours, Cass thought. Her eyes were tired, as if she'd been up all night. She could hear weariness in her voice. It was as if she was carrying a weight too heavy for her small body.

Lucky noticed it, too. "Hey, I've got my truck limousine over there," he said. "Want a lift? We can throw your bike in the back."

"*Throw my bike?* Not on your life," Tess said. She lifted a leg over the bike frame, the other foot on the ground. "You girls are the best," she said to Gabby and Daisy. "And you, too, Cass. Thanks so much." And then she was off, pedaling into the wind as she moved across the parking lot.

Cass threw her car keys to Gabby so the girls could climb in and get warm.

Then she caught a final glimpse of Tess as she disappeared from sight.

"She's a strange person," Lucky said, looking at the track in the gravel lot made by Tess's wheels.

"Strange, how?"

"Well, not strange. Bad choice of words. Tess is sweet and nice. Here's the thing. I don't know her very well, but it's her actions that are a mystery. That whole thing with the Harbor Club —"

"What thing?"

"It started out being simply a push against dumping materials, like plastic, in the ocean. Tess tried to explain it to all the restaurants, not just the Harbor Club, how destructive simple things like that could be.

But for some reason, it was different with Bobby. Like you nicely pointed out, I hang around there a lot. So I saw a lot. It wasn't just that Tess didn't like some of the vile things the guys there did. And, sure, Bobby didn't eagerly embrace her ecological efforts to educate them, but there seemed to be something else. I don't know what. Bobby didn't seem to have the same antagonism, or whatever it was, toward her, even though others could set him off easily. Like one day I was in there and we saw her walking along the wharf, handing out flyers. Bobby stood at the window for a long time, watching her go, with this odd look on his face."

"What kind of look?"

"I don't know. I couldn't figure it out. Almost like, I don't know, like he admired it. I asked him if Tess was getting to him. He shrugged. And then he said no. She was just doing her thing. So that's the mystery. We have Tess, who basically seemed to have a problem with Bobby, and probably would still dislike him, even if he cleaned up his act and the whole friggin' ocean as well. And then there was Bobby, who, especially recently, didn't seem upset when she came around. Even when she was tough on him. A conundrum."

"That's a big word for you, Lucky."

"Watch it!" Lucky laughed.

"So, is that what you were talking about when we interrupted?"

"Sort of. I ran into her by accident. With Bobby dead, I thought maybe she'd want someone to talk to. Mostly, I guess, I wanted to know her better." He pulled his keys out of his pocket and shook off the serious note, bringing the smile back. "I didn't get very far. Tess is still mysterious. Now you, Cass? You, I understand completely."

He waved at her again and strode off to his truck.

Tess rode around a bend in the road, through downtown, and finally reached the woods. She turned onto the winding path that would take her through the trees and underbrush and sweet-smelling pines to the small cabin near the sea. *Home.*

She'd been surprised that her mother had left her anything when she died. She'd ignored claiming it for a while, but when she finally came to see it, she knew she'd found a haven. What her mother might have meant as a reflection of what she thought of her daughter — broken-down and worthless — had turned into an inestimable gift. Maybe the only place Tess had ever really called home. A place she felt safe.

The wind whipped against her face as she maneuvered her bike along the path. Her eyes began to water and her cheeks stung. She blinked away the tears and pedaled on, ducking her head to avoid a low-hanging branch. The path was thick with beechnuts and mounds of leaves that only weeks ago were clinging to the branches, thick and lush, shading the path so completely that Tess sometimes had to turn on her bike light in the middle of the day.

Although the beech trees inspired the name of the woods, Tess was happy they had generously shared their soil with evergreen magnolias and hearty hemlocks. They'd keep their coats in the winter months, making the woods feel less bare, more private. More her own.

She sped up, the leaves crackling and snapping beneath the tires, releasing the pungent smell of late fall and winter holding hands — fresh, earthy smells and the scent of green needles. Soon, any minute, the crunchy path would be soft with snow and new smells to sharpen Tess's senses.

The vibration of her phone in her jeans pocket startled her for a minute. The school, maybe? The school she was coming to like a lot. And the students, too. They made her feel alive in a whole new way, their faces bright and eager to believe in things, to better their world. She loved the wise headmistress, Dr. Hartley, too. She seemed to respect Tess and the knowledge she brought to the curriculum. The headmistress liked her passion, too, and had told her so the other day. "It's good for the girls to see," Elizabeth Hartley had said.

Some of the teachers were slower to accept the part-time science teacher who initiated unusual projects and went through the cafeteria's garbage cans for items better composted. But over the weeks most of them had come around, their minds changed by the girls themselves. By their zeal and good works. She knew she was good for Sea Harbor Community Day School. And she was happy they were realizing it, too.

But today she had to stay away. She wouldn't have been good for the school, for her girls. Her emotions and thoughts were smothering her, tangling her into a knot that made it difficult to breathe. She couldn't impose those vibrations on the kids. Walking along the ocean was what she needed, and being alone in the woods. Connecting. It helped her, calmed her, and pulled her into a better place.

Tomorrow she'd be able to face the day, the school, the students. Tomorrow would be better.

The path split in two and Tess took the path less traveled, as the poet directed. The one that led straight down a short incline to the little, one-room cabin that was nearly invisible, gray-brown shingled and tucked right into a copse of magnolia trees, as if they had all grown up together.

She parked her bike next to the front door, leaning it against the house, and pulled out her phone, remembering that she'd had a call. She didn't recognize the number, then noticed a voice message had been attached.

Tess tapped to listen.

Her legs began to wobble and she sat down hard on the wooden step.

She dropped the phone down beside her and rested her chin on her hands staring through the bare branches to the incoming tide, pounding against the rocky shore.

She took deep breaths, forcing the stinging cold air in and out of her lungs. And then, in and out again. And again. And again.

CHAPTER 16

"The investigation isn't going as fast as Jerry hoped." Ben stood in front of the mirror in their bedroom, wiggling the knot on his tie. "And people in this town are letting him know it."

Nell sat on the edge of the bed, watching him get ready for a board meeting in Boston, her thoughts on THE HARBOR CLUB HOMICIDE, as one of today's headlines stated. "I'm sure they are all working nonstop." But even her tone spoke to how she really felt. Jerry had assured people that there wasn't a mass murderer loose in their town. But there was a murderer, just the same. Someone they might even know.

"A few days can be a long time in an investigation," Ben said. He frowned into the mirror, tugging on the two flaps of the tie.

"And probably about as long as people are willing to live with uncertainty. Frightening uncertainty, anyway. Especially parents." She got up and walked over to the mirror, looking at Ben's collar, then his tie. *How can this man, who is so wise and smart and clever, fail so miserably at tying his own tie?* She quickly took over, undoing Ben's attempts and maneuvering the silky material into a perfect knot. She stood back, admiring her handiwork, then moved beside him and looked into the mirror. Her face was next to Ben's, their smiles meeting.

Ben cocked his head and touched his tie, then stepped away from the mirror and lifted his suit coat from the back of a chair. "I saw Jerry briefly today and he showed me a copy of Mary Pisano's 'About Town' column. She subtly brought the police to task. Gently, of course."

"I haven't seen it, but I'm guessing Mary launched into a reminder that it's the holiday season. *The season of children.* Santa coming to the wharf on his lobster boat, Christmas tree lightings and carolers, holiday performances, and the bright beautiful faces of children all over town."

Ben chuckled. "Exactly. But the thing is, we both know that Mary is usually echoing what she hears. Parents worry. There's a cloud. And it'll get worse. Jerry knows this, too. Small towns bear a heavy burden to take care of their own." He slipped into his suit jacket and rotated his shoulders until it felt comfortable. "How do I look? Suitable for the semiannual Endicott Family board meeting?"

Nell smiled. Nothing could totally prepare Ben for the semiannual board meeting in Boston, the only vestige of his former life he couldn't shake loose of when he retired. And it was one of the few times he had to put on a suit. When they'd packed up their Beacon Hill townhome to retire in Sea Harbor several years earlier, Nell allowed Ben to take two good suits. "Sea Harbor was a two-suit town," she had said.

But she was wrong. Ben could easily have gotten by with one.

She straightened the lapels on his suit and smiled into his warm brown eyes. And she told him exactly how he looked in a suit. Or out of one, for that matter.

They headed down the back stairs, Nell making sure Ben had his phone and reading glasses, then handing him a small overnight case. He reached for his winter coat and started to say good-bye, then paused briefly, his brows pulling together.

"That's the look you have when you know something that I don't. And you're not sure you want to tell me or not," Nell said.

And then she remembered he had seen Jerry Thompson earlier that day. Surely, they had discussed more than Mary Pisano's column. "What else did Jerry say?"

"I'm not a worrier, you know that. We both joke about Mary Pisano and her nice holiday treatise and wanting the season to be free of bad people —"

"And?"

"There's some truth in it. Someone in this town, maybe someone we know, murdered Bobby Abbott."

Of course. And Nell knew the message in his words: *Be careful. The person who did it may not be out to get anyone else. But he or she also doesn't want to get caught. And someone who murdered once could murder again.* "What is Jerry concentrating on? Is he at all close?"

"He isn't targeting a bar filled with strangers, though some he is still talking to. The person who did this was someone Bobby knew. Someone who, for whatever reason, wanted him dead."

"This has to be difficult for the police. People don't seem to know him that well. Did he mention Helen Getty? It seems she would be able to give them some direction."

Ben had been as intrigued as Nell when Jerry told him about meeting her. "In his very discreet way, Jerry said it was an interesting talk. He suggested I give her a call, since she's stuck here for a while and wasn't very happy about it."

"Interesting?" It wasn't how she and Birdie would have described their time with Bobby Abbott's wife.

"That's what he said. Which usually means there's a story behind it, one he can't talk about."

"I suppose he's talked to staff —"

"There doesn't seem to be much there. Some liked Bobby, some didn't. But nothing unusual, nothing hateful. He paid well. The customers liked him. He was a good host — cordial, remembered faces and names, offered free drinks to let customers know they were valued. He knew how to play the game. One thing that was clear, he was definitely a ladies' man."

Nell thought about Izzy and Cass's description of their one evening spent at the Harbor Club bar. "Penny Turner —"

Ben nodded. "Penny was in there often, according to the staff. They all knew her. Liked her, actually. But apparently she held her own. No one messed with her, even though she was definitely flirtatious. There were some who mentioned her name alongside Bobby Abbott's. But there were others they mentioned, too. Bobby had more groupies than a rock star, apparently."

"But those people don't sound like people who would want to kill him."

"Probably not, but who knows? Everyone has a story. And you know what they say about a woman scorned."

"Garbage," Nell said.

Ben laughed. "Jerry said some of the waiters were happy to talk. They hear a lot, see a lot. And with the bar owner gone, there's no reason to be quiet. They pick up things. People who might have seen or heard arguments or people voicing a grudge against Bobby. People who really might want him dead."

People like Tess Bean. That's what Ben was getting at. Gabby's teacher and mentor, Tess. But not just Gabby's role model. Izzy and Cass liked her, too. In fact, they'd all begun to embrace the woman who didn't try to make friends, but who had somehow become entangled in their lives.

"As I left the police station this morning, I saw Tess heading across the street toward the department," Ben said. "Her head was down, hands stuck in her pocket. And wearing that god-awful sweatshirt. Someone needs to get her a good winter coat." Ben smiled, trying to lighten the image.

"Did you talk to her?"

"I wanted to. I called out to her, but she kept going. I'm not sure if she heard me or not."

Nell found herself hoping that the Tess who talked to Tommy or Jerry was the Tess who was strong and passionate about the world. And not the lost-looking woman Izzy had described seeing on the wharf after the murder. Lost, guilty, sad. Not words that went together easily, but all that had somehow merged together in their description of Tess.

"Who else might have a motive?" She needed to block out the image of Tess, having to face rumors and innuendos, some by well-meaning people simply wanting the investigation closed. Wanting someone connected to it other than their next-door neighbor. Surely, there were other people who had good reasons to dislike Bobby Abbott. Maybe some who feared him? And just maybe some who loved him?

Of course there were others. Nell understood that Tess would be questioned. But there was little motive. Pushing someone off a deck didn't stop people from doing damage to the ocean or the earth.

"Jerry leads a tight ship filled with smart guys. This will work out, Nelly," Ben said.

"They'll find the person."

Ben stopped talking, his hand on the back door leading to the garage.

Nell waited. But she knew before Ben said a word that there was another person the chief had talked to Jerry about. Someone who had a good reason to want Bobby Abbott gone. Someone they both cared deeply about.

Gracie Santos.

Harry Garozzo saw Nell and Birdie walking up to the door of his deli and hurried to open it, his apron flapping and his ruddy face pulling into a smile. He waved them quickly out of the cold night air and into the savory-smelling warmth of his and Margaret's deli. Next came a Harry hug, one that the women were prepared for, hoping the stains on his apron were not fresh. Finally Harry pulled away.

Birdie straightened up and looked into the warm eyes of the man that she'd known and loved as a friend for more years than either of them could count. "What am I seeing in those eyes, Harry? You're worried about something."

"Nah, Bernadette, you know me. Worried about the desserts for the mayor's party, the holidays, the snow we will probably get. The

Pats losing." He spread his arms wide and scrunched his shoulders up to his ears. "Somebody's gotta do the worrying, right?" He forced a smile and chuckled, loud but unconvincing.

"Come on, come on, come on," he said, "enough about me." He waved for the women to follow him, past the deli cases and into the cozy restaurant area. He led them back to their favorite table, pushed right up to the windows, where the seagulls could sit on the outside ledge and watch them eat. Beyond the gulls, boats sailed up so close that in the warm season, when the windows were swung open, one could almost reach out and touch them. In the winter, snow collected on the moored boats and the restaurant ledge, creating soft works of art while customers dined.

Nell knew another reason Harry saved the table for them: it was the most private, out of the way of listening ears. And he knew they sometimes had private things to talk about, even as they pulled out their needles and yarn.

Harry placed two menus on the table.

"Two more, dear," Birdie said.

"The young'uns," Harry said with a chuckle. "*Perfetto.* So, what's the occasion, besides a taste of the most magnificent *strac-*

ciatella this side of the homeland?"

"Seeing you is reason enough, Harry," Nell said. Then she leaned to the side and looked beyond his ample figure as Izzy and Cass approached, their faces pink from the cold.

Harry grinned. "And here they are. A perfect night."

"No night is perfect, Harry," Cass said, giving him a peck on the cheek and sitting down next to Birdie.

"Oh, and isn't that the truth!"

"What's the truth?" Gus McGlucken came up beside Harry and elbowed his friend in the side. His jacket was stuffed beneath his arm, a napkin still in his hand. "This guy never tells the truth. You all know that."

Harry took the napkin from his friend's hand. "And *this* guy tries to walk off with things. Thinks he owns the place."

"Gus, you look like you've been in a bad fight and lost," Nell laughed.

They looked at the hardware store owner and the gooey Rorschach-looking splotches covering the entire front of his white shirt.

Gus pulled a pair of readers out of his pocket and put them on, ducking his chin to his chest and looking down at the shirt. "Well, what have we here?"

Cass leaned in for a closer look. "Chicken cacciatore," she said.

Gus gave a belly laugh. "How'ya know that, Cass?"

"It's a gift, Gus," Cass said.

Still laughing, Gus grabbed his napkin back and dipped it in Cass's water glass, then dapped at the most dangerous-looking spot. "It was worth every stain," he said, dropping the napkin and slipping on his jacket. "Old Harry here still has it, believe me. Or maybe it's Margaret. What matters is that I get fed well."

The women all knew that Gus spent more nights than not eating at the deli. Margaret's orders — she hated the thought of Gus eating alone every night. The two men, along with Mario Palazola and the recently deceased Anthony Bianchi, had been friends for at least fifty years.

Gus turned serious and looked Harry in the eye. "I heard you talking. You told 'em, didn't you, Harry? That's good. They should know what's goin' on."

"Told us what?" Izzy said.

"Nah, it's nothing," Harry said.

"It's something, Harry. Something to our mayor, anyway. Just ask her," Gus said.

"I don't have to ask her." Harry stared down at his wide hands, now flat on the tablecloth, leaving a perfect imprint.

Gus went on, ignoring Harry and talking to the women. "You know that silver contraption that the mayor always has in her purse?"

"You mean her compact," Nell said. "It's a powder compact, Gus." Everyone knew Beatrice's silver compact. It was beautiful, complete with the raised Tiffany bow on top. She pulled it out often to refresh her face, as she put it. Beatrice loved the compact, especially because it had been a gift from the city council in recognition of all she'd done for the children of Sea Harbor: crossing guards, playground improvements, computers in classrooms, and learning labs. Beatrice had been so touched at the awards ceremony that Nell wondered if anyone had ever given her a personal gift before, jewelry or similar things. She'd vowed that night to make sure Beatrice got something every year she was mayor. To make sure, Nell had already commissioned a Canary Cove artist to make her a silver-tooled bracelet — and had Ben submit the receipt to the council. "Well deserved," Ben had said, prouder of his wife than the mayor.

"Yeah," Gus said. "That's it. The one with the mirror."

"It's beautiful. I asked Sam to buy me

one," Izzy said. "But he reminded me I don't use compacts. Or powder. What's wrong with Beatrice's?"

"Nothing, I hope." Harry looked around out of habit, to make sure no one was listening. "She forgot her purse in here the other day after she'd lunched with some biggity wig from the state. I called, left a message, and she came back later to pick it up — I'd kept it safe, I swear. But when she looked through it, she said that darn silver compact was missing."

Harry looked so sad they all wanted to tell him it was nothing and, surely, Beatrice would understand. But the bigger thing, what they were left wondering, was why someone would take a compact — even a Tiffany compact — when a wallet and credit cards and probably plenty of cash were well within reach.

"Another theft," Izzy said, frowning.

"This must be disturbing to all of you. What else has happened?" Nell said.

But she knew before the question was out what the answer was. Theft simply wasn't as disturbing as it was a week ago. She glanced at Izzy, who had barely mentioned the word *thefts.*

Harry said the same. "A murder has kind of pushed penny theft or whatever it is to the sidelines. That's what folks are caring about. That's what's taken over the town."

He looked at his friend Gus and looped one arm around the man's narrow shoulders. It was a year ago, but seemed more like yesterday, that Gus's own son had been involved in a murder. The wound was raw and showed on the older man's face. Lines were deeper, and Gus's eyes held a sadness that only a parent would understand.

But despite his sorrow, Gus was a practical person and saw things for what they were. "Harry's right," he said. "That's exactly what people care about. I've sold more door locks and home security cameras in three days than in all of last year. That's not what Sea Harbor is about."

Harry nodded, his jowls moving. "I noticed people were really calm at first, not willing to let go of the holiday spirit. And some of them not even sure who the guy was. Somehow being killed at a bar put it into a not-as-important category, especially for people who didn't go there. Kind of like another world, you know? But then it gets written about in the paper, talked about at Coffee's, on the street, in here. And it becomes this *thing,* this kind of awful thing that we need to get rid of. Like a contamination. It needs to end."

It was as if all their thoughts had come together in what Harry and Gus said. They were right.

Gus checked his watch. "Speaking of end, I need to walk off some of this meal and get home to watch my saved *Homeland* show before bedtime. See you ladies later." He gave Harry a punch in the arm, then a clumsy hug before disappearing beyond the deli counters and out the front door.

"You and Gus are right," Birdie said thoughtfully. "What was impersonal at first becomes far less so when people get around to realizing that they may be sitting in Coffee's or in here or walking down the street next to a murderer. So, what are you hearing, Harry?"

Many conversations flowed through Garozzo's Deli, even at the more private tables in the back. Harry always had his finger on the pulse of the town. Nell sometimes thought it was the cozy, home-kitchen kind of feeling that he and Margaret created in their deli and restaurant. Homemade soups and sauces, dishes rattling, and friendly voices everywhere seemed to create a comfortable place to talk. And people did.

When they did, Harry listened, even when Margaret tried to get him to turn the other way.

"A lotta people went over to that bar. My buddy Jake Risso had a major gripe about it, thinking it'd steal his regulars away. But that wasn't going to happen. Jake's Gull Tavern is a fixture in Sea Harbor. Guys go in there right from the boats, the studs on their jeans practically engraved into the bar stools. Those guys won't desert Jake for another place, especially if the other place is polished and the floor isn't covered with peanuts. And even if the TVs are bigger, who can compete with a roomful of beer drinkers linking arms and singing 'Sweet Caroline' in the eighth?"

Nell knew he was right. Cass had told them she'd heard it from the guys on the dock, even though the younger ones — those who still danced — were splitting their time between Jake's and the Harbor Club, depending on the night. But never really deserting the Gull. There seemed to be enough of them to keep two places happy.

"There're others who had bigger beefs about that bar than Jake's worry," Harry went on, his hands on the table, leaning in. "When Beatrice came in to pick up her new compact, she started chatting with a councilman about petitions and letters and whatnot, things that had crossed her desk. All complaints about environmental things, but the worst, she said, were directed at Bobby Abbott. About how he was ruining our town, killing our ocean."

Nell felt Birdie shiver, knowing where Harry was going.

"I interrupted both of them," Harry went on, his thick brows lifting. "I told Beatrice to be practical. I knew who she was talking about. I told her Tess Bean couldn't throw a lobster over a railing, much less a man."

"How did you know they were talking about Tess?" Izzy asked.

"Who else?" He pointed to a littered bulletin board behind the hostess station. "We all know Tess. None of us have escaped her. But me? I think she's a darlin'. So do Gus and Jake. Hell, I'll get rid of straws if it helps the fish. Jake's already doing it. And my Margaret will show anyone the door who speaks badly of her. Which is what she did with Beatrice."

"Margaret kicked the mayor out of your deli?" Cass laughed.

They all tried to imagine the scene: Gentle Earth Mother Margaret and straightlaced, elegant Beatrice Scaglia.

"Well, maybe not exactly. I exaggerate. Tess comes in every now and then to see Margaret. I think she never had much of a mother, and my Margaret holds her tight to her bosom in that way she has. Anyway, Margaret explained to Beatrice that Tess was a good woman who loved our town and our earth, and Beatrice wasn't to say a bad word about her to anyone."

Harry straightened up and rubbed the back of his neck, looking around. He spotted Margaret on the other side of the restaurant. Her hair was slightly in disarray, gray hairs pulled loose from a haphazard bun. She was looking out the window at Harbor Road. Her brows were pulled together in deep concentration, as if pulling thoughts together carefully. She rubbed her cheek absently with two fingers.

Nell tried, but she couldn't read the look on Harry's face or on Margaret's. She wondered again about Harry, about his health. Had that been a cause for worry? But he didn't look sick. No weight loss. Birdie would know if there was a problem and would have said something. She kept in close touch with Harry and his buddies.

Harry turned back to the table. "Margaret's a little out of sorts today. Somehow we didn't order all the ingredients for the soup. Forgot the organic spinach, which, hey, who cares, right? We go over to Market Basket and we get us a bunch. But Margaret likes the organic. Grows it herself in season. She's over there scolding herself crazy, I can tell."

"Margaret's conscientious," Birdie said. "I understand where she's coming from. When I forget things, Ella covers it up as if it were her fault." She smiled sweetly at Harry, sending a message. "And I let her."

Nell was still watching Margaret, her thoughts moving away from organic spinach to Tess Bean and Margaret's affection for her. The thought was sweet and made her smile. It didn't surprise her. Margaret Garozzo was kind and compassionate. Over the years she'd been involved in everything from making sure all kids in Sea Harbor had healthy breakfasts to knitting head huggers for cancer patients. So it made sense she had taken someone like Tess into her warm and protective embrace.

Margaret was a loving woman. And then she remembered something that came back to her in fits and starts.

"Harry, did Margaret know Bobby Abbott?" The words that had been pushed to the back of her head had suddenly inched forward. The words Margaret had murmured to her that cold day — hours and hours before most people in Sea Harbor had awakened to the awful news that a man had been killed in their town.

He was a bad man, and then something else that Nell couldn't quite pull into memory. But those words had been clear. *A bad man.* She and Ben had picked at them, come up with nothing much, and dismissed them. But not completely.

"Abbott?" Harry laughed. "You think my Margaret's been hanging out in a bar on the wharf? The only things that bring us over that way are Gracie's lobster rolls. And Margaret tried that free yoga on the wharf last summer. They gave her a chair, but she refused it. Did fine. That's my Margy."

The yoga they could visualize, but they all laughed at the incongruous image of Margaret in Bobby Abbott's bar.

"I just wondered," Nell said. "I know Bobby Abbott has been a thorn in Tess's side. I just thought maybe Margaret said something to him. She protects her flock." Nell smiled.

"Sure, sure, I get it. Tess knew the guy, I see where you're going. Maybe she'd have talked to Margaret about it all. So maybe she knew *of* him. But talking to him? Nope, I don't think so."

Nell nodded and tucked the information away. When she looked back to where Margaret had been standing, she was gone.

But walking through the door, looking

slightly wan and without the red dress with the plunging neckline, was Penny Turner. She was alone, her head low, as if she didn't want to be seen. She leaned in and murmured something to the man standing behind the counter. He nodded, disappeared for a minute, then returned with a heavy white sack that he handed across the counter.

Harry followed Nell's look and grinned. "That's Penny, right on schedule."

"On schedule?" Birdie asked, looking over as Penny headed for the door. "Don't tell me you have Penny Turner doing deliveries for you, Harry."

Harry chuckled. "Okay, ladies, between you, me, and the fence post —" He turned back to the table and leaned in. "Here's the thing," he said in his low, husky voice, "but you can't breathe a word of it, cross your hearts."

Before they could cross, he continued, "The thing is, Penny Turner can't cook. Nothing. She's probably even worse than you, Cass. So she comes in every few days and we load her up, along with promises that Clark Turner will never find out from us. *Ever.* And I make sure it's always when Margaret is in the back or not here."

"Why's that?" Cass asked.

"Well, you know how Margaret loves everyone?"

They nodded.

"Well, Penny's an exception. Margaret thinks she is shameful. I guess it's the way Penny looks sometimes. A little like a barmaid. Margaret doesn't like bars."

Harry's wrong, Nell thought. *There're two people Margaret doesn't like.* Her words came back: *He was a bad man, Nell . . .*

Harry wasn't through. He looked around again, then returned to his hunched-over position, his fingers splayed out on the table. "But you want to know what else about Penny Turner? Something even more interesting."

They were silent, each of them resolving once again never to tell Harry Garozzo anything in confidence.

His bushy brows lifted and fell and lifted again.

"She's allergic to animals."

Chapter 17

Izzy opened the door to the clinic and carried Purl's bright purple carrier into the waiting room. She found a seat near the reception desk — empty at the moment — and glanced back at the small alcove in which Tess had performed her magic on Red.

The cushion was still there, but it was missing both a dog and a dog whisperer. She watched, anyway, as if seeing them there, Tess's fingers settling into Red's coat. But mostly she was seeing the look on Red's face that day. It was as if Tess's massage had been delivered both in whispers and gentle touches, and was healing his body and soul.

A loud meow brought her attention to the carrier and she looked inside to see Purl looking out at her, wondering why Izzy was doing this to her.

"It's Purl, right?" Tess appeared from nowhere, crouching down on the floor and smiling into the cage. "May I?" she asked, unhinging the door. She settled back on the floor, crossing her legs and settling Purl into the donut hole.

Purl thanked her with a sweet purr and buried her head in her paws, closing her eyes.

Izzy settled into the chair, watching Tess's face as she focused fully on the cat. "Have you ever thought of becoming a veterinarian, Tess?" she asked.

Tess looked up. "No. I love the animals, but I would rather work in the kennels, where I can give them love, not shots."

"I think Purl heard you. And she is never ever going to leave your lap, you know that, right?"

Tess smiled, her fingers caressing the underside of Purl's chin, the base of her ears.

"Do you have a pet?" Izzy realized that she didn't even know where Tess lived, unusual in such a small town.

"I don't. I live near the water, and I worry about all the wildlife down there. But I may someday."

"Where?"

Tess looked up. "Where? Oh, *where* I live. On the shore edge of Beech Tree Woods."

Izzy thought for a minute, imagining the

area. Abby loved walking through the woods, jumping off tree stumps and swinging from some of the old vines that looped from one tree to another.

"I think I know where. Down the path where the main trail splits. One goes to a small beach. The other one —"

"Yes," Tess said. "That's it. The other one."

"Sure. I even know the cabin and that small little shack behind it. It's been there for a long time. Well, as long as I've been here, anyway. It must have been quite a job, fixing it up."

"It's good therapy," Tess said. "I loved fixing the roof, the windows. There was some damage from animals that had found a refuge from the cold. I kind of hated to take that away from them."

Izzy looked over at Tess's diminutive form, but also noticed the firm muscles beneath her T-shirt, the controlled movement as she massaged the cat. "Sam and I often talked about that cabin by the shore. We thought it looked like it needed love. I'm glad it's getting it now."

"It's the first place I've ever had of my own. I mean, something that was actually mine. Walls that held me in, welcomed me."

"So you bought it?"

"No. It was given to me. Well, I inherited it, I guess you'd say."

Tess concentrated on Purl, her posture indicating she didn't especially want to talk to Izzy about personal things. Or, at the least, how she managed to own a broken-down cottage with an ocean view. She would much rather be whispering to Purl.

Izzy glanced at the desk, realizing that no one had been standing there since she'd come in. Penny had always been at the desk. Almost like a guard. "Where's Penny?" she asked.

Tess stood and looked over to the desk. "That's a good question. I came in to tell Clark I needed some supplies for the kennels. Let me check."

Izzy tucked Purl on her lap.

"Also, I haven't forgotten to come by and show you some tricks to make Red happy. I'd like to see him again. I need dogs in my life right now. They don't judge. They just love." She stood still for a second, her face thoughtful. Then she hurried around the reception counter and into the medical section of the clinic.

A minute later, Clark Turner appeared in the lobby.

"Hi, Izzy," he said with a broad, happy smile. "Tess said you were out here. Who do we have here today?" He spotted the carrier. "Ah, Madame Purl."

He waved for Izzy to follow and ushered her into an examining room. "Make yourself comfortable while Purl and I have a chat." He lifted the calico out of the carrier.

Purl meowed but offered only minor resistance. Izzy watched her calm cat. Purl had convinced her long ago that all cats should live in a yarn castle surrounded by knitting. It made them peaceful and calm. Cats understood *hygge.*

Clark began his examination, feeling behind her ears and palpitating her chest, then listening through a stethoscope, then letting it hang from his neck. "So, how are you doing, Izzy? How's Red?"

"Both of us are fine, thanks. Abby and Sam, too. And you? I missed seeing Penny out front. Is she okay?"

Clark continued his examination, a loose, happy smile on his face.

Izzy thought he looked a little giddy. A lovesick kind of smile.

"Penny's fine, Izzy." Clark paused, still cuddling Purl, kneading her belly. "She's just not feeling one hundred percent today, so I insisted she stay home. Rest is good. She put up a fuss — she likes being here. But we live so close that I can check on her." He nodded toward the window in the rear of the examining room, looking out over a modest two-story house that sat on a slight hill on the clinic's property. "I'm thinking of building a new house, one with all the comforts Penny never had. I have it all planned in my head. Over in that new area, maybe. A place with plenty of room for us all. As soon as she's up to it, we're going to look at plans."

"You're a thoughtful man, Clark. I hope she's better soon."

"She will be. She's not sick, just tired. She's changed my life, you know. We are a good pair. Penny is . . . well, she's amazing."

Izzy watched emotions fill his face. They were so naked she felt she should turn away. This wasn't the same man she knew pre-Penny. When she moved to Sea Harbor, and Red came into her life, she'd brought him in to be checked. Clark's cousin, a classmate of hers, had recommended him. Clark had talked to the dog the entire time, but barely managed a hello to Izzy. His shyness — at least that's what Izzy assumed it to be — was nearly painful to watch. When they talked, it was about pets and dog food and vaccinations.

Clark didn't talk much at pickup basketball, either, Sam had said. They figured he did his talking by crushing them on the court, slamming in basket after basket. The guy was good, Sam said. And Izzy remembered a few times when Clark's cousin came to town and solicited Izzy's help in going out to a bar with her and Clark. Just to have someone else to carry the conversation, his cousin Jill confessed.

This same man had turned into a love puppy with Penny Turner. Night and day. "We saw you and Penny the other night at the Harbor Club," Izzy said. "We would have said hello, but the place was packed. You're an awesome-looking couple, by the way."

Clark ducked his head, his attention back to Purl. "Well, that's Penny's doing. I may not be totally comfortable with it all, but, hey, I'll get there. She's worth it." He looked at Izzy and stood up, stretching out his back. "She's even an amazing cook. I've gained ten pounds this past year. I've found the perfect wife. How did I get so lucky?"

Izzy held back a smile. She'd have to tell Harry what a good job his pastas were doing at the veterinary clinic. They'd soon have a chubby vet if he didn't hold back on those sauces.

"It's a new world for me, and I'm figuring

out how to make it all work." Clark continued his gentle rubbing of Purl's neck. "She's my one and only love."

"It's a gift when you find that person," Izzy said, not sure if she was expected to be a part of the conversation.

Clark nodded. "I never dated much. I decided early on I would never get married — and for good reasons. But then I met Penny. And I knew, no matter what, it'd somehow work out if I married her. She's even helping me socially. People know her over at the Harbor Club and she's introducing me all over town. Used to be if you didn't have a pet, I didn't know you. It's nice meeting the rest of the world."

Izzy smiled and checked her watch. She wondered if Clark had forgotten about Purl's vaccination. But if nothing else, her cat was being greatly loved in Clark's large hands.

Clark went on. "I know Pen can be grumpy in the clinic sometimes — she's a little overprotective of me, I think. A little controlling. But she insists on being here. She says she didn't marry me to spend her days away from me."

Harry's words came back to Izzy and she wondered briefly if now was the time to explain to the doctor that his wife's grumpiness might well be discomfort as she exposed herself daily to cat dander.

Clark fell silent, lowering his head and concentrating on Purl. He gave the injection almost before the cat realized it. Vaccination complete. One hiss was all Clark Turner got, and he quickly made amends with a cat treat.

Izzy sat in the chair, watching his face, his caring for her cat. It was like reading a book for the first time, each page revealing something new about a man she'd known for years. But maybe not at all . . .

It didn't fit neatly in her head: exchanging the old Clark for the new, but she would give it time. And she'd be more patient with Penny, too, knowing the poor woman was probably itching her way through her working days. "I'm happy for you, Clark. And I'm happy for Penny, too. She's a lucky woman."

"We both are." Clark Turner beamed. Over his shoulder Izzy saw a framed photo, right beside his veterinary license, but larger. Clark and Penny, standing beside a waterfall, arms wrapped around each other. There was something Old World about the image of Clark. A protector, tall and resolute, holding his loved one close. And Penny sinking into his arms, as if she'd drown if she let go.

CHAPTER 18

They all agreed that what they'd been missing that week was time alone — *alone together* — to knit and to talk. It was like a deep hunger, one that needed to be fed. A Thursday *hygge* all their own.

Nell took the cover off the Crock-Pot while Cass breathed in the enticing aroma of garlicky potatoes and wine and bacon, reciting the ingredients down to the last sprig of parsley and the nutmeg sprinkled on top.

"It's a Danish recipe," Nell said. "I thought we might consider a Danish holiday soupfest at our holiday *hygge* this month."

"Anything that breathes of peace, harmony, and happiness, along with soup, has my vote," Birdie said. She filled the wineglasses and glasses of water on the coffee table and sat down near the fire, pulling her needles from the basket sitting at her feet. The cuffs of an orange sleeve appeared and

Birdie began to knit, her small worn fingers working in perfect harmony with each other. She gave Cass a smile. "Everyone needs a hugfest."

Birdie's voice was soft and hopeful, even though she knew that the town needed more than that. But she would hold firm in believing that what she wished for would happen. It almost always did.

But Nell wondered if finding a murderer would succumb so easily to Birdie's wishes. She wasn't sure even Birdie believed it.

She carried a bowl of soup across the knitting room and set it down in front of Birdie, then returned for her own.

Beyond the mullioned windows it was already dark, a round moon lighting a sprinkled path along the harbor. Sounds of soft jazz floated through the room and the heat of the fire cast a warm glow across their faces and the glasses.

Izzy brought a wrapped baguette to the table, along with salad bowls and a pistachio-and-walnut salad she had picked up on her way over.

"Did you make it or 'pull a Penny'?" Cass asked.

Izzy laughed and confessed she'd picked it up at the yacht club's restaurant. "But speaking of Penny, I saw her husband today."

"Did he have his bolo tie on?" Cass looked at Nell and Birdie and described the incongruous look Clark had presented at the bar on Saturday night. She wasn't sure she'd ever get the incongruity out of her head, she said. "It was a little bit like me wearing a frilly pink dress."

That image brought loud laughter.

Izzy kicked off her shoes and sat down, curling her legs up beneath her. The fire leapt and crackled. "Nope, no bolo. The original Clark was back today, straightlaced, starched white jacket. At least his appearance was the old Clark. But we had an unusual talk. He and Penny may be the most unlikely couple in town, but that man is absolutely, totally in love with her. It was touching to hear him talk."

"I wonder if the love will be dented when Clark realizes his weight gain is because of Harry Garozzo's lasagna and not his wife's cooking," Cass said. "Why do you think Penny does that? One of the first things Danny discovered about me was that my three-course dinners consisted of Nell's leftovers, frozen pizza, and peanut butter."

"Maybe it's a matter of pride with Penny," Birdie said. "Maybe she equates cooking with being a good wife, or at least a part of what a good wife is."

Izzy stirred her soup with the spoon, the thick potato base creamy and perfectly seasoned. She took a giant spoonful. "Maybe," she said, wiping her mouth. "She wasn't in the clinic today. Sick or something, Clark said."

"She shouldn't be in there at all. Pet allergies can be serious," Birdie said. She broke off a hunk of the bread and dipped it in her soup.

"Nothing to sneeze at, for sure," Cass said, then grinned as they groaned.

"I know people handle relationships differently, but apparently Penny spends a lot of time in bars," Izzy said. "Don't you all think that's odd?"

"Lucky Bianchi said she loves bars," Cass said. "We've all joked about her lack of experience in a veterinary clinic, but she has lots of experience in bars. And I'm half serious about this. She probably feels at home there. Comfortable. Lucky said all the regulars know her, like her."

They pondered the thought of feeling more at home in a bar than cuddled up in front of a fireplace at home, music playing softly in the background.

A foreign concept, but apparently not for

Penny Turner.

"Comfortable or not, it's put her in the middle of a murder investigation. Spending so much time with Bobby Abbott will be questioned and probed," Izzy said.

"From what Lucky says, Penny was controlling even in the bar. It was her way or the highway sometimes." Cass twirled her spoon around in her soup bowl, her voice thoughtful.

"And she was there the night he died," Izzy added. "She seemed friendly with everyone that night, though who knows?"

"Too friendly?" Birdie asked.

A question the police would probably wonder, too.

"Clark didn't seem worried when we saw him," Izzy said.

"I doubt if Penny will be intimidated by the police," Cass said. "They're talking to the bar regulars who might have heard something or seen something, too. Penny knows them all. Lucky knows he'll be on the list. He spent almost as much time in there as Penny. It relaxes him, he says."

"If Penny truly loves that kind of atmosphere, I wonder what she will do, now that the Harbor Club is closed," Birdie said.

Izzy held up one finger for them to wait a minute. She swallowed her mouthful of soup. Then she gave her news. "It's reopening."

"Really?" Nell said. "That's surprising, after having met Bobby's wife. Helen Getty seems like an unlikely bar owner."

"No. It's not his wife, Gracie said. Apparently, Bobby wasn't the sole owner and either one gets full ownership if the other backs out or doesn't give it to someone else. Or dies, I guess," Izzy said. "Bobby's wife wasn't an owner at all. He had a silent partner."

Nell mulled that over in her head as she spread butter on a piece of the baguette. She knew about silent partners in business transactions; Ben's family had sometimes invested that way. But for some reason, the Harbor Club having a silent investor seemed odd. "Who is it?"

"Gracie didn't know. She guessed it's an out-of-town investor. If it were someone from around here, we'd probably know it," Cass said. She cleaned the bottom of her soup bowl with a piece of bread, then got up for more.

"It adds a layer to his murder, no matter who it is," Izzy said.

Nell agreed. "Another person with a motive. Maybe a silent partner who didn't want to be silent. Silent partners usually don't have much say in decisions. That could cause friction."

The thought of another suspect being brought into the mix brought a surprising feeling of comfort to the knitters and they imagined several scenarios that could have led to Bobby's death. A stranger being the suspect was far better than those they loved or even knew.

"Maybe this new development will help the case along. Ben says the chief has been perplexed. What seemed relatively easy — a time, a place, and maybe even witnesses — isn't turning out that way. Nothing is clicking."

"And what about this wife that no one but you two and M.J. at the hair salon seem to have met?" Izzy asked, looking at Birdie and Nell. "M.J. said she has great hair. Not much help in a murder investigation, I guess." She set aside her soup bowl, wiped her hands, and took out the slouchy pink hat she was knitting for Abby, a pom-pom as big as an apple at the end.

"The police have met her, too. They questioned her almost immediately and will do so again," Nell said.

"It's Tess I worry about." The comment came from Birdie. They looked at her, surprised. Birdie had yet to embrace Tess in a way the others were beginning to do.

Izzy got up and began collecting bowls, stacking them on the library table, then plugging in the coffeepot. Cass refilled wineglasses.

Nell pulled out the holiday cowl she was working on, knitting and purling. Waiting for Birdie to say more.

Birdie drank the remaining trace of pinot gris in her glass and set it down. "Yes, I've been resistant to Tess, but that was because I was worried about Gabby. Worried about having her involved in something that was beyond my reach. My world, maybe. And I didn't understand exactly what it was all about. Having her under the influence of someone I didn't know was unsettling. What boundaries did I need to set? I've done a lot of listening and reading and even googling about all this — and some quite serious soul searching, too."

She smiled and continued. "It was never about Tess. Not really. It was about my coming to grips with being everything I need to be for my quite amazing granddaughter. And to letting Gabby *be* Gabby. To letting her grow." She turned her head and looked into the fire, her deep love for Gabby hanging right out there for all of them to see. She looked back. "It's new for me, you see."

But what was new for her three dear friends was watching the wisest woman they had ever met grapple with her own heart.

Cass took a drink of water, then ripped out a lopsided row on a heavy winter beanie. A not-so-discreet cover-up for the emotion she was feeling. "In my humble opinion," she said, glowering at her needles, "your granddaughter is truly amazing. And her spirit is thriving in her present home."

They agreed in the silent way of friendship, and for a few minutes the only sounds in the room were the crackling and popping of the fire and the easy voice of Carole King singing in the background.

Finally Nell finished the first round on her soft cowl and brought them back from listening and knitting to what was on their minds. "Birdie, how *is* our Gabby doing with all this? Murders captivate all of us — our fears and imaginations — but I hope the girls are free of it. I hope they have other more important things filling their days. Like tests and friends and sleepovers."

"I wish that were true. And it might well be the case if this were far removed from us. But it isn't. I can tell that Gabby's concerned," Birdie said. "She and Daisy helped Tess deliver flyers on the wharf, they know where the bar is, where the homicide occurred. Mostly I know that the smile that explodes and lights up our whole house for no reason doesn't appear quite as quickly, not since our town has been grappling with this."

Nell had wondered about Gabby, too. She thought back to the day on the wharf when Bobby Abbott had run into little Abby, toppling her to the ground. But the image that stayed in sharp focus from that day was the look Gabby had thrown at the man like an arrow. Fierce, somehow. "Did Gabby know Bobby Abbott at all?" she asked. She described the scene on the wharf, trying to bring some clarity to the look she'd seen on Gabby's face.

Birdie didn't think so.

But Izzy had an idea, one that seemed easier to accept than Gabby having anything at all to do with a man who had been killed. "It makes sense to me. Gabby is so devoted to Abby that I suspect she would have stared down the pope if she thought he'd made Abby cry."

It was a comfortable explanation. But Nell wasn't sure. The look she had seen was almost accusatory. And she wasn't completely convinced Gabby was accusing a man of causing a little girl to fall down. "Do you think Tess has talked to the girls about any of this?"

"Tess is their teacher," Birdie said. "Not their friend. I think Tess probably keeps good boundaries. Whatever there was between her and Bobby Abbott doesn't have anything to do with Gabby, Daisy, and the others."

"But they would have known how she felt about him," Cass said.

"We know they were at the council meeting when Tess talked about things — and probably mentioned Abbott," Cass said.

Nell watched the thoughts as they formed and as Birdie spoke them. *This is what would be wise, this is how Tess should act,* Birdie was saying. Nell suspected that however she might worry, Birdie's wisdom was alive and well in the young woman Gabby admired so.

"Gabby is with the group tonight — the environmental club — but, hopefully, a man pushed off a deck is the furthest thing from their discussion."

"What are they doing? It's a school night, right?" Nell asked, a sobering image of the girls out in the dark, delivering flyers flashing across her mind.

"It's a school-sponsored event at Percy's Old Theater down the street. Someone talked Percy into showing the documentary

A Plastic Ocean to the environmental club. Tess is chaperoning, along with Laura Danvers and a couple other moms."

"Best popcorn on Cape Ann," Cass said. "I love that theater. Danny does, too, even though he usually falls asleep the instant he hits the sofa."

Nell chuckled. Ben did the same. The theater consisted of a room above the wine-and-cheese shop, up a rickety set of stairs and filled with old couches and chairs scattered around the room, all facing the theater's screen in some fashion or another. Homemade popcorn, drinks, and Rice Krispies bars filled a counter in the back, along with Percy and his wife, Sarah. Occasionally the words *health regs* were mentioned in connection with Percy's Old Theater, but even Mayor Scaglia seemed to turn a blind eye to it.

"It's a good choice of movie, considering their efforts," Izzy said.

Birdie nodded. "But something else was going on with Gabby. I'm not sure what. There was an urgency about her, like she had to be there. She had to see Tess. And I think it was for reasons other than the movie. She said she had something really important to talk to her about and she hadn't been able to catch her at school. And whatever it was, it was troubling her terribly."

Birdie picked up her knitting again, smoothing out the rows and beginning a new one, the orange yarn looping across her lap and on down to the ball in her knitting basket. The rhythm and sound of her needles soothed the concern that had come with her words.

Cass picked up her bulky hat and stared at it, as if she wondered how it had gotten in her hands; then she began her decreases, slipping and stitching together as she moved toward the crown of the hat. She did it every year for the lobster crew, paying little attention to size, knowing there'd be a head to fit each. "Birdie, I watched Gabby and Daisy the other day when they brought their flyers and little eco shtick to our dock. They are learning a lot from Tess, but the impressive part was how they passed it along to my motley crew." Cass looked down to her lap, picked up a dropped stitch, and continued. "Honestly, they were a bright light down there. The fishermen loved them — not to mention that their presence cleaned up the language like you wouldn't believe. But more important, those guys and gals love the sea, and they think they know everything about it. But they don't. Whatever these kids are learning from Tess is capturing the crew's attention. They actually listened to the girls, even asked questions about how they can help their ocean survive. Not to mention their fish."

Birdie loved the story of the fishermen listening attentively. "It's all wonderful, what you say. But the truth is still there that this interest, or passion, however good it is, has brought Gabby too close to a homicide. And that's what is so troubling."

The fact that life did that — made us grow up a little faster because of death or disaster, or sadness or joy — didn't change anything, and they all knew that of all people, Birdie knew that. But all people weren't her granddaughter.

Finally Birdie said, "I can't get my arms around Tess having anything to do with the homicide."

"Well, can any of us?" Izzy asked. "Could she be involved?"

It was a thought that hung there, refusing to go away, and one they didn't want to answer.

"We don't know," Izzy answered herself. "We want the answer to be *no.* So we need to find that answer. That *no.* That's the only way. We are good at finding answers."

Nell agreed. "For Gracie, too," she said softly.

"Gracie is absolutely *not* involved," Cass said, almost before Nell released Gracie's name.

"Of course she isn't. We all agree, Cass," Izzy said. "Gracie even hates the idea of killing lobsters and she owns a lobster shack. We know her and we love her. But to the police she has motive and opportunity. Stronger maybe than Tess's — at least what we know of it. Bobby Abbott wanted to put her out of business. He was a bad guy."

He was a bad guy. Izzy's words made Nell shudder. Margaret's comment had strayed from her mind. But it kept coming back, only to be pushed away again. She would deal with it later. She'd talk to Margaret and it would be cleared up.

"Tess's motive isn't very strong," Izzy went on. "The police will need more than her environmental beliefs. I mean, think about Wendell Berry, John Muir, Rachel Carson. Thoreau. All passionate about our earth. And not a killer in the group."

And yet they all knew that motives were given strength by the person who had them, not by bystanders. *Motive, opportunity, . . . and . . .*

"Emotion," Birdie said. She sat up

straighter, the way she did when it was time to consider things in an orderly way. "We're asking good questions. What did Bobby Abbott do to someone to cause an emotion strong enough for that person to kill him? That's the question —" She pulled her glasses from the top of her head and put them on. Not to read, but because they helped her focus, she said. "Murder involves emotion."

The room grew silent, but they all sat up straighter, buoyed by the resolution in Birdie Favazza's voice.

Izzy leaned over and placed one hand on Birdie's smaller one. "And we do *emotion* well."

Birdie smiled at her. She looked around at the others. "We all have our reasons for wanting this over. The whole town does. The girls idolize Tess — they are being hurt by this, not to mention how rumors and this kind of adverse attention will affect Gracie and Tess. Good, strong women, both of them. The sooner we can find the person who did this, the less time it will take them to heal."

Good, strong women. They sipped their wine and appreciated that Birdie had included Tess fully into the fold. She was important to Gabby. And that was now enough.

"Tess is a mystery herself," Cass said. "Why did she dislike Bobby so much? Even Gracie admits to being puzzled by the strength of Tess's emotion when it came to Bobby Abbott. And then there's Abbott himself. Lucky says he was tough on Tess when she first came around, then mellowed a little. What do we know about him? Where is he from? Who knows him well? We're thinking about this all through dark glasses."

Birdie nodded. "Through a glass darkly," she said softly, quoting Paul the Apostle. Imperfectly.

Cass went on. "Maybe once we find out more about these people and what makes them tick, we will be able to think more clearly about this, to sort through it all. Bobby himself should have plenty to tell us once we get to know him better."

Cass had walked over to the bookcase and poured four heavy mugs of coffee. She carried them back on a tray with a pitcher of cream and sat down. She grabbed her knitting as if maybe the answer was somewhere in her latest ripped out tangle of yarn. Then she looked at the others. "So, what do you think?"

They lifted their coffee mugs in unison. Challenged. And ready to go.

Chapter 19

Gabby walked up the wooden steps to Percy's Old Theater — the theater's actual name according to the painted marquee on the lower level. Harold had dropped her off, and she knew she was a little bit late. But still she moved slowly, counting the steps as she climbed. Ten. Thirteen. Fifteen. She wished there were twenty more. Maybe fifty. She wondered why she'd even decided this was the right thing to do. She'd seen the movie before. But that didn't really matter. Daisy had seen it, too. And she knew she was already there, happy to be with everyone. Truth was, the movie had little to do with why she was there.

From the theater room at the top, she could hear Melissa Etheridge's voice pouring out, probably from someone's phone, the words pulling the girls together. The club had adopted Melissa's "I Need to Wake Up" as their motto. And when they sang it, their voices joined, it made them feel strong and committed. She thought she could hear Daisy's voice above the others, singing along with Melissa, loud and clear: " 'Take me where I am supposed to be . . .' "

Gabby hummed along, feeling calmer as the words and the music and her friend's voice took hold.

She thought back over the day. At first, she had thought Tess was avoiding her. She had tried to talk with her after class. Then she tried after school. But somehow missed her both times. But it didn't make sense that Tess would do that. She didn't know why Gabby wanted to talk with her. And even if she had, Tess taught them to face things directly. To be honest. That's what Tess herself always did. Not avoid things. The singing grew louder as she got closer to the top, the words ringing in her ears: " 'I need to speak out . . .' "

Speak out. Yes, she would do that. She had gone over it in her head a hundred times.

But then, briefly, she had changed her mind. Maybe, instead, she would talk to her *nonna.* Her *nonna* always listened intently — and she was wise. She knew so much. And she loved Gabby a lot.

She'd go to her *nonna*'s room and sit on her wide white bed and pour it all out to her. She'd tell her she'd been having trouble sleeping. And then she would tell her why.

Her *nonna* would be calm and attentive, propped up against huge, puffy pillows, and maybe she'd put her glasses on, like she did sometimes to hear better. She'd listen and she'd take Gabby's hand in hers and she'd tell her she loved her and it was going to be okay. She would even smile, and she'd kiss Gabby good night and tell her to take deep, deep breaths. Then she'd tell her to climb into her own bed and dream about things that swept her up, made her soar.

And Gabby would. She'd crawl into bed, feeling safe, and she would go to sleep. She wouldn't be troubled anymore about doing the right thing or the wrong thing, because she'd have dumped the whole dilemma on her *nonna*'s bed. On her *nonna*'s shoulders. And on her *nonna*'s heart, knowing she would now take it all on herself.

So Gabby could sleep.

But it didn't take her long to uncover the problem with all that.

It wasn't her *nonna* who had watched Tess Bean push Bobby Abbott into the ocean that day. It was Gabby who kept that locked up in her head and her heart. It was Gabby's painful dilemma, not her *nonna*'s.

A sound from above drew Gabby's attention to the top of the stairs. Winter boots and clunky shoes were hammering the old wood floor. She heard voices, kids talking louder over each other, grabbing bags of popcorn and cans of Coke and scrambling to get a place on the least bumpy couch.

She reached the top step and rounded the corner into the theater just as the lights flickered, the crowd hushed, and the room grew dark. Music filled the room as the movie began — images of a deep majestic ocean, mermaids and fish swimming in its depths.

Gabby squinted into the darkness.

Then she felt a soft tap on her shoulder and a familiar voice whispered into her ear.

"There are some chairs behind the popcorn machine, Gabby. We can talk there. I saved you a bag of popcorn."

Gabby turned toward the dim light of the popcorn machine. She nodded. And she followed Tess Bean to a quiet, shadowy spot behind the blinking lights of an old popcorn machine.

Cass had sworn the spirited conversation had been the best thing for her knitting in a long time. Her needles moved at a rapid clip as possible scenarios and names and motives were tossed out and dissected, edges smoothed, and inconsistencies pointed out — just like the beanie she was working on. "I'm getting so good at this that I'm going to move on to knitting new things. Special things. You just wait, all of you." She smiled, a soft, slightly mysterious smile, and then she went back to the issue at hand, pulling their ideas together and repeating them out loud as the flames died down into glowing embers.

It wasn't only Bobby Abbott's death that was a mystery. His life was mostly unknown. "All victims have a story," Birdie had said. "Surely, Bobby Abbott has one."

It was certainly a logical place to start.

"His bar may have a story, too," Nell had said, examining her holiday cowl and the intricate pattern it was creating. *Intricate.* Like all these stories would do.

"And Tess Bean," Izzy had said, knowing they were all thinking the same thing. It wasn't only Bobby who had a story.

Many questions had been brought to the table, weighty and complicated, warmed by the fire and glow of the candles Izzy had put around the room.

While answers were negligible, some words rang clear: *motive, opportunity.*

But there was one that echoed the loudest, that kept coming back again and again as they tried it on each person who might have motive and opportunity to kill Bobby Abbot: *emotion.* It sometimes drove decent people to perform horrible acts — the thing that might cause that person's humanity to collapse.

Nell began blowing out candles, feeling buoyed by the evening of knitting. But it wasn't just their hats and cowls and sweaters that had come alive in the warmth of the fire, it was the resolve that there were answers to all the questions they had pulled apart in the yarn shop's cozy knitting room. And once they got the answers to them, once these clues were laid out, side by side, overlapped and stitched together, they would know who murdered Bobby Abbott. And why.

A knocking on the front door interrupted Nell's thoughts. Loud and intrusive, or perhaps it was the calm that had settled on all of them that made it seem that way.

Izzy started at the sound, then rushed up to check the locked door.

Standing together on the step were Tess Bean and Gabby Marietti, an inch taller than her favorite teacher.

CHAPTER 20

Tess had insisted they walk down and talk to Birdie first. They'd explain everything to her, and then she'd leave Gabby in the arms of her grandmother, safe and loved.

And then Tess would head over to the police station and tell them about the "forgotten incident."

But Izzy had a different idea and suggested calling her uncle Ben first — he knew the chief better than anyone, and he seemed to have an access few others had. Although she herself had legal expertise, this needed something more than that.

Tess seemed grateful for the advice. Her only concern, which was clear to Nell and Izzy, was Gabby — and relieving her of the guilt that burdened her so heavily.

Now, with Birdie and Ben, they all gathered back in the knitting room while Tess repeated the story of what Gabby had seen that day, something Gabby hadn't told a soul. Except for her friend, Daisy Danvers.

Even Tess didn't know, having been completely unaware of Gabby being there.

"After Bobby Abbott died, Gabby didn't say anything because she was trying to protect me," Tess said, her voice strong and matter-of-fact, but the hand she extended to Gabby was filled with feeling.

"Your granddaughter is an amazing young woman," she said to Birdie, "and she needs to be free of this burden she's been carrying. We need to tell the police what Gabby saw, and let her go about her life." Tess looked at Gabby again.

"It's not a betrayal of me, Gabby," Tess said, her eyes holding Gabby's and refusing to let her look away. "It's simply the truth. We can deal with that."

The *that* was quickly understood. Gabby's understanding that what she had accidentally witnessed that day at her private cove — what had seemed like an argument between two people — had taken on serious overtones when one of the people had died.

Nell glanced over at Gabby. She looked so sad, it was difficult to look at her. It was clear now that she had wanted to protect Tess so fiercely that she had kept the incident bottled up inside her, where it clawed and gnawed away. But she couldn't — wouldn't — go to the police.

So, instead, she finally met with Tess, hoping — praying — that a simple explanation would make what she saw seem silly, inconsequential. Certainly nothing that would connect Tess to a murder.

They all listened carefully while Tess talked; Ben leaned forward, his elbows on his knees, his eyes lacking judgment.

The implication of what Gabby had witnessed was significant — they all knew that. And Tess might not be able to make it go away easily.

Ben finally convinced Tess that going to the station right then was not a good option. The night shift wouldn't have the right people there, and he thought it'd be good for Gabby to go along.

Instead, he'd pick Gabby and Tess up at Sea Harbor Community Day School the next day, during lunch hour. He'd take them both to a little out-of-the-way diner where he and his good friend Jerry often met to escape from inquiring minds. In fact, the two men were already planning to meet there the next day. Ben would simply change the reservation to a table for four.

All of them walked out together, standing

for a few minutes on the sidewalk, breathing in the bracing evening air. Up and down Harbor Road, small trees sparkled with lights, and lampposts, wound with lush garlands and brilliant red bows, stood like stately sentinels of the holiday. In the distance music streamed out of the Gull Tavern. Jake Risso had already begun his holiday medley of tunes. Strains of "White Christmas" escaped when the heavy front door opened and closed. Soon they knew the voice of Jake's all-time favorite singer — Elvis Presley — would be singing about a blue Christmas.

Finally good nights were murmured and the group broke apart, walking to separate cars. Nell and Izzy were the last to go. They stood for a minute, watching Ben walk three women to his car. Birdie's arm was hooked through his, and Ben's other arm was wrapped around Gabby's shoulders. Tess Bean walked slightly apart, her head held high and her eyes looking straight ahead.

Izzy gave her aunt a hug, holding the embrace for a long time. "We left the elephants in the room, Aunt Nell," she whispered.

Nell nodded into her niece's shoulder. They'd done exactly that. No one asked, no one answered, leaving the *whys* hanging like storm clouds over Tess Bean's head.

Why was she meeting with Bobby Abbott in such an isolated place?

And why in heaven's name had she pushed him into the freezing waters of the cove?

CHAPTER 21

Although the temperature dipped the next day, a brilliant sun was luring people from the shadows of their homes and into the day.

Izzy called Nell early. She was taking the day off, but had overslept and missed her morning run. Next best was a walk in Beech Tree Woods with Abby and Red and Aunt Nell. Would she come?

Nell poured a second cup of coffee, answered a few emails, and then headed for her coat and boots.

The pinging of her phone announced another text, this one from Birdie. She paused for a minute at the door to read it, smiling in surprise. And then she answered it with a thumbs-up gesture. Of course she'd meet them for lunch, and she headed outside to wait for Izzy.

A short while later, bundled up like polar bears, they piled out of Izzy's car and headed down one of the paths into Beech Tree Woods. The sun was pouring through the bare branches of the beech trees and filtering through firs, lighting patterns along the trail. Needles beneath their boots released the crunch of fall and the smell of Christmas, the solid ground of winter.

Abby, her cheeks pink from the cold, ran ahead. Red lumbered in the rear. Happy to be out.

"I don't suppose Ben has said any more about last night," Izzy asked.

"There's nothing to say, really. Gabby was right to be concerned about what she saw. Tess knows that, too. It's awkward, for sure."

"Unless there's a perfectly logical explanation for it."

"For pushing someone into the ocean?"

Izzy chewed on her lower lip. "Yes, that's a little extreme, isn't it? Even if you don't like the guy. But we don't know, right? We don't know if he was trying to threaten her? It could have been self-defense."

"Maybe." But it was a weak *maybe.*

"The thing that impressed me last night was that Tess showed absolutely no concern for herself. It was all about Gabby — her worry, tearing herself apart because she was caught between her loyalty to Tess and what she thought was right."

Nell nodded. "Gabby could have stayed quiet and no one would have known any better. It must have been awful for her."

Izzy called out to Abby, who slowed and turned around, beaming, a bunch of slender sticks clutched in her mittened hand. Red sat proudly beside her as if he'd chosen them himself. "We can build a house," Abby said.

"It's a start," Nell said, grinning. "Maybe start with a hut?" She looked around at where they'd stopped. "Speaking of huts, Ben and I have come across a few in these woods. Not huts exactly, but abandoned, bare-bones cottages that over the years have begun to crumble. Their windows broken or removed, and animals have made some into happy homes. Ben thought he remembered a couple that were built as summer places when he was a kid."

"Tess told me she lived down on the edge of Beech Tree Woods, down near the water. A little cottage with a shed in the back. Sam and I happened upon it before Abby was born."

"Tess? I never thought about where she lived. But I know where you mean. Those were pieces of private property grandfathered in when the town took over the woods." Nell vaguely remembered it. "I think I saw it once when the regular path had flooded after a storm, and Ben and I took the narrow, winding one. It's tucked away in the trees, right?"

"That's the one." Izzy looked ahead where Abby was starting to run. She had spotted another walker on their path, coming toward them.

The hiker was a large, lumbering figure, her white hair sneaking out from beneath her hat. A thick walking stick was clutched in one hand, and in the other a leash attached to a fat basset hound waddling beside her.

"Look, Mommy," Abby called out. "Mugrat and Figo." She took off, running toward the deli owner, the wonderful lady who always picked out the biggest cookie for her on Kids Eat Free night. Red followed, only mildly interested in the dog who seemed to have legs no self-respecting dog would leave exposed.

Margaret Garazzo beamed at the child, awkwardly leaning down to give her a hug, then walking with her to where Izzy and Nell waited.

"It's a lovely morning for a walk, ladies," Margaret greeted them. Her round cheeks were bright red. Several drops of moisture rolled from her nose and she wiped them away with one glove, smiling.

"It sure is, Margaret. Have you been all the way down to the ocean?"

Margaret nodded happily. "That's my favorite trail. I know that area well. Where are you headed with my sweet pea here?"

She patted Abby on the top of her pigtailed hat.

Nell pointed to the path beside them that turned off to the right. "I was telling Izzy about some of the rustic cottages tucked in the woods. Ben and I have found a few out this way. There's one down this path, if I'm remembering correctly."

Margaret took off her sunglasses and looked in the direction Nell was pointing, squinting into the trees. Then her face changed, the quick smile fading into a worried frown. "No, don't go down that way. The sea is more beautiful."

"You've been down this path? Did you see the small cabins?"

Margaret looked down the path again, shaking her head. She looked back at Nell and Izzy, the worry still in her eyes. "I need to be going." Her tone was hushed, as if the trees might be listening. "Take yourselves down to that little beach, just a bit farther on this path. Let the child throw stones in the water. But that way" — she pointed again to the side path — "that way is no place to take a child."

She gave Abby another pat on the head and walked around the two women, nodding good-bye.

They watched her for a minute, hearing a mumbling as if Margaret were talking to herself.

"What do you think she meant?" Izzy asked.

"I'm not sure. If she were out here after a rain, it might have been too muddy for Abby. I think Ben and I made that mistake once. But today should be fine."

Abby had already decided where she was headed, and with Red at her side, she skipped down the path that was tucked in between an endless forest of beech trees. The trail was a makeshift one of trampled leaves, the earth pounded smooth by boots and heavy shoes. Branches hung over the trail and Izzy hurried ahead, holding them out of Abby and Nell's way.

They walked a short way before the path turned deeper into forested land, the trail only negligible now. Just as Nell was about to suggest they go back, Red moved on ahead, around a bend. He gave a single bark as they caught up with him. A small dwelling appeared in the distance. It stood in a clearing, looking less like a shack than a cabin, with an intact chimney, unbroken glass in the windows, and a step leading to a front door.

"It looks like we found it," Nell said. "Although it looks much nicer than I remember."

But Red wasn't looking at the cottage. He was moving off to the side of the clearing, tail wagging, with Abby at his side.

A small figure was sitting on a granite boulder, near a half circle of hemlock trees. She was doubled over, her head buried in her lap. The small body vibrated with sobs as it rocked back and forth, unaware of the hikers approaching.

Izzy and Nell spotted her at the same time as Red, but before Izzy could hold her daughter back, she followed Red, running across the small clearing, not stopping when they reached the woman's knees.

Abby cocked her head and smiled at the woman's buried face. "Hi," she said. "I'm Abby. Who are you?"

Penny Turner lifted her head and stared into the little girl's face, their noses nearly touching. Abby reached up and touched the woman's cheek with her small fingers. "Don't cry," she said.

Penny forced a smile, the river of tears

collecting at the corners of her mouth and down her chin. She looked over and saw Nell and Izzy approaching.

Izzy moved quickly to Abby's side, crouching down beside her. "Oh, Penny, I'm so sorry. We didn't know anyone was here."

Penny straightened up, but made no attempt to stop the steady flow of tears cascading down her cheeks, her chin, and onto a scarf wrapped haphazardly around her neck. She wiped her nose with the cuff of her jacket and looked at the two women. Without makeup, her jeans torn, and her parka swaddling her, she looked like an abandoned child herself.

Izzy wrapped an arm around her daughter. Then she scanned Penny's body to see if she had fallen or cut herself, though the cry seemed to be coming from a less visible source. "Can we help?" she asked. "Are you hurt?"

Penny wiped the tears from her cheeks with her hand. "No, I'm fine. I wasn't expecting company, I guess." She shook her head, a movement that seemed to bring a few tears, dislodging them, along with a sob that Penny didn't seem able to control.

Abby clutched her mother's hand tightly, staring at the woman.

Red pressed up against Izzy and Abby,

somehow knowing he was dealing with a human that might not appreciate his licks. Abby looped her arm around his neck.

"Please let us help," Nell said softly. She rested a hand on Penny's shoulder and fought against the urge to wrap her in a hug and tell her they'd fight off the beasts, wherever they were. Instead, she kneaded her shoulder lightly.

But Penny shrugged off Nell's hand and sucked in gulps of air, expelling them slowly, her shoulders moving up and down. She looked down at the twigs and rotted leaves at her feet, moving them with the toe of her boots. "I appreciate your concern, but I don't need help. I'll be okay. And if I'm not, well, that's my fault, then, isn't it?"

"In my experience, blame is overrated," Nell said. "Finding solutions usually works better for me."

Penny looked up then, her face puffy from the tears. Finally she said, "You wouldn't understand. I live an orderly life. I plan and control my days. I make decisions. I keep things working."

At first, Nell thought she was talking about managing the clinic. What she said made sense. Sort of.

Talking seemed to bring her to the brink of tears again, but there was a steely determination in her face to fight them off. "But even then, things don't always work out, even when they should. Sometimes it even breaks your heart, in a way you never expected. It isn't fair, you know."

Penny seemed to have shrunk as she talked, her gloves too big for her hands, blond frizz escaping from a red beanie that nearly swallowed her head.

Nell wondered how long she'd been sitting there in the cold. She must be frozen. And it wasn't just her body. She looked cold inside and out. Broken.

Finally, Penny stood and brushed off her jeans. She looked around the clearing, then over toward the cabin.

"Why don't you come with us, Penny," Izzy said, trying to find a light tone to her voice. "We're about to head back. My car's at the trailhead. We'll warm you up, and Abby will sing 'The Itsy-Bitsy Spider' if you're good."

Penny fidgeted with the zipper on her jacket, her face unreadable. It was hard. A mixture of so many emotions that she came out looking gray, as if the emotions were colored and blended into one.

"Dr. Turner will be worried about you," Nell said.

At the mention of Clark's name, Penny

gave a slight gasp, her chest moving beneath the pink jacket. "Clark," she said, looking off into the woods, as if maybe he was there and would appear. Rescue her.

"Clark Turner means everything to me," she said.

The words were spoken so softly, Nell and Izzy weren't sure they were hearing them correctly, or that they were coming from this usually self-possessed woman who had suddenly turned vulnerable.

Penny picked at a tangle of burrs on her sleeve, then wrapped her arms around her body. She forced a smile to her face and wiped some stray tears away with her hand. "I did everything in the world for him." She looked at both women. "Remember that. I made things that weren't possible, possible. To make Clark happy."

"That can be a good thing," Nell said, puzzled, but trying to lure Penny to the warm car. "Let's go, then. We can talk more in the car when we thaw you out."

Izzy clipped Red's leash to his collar as Nell took Abby's hand. They turned and began to walk toward the path.

Abby stopped first, then Red. "Aunt Nell," she cried, pulling her hand away and pointing toward a fleeing Penny.

Instead of joining them, Penny had turned

in the opposite direction and was running toward the woods behind the cabin.

"Hey, Penny, wait!" Izzy called out, starting to follow her.

But at the sound of her voice, Penny sped up and soon all they could see was a red beanie, moving in and out of the ghostly shadows of the beech trees. A minute later, the beanie, too, disappeared.

"Gone she went," Abby said, looking up at her mother, her eyes huge and questioning.

Izzy looked down and smiled. "Yes," she said. "I guess she didn't have time to play today. Maybe another time." She kissed the top of her little girl's head.

Nell looked over into the thick copse of trees that had swallowed Penny whole. There were few paths in that direction, a nod to the development just beyond Beech Tree Woods and the homeowners who lived there, most of whom weren't amenable to walkers and hikers trampling the woods that bordered the backyards of their huge houses.

The area between where they stood and that edge of Beech Tree Woods had been purposely left wild, a tangle of bushes and magnolia trees and thorny bushes. Difficult to get through. But Penny ran as if she knew where she was going. Or didn't care.

Izzy followed her aunt's look and read her thoughts. "I don't think she'd welcome us coming after her, even if we could catch up. I think Penny gave us all she could. She'll be okay — it's not far to the road and the clinic. Close to her home."

Nell nodded, knowing that most of what Izzy said was true. But she wasn't at all sure Penny would be okay. She had wanted to let them in, at least an inch. Nell thought she saw that in her face. She wanted someone to help lessen whatever pain was gripping her heart. But she couldn't. And so she had fled.

Suddenly Nell looked around.

Red and Abby had fled, too.

Izzy was already headed across the clearing. "They're in there," she called back over her shoulder, pointing to the cabin.

Abby's bright purple jacket was just visible through the smudged window of the cabin, and Red was standing at the door, guarding his princess.

"Abby," Izzy called, leaping over Red and into the room.

Abby turned around and grinned. She was holding a squat candle, partially burned, between her hands. "Look what I found!"

Nell was close behind Izzy. She stood just

inside the door, scratching Red's head and looking around the shadowy space. Abby had found more than a candle. She'd found a surprising one-room cottage, not much larger than a child's fancy playhouse, but not a shack at all. Red followed her over to a woodburning stove in the corner, filled with firewood, a bed of ashes beneath it. A couple of small rugs softened the wood floor, and across from the fireplace, close enough to feel its warmth, was a bed, with blankets and pillows piled at one end.

"It's a love nest," Izzy said in a hushed voice. She took the candle from Abby and set it on the window ledge.

"My playhouse," Abby said.

Nell smiled. "Take the stove out and it would be a perfect playhouse, Abby. We'll have to get Uncle Ben and your daddy to build you one."

Abby danced around the bed.

There wasn't much else to see — a windowsill filled with more candles, box of matches near the stove, and a lantern on an old dresser. A round table with two chairs stood beneath a window. A bottle of wine in the center.

"Is this the same place you and Ben saw on your hike?" Izzy asked. She went over and checked the door. It swung open easily, which, apparently, was how Red let himself and Abby inside. A heavy doorstop beside it would hold it securely closed from the inside, along with a thick metal latch.

"I'm pretty sure it is, but we never went inside. We haven't been this way since last summer. I don't remember ever seeing any signs of life."

"Did you look inside?"

"No. It looked run-down. A broken window, I think, and trash piled up on the side. In fact, we picked some up. I remember now because Ben used his backpack to carry it out and his pack needed a thorough scrubbing later. It was normal stuff — old pizza boxes, some cans and wrappings, an old sock, that kind of thing. The things you'd expect seeing if someone without a home had been staying here for a night or two, trying to stay warm or dry."

Izzy went over and touched the thick comforter, clean and soft, and the pile of pillows at the head of the bed.

Nell looked around, too, noticing a broom in the corner with a store sticker still attached. "Even if we had come inside, it didn't look like this, that I'm sure of."

"Someone has definitely been here recently." Izzy took a stick and poked inside the woodstove, releasing the scent of ash.

Abby had tired of the cold, dark room and skipped through the open door with Red at her heels. Izzy and Nell scurried to keep up with them.

Izzy bent down and tightened the Velcro strip on Abby's boot, glancing back at the dwelling several times.

Nell did the same, trying to figure how it'd been used. She hesitated for a minute, wondering if there was more to it — things they should have seen inside, that they had missed. It was a mystery, maybe one left untouched. After all, they weren't out looking for anything except sunshine, fresh air, and woodsy paths. And none of that had anything to do with an old cabin.

The fixed-up room was probably a clever project some kids had embarked on, creating a secret place, a private fort. A place to sneak a beer or a cigarette. Or maybe college kids, or older than that, someone wanting to get away for a night.

Nell noticed several pieces of tissue and a crumpled cigarette pack stuck up against a tree, evidence the recent storm had left its mark. But it didn't seem to have done any damage to the one-room dwelling. She shoved the trash in her pocket, then looked back at the cottage one more time. She told herself she was making mysteries where there weren't any. Perhaps that's what murder did to someone. She hurried to catch up with Izzy, Abby, and Red as they walked back to the main trail. The sounds of Abby singing to the birds caught her attention and she tried to push other thoughts from her mind, especially the image of a troubled woman sitting on a cold granite rock.

And an old cabin not far from where she sat.

Chapter 22

Birdie walked briskly down her driveway, just as the sun was beginning its climb into the sky. A sunny day. A good omen. The early-morning walk was a routine she tried to build into her days, getting in her "morning constitutional" before Gabby was up and showered. Then back in time to have breakfast with her granddaughter before the school bus lumbered up Ravenswood Road.

She headed up the nearly deserted road, through the neighborhood of decades-old family estates, their grandeur hidden behind low granite walls, and the sound of the ocean in the distance.

It was her time to be alone, she had explained once to Nell, and Nell understood what Birdie really meant: Despite Birdie frequently being alone, this was her time to be mindful. To be thankful. And everyone who knew Birdie well knew what she'd be grateful for, and they knew her friends were tucked right there in the middle of her list. Right alongside peace and health and books and good eyesight and music and birds — and people she'd never met who might need an extra bit of grace that day.

Birdie lifted her face to the sun, soaking in its strength. She wanted so desperately for Gabby's day to go well, for her and Tess to weather this new storm — and for her promises to her granddaughter to get moving in the right direction. Today. Now.

When they got home the night before, she'd prepared for bed and then gone into Gabby's room to say good night. Gabby was propped up against a pile of pillows, her knees up, looking out the window into the moonlight. Birdie sat on the high bed, then pulled her legs up and settled in next to Gabby. She took her smooth hand in her own, rubbing it gently. Gabby had seemed relieved she'd come in. Relieved to let out the words bottled up inside her.

Birdie turned off the bedside lamp. A path of moonlight had fallen across their legs as they began talking softly about Tess Bean.

Gabby's burden lessened as the words flowed. She told Birdie all about her secret cove, how she loved it, and how she had felt that day when she thought strangers had discovered her spot. She talked about the mix of emotion that had washed over her when she realized it was Tess, and then watched the couple arguing, first wanting to help Tess, and soon after being seriously proud of her as she bested the man who had been rude and disrespectful. At least that's what Gabby had thought that day. It wasn't until days later, when she saw the awful headlines on the breakfast table — along with the photo of the same man she'd seen Tess push into the cove — that the incident took on implications that weighed heavily on her mind.

Gabby talked more about Tess, about what she meant to the girls, about how caring she was about everything — from the girls, to what people were doing to our earth, to old people.

"Old people?" Birdie had asked.

"Like Margaret." Gabby shared how Tess's kindness to Margaret Garozzo affected all the girls. Margaret had told Tess she wanted to join them, *to be helpful.* She'd pleaded, and Tess welcomed her. So the girls did, too. Tess always covered for her, Gabby had said, even when Margaret sometimes forgot or messed up where they were meeting to clean up the beach — "She'd go find her" — or when Margaret forgot to wear warm hats and gloves — "Tess would just give hers to Margaret."

Gabby spoke softly, with a clear head — and with awe and admiration.

Birdie listened carefully, her eyes moist and her bent fingers caressing Gabby's hand as her own insight into Tess Bean grew through the words of her grandchild.

Finally she asked Gabby the question she'd been holding on to.

"Do you think Tess had anything to do with Bobby Abbott's death?"

"No," Gabby said.

Gabby had answered so quickly and earnestly and soulfully that, had Birdie been on a jury, her vote would have been determined in that instant. She told Gabby that was all she needed to hear. And as she kissed her granddaughter's forehead, she promised her it would all work out.

Gabby had squeezed Birdie's small hand, and then she sat up and wrapped Birdie in a hug so warm and tight and long that Birdie vowed to the heavens that it *would* be all right. And she whispered her promise again.

The promise came back to her now as she walked around a bend in the road. It was the place where the trees fell back and the land cleared, as if one were walking out of a forest and into a field. It was where the newer houses were being built, taller than the trees, one beside the other. It was at this bend that she usually turned around and headed back toward the comfort of the older section of Ravenswood Road.

She stopped to catch her breath and looked over at the new homes, expensive and expansive, with ocean access, all looking similar to one another. Each rooftop held a Santa, and decorated Rudolphs and sleighs stood in the yards, ready to take off. All freshly painted. She thought of her own decorations, some made by Sonny himself, reindeer that were put together like puzzles, paint worn off with love, just like the Velveteen Rabbit. Old and worn and loved.

This neighborhood was new — *A whole new world,* Birdie thought. She wondered briefly about the fact that she knew only a sprinkling of people who had built houses here. Clearly, these were people she didn't know well, since she had never been invited inside one. She smiled at the thought, hoping they were all happy and enjoying their ocean view as much as she enjoyed her own. She silently wished them a happy holiday, then turned to head back to her own comfortable home.

She started back, establishing a rhythm. She rounded another bend, then slowed, noticing another early riser walking toward her. An unfamiliar face, probably a new homeowner. Such resolve in her step, Birdie thought, watching the woman come closer. Her own walks were far less determined.

The woman was dressed in leggings and a yellow neon jacket, her hair pulled back severely and a heavy woolen hat pulled over her ears. She wore large sunglasses and walked with energy and purpose, her arms rotating back and forth and her face fixed in a grave expression. Her breath came out in white puffs.

It wasn't until the woman was a few feet away that Birdie realized who it was. And she realized quickly that the woman wouldn't notice her unless she called out to her or put out an arm to stop her.

So she did both.

"Good morning," Birdie called out. And without thought or planning, she told a surprised Helen Getty that she and Nell Endicott would like to take her to lunch that day.

Nell showered quickly, then pulled on a pair of wool slacks and a cowl-necked sweater. The image of Penny Turner sobbing on a cold granite boulder had stayed with her, and she had almost forgotten about Birdie's plans.

The shower had helped clear her head, and she re-read Birdie's text as she absently ran a brush through her silvery-streaked hair.

Glancing in the mirror, she noticed the damp ends from her shower and set the phone down, pulling her hair to the back and securing it with a clasp. *Good enough.* That was her motto these days as the list of holiday tasks lengthened and the time grew short. And as a thick, suffocating cloud hovered over the town.

She had seen the text from Birdie shortly before she'd headed out with Izzy and Abby. Brief and without much explanation: Lunch at the yacht club.

The reservations were made, the text read. She and Helen Getty would meet Nell there at noon.

Helen Getty. Nell was surprised and wondered how Birdie had arranged the lunch. The text read as if she and Birdie had planned it together. However it happened, it was fortuitous. They had all agreed the night before that if anyone could start them on the journey to understand who Bobby Abbott was, it would surely be his wife. Or so they hoped.

■ ■ ■ ■

Nell reached the club minutes before Birdie and Helen and was already seated when the two women walked across the room and joined her. Birdie had requested a window table toward the ocean side of the dining room, overlooking the veranda and the beach beyond. It was a beautiful view, but also a quiet spot that was far enough away from adjoining tables to talk comfortably. If others in the dining room recognized Helen, ears would surely be tuned in.

Helen looked much like she had that day in Coffee's, but the tension that had made the encounter so awkward seemed lessened today. Her face was more relaxed, and even her attire was more accommodating to Sea Harbor — a cashmere turtleneck, comfortable wool slacks, and low-heeled boots.

After the greetings they sat down and Helen took off the enormous sunglasses that nearly covered her whole face. She seemed pleased — or at least comfortable — to be with them.

"I'm not pretending to be a movie star," she said, glancing at the sunglasses. "Somehow my face keeps showing up in the local paper. I'm hoping it hasn't reached the post office wall, too."

Helen had a sense of humor. A good thing to have during difficult times, Nell thought.

The waitress set a basket of small rolls and pots of flavored butters on the table, along with a bottle of sparkling water.

"It must be awkward being recognized in a town where you know so few people," Nell said.

"I mostly pretend I don't see the flickers of recognition. And for the most part I don't. But I do feel them." She fiddled with a long string of turquoise beads. "My behavior may seem rude, but I don't mean it that way. It's just that it's difficult. I don't fit in here, although, I'm told to stay around for a bit. I know that's police talk, and I know what it really means. I've watched too many police dramas *not* to be aware that the prime suspect is always the spouse."

Birdie flagged the waitress and suggested drinks might be in order.

Helen finished the comment she'd left hanging. "But of course I didn't kill Bobby. I would have had no reason to do that. Nor would I ever have gone back on my word to his father."

Birdie and Nell glanced at one another; then Birdie asked quietly, half in jest, the other half in wonder: "You promised

Bobby's father you wouldn't kill his son?"

This time Helen chuckled. "That was poorly worded, wasn't it?" She looked over Birdie's head to the ocean, as if collecting her thoughts, then explained.

"Bobby's father, Robert Abbott, hired me when I was practically a newborn, at least in the business world sense. He recruited me right out of Harvard Business School, and we became a pair, the two of us. A powerful duo, he used to say, although he was already a business success and years older. But none of that mattered. We worked together nearly every day for the rest of his life. I was in love with him."

"With Bobby's father?" Nell was trying to process what Helen was intending. It seemed muddled, almost sordid at first.

"Yes. Robert was the first person who ever looked beyond my bland appearance — I was quite dull back then. Maturity and money can do wonders for one's appearance. Robert encouraged me, and he had a deep appreciation for my mind."

There was emotion in Helen's words. Even her expression changed, filled with something more than simple caring for this man who had apparently been her whole life.

"You loved him," Birdie said. Her words

holding a question.

"Yes, I did. And yes, it was *that* kind of love. I loved him terribly. Painfully. I don't know if he ever knew it or not. He certainly knew that I would have done anything for him, that I was devoted to him. I was young and brilliant and socially awkward when we met. I had never had a boyfriend in my life. Robert became my life."

Nell marveled at the raw honesty of the woman sitting across from her, spreading her life out in full view. To almost strangers.

And she wondered why.

Helen went on. "I knew that I was important and valuable to Robert — that in some way he considered me integral to his life and his family. That was enough for me. I probably had more assurance from him than many husbands and wives give one another."

Nell wondered what kind of assurances Helen was talking about, but before she could pursue it, Birdie focused in on the person they really needed to learn about.

"How did Bobby fit into this?" she asked.

"He was the crown prince. He was Robert's only son, his pride and joy. I've never seen a parent love a child the way Robert Abbott was devoted to Bobby. It was as if Bobby was his hope for immortality. Does that make sense?"

But Helen didn't wait for an answer. It was as if she was figuring this out for herself as the words formed.

"Robert had several companies in Europe, so we traveled together — Robert, young Bobby, and me. So I got to know Bobby well, even though I had zero interest in or knowledge of kids, which is what he was for those early years. But he was Robert's only family. And I also knew that if I wanted to be close to Robert, I had to get to know Bobby, too."

"So you were close?"

Helen paused. Finally she nodded. "I knew sides to Bobby, especially once he hit the teenage and college years that his father never saw. Bobby had a mean streak. But he never once used it on me, or in his father's presence. It came out when he was afraid someone would best him in something or be better than him. I'm not even sure he could help it."

Nell sat back as the waitress placed steaming bowls of clam chowder in front of them. She was listening carefully, trying to work through the puzzling story Helen was telling. It wasn't quite adding up.

Helen took a long drink of the Bloody Mary she'd ordered. "I'm sorry if this is beginning to sound sordid. It's not — not really. Different, maybe. But it was my life. And Bobby's."

"How did Bobby's mother fit in?" Nell asked.

The question seemed to surprise Helen, as if Bobby's mother didn't have a role in her story. She took a spoonful of soup, thinking about it. "I knew she existed, at least at first, but she was never a real person, only a name. Early on, Robert told me he had severed the relationship. At first, I wasn't sure if it was his own relationship with the woman he was severing, or Bobby's, but I later figured out he probably meant both. Bobby was about ten when I came into his life, and he rarely talked about his mother, though I think he may have seen her once or twice. He was so spoiled by his father that anything less than that wasn't especially welcome, at least that's how I interpreted it."

"It's unusual for fathers to get custody," Nell said.

"Maybe, but it wouldn't have been difficult for Robert. He was rich and powerful and charismatic. He never questioned what was his due. Bobby was his. It was almost as if he had given birth to him in all ways."

"Did you wonder about the mother?" Nell

asked. “I wonder if she tried to get him back. Were you kind of a surrogate mother to him?”

“Oh good grief no! Not anything like that. There was never a hint of that kind of relationship. Robert never envisioned that for me, nor would I have allowed it.”

“Even if his mother wasn’t a presence in his life, it appears Bobby didn’t lack for love,” Birdie said.

“No, he didn’t. Maybe it was too much, I don’t know. Can a parent love a child too much?”

Nell scooped up a chunk of creamy potato from the bottom of her bowl and savored the last bit of flavor. She thought about her niece Izzy, and the love Izzy and her brothers had been given. Buckets full. From parents and aunts and uncles and other relatives. But somehow the love that smothered Bobby Abbott didn’t sound the same. “Was Bobby close to his father?” she asked. “Excessive love might be difficult for a child.”

“Bobby adored his father. But yes, being given the whole world can create weaknesses and difficult behavior patterns. When Bobby graduated from college, Robert took him into his businesses. But more than once, Robert had to rescue him from financial messes. Bobby cheated people when he felt backed into a corner."

Helen's words dropped off and she concentrated on her soup, pushing pieces of clam meat around with her spoon. She seemed to be deep in thought. Nell wondered if she was regretting the way she had bared her soul to them.

But after awhile, she began speaking again, her words soft and coming more slowly than before. Her eyes were sad.

"A few years ago — or was it yesterday? — the bottom fell out of all three of our lives. In one hour, sitting in a physician's office beside Robert, my life began to unravel. Robert was diagnosed with an incurable cancer."

She paused for so long, Birdie broke the silence by waving over a waitress and ordering a plate of lemon cake slices. A diversion.

But before the waitress returned, Helen dipped into her story again, her eyes moist. "All Robert could think about was Bobby. Protecting him. Mapping his future while he still could. All his thoughts were with Bobby. Every single one of them."

Although her voice was steady, her words were filled with an emotion so raw Birdie and Nell both dropped their eyes, then wrapped their fingers around wineglasses, sipping slowly.

"I know that such a relationship is difficult to understand, I know that. But in spite of everything, when Robert became ill, I was his only dependable connection to life. By then, Bobby was in his twenties, a ladies' man. Careless. I tried to keep some of it from Robert. But he was obsessed with his son. Wanting to make sure his life was whole. I would have done anything to keep him alive, to console him, or to let him die with peace in his heart."

Helen smiled and looked down at the chowder, then took a sip of her cocktail.

"It almost seems sacrilegious to sprinkle this fine soup with my tale of woe."

"I think your life with Robert Abbott was satisfying, not woeful," Birdie said. "In between your words I sense joy."

Helen's face registered both surprise and gratitude. "It was Robert who suggested that Bobby and I marry. And the odd thing was, it didn't come as a surprise. Bobby needed someone, a protector of sorts. It would make it easier to solidify financial interests, he said, but mostly to keep Bobby safe in some unexplainable way."

"So your marriage was a business arrangement," Nell said. "Why did you agree to do it? You're attractive, smart. You have a whole life ahead of you. And —"

"And the age. Yes, there's that. I'm almost fifty. Bobby is 33. But our ages were irrelevant. And yes, I am smart and accomplished and polished. But marriage in the normal sense didn't interest me. I had been a part of the Abbotts' life for so long that for Robert, the agreement was keeping his family intact." A parade of emotions passed across Helen's face as she thought back on the most difficult days of her life.

"Robert saw goodness in me, God only knows why. And he wanted me to help Bobby find goodness in himself. That's one of the reasons I loved him, I guess. He had faith I could perform miracles.

"But at the heart of why both Bobby and I went along with Robert's idea was because we both loved him, and it was the one thing we could do to bring him some peace as he was dying. And for the time being it suited both of us."

"Did you own the bar with Bobby?" Nell thought about the issues with it, about Tess and Gracie.

"No. Robert had friends here in Sea Harbor. He lived close by, on and off, in Hamilton, and he had made some investments with people here. They owned property together. I agreed with Robert that the upscale bar might be a good idea for Bobby. But it didn't involve me — it was the last birthday present Robert gave his son."

"The Harbor Club seemed to be a success," Birdie said.

"And that would have made his father inordinately proud. Bobby was happy here so we bought one of those houses up near Beech Tree Woods for him. I hired a couple to take care of the house. I'd come up occasionally to check in. Bobby was fine with that. He didn't spend much time in the house, according to the help. But he wasn't as reckless as he'd been before."

"Not that we're a gossipy place, mind you," Birdie said, "but I don't remember seeing you around town before, not until now."

Helen smiled. "You're right. I usually come up when the crazy life I have in New York begins to consume me. I've never been a socializer. Instead I go for runs along the ocean, read, relax. It puts me back in a good place." She paused. And then she said, with a semblance of a smile, "If I had known of you two, I might have been less reclusive and invited you both over for a Bloody Mary."

Nell smiled. Helen was almost fifteen years younger than she, and many more years younger than Birdie, but she felt a similar sentiment. There was an old soul in Helen, or young souls in Birdie and herself. But either way, she was beginning to like this woman, even though she would never completely understand the life she'd lived.

Birdie had been quiet, but Nell knew she was listening to every word, committing the conversation to memory, and trying to find something in the unconventional pieces of Helen's family story that might help explain what they needed to know. What was pressing on all of them.

"Helen, you have been remarkably open with us and shared difficult moments. You've known Bobby for most of his life. A long journey for you. But there's a question out there, one that none of us have the answer to, an answer that our small town desperately needs.

"Who do you think would have wanted him dead?"

CHAPTER 23

Nell looked around the kitchen, her mind cluttered with the events of the day and the remains of the Friday night dinner. Her body weary.

Across the kitchen island, Ben used one finger to scoop up the last remnant of the casserole — tender chicken smothered in olives and capers and wine. The food — and Celtics overtime win — had been huge hits with everyone and contributed to a Friday evening ending happily, even in the midst of a murder weighing heavily on the town.

"I barely had a chance to fill Izzy and Cass in on our lunch with Helen — except to tell them it was a stark lesson in not always trusting first impressions," Nell said. She began putting away drink glasses. "She's a nice person."

"Good to hear. A neighbor stopped me in the wine shop and told me that she'd been pegged a Black Widow by one of the local online writers."

Nell cringed. The Helen she had had lunch with was completely undeserving of such a reference. But it was a vivid description, and she knew it would unfairly be repeated by many.

"I'm assuming she wasn't helpful in suggesting who might have killed her husband," Ben said, filling in the blanks of what Nell had told him earlier about the lunch.

"No, she didn't," Nell said. Her voice was weary.

"Sit for a minute, Nellie." Ben walked over and took a glass from her hand. "I'll get this. And whatever is left we can clean up in the morning."

"Thank you," she said softly, pulling out a stool.

Nell rested her arms on the island, grateful for the quiet moment. She watched Ben moving around the kitchen, putting back martini glasses, platters, salt and pepper shakers. Opening and closing cabinet doors.

Observing him was a luxury she didn't get often enough these days, and she loved it. It took her back to sitting in a café in Harvard Square, watching a tall classmate walk by every day on his way to a philosophy class. Until the day he stopped right in front of her, smiled, and sat. And for the rest of that semester they walked together to class and many other places, arms linked, their heads bent in discussions about everything from *Aristotle's Ethics* to politics, their minds awakened and excited by the other. And their youthful libidos, too.

Since then, they'd each added a few pounds, a few wrinkles, more than a few years. But what brought them together was still there, still holding them close. And as for the years, they both wore them well — at least that's what they told each other. They had settled happily into the retirement rhythm of their life.

"I haven't heard about Tess and Gabby," she said finally, knowing the counter Ben was now cleaning would still have crumbs on it in the morning. But he wanted her to sit, not fuss with it. And she loved him for it.

"It was interesting," he said.

Nell had seen Ben walk into the den with Birdie when she'd arrived that evening, and knew he was filling her in on the lunch he'd had with the girls and the chief. And she suspected from the few words Birdie had shared with her that Gabby was fine. She wasn't at all sure about Tess.

" 'Interesting' is better than 'disastrous'. Let's start with the easy part," she said.

"Where did you go for lunch?"

"A small mom-and-pop place, out near the highway. Jerry was comfortable bending the rules, if there are rules about these things. And I suspect from the treatment he got from the owner and the out-of-the-way booth that the friendly waitress led us to, that it wasn't the first time Jerry had done business over burgers and fries."

"Were the girls at ease?"

"If Gabby's appetite was any indication, she was fine. She wolfed down a burger as if Birdie and Ella hadn't fed her in weeks."

"That could have been nerves."

"Maybe. But the hardest part for her was already over. What had been awful for her was holding in something she saw happen, something that might reflect poorly on Tess. That was tearing at her. Finally going to Tess herself was very smart."

"Tess's decision to go to the police immediately was smart, too. Was Jerry impressed?"

"I hope so."

"You sound hesitant."

"I'm just not sure. Tess insisting she and Gabby tell the police the whole story was admirable. But there's something else going on with her. There was something missing from her answers."

"An explanation for why she pushed him into the cove?"

"No. She explained that easily. She verified everything Gabby saw. Denied nothing. She was upset that the schoolgirls had seen Abbott tossing trash into the ocean and had argued with Bobby about it. It really angered her, and she was letting him know it. He was making light of it, teasing her. Gabby had seen that, too. He called Tess a 'tree hugger' or some such thing."

"That seems believable."

Ben shrugged. "Maybe. Tess said that she rarely acts on anger. But that day she did. And she apologized, more to Gabby than Jerry and me. But it was sincere."

"So then what's bothering you?" Nell watched Ben's face. His prominent brows moved together, the tension visible. "What is the *but*?"

"Maybe there isn't any. I just had the feeling — intuition maybe — that Tess is holding something back. She did a good job of spelling out facts. But I had the feeling a layer was missing, one that wasn't addressed by any of the questions asked."

Nell sat quietly, listening and playing it out in her head. She trusted Ben's intuition.

"Did Jerry sense that, too?"

"I don't know. I know he appreciated her

cooperation. And I suspect he believed the things she did say. It's what she *didn't* say. I hope Tess isn't digging herself deeper into a very serious hole. One she may not be able to dig her way out of."

Nell felt a sadness seep inside her, mixing with an enormous weariness.

Ben did one final swipe of the island and began to turn out the lights, then walked over to Nell's side, slipping one arm around her shoulders and nodding toward the stairs. "We'll think better in the morning, Nell. You're about to fall asleep on that stool. And I'd much rather it be beside me."

They walked up the back stairs, tucking away the worries of those they cared about for a few hours.

Trying to put the world, the town, the worried neighborhoods of Sea Harbor at bay.

But sleep didn't come to everyone. Not to the reporters out scouting the night for something — anything — to give them inches of space online and in print. Some news to encourage a reading of the Saturday *Gazette.*

One lucky reporter followed the sirens and won the lottery that night. Hauling his photographer out of bed to get photos. Writing it up, and scoring the breaking-news headline for his paper: LOVE NEST IN BEECH TREE WOODS GOES UP IN FLAMES.

CHAPTER 24

Cass, Izzy, and Gracie ran abreast of one another, waving to gulls and stopping only briefly when Gracie needed to snap a photo. #Distractions while running she typed, hashtagging them on her restaurant's Instagram and website — photos of waving sea fronds, sunrises, and hovering fog across the water, as soft and quiet as a cat.

"You should try it," Gracie said. "Photography is helping me see things differently."

Izzy nodded. "Sam says that, too. But there needs to be some talent on the other side of the camera, Gracie. The pictures I take of Abby have her eyes shining red and strange streaks here and there, sometimes two sweet little noses."

Gracie laughed and picked up her speed.

At that hour — before most people had had their first cup of coffee — the women had the beach — the whole ocean, it felt like — to themselves. Even dog walkers waited until the sun had taken the early frost off the sands. And the three runners loved it that way, the world of Sea Harbor being all their own.

Cass huffed and managed to ask if they were almost there, wherever *there* was.

Gracie was taking them on a new jogging path, around the back of the shore, then down to Paley's Beach. The sand was hard as they ran along the curved beach and across a footbridge, then up a short hill, through a seaside neighborhood, and back to the beach.

"Are you getting too old for this, Cass?" Gracie yelled over the sound of the waves.

"Ha, you wish!" Cass yelled back, catching up with Izzy and Gracie as they rounded the next bend.

Izzy looked across the hard sand toward the water's edge and spotted a group of girls with large bags bending and rising and bending again. "What are they doing up at dawn?" she wondered out loud.

One of the girls broke loose and ran their way, waving her arms, a black braid flying in the wind, her long legs covered in heavy sweatpants.

"Gabby," Cass called out, and the threesome slowed as Gabby came close. "What the heck are you doing out here?"

"It's Saturday cleanup time," Gabby said with a grin. "Trash waits for no man. Gotta get it before it floats away to wherever."

"Geesh," Cass said. "When I was your age, this hour would have been the middle of my night. You're weird."

Gabby's laugh startled a lone gull searching for food.

"Is Margaret still helping you out? She's probably used to these crazy hours." Izzy looked back toward the group. She spotted Tess in the middle of the girls, her body bending and moving like the Energizer Bunny.

"She is. She was. Well, she's supposed to be. She's the earliest riser I know. I think it was all that bread she baked for the deli. She'll find us eventually. If not, Tess will find her. Margaret likes to clean up over near your place, Gracie. She says it's the messiest." She grinned as Gracie moaned. "We found her there a couple times last week, down near that tiny stretch of shore near your deck."

"That's good. It can be a mess," Gracie said.

Although, in fact, they all knew that wasn't entirely true. Not anymore. The man who tossed the most debris down to the sliver of beach beneath his deck — toxic food for the incoming tide — was dead. His bar closed. Debris from the Harbor Club nonexistent.

Gabby picked up a sandwich wrap, stuffed it in a sack, and started moving again, explaining that they had miles to go before pancakes at Annabelle's Sweet Petunia restaurant.

The three women waved her off and picked up speed themselves, heading toward a narrow stretch of beach with the ocean on one side, a steep hill and several elegant homes on the other.

"Almost there, Cass. Coffee awaits." Gracie led the way around the bend and they slowed as the beach narrowed to a sliver, allowing only a single runner at a time. When they rounded the curve, they stopped, resting for a moment.

"Nirvana," said Cass, bending low, stretching, and breathing in the cold air. She lifted her arms, palms up, to the scene around them: a few small boats bobbing on the water, and the long wharf above. "Home," Cass said, looking up at the deck of Gracie's Lazy Lobster & Soup Café.

Izzy looked up, then took a few steps along the wet shore, ragged with boulders half covered with tide water. Unconsciously, she backed closer to the bramble of sea grass along the incline, planting her running shoes in the narrow strip of shore. Above her, a newer fancier deck jutted out.

She pointed to the rocks beneath the large deck. "That's the spot, isn't it?" she asked, her voice soft.

"Yes," Gracie said. "It's creepy. That's where he landed. I'm glad no photographers showed up while the body was still there."

"But you saw it?" Cass asked, hoping the answer would be *no.* Every now and then, her protective instincts emerged. Like now.

Gracie nodded. "Briefly. From my deck. Tommy Porter was quick to move me away."

"I used to babysit him," Cass said. "That's why he has such good sense." She gave Gracie a brisk hug.

Izzy was looking back up at the newer deck. Imagining that night, trying to remember the sparkling lights and laughter and music that had filled the bar and poured out to the deck. She could almost see the bodies dancing.

And trying not to imagine the dead body of Bobby Abbott sprawled on the rocks just footsteps away from where she now stood.

Izzy frowned and took off her sunglasses, still staring at the Harbor Club. "Gracie, I think someone's in there."

Gracie and Cass shaded their eyes from

the morning sun and looked intently at the darkened club.

"I don't see anything," Gracie said.

Cass didn't, either. And when she looked again, neither did Izzy.

"Morning light," Cass said. She looked at Gracie. "Do you still think it's going to reopen?"

Gracie shrugged. "The rumor is still going around. But who knows? I did hear that Bobby's wife has no financial interest or claim to the bar. So that brings us back to the elusive silent partner that I keep hearing about."

"Maybe the guy doesn't want to show his face and become a suspect in Bobby's murder, which would happen, I guess," Cass said.

"I'm not sure that follows," Izzy said, still looking up at the bar. "If someone killed Bobby because he wanted the bar to himself, he would have to come forward eventually."

"Okay, okay. I hate that lawyer part of you, Iz," Cass said.

Izzy started to tell them what Aunt Nell had told her the night before about Bobby's father and a local man financing the bar.

But a rustle of sea grass and beating of a stick from a small, nearly hidden path distracted all of them.

Gracie pointed to a narrow, bramble-strewn path that wound its way up to the parking lot.

In the next minute a branch was pushed aside and Margaret Garozzo appeared. She grasped a long stick with a pointed end in her gloved hand, and a garbage bag in the other.

Margaret looked startled to realize she wasn't alone, but quickly broke into a smile when she recognized the three women staring up at her.

"That looks lethal, Margaret." Cass pointed to the stick.

"My weapon of choice," Margaret said, holding it up and looking at the pointed end. "Are you girls helping us today?"

Gracie laughed. "Margaret, none of us can compete with you. No, we are selfishly out to keep ourselves fit and then find food and drink."

Margaret's smile stayed in place, but she looked distracted for a minute, her gaze falling on the rocky pile beneath the bar's deck.

There had been blood on the rocks, but with assistance from the police and the tide, it was gone, along with Bobby Abbott's body. There was nothing there. But Margaret was staring at the spot as if a dead man was there. Her eyes grew large as she sucked in a breath. With the tip of her stick, she traced an invisible line on the rock.

Finally she looked away, shook her head, and spotted a plastic drink cup, which she stabbed with mighty force.

Izzy watched the puncture, grateful her feet weren't anywhere near Margaret's weapon. She wondered if Margaret might have been a spear fisherman in another life.

"We spotted the girls around the bend on Paley's Beach," Cass said. "Gabby said you'd be meeting them there."

"Mornings are a good time for me. I'm at my best," Margaret said, her head nodding and her smile back. "But this silly old head of mine sometimes mixes me up and puts me on the wrong path." She looked around. "Like here. Again." She looked up at the path she'd come down and frowned, as if wondering how she'd gotten there.

Gracie quickly stepped in to relieve Margaret's embarrassment. "You want to talk 'mixed up'? I can match you, Margaret. Your sweet Harry stopped me just in the nick of time from going into the men's room in your deli last week."

Margaret chuckled. Then she said, "Ridiculous. I told Harry we need to make them unisex." She rubbed the back of her neck, working out a kink, her face registering a moment of pain. "But that old man of mine. He's from the old school, you know." She tucked a strand of gray hair beneath her thick beanie and began walking back up the short path, the way she had come, humming a tune about a red-nosed reindeer.

They watched her maneuver her way up, using her stick to help her on the incline. "She looks happy," Izzy mused.

Gracie nodded. "Tess brought her in for soup this week. I think Margaret needs breaks from the deli now and then, and Tess is attentive to her needs. It's interesting to watch them together. She's a sensitive woman."

"Margaret?" Izzy asked.

"Yes. But I meant Tess."

Cass was looking after Margaret, too, her face thoughtful. "They're an odd couple, but maybe it's good Margaret is involved in Tess's group. My mother-in-law and Margaret have been friends forever, and I can tell that Danny's mom has concern about her friend. 'Working too hard, tensions in the deli' is all I can get out of her. Harriet Brandley has the tightest lips in town so she doesn't say much more. But anyway, everyone loves Margaret, so I'm happy Tess and her little band of preteens are giving her a cause. Something to give her new life."

Izzy smiled. "Well said, Cass. I agree."

"Me too," Gracie said. "But I'm freezing. I'd agree much better away from this spot. How about you two? Coffee or hot chocolate?" She looked over at Cass. "I'll even add a spot of Baileys if you behave."

Gracie lit a fire in the hearth and turned on the coffeepot while Cass and Izzy settled in the half-moon of chairs, chugging down bottled water. The Lazy Lobster was eerily quiet, waiting for the town to wake up. In an hour or two, the wharf would be alive with people coming out for a Saturday stroll, smiling up at the garlands hanging from lamps, the schooners festive in holiday colors. The holiday music pouring forth from the maritime museum's outdoor speakers, and occasionally Santa would stroll down the wharf, his sack filled with lollypops.

Even a murder couldn't totally crush the Sea Harbor holiday spirit, although it was trying hard.

Before Gracie had a chance to fill their mugs with coffee, the front door rattled as if a nor'easter was trying to get inside.

Gracie pulled it open and stared at Nell and Birdie standing on the stoop.

Before Gracie had a chance to say hello, Birdie gave her a peck on the cheek and the two women walked by her and over to the fire, pulling off their coats.

Nell put a folded newspaper down on the hearth in front of them.

Gracie scurried behind them, pulling over two more chairs. "How did you know we were here? The café doesn't open for hours. I don't even have a donut to offer you."

"It was Sam," Nell said. "When he said Izzy and Cass were running with you, we figured you'd be warming up right here, where it's toasty and quiet and far away from the rest of the world."

"And we saw smoke coming from the chimney," Birdie added.

"And where there's smoke . . ." Cass laughed.

But Nell wasn't laughing. She leaned over and unfolded the newspaper, spreading it out on the stone hearth.

Izzy shifted in her chair and stared at the page. She read the headline out loud: " 'Love Nest in Beech Tree Woods Goes Up in Flames.' " She looked up at Nell. "What is this, Aunt Nell? What are they talking about?"

But almost before she had said the words, she knew exactly what the reporter was talking about. She knew the cabin — and so did Nell, Abby, and Red. They'd seen it just days before.

Birdie had brought along a still-warm blueberry coffee cake with a vanilla custard topping. *Brain food,* she insisted. "And we need it. I feel we've been gathering nuts as eagerly as squirrels. And just like they do, we've been dropping them along the way."

They chuckled, knowing Birdie wasn't fond of the squirrels that ran wild on her estate.

But the laughter was brief as Izzy and Nell relayed their encounter with a desolate Penny Turner sitting on a rock in a small clearing in Beach Tree Woods. And a stone's throw from a cottage that just a couple days ago could have passed for a fairly decent Airbnb.

Cass wrinkled her forehead. "So, what's the significance of you finding Penny near a cabin that burned down? I don't get it?"

"That's the question, isn't it?" Izzy got up and refilled coffee mugs, pondering the question both she and Nell had grappled with on the way home.

"From what you've told us, there has to be a connection," Birdie said. "The poor girl was suffering, and maybe it was from something that happened in that cottage."

It seemed a leap, but no one argued with Birdie.

"All right, then, what happened?" Gracie asked.

And *with whom* went unsaid.

"It wouldn't have made sense for her to have met Clark out there. They have a lovely home, walking distance away," Birdie said. "And somehow Clark doesn't seem the rustic type."

"But unless Penny Turner is a superb actress, she completely convinced Izzy and me that she loves Clark Turner."

"I don't think it's an act. I think she loved Clark," Izzy said. "But she and Bobby Abbott certainly knew each other, too. There seemed to be an attraction there, or a connection. Cass, you and I saw it that night, right? And Lucky had indicated as much." Although, Lucky's description was slightly ambiguous, she knew. And Penny seemed to be in control of her own life, not easily used by womanizers or anyone else.

Their thoughts collided in the heated air, wondering if they were pulling at straws, connecting things that didn't go together, but they wanted them to, so they were forcing one on the other. They needed connections to somehow get them a step closer to making sense of a murder.

"Bobby and Helen own one of those big houses just adjacent to the woods," Nell said. "It seems unlikely Bobby would need to rendezvous with anyone in a deserted cabin."

"But Helen had hired live-in help," Birdie reminded her. "And she said Bobby was rarely home."

"Not to disparage Penny," Gracie said, "but Bobby had a whole harem of women who were very interested in his attention. They were like groupies. I didn't understand it."

Izzy looked back at the paper. "I wonder how the fire actually started. It may have absolutely nothing to do with our seeing Penny out there. Or that the cabin looked like it was some kind of love nest. For someone."

"It was arson," Birdie said. "I don't quite know how firemen can figure that out so quickly, but they can. Ben, with his multiple connections, confirmed it. And since Bobby Abbott was already dead, he wasn't the one trying to get rid of a love nest."

But it could have been some woman, sad and desolate, thinking her life was over.

Izzy glanced at Nell, who was thinking the same thing.

But Penny had fled from the area. And

something in that image of her disappearing in the woods made both women think she had no intention of coming back. Even to set a fire.

"So you said Bobby and his wife lived near this place?" Cass pointed at the photo.

Nell nodded, and she and Birdie quickly filled the others in on the unique marriage that Helen had described. Unique, but in Helen's telling, it seemed almost normal.

"Unfortunately, we learned little about Bobby's life here, at least about things he'd done that would make someone want to kill him," Birdie said. "Helen said in his father's eyes, he was a prince, albeit one who needed help to becoming a full-fledged king."

"So he was spoiled. That fits what I knew of Bobby," Gracie said. She looked through the windows that looked across to the Harbor Club. "He was charismatic. But I was never sure if there was much beneath that. It was like a coating, a thin shell. I'm not sure he was even capable of being more than that."

"The fact that his mother seemed to be absent from his life may have been a factor. Why was she absent? Maybe there's something there that might help us understand him better. And what he might have done to provoke someone to kill him," Nell said.

"You say Bobby grew up over in Hamilton?" Birdie said. "I will happily do some scouting around. I have relatives there."

"Birdie, you have relatives and friends everywhere," Gracie said, leaning over and hugging her tight. "And I am forever grateful to be one of them."

There was something in the tone of Gracie's voice that reminded them all that she knew she was one of the reasons they would drive to Hamilton or Alaska or Timbuktu if it would help remove the cloud of suspicion hanging over her head. Although she hadn't been accused of anything, she had motivation for killing Bobby Abbott. She didn't have an alibi for that Saturday night, other than being asleep in her own bed. Alone.

But she also had a group of wise, loving women who held her close and would never let her down.

"I know we are jumping around worse than Abby on a sugar high, but maybe that's how we'll piece this all together," Izzy said. "Just throw everything out there and then piece it together. Like gathering those nuts Birdie talked about. But here's something that's been bothering me." She laughed. "Well, like for at least thirty minutes, anyway. It's something that happened this morning."

"Margaret," Cass said, almost immediately. "Me too."

"Margaret Garozzo?" Nell asked.

Izzy quickly explained about meeting her down at the shore, just beneath the wharf.

Birdie was frowning, thinking about the lovely woman she'd known for nearly her whole life, and whose husband had been her dear friend for nearly as long. "Harry worries a bit, I think. He sees a change in Margaret recently. The deli was always her passion, and now she has other interests. These new chapters as one grows older can bring surprises. I've had a few myself." Her frown softened into a smile.

"She seems happy helping out this way," Izzy said. "But here's the thing that confuses me." She looked at Birdie and Nell. "You two read the paper more dutifully than the rest of us. Tell me this. Was there ever a photograph in the paper or on the news of Bobby Abbott's body down on the shore?"

Birdie and Nell thought for just a short minute before answering no.

"I'm confident of that," Nell said, "because Ben and I talked about how determined Jerry was that there *not* be one. It wouldn't have been good for the investigation, but especially not good for people to see. Those images are difficult to expunge from the mind."

She looked over at Gracie, knowing the police had been quick to remove her from the scene that morning.

Gracie nodded, her expression telling. Even the brief image had been too much, and probably drifted in and out of her mind at unexpected times.

"Then how did Margaret know exactly where Bobby landed? How was she able to practically trace his head on that rock with the tip of her walking stick?"

The silence was heavy. For a minute the only sound in the room was the pop and crackle of the fire that Gracie had lit.

He was a bad man, Nell. There they were again, the words that refused to be silent inside Nell's head. That shivering night, when Margaret Garozzo had whispered them to her, hours before most people in town knew that a man had been found dead on the cold shore beneath the Harbor Club deck.

They might have spent the entire day huddled in front of Gracie's fireplace, struggling to pull together everything they knew as they tried to make sense of a murdered man. The web spinning out from Bobby Abbott was growing, catching good people in its sticky orb. But a burst of cold air bringing in two of Gracie's lunch staff made them all check the lobster-shaped clock on Gracie's wall.

"Oh geesh," Gracie said, jumping up from her chair. She looked down at her running tights and jacket.

"Need me to bring you some clothes?" Cass asked.

But Gracie was already heading for her office and called out as she opened the door, "I'm always prepared! One never knows when a pot of lemon butter is going to land on one's shirt."

Nell and Birdie quickly picked up napkins and got rid of coffee cake crumbs while Izzy and Cass took care of the coffee mugs.

In minutes the four of them were headed for the door.

They stood on the wharf for a moment, noticing the town had fully awakened as they sat in Gracie's warm café. Families strolled down the wharf to look at the decorations and play on the lobster traps, and the maritime museum had opened its door, carols spilling out from the outside speakers. A jolly Santa who looked vaguely like Harry Garozzo's older brother ho-ho-hoed them as he passed by.

It was almost normal.

And then Cass pointed over to the Harbor Club. "Iz, I think you were right earlier. Someone is in there. The police, maybe?"

They all turned and stared at the bar's tall, narrow windows. The shades were down, but a single light from within created an eerie ghostlike shadow. A moving shadow.

"Sure. Probably, police," Izzy said.

As they watched, the light went out, somewhere inside a door opened and slammed shut, and finally the heavy front door opened.

Cass stared at the man coming out.

He looked her way. Then grinned.

"Good grief," Cass said. "What are you doing in there?"

CHAPTER 25

Lucky Bianchi strode over to where the women were standing, a crooked grin on his face. "Hey, Cassiopeia, what's up?"

He wrapped Birdie in a bear hug — reminding everyone, as he always did, that Birdie was his godmother — and then greeted Nell and Izzy.

"What's going on?" Cass asked. "Did you miss your old haunt so badly that you broke in for a beer?"

"Nah, I might have been tempted, though." Lucky held a big silver ring of keys in his hand. He glanced back at the bar.

They all stared at the keys. Lucky was funny and entertaining and even known to perform a prank or two. But always the gentle kind. Surely, he wouldn't have fooled with a crime scene — even if the yellow tape had been taken down.

Lucky saw the look on their faces and shook his head. "You're wondering if I need a lawyer — I can see it in your eyes, Iz. You ex-lawyers, always looking for a job."

Izzy laughed, but Birdie had read her godson differently. She looked up at him. "Luigi Anthony Bianchi, you're the silent partner everyone's been wondering about, aren't you? It makes sense. I just didn't put it together. It's your father's doing. Anthony Bianchi is still meddling in our life in that loving way of his."

"No, he's not," Cass said. She looked at Lucky. "Don't lie to your godmother."

"I don't think he's fooling this time, Cass," Nell said.

Lucky was still focused on Birdie. "I thought maybe you knew about it. My old man loved you, Birdie. I figured he told you and those old cronies of his all his secrets before he died. Like how he was mad at the mayor about something or other and refused to clean up his properties. This was one of them. Italians, I dunno. What can you do with them?" He grinned.

"*You're* Italian, Lucky," Cass reminded him.

"So Anthony owned this, did he?" Birdie asked. They all knew Lucky's dad, although Birdie knew Anthony Bianchi the longest. Anthony, Harry Garozzo, Mario Palazola, and Gus McGlucken were the "old four horsemen," or so they called themselves, and they always included Birdie in the group. "Our spiritual adviser," old Anthony called her.

His recent death had been grieved by the men — and Birdie, too — but if people truly lived on in loved one's hearts and in memories and stories and frequent toasts, Anthony Bianchi was very much present.

"My dad had some business dealings with Abbott's dad. Did you know him, Birdie? Lived over in Hamilton. Somehow this bar was the outcome, something Mr. Abbott thought would be good for his son."

"And you?" Izzy asked.

"You guys know me. I kind of fall into things. Like an accident. Since they invested together, Pop wrote me in as a silent partner when he knew he was dying. He didn't much trust Abbott."

"Why silent?" Cass asked. "What's that about?"

Lucky looked at Cass and chuckled. "Come on, Cass, you know me. If I had taken an active partner role, I might have had to *work. Work,* Cass. Think about it. Silent partners have different responsibilities, giving the money — which Pops took care of — and sitting at the bar, drinking good beer and having great conversations with people I like."

"So you were Bobby Abbott's partner . . ." Izzy was thinking out loud as she pieced it together.

"*Silent* partner, Iz. That's important. I didn't like the guy, like I told you before, so it worked fine — we didn't have to have a lot of dealings together. I didn't trust him much. Another reason, I guess, that I hung out at the place. I could keep an eye on him — though he seemed to have put together a decent place. And I didn't care about his personal life, which would have been impossible to control. I got to watch the drama, the ladies make plays for him, make sure it was all handled okay."

"Like Penny Turner?" Cass asked.

"Penny, well, Penny handles herself. Tough lady. Sure, she and Bobby . . . Well, who knows what others are up to, right? Sometimes she's perfectly content to just talk to people and sip her pretend martinis. And other times, well —"

Cass broke in. "*Pretend?* I saw her handle a few the other night."

"Ginger ale," Lucky said. "Clark — her guy — didn't drink much, and I think she had changed habits recently, maybe wanting to be a good wife. Turning over a new leaf, she told me. But she likes the looks of the martini glass."

"So, are you feeling good about this? Are you keeping it?" Cass said. "Sounds like you'd have to give up your bar stool. Like you'd actually have a job."

"I know. Can you believe it? I didn't jump into it right away. But then I thought, well, someone has to do it. I guess I'll give it a try and see what it's like to work for a while."

"That's a good plan, Lucky," Birdie said. "Anthony would be proud."

"And if I mess up, isn't it kind of your responsibility, right, Birdie? Being my godmother and all?"

Birdie chuckled and patted his arm. "You won't mess up."

"We'll see," Lucky said, but he smiled as he said it.

They talked a few minutes more, Lucky confessing that he hadn't mentioned it sooner because he was trying to figure out what he was going to do. "I knew there'd be repercussions, no matter what I decided, with Bobby being killed and all. I now have a motive for wanting him gone. I know it looks like that.

"Besides while all I was doing was sitting in bars and pretending to help out the Hallorans, I had plenty of time to read every one of Danny Brandley's mysteries. I know how these things roll out." He looked back at his keys and turned serious again. "I talked to Chief Thompson yesterday and told him the deal. And told him no matter how it looked, I didn't knock the guy off. I mean, no one deserves that. Birdie, you know that's not the Bianchi way. And I wasn't planning on taking the bar away from him before it happened. I kind of enjoyed my role of hanging out — free food and beer, good music, great people to talk to. It was a good life."

"But you've changed your mind. You're going to reopen? Be the boss?" Cass asked.

"Eventually. There are some surprises I gotta work out first." He checked his watch. "For right now, I'm headed to the pier to help your brother paint some buoys. My talents know no bounds."

They started walking toward the parking lot, Nell in the lead, when she stopped abruptly and looked over at Lucky, now headed in the opposite direction. "Lucky, have you met Helen Getty?"

Lucky slowed down. He nodded and turned toward her. "I went over a couple days ago to pay my respects. I knew she wasn't involved in the bar, but I told her my role. She said she didn't much care if there was a silent partner or twenty who talked. I laughed at that — the lady looks as stiff as a stick, but she has a sense of humor. I liked her."

He began to walk away, then stopped and turned back again, looking over at the women now ready to pile into Nell's SUV and turn on the heater. He began walking back. His grin was faint, his face serious. "Hey, friends," he said, "there's something else I didn't mention."

They turned, surprised by the serious tone in Lucky Bianchi's voice.

"There's one more thing going on here," he said. "Something you'll find out about sooner or later."

That stopped them all exactly where they were.

"I found something in a mess of things that I had to go through. It was a surprise. A total surprise, believe me. Something Bobby did before he left these surly bonds. There's another partner or part owner or whatever. Surprised the heck out of me. Abbott willed his half away, an option in the agreement our dads had made."

"His half of what?" Nell asked. The house would surely be Helen's. At least she hoped so. It seemed right, somehow.

"His half of the bar. A partner. Silent or

talky, I don't know yet."

He hesitated again, just for a moment, and smiled into Birdie's wise face as if for some kind of affirmation.

Then he told all of them who it was.

No one spoke. They simply stared, suddenly oblivious to the cold.

When Lucky walked away this time, he seemed to be lighter, as if a burden had been lifted off his shoulders, just by sharing a small piece of news. He climbed into his truck and drove off, waving to them as he turned into traffic, and looking like the biggest thing on his mind was painting buoys with Pete Halloran.

The women watched until he was completely out of sight, wondering if Lucky Bianchi was playing a gigantic joke on them.

Or not.

CHAPTER 26

"How about a spin to Hamilton on a bright sunny day?" Birdie asked Nell.

Izzy and Cass were eager to get home and out of their running clothes, thaw out in a shower, and head into their day: Izzy to an annual checkup and Cass to check on the buoy-painting project. But mostly to check on Lucky. Maybe what he'd said was a big joke. It had made no logical sense to any of them.

"Hamilton? Interesting," Nell said. "I was thinking the same thing. We need to know more of Bobby's story, try to walk in his shoes for a mile to make sense out of any of this." *And maybe farther than a mile,* Nell thought. *The victim always has a story.* And they were only beginning to piece little bits of it together.

They turned off the highway and onto the winding route that would take them along narrow roads, past rolling horse farms and stately homes with magnificent views. The drive was slower here, with no one in a hurry to get to malls and Saturday shopping. Peaceful. Even in the cold beginnings of winter, it was a lovely drive.

"Sonny's second — or maybe third — cousin Eunice used to live in one of those houses," Birdie said, pointing to wide, sprawling homes, surrounded by freshly painted white fences on rolling hills. "Her family owned horse farms, but Eunice now spends most of her time holding court in a little downtown bookstore that offers free coffee and hot chocolate. Eunice is the self-appointed town historian. She bought herself the bookstore as a birthday present. I think she bakes brownies and brings sandwiches in. Everyone knows her, and Eunice knows everything. At least that's what she says."

It didn't surprise Nell that Birdie would have connections in Hamilton. And she couldn't imagine not liking — or at least being fascinated by — a member of the far-flung Favazza clan that Birdie had married into. There were few towns on the North Shore and all the way up to Maine that weren't connected to the family in one way or the other. Every Favazza that Nell had met had fascinated her the way old Hollywood movies used to do. Intrigue. Romance. Not to mention the great wealth the family had accumulated.

A short while later, they pulled up in front of an old-fashioned two-story bookstore right in the center of town. Nell found an empty spot and in minutes they were wrapped in the arms of one of the largest women Nell had ever seen. And every inch of her welcomed them. Her curly blue-black hair smelled of a recent perm and dye.

Birdie finally extracted herself from Eunice's embrace and managed the introductions, although it didn't seem to matter to Eunice. Nell was with Birdie. That equaled family, or, at the least, lifetime acceptance.

Nell walked around the store, leaving Birdie and Eunice to catch up on "family scandals," as Eunice called it. The store was long and narrow like a town house, with bookcases that rose up to a ceiling Nell could barely see. Narrow staircases hugged each side of the room, leading to a balcony that circled along more bookshelves. More books. Old and new. Musty and some stiff with unbroken spines.

Heaven, Nell thought with a smile, vowing to bring Ben back for an hour or three or four. She moved down the skinny rows, past several customers, and stopped beside a section set apart with a sign that read TOWN HISTORY. In between the books were old photographs, awards, framed art, and down toward the end, a long wooden plaque of contributors to the town. Nell traced her finger down the dozens of names, then stopped when it came to Robert Abbott. *Good,* she thought. Surely, Eunice would know something about a resident who had made it to the bookstore hall of fame.

When she wandered back to the front, Eunice had magically produced three mugs of hot chocolate, a swirl of whipped cream on top, and a plate of small turkey and Brie sandwiches beside it.

"I don't think I will ever leave here. Thank you, Eunice." Nell sank into the soft cushioned chair that had been pulled over for her.

"Bernadette tells me you are interested in one of our families. The Abbotts. A man as generous as King Tut." She chuckled. "Was King Tut generous? Well, no matter. He was rich." She waved a plump hand in the air, her jeweled rings flashing in the sunlight. "Robert Abbott was a towering figure here before he became ill." She leaned in, her free-flowing flowered caftan allowing her to fold forward and reach Birdie's knee with her hand, patting it gently.

"I noticed that Mr. Abbott made your hall of fame," Nell said, nodding toward the wall display.

"Yes, he did. As I was telling Birdie, Robert was a charming and wealthy man — and generous to the town. We claim him as our own, even though, as you may know, his businesses were based other places and he was gone probably more than he was here. A very successful man, although some people believed half of the credit went to the young woman who seemed to take care of his life in a most efficient way. That's quite a long dissertation for your simple statement about Robert Abbott being on a plaque, isn't it?" She chortled, hundreds of tiny lines fanning out from her still-clear eyes.

"From what we know of Bobby, he had a kind of charm, too," Birdie said.

Eunice helped herself to a sandwich and swallowed it in two bites. "My niece Greta was about the same age as Robert. Her son went to Phillips Academy with the young Abbott boy. Now, Bobby wasn't the brightest crayon in the box, but he was a legacy and his father made a new library possible. So there you are. You know how those things go. There were few things in life not made available to Bobby Abbott. Traveled the world."

"Was Bobby's mother from here?"

"No. Lenore, that was her name, was from someplace else. Ipswich, I think. That's where the boy was born. She was a beauty, they say. Though by the time Robert left her and came back to the Abbott estate with Bobby, people say she was looking like someone had discarded her. Cast her off like used furniture.

"It was very sad. Apparently, she got little to nothing from the divorce, and almost nothing of her son. Robert took Bobby away from her, lock, stock, and barrel."

"What a very sad story. A boy needs a mother," Nell said.

"But maybe not that mother, although she might have been different before he left her. She moved here briefly to try to get Robert back. I'm not sure the son mattered as much to her as getting the husband back. She lived on the edge of town and she worked at the donut place. She was determined and rather frantic, causing scenes when they met. It was very sad. I only saw her once or twice, but others said she was nervous, determined, sad, and angry — all those things mixed up together. Jittery. 'Mexican jumping bean,' the other workers at the donut place called her."

"What happened to her?" Birdie asked.

"She finally couldn't afford to live here anymore and they moved away. That may have been a blessing for the boy and Robert. And maybe for the poor woman, too."

"Do you know where she is now?" Nell asked.

"I heard she died," Eunice said. She picked up the plate of sandwiches and passed it around. "Sad. It was all very sad."

It wasn't until Birdie and Nell were in the car headed to Sea Harbor that something else Eunice had said registered with both of them, nearly at the same time.

"They," Birdie said it first.

"Yes. Eunice referred to Lenore in the plural a couple times. Curious. I wonder if she remarried. Or if she meant something else."

Birdie pulled out her cell phone and punched in Eunice's number. Her cousin answered on the first ring.

"Yes, Birdie, she did marry again, according to a customer who was eavesdropping on our conversation. Julia Simpson. A lovely lady."

"Lenore married Julia Simpson?"

"No, no, no. Julia is here in the shop today

and she was listening in on our conversation. We talked after you left. Julia knew Robert Abbott well — they shared cooks or maids or some such thing, and she said Robert's ex-wife — that would be Lenore — finally married a man named Graves from Ipswich. And, yes, it seems she died relatively young, Julia said. She had a difficult life. In marriage, in parenting, in divorce. Her mind and body grew weak, Julia said. And then she died."

CHAPTER 27

Izzy stood at the counter in the Women's Clinic, apologizing to the receptionist for being late. "It's my dog, Red," she explained to the young girl whose nametag read *Sherry.* "He's having trouble today. Arthritis."

"So maybe you should have brought *him* in," Sherry said with an awkward giggle. She looked around at a pile of folders on her desk, and then glanced at her computer. Then looked up at Izzy, frowning. "So, are you pregnant?"

Izzy shook her head. "No, sorry. I'm just here for my annual checkup."

"Oh. Well, it helps me find the right stack if I know," she said, looking worried. Then her face brightened. "Okay, okay. I see your name right here." She pointed to a file on her desk.

Izzy looked at it. She shook her head. "I'm sorry, Sherry. That's not me."

The girl frowned. "Are you sure? Oh shoot. Sorry. I'm new, just learning. And not doing a very good job at it, am I?"

She looked frazzled and Izzy felt sorry for her. She put her elbows on the table and leaned in, friend to friend. "You're doing fine, Sherry. It has to be difficult to keep track of all this." She looked around the desk, then at a file holder hanging on the wall. She pointed to it. "There I am, Sherry. No problem. I'm not lost, after all. My husband will be happy. My little girl, too."

Sherry threw Izzy a grateful smile and pulled the file from the rack, then jumped as a nurse came up behind her and tapped her on the shoulder.

Sherry spun around in the swivel chair and looked up. "Yes'm?" she said.

The nurse was holding a patient's folder in her hand. She showed it to Sherry, her voice soft. "The doctor suggested a follow-up with this patient. We were wondering if you'd called yet?"

"*Follow-up?* But . . ." Sherry took the file and looked at it as if she wanted to cry. "Oh geez — sure, I remember now."

"It's all right," the nurse said quietly, her tone suggesting Sherry lower her voice. "Please give her a call when you get a minute. Ask her if she would like to talk with the doctor again." She smiled and walked back into the inner sanctum of the clinic.

Izzy half listened, thinking of Lily Virgilio and how often the kind and generous doctor had made time for her when she was worried about anything, especially when she was pregnant with Abby. Calming worries and fears, assuring her the baby was healthy, she was healthy, Sam was healthy. She smiled to herself, the memories still fresh and one hand instinctively moving to a nonexistent baby bump.

Sherry spun back around and dropped the file on her desk. She looked up at Izzy with cocker spaniel eyes. "It's been that kind of day."

"I get it, Sherry. Some days are like that. I have them, too."

"And your dog, too," Sherry said, a weary smile on her face.

Izzy laughed. "Yep, Red too."

"But not as bad as this lady. She was way upset. But life, hey? Sometimes things don't work out exactly the way you want. My mom used to say it was nature's way, just like with planting seeds. Some grow. Some don't. But this lady was blaming everyone. But you know what the saddest thing was? The very saddest thing was that she was mostly blaming herself. And no matter what the doc says, this woman isn't coming back to talk to anyone. I'd bet my job on that."

Without meaning to, Izzy followed the receptionist's eyes down to the file to commiserate with her. And hoping she wasn't really betting her job on anything — that might be a foolish wager.

Then her thoughts went *poof* as she focused on the file.

The name seemed larger than life, the words jumping right off the file and hanging in the air in front of her eyes.

She read the computer-generated label glued to the private folder once. And then again: *Mrs. Penny Turner.*

Ben and Nell walked into the Sea Harbor Yacht Club with Abby Perry skipping between them. "Santa is here!" Abby shrieked. "I hear his jingles. We better be good."

Nell assured her that was the plan and she headed for the coatroom, her arms piled high with their coats as Ben hoisted Abby up on his shoulders so she could see over the heads of the milling crowd. All the way to the far wall of the dining room, where a towering spruce tree was lit with hundreds of tiny lights.

As a yacht club board member, Ben was

expected to attend the annual grandparents' event, which benefited the Holiday Toy and Clothing Center, but having Abby for the evening and an overnight made it a treat he'd never miss. And it was his favorite kind of event these days. Kid food, plus drinks and appetizers for the gray-haired crowd, and they'd be home before the football game started.

Birdie had decided to come, too, and met them in the foyer with a wonderful surprise: Gabby, all dressed up in a soft red sweater and jeans, her black hair in a thick braid falling down her back, and big furry boots that went nearly up to her knees, delighting her almost-namesake, as Izzy often called her daughter, Abby.

"Me too!" Abby grinned, sticking out one of her own fur-trimmed UGG boots as Ben lowered her to the ground. She immediately attached herself to Gabby and began pulling her through the crowd to the tree, where baskets of ornaments were ready to be hung, and a jovial Mr. and Mrs. Santa Claus were ready to greet them, peppermint sticks in hand.

"Abby's loving every bit of this," Nell said. "She thinks Gabby is hers, you know."

"It's a mutual thing. Gabby decided she needed a touch of Christmas, and Abby would be exactly that." They watched Gabby holding Abby's hand tightly in her own, walking into the festivities. "She offered to come to help keep track of our sweet munchkin. A break from the real world, she said."

A world closing in on them, Nell thought. Hopefully, an evening of holiday cheer would release Gabby from concerns that didn't belong in her world right now. "How is she doing?"

"She's relieved to have the painful 'secret' off her chest, but also worried and confused," Birdie said. "At least that's how I read her. I think through all of this, Tess has taken on an even more important presence in the girls' lives. Maybe mine, too. She's handling this with grace. But Gabby mentioned one thing that has preyed on my mind." Birdie hesitated, then moved over to the side to let a group of children wind around in the quest for Santa.

"What's that?"

"She said Tess is sad."

"Well, I'm not sure that's unexpected. She's being questioned by the police, and I heard from the headmistress that some parents are reluctant to have Tess teaching at the school. That's a lot to have on your shoulders."

"But wouldn't that make you angry instead of sad? Tess has always seemed self-reliant, not the kind of person who would take time to pity herself. If anything, she'd be mad about it, but maybe not even that. Maybe she had had hard knocks in her life and learned how to deal with them and move on."

Nell thought about that as she looked around the room at the happy children, with their wide eyes and dreams, racing and playing and greeting Mr. and Mrs. Claus. She wondered if the grandparents and parents watching them were troubled by the juxtaposition of emotions that she and Birdie were sorting through: innocent joy — and a vicious act that coated the town in suspicion and fear as they passed people on the street, in their churches and schools. Suspicions that even in this happy, celebratory room, someone who had taken another's life might be sitting at a table, watching the festivities.

And then she thought back to Tess Bean. Relatively alone in Sea Harbor, having people look at her with suspicion and distrust. *Sad?* Nell had no idea how she would feel in that situation, but she suspected Birdie was right that anger might have been a more likely emotion for Tess. But she hadn't seen a trace of it.

Those who cared about her were dealing with their own emotions, frustration topping the list. The trip to Hamilton had been interesting but perplexing, a sweater with too many hanging yarns. But both women felt it had been worthwhile, although they hadn't had time to figure out exactly why.

Ben spotted a table not far from the Christmas tree festivities and led them toward it.

Alex Arcado, the fire chief, was standing not far from the happy crowd of children, talking to his wife, M.J.

Nell noticed that the Arcado grandkids were there as well, playing around the tree.

But Alex had a serious look on his face. And his body leaned a bit, shoulders sagging, as if he hadn't slept in a while.

Nell walked up and hugged M.J., her hairdresser and friend for as long as she'd been in Sea Harbor. She greeted Alex. "I can see you've had a night of it. We heard about the fire."

Alex nodded. "It's under control," Alex said. "Extinguished, actually, though there are still a few hot spots."

"It's kind of surreal. Izzy and I were hiking over there just yesterday." She paused for a moment, wondering if, in fact, it had been yesterday. The days were as tangled as the confusion of facts rattling around in her head.

"Were you hiking near the place that burned?" M.J. asked.

"Yes, as best I can figure out from the newspaper. Maybe we were even in it." She briefly described the clearing and the cabin. "Ben and I had been on that path before, but the place had been vastly improved since we last saw it."

"That's the one, then," Alex said. "Someone in one of those new houses not far behind it noticed the flames. One burned down not far from there a couple years ago."

"I remember. A homeless man was trying to keep warm," Ben said.

Alex nodded. "But unless this homeless person had some bucks to spend, I think something else was going on."

"How did it start?" Birdie asked.

"The initial report is probable arson. And a clumsy attempt at that."

"That's strange. I wonder why," Ben said. "An accidental fire I can understand. But a deserted cabin? Clearly not for an insurance payout."

Alex managed a laugh. "You wouldn't think."

"The door had been left open, so Izzy and I walked in," Nell said. "In fact, if there's enough of the structure left, our prints might be around. Abby's too. She was playing with a candle she found. We were surprised at how nice it was. Rudimentary, but nice."

"As if it had one purpose?" M.J. said.

Nell admitted it looked a little like that. "Someone had definitely been there, although it wasn't clear how recently. I smelled a trace of wood smoke, although the embers in the fireplace were cold."

"They're not cold any longer," Alex said with a shake of his head. "But M.J. and I don't quite agree on the suppositions. I didn't like the headline — it was clearly to get people to read the article. It's too soon to know what was going on in there. And maybe we'll never know."

Beside him, M.J. was silent.

"Do you know how it started?" Birdie asked.

"The bed was drenched with gasoline. But accelerant was also used near a table, the door — telltale signs of arson. Natural fires don't burn that way."

Nell looked over at M.J. Her salon almost always had the inside scoop on Sea Harbor happenings. Although Nell knew M.J. herself was discreet, her staff didn't always follow suit.

"Are you two okay if we round up some food and drinks?" Ben asked. He and Alex headed toward the other end of the dining room and the comfortable lounge.

"You look bothered, M.J.," Birdie said.

M.J. smiled. It was what people did with Birdie, smiled. And confided.

"You know how kids are, always looking for a private place with no parents within shouting distance. Beech Tree Woods has hosted more than its share of that sort of thing."

"Do you think the cabin was fixed up by teens?" Nell asked.

M.J. shook her head. "No. That isn't what they did. But the kids knew of a place that had been fixed up. And they knew it was being used. Some of my girls at the salon have kids that age and they've been talking a lot. Sometimes the kids would head down to the beach at night, just for fun, and would see activity off that side trail."

"Did they see people?"

"Apparently, they snuck around, like kids do. But it was after dark, so mostly they heard sounds, I think. It was early fall when they were hanging out around there, when the beach was still fun. I suppose they'd sneak a cigarette, a beer stolen from some parent's fridge. Kiss a little. But once it got cold, the kids had sense enough to stay home. And that probably provided more privacy for anyone interested in that place. But that's a guess. And a guess of some of my customers, too. The reporter wasn't the first to call it a love nest, you know. The title was in place before the fire ever happened. Alex is just being cautious. We're a good balance that way." She smiled.

"Well, I suppose it's not the first time for shenanigans like that," Birdie said. "Though, frankly, it wouldn't be my choice of a nest."

Nell laughed and gave Birdie a hug. "You always bring us back to common sense, my dear friend."

M.J. laughed, too. But only for a moment. When she spoke again, her face was grave.

"If a love nest burned, that's one thing. But with a murderer loose in our town, it takes things like this to a different level. A heightened one. Bobby Abbott liked women. A lot, from what I hear. And they liked him. According to some of my customers, he fit the bill for women who were not at all interested in commitment, just fun."

"What about the fact that he was married?" Birdie asked.

"Did you know he was married?" M.J. asked, her brows lifted. Then she answered her own rhetorical question. "No one did. It was not a factor."

"But a rustic cabin in the woods?" Nell asked. The very thought made her shiver.

"As Birdie said, maybe not a sane person's choice. A hotel, a B and B, there'd be lots of other choices. But what if the women liked that? Impromptu. Close. Private. A bed warmed by a fire. Or maybe one even insisted on something not traceable in any way? What if that was why the cabin grew a bed and windows and a door that locked?"

As M.J.'s theory floated around them, Alex and Ben arrived with a tray of wine, apple juice, soft drinks, and a basket of calamari. Others joined the group and the conversation soon changed to things going on in the town, football, and a new exhibit at the Cape Ann Museum.

Nell helped herself to a glass of wine, handed one to Birdie, and the two walked over to check on Gabby and Abby, to bask in the magic of children. *A break from the real world,* Nell thought, recalling Gabby's intention.

But before that, there was still business to conduct. Birdie pulled Nell into the shadows of the tree. She had a bit of sleuthing she needed to share.

"I had a little time to check on Eunice's

tidbits," she said. "You never know if that information has been altered as it passes from cook to hairdresser to whomever. So I googled obituaries. And I found Lenore Graves. Although the obituary didn't mention Robert Abbott, it was clearly the same person Eunice was talking about. She lived in Hamilton, but died in Ipswich. Apparently, her final days were in a memory care unit near there. It asked that donations be sent to that place."

"Did it mention Bobby?"

"It said she had been previously married, and that she had two children."

"Two . . . Bobby Abbott had a sibling?" Nell's face filled with surprise.

"Younger. I called Eunice back. She had forgotten to mention it because somehow the child was always in the background. Neglected. That's how people who worked in the donut shop looked at it. It was the older son Lenore talked about. The son Lenore tried to get back. She'd have swapped the kids in a heartbeat, if she could have, though apparently Robert had no use for the younger one. Perhaps it was a son from Lenore's second husband. It was never clear."

"How awful. The whole scenario. I wonder if they kept in touch."

"Eunice didn't mention that. The child was sort of a nonentity — people weren't even sure if it was a boy or girl. Other people didn't even know Lenore had another child."

"Not even Helen Getty," Nell said. "Now, I wonder why that was."

CHAPTER 28

"It's one of the first things new parents learn," Izzy was saying to Danny Brandley. They were sitting at a tall table near a window at the Ocean's Edge restaurant bar.

Izzy was stabbing a cherry that she'd spotted at the bottom of her drink, something fancy that Sam had ordered for her. "This is very good, Sam," she said, waving a toothpick in the air.

Sam reached over and touched her glass with his own. "Enjoy, Izzy. And relax."

Izzy knew he meant more than that. He meant to shake it off, to let go of Bobby Abbott. RIP. Which, of course, she couldn't. Not completely. Not yet.

"So, what's this important thing you're telling Danny?" Cass asked.

"It's that when you have an amazing grandaunt and uncle or grandparents who love your child almost as much as you do, who want to whisk her off to be just with them, to love and cherish her all by themselves, you gratefully welcome it, and then you call your best friends to meet you for a grown-up hour or two."

"Is that what this is?" Danny asked. He looked around the elegant lounge.

"It's that, yes," Izzy said.

"Hmm. Maybe I will have to get me one, so I can understand this whole getaway thing more intimately."

Izzy laughed and looked over at Cass. She was giving her husband "*the* look," but it was more from habit, Izzy thought, than genuine. It's what Cass did without thought when she was teased about being Irish and, good grief, *where was the baby carriage?* Izzy pushed the thought away. Cass could live her life the way she wanted. No matter that they all thought she'd be a great mom. And no matter that the stare at Danny was softened almost to be something else entirely.

"I agree it's been a heck of a week," Cass said. "And this is good. We all needed a break. I'm not sure from what, but I'm sure we needed it."

They were quiet for a moment, sipping their drinks and looking out the windows into the harbor. Weariness drained away as they watched fishing boats bobbing in the moonlight. In the distance a lone lighthouse blinked on and off, and on again. Quiet and peaceful.

A peace that was temporary, just for right now. This moment. This place. And then they would go back to real life, and to pulling together loose strands, gathering scattered, tangled pieces of information, and trying to find in the morass a person who feared or hated Bobby Abbott enough to kill him. Tomorrow.

When her aunt and uncle had picked up Abby earlier that evening, Izzy had had a moment alone with Nell, just long enough to share what she had discovered that afternoon. Seeing Penny Abbott's name on the file in Dr. Virgilio's office had stunned her. It wasn't because Penny Abbott had miscarried. That was a truly sad and difficult thing to handle. It was pairing it together with the heartbreaking image of Penny Abbott, alone in a clearing, mourning her loss. And blaming herself for destroying what couldn't be fixed. It didn't fit. Not with a husband like Clark Abbott, who loved her so much he would fight demons for her.

"Izzy?" Sam said, pulling her back to the group. "Clams?"

Izzy tuned back in, sipping her drink and

piling a generous helping of the restaurant's crispy fried clams on her plate. Never over-battered, always plump and succulent, the Ocean's Edge claimed them as a specialty of the house. Of the town. Perhaps the world. She dipped one in a pot of tangy sauce and waved to friends across the lounge, pushing away the afternoon and the week. She wrapped herself in friendship and the smell of the holiday garlands, which were looped artfully around the edges of the lounge and restaurant.

The sound level in the lounge had risen as more people crowded in. Groups of friends and couples came by their table and left again, circling around. Danny and Sam disappeared to get more drinks, and Cass was pulled away to look at photos of a relative's wedding on a tiny phone in dim light. She threw Izzy a look that begged for a rescue soon.

Izzy smiled and turned back to the windows, enjoying the solitary moment and the moon's silvery sparkles on the water, dancing like woodland fairies.

"Hey, Izzy." A familiar voice behind her pulled her back and she looked up into the face of her old college friend.

"Jill," Izzy said, surprised. "Hey . . ." And then she stopped, looking behind Clark Turner's cousin to see if he was there.

"Are you here with Clark?"

"Ha, I get it." Jill laughed. "You're wondering if I'm wanting to lure you into joining us to keep the conversation going. I'm right, aren't I?"

Izzy's laugh was awkward. "Well . . ."

"I know I know. I've put you in that role once or twice. Helping to balance the conversation with Clark. He wasn't the greatest conversationalist back then."

Izzy smiled. "But a nice guy."

Jill went on. "No, you're off the hook. I'm here for a couple weeks. My aunt is sick and I'm helping out. But I barely see Clark. He used to depend on me, you know, for social things. But I barely see him when I'm here now. My aunt noticed the same thing. Clark has always been a little odd, but he's a different man now. Do you see him?"

"I do. He's my vet, so I —"

"Sure, I know that. But I mean have you seen him with Penny? He's over the moon in love with her. I think it's totally mutual. She dotes on him. Cooks amazing meals, he says. They're thinking of building a new house. It's pretty cool." She took a clam from the basket in front of Izzy and chewed on it, still thinking about her cousin and his marriage.

"We knew Clark would never get married — he'd decided that, well, twenty years ago now, when everything happened," Jill said. "But then he met this Penny from Hooters and *bam!* He fell for her hard."

"They seem happy," Izzy managed to say, finding the conversation a little strange.

Cass saved the day, coming back to the table after looking cross-eyed at the tiny wedding shots of a relative she barely knew.

"Who's that?" Cass asked as Jill walked away.

"Someone I went to college with. She's Clark Turner's cousin. It's obvious they must be blood relatives, because I think they share similar genes."

"Weird?"

Izzy nodded.

CHAPTER 29

The morning was brisk and bright, with a scent of snow in the air. Izzy stood at the front door of her house, worrying about whether the pajamas she'd packed for Abby had been warm enough. And if her aunt had remembered to help her brush her teeth. Worries intended to erase other things from her mind: silent partners, miscarriages, fires, and angels from heaven.

Hygge events were nearly forgotten, but Mae had assured her yesterday that their knitting gathering would rise above the ashes. Delayed a few days, perhaps, but it would rise.

Finally Nell drove up and Izzy crouched down as Abby raced up to the door and threw herself into her mother's arms. She was jabbering about a million things, including the tiny reindeer that Santa had given her, all for her own.

Nell stood beside her, beaming at this tiny

person who had changed all their lives. She was reluctant to let her go. But in the very next instant, Abby had circled her mother and had run off to find others to hug and to share a reindeer with — a daddy and an old dog.

Izzy hugged her aunt, pulling her into the warm house and closing the door behind her. "Please stay, Aunt Nell. For a while?"

It took Nell three seconds to agree.

Izzy busied herself with her daughter, planning Abby's next event, while Nell retreated to the quiet family room, where Red was lying in front of the fireplace, the glow turning his coat a golden color. Rich and silky. She called Ben to check in, and explained she'd be home later. Perhaps they could have a quiet Sunday night together. It seemed those had been dwindling, as of late.

She almost didn't hear the doorbell, but noticed the twitch in Red's ears, then the rush of Abby's small feet racing toward the front door, expecting, hoping, Santa had come early.

Nell heard the familiar voice, the sweet words to Abby, and in the next minute Izzy led Tess Bean into the den.

"Red has been dragging," Izzy explained. "I'm hoping it wasn't the hike that did it. But Tess agreed to come by to perform some magic on him."

"This is serendipity, then," Nell said. "I've been thinking about you, Tess. Wondering. Hoping you're okay."

She moved over on the slipcovered couch, but Tess smiled her hello and immediately moved to Red's side, her petite body folding down next to him.

Izzy told them coffee was brewing and filled Nell in on the Perrys' crazy day. "Danny's parents are holding their annual holiday book fair for kids at the bookstore. Hot chocolate, Harriet Brandley's famous Christmas cookies, carols, and a visit from elves. Sam is taking Abby. I only hope he and Danny aren't the elves Harriet and Archie have advertised."

Nell laughed at the image, while Tess listened, taking it in, her fingers beginning to gently circle Red's head, then his neck.

Izzy went on about another party, another event to confuse a child about how many Santas actually existed in Sea Harbor. Nell watched the expression on Tess's face as the day played out in front of them. Pensive, a slight smile on her face as Abby's voice in the background was filled with excitement and Sam pulled jackets from the closet. She wondered about Tess's own childhood. Had there been any magic in it? Joy? For reasons unfounded, she guessed not. And she wondered about her life in Sea Harbor. The school. The cabin by the shore. Had she found peace there?

And her future.

A round of good-byes filled the house, along with a child's energetic hugs, delivered profusely to everyone in the room, including Red and Tess. And then utter quiet as the door slammed closed behind them.

"Sam said Birdie called and is on her way over here with Cass and a cheesy egg casserole that Mae made this morning, then discovered there was no one there to eat it. Apparently, Gabby is with friends getting ready for some kind of gathering of their own.

"Also, Birdie needs help with the hood she's knitting on Gabby's sweater. There" — she stopped talking and grinned at Tess — "that's all I know."

Tess was whispering in Red's ears, but looked up and smiled back, looking contented, Nell thought. As if she would be happy sitting in front of the fireplace with Red's head in her lap for at least a month or two. Perhaps longer.

She and Ben had spent a quiet hour the night before, once Abby had fallen asleep, catching up.

Lucky had called him almost as soon as he'd found the makeshift will that Bobby Abbott had signed, Ben said. It was legal, witnessed by two dishwashers who had no idea what was in the will, but that didn't matter. The will offered no explanation. Just the bequest and Tess's name. That was it.

And now Tess knew. Ben and Lucky had gone down to the small cabin and told her later in the afternoon.

Nell watched Tess's face closely while Izzy went back and forth, turning on an oven to heat up the casserole when it arrived, filling coffee mugs, and putting on some soft, soothing music.

She couldn't read anything on Tess's face that indicated Bobby Abbott had left her his share of a bar. A bar she had protested with posters and words, and a man she had badgered and scolded and pushed into the ocean.

All she saw was concern for an old dog whom she wanted to feel better.

Ben said she had shown little reaction when they told her, definitely not the surprise they'd expected. Ben suspected Tess Bean knew that she had inherited a bar — or something — before they told her. And he also suspected she wished no one had found out about it and that it would all go away. The only expression Ben and Lucky had seen on her face was a look of deep sadness and regret.

And acceptance.

That was all, even when she realized the next person they would have to tell would be Chief Jerry Thompson.

Birdie and Cass arrived in a flurry through the side door, tugging off boots and hanging coats on racks in the mudroom. They were surprised to see Tess on the floor beside Red, but welcomed her warmly, as if Izzy's house were their own.

In no time the casserole was heated and served up, and knitting baskets were set aside momentarily.

Cass walked over and knelt down beside Red, looking into his face. His eyes were closed, his body in a kind of repose as Tess's hands continued to gently circle his neck, the base of his ears, around to his shoulders. Firm, then gentle. A steady rhythm of comfort.

Cass looked across Red's contented body to Tess. "I don't suppose you could do that with my hens so they'd lay more eggs?"

Tess laughed. She'd never tried it on a hen, she said, but it relaxed people and dogs.

Nell thought Tess seemed relaxed. But vigilant. As if keeping a watch out for something. But she couldn't figure out what it was.

Cass picked up Tess's plate and took it to the sink. Nell rinsed off the finished plates as Izzy came in for another pot of coffee.

"Hey," Cass said, "we never heard about your trip to Hamilton?"

"It was interesting," Nell said. She looked over and noticed Tess had looked up, then lowered her head again.

"It was a beautiful drive," Nell said. "Birdie's cousin lives there and she told us a little about Bobby Abbott's family. About the son and father." She closed the dishwasher door and turned to the sink. Something was settling down inside Nell's head. Connections.

It clicked, like an electric shock. She took a deep breath, releasing it slowly, steadying herself.

Was it Cass's reminder of the trip that caused her mind to clear?

It was as if the conversation in Hamilton had needed some hours to percolate and brew. And when it did, a veil was torn off the confused pieces of memory — a bandage jerked off quickly — shifting the comments and images, even the retelling of an irreverent comment made about Robert Abbott's wife. And it had arranged them all into a sensible, horrifying order.

Across the room she caught Birdie looking at her. It shouldn't surprise her. It happened frequently. Brainwaves or karma or some kind of psychic energy brought their thoughts together. She calmed herself, then walked back to the others, sat down, and picked up her knitting.

"That's beautiful," Tess said, glancing at the nearly finished pink hat in Izzy's lap and the remaining yarn, soft and plush.

"Come into the yarn shop," Izzy said. "I will fix you up with everything you need. I owe you big, Tess. It would be my pleasure. We have plenty of organic yarns, too. See Birdie's orange sweater? Beautiful, sustainable, and ethical."

Tess laughed. "I lived with my grandmother for a while and she tried to teach me. I'd love to make something organic, bamboo yarn, maybe? I think I learned a little from Grams, but it was a long time ago."

"It comes back," Cass assured her. "Like riding a bike. I'm Izzy's living example that anyone can do it."

"Where did your grandmother live?" Birdie asked, grateful for the comfortable segue. It was meant to be. Nell smiled at her.

"A little north, northwest of here," Tess answered, turning back to Red.

"So close by, then. Ipswich?"

"Yes. For a while." She began working on Red's hind legs.

"Tess —" Birdie spoke the single name so softly and with such respect that when Tess looked up into her warm gray eyes, there was a trace of moisture in her own.

"Tess Bean Abbott," Birdie said.

Izzy and Cass sat silently, but without showing total surprise. The connection between Tess and Bobby had been there from the beginning. All along it had defied the simple explanation of an activist protesting an establishment's bad habits. It was far more than that. It was personal.

Jittery, Eunice had told them about Tess's mother. And some other things. Nell had recoiled at the way Lenore was treated when she'd heard the story. But she had skipped over connecting the dots. They called Lenore *The Jittery Mexican Bean. Bean.* Her maiden name. Tess's name.

"I had decided to talk to you — you're kind and I knew you would be understanding. I didn't know when or how, but the intent was there. Also, I didn't want the girls — Gabby, especially — to be caught up in any kind of rumor-mongering vortex. I waited, as if the moment would tap me on the shoulder."

"Sometimes talking helps to lift burdens. Friends do that, too," Nell said. Tess hadn't had much friendship in her life. She looked around the room at those who knew her own heart. Who held it in their hands.

"My story isn't long," Tess said. "It's unsavory, messy. But not long."

Izzy refilled their cups. "Those adjectives don't fit my dog whisperer. So let's exorcise them."

Tess nodded and looked around at a circle of open faces. She focused in on Birdie. "I think it may have been difficult for you having Gabby attach herself to me the way kids that age do with teachers. And the rest of you — none of you seemed to condemn me after Bobby died and the whole town knew I had railed against him. At least I didn't feel you were judging me. Why?"

Birdie smiled. "Gabby said you didn't do it."

Tess laughed softly, then sat back, seeming to find comfort in the dog at her side. She told her story evenly, as if she had practiced it. Or maybe over the years, she had removed herself from the pain of a father who didn't want her, and a mother who blamed her for every wrong thing in her life.

"They married young. My mother was beautiful, and he was handsome. The one thing in life he wanted was a son. As an adult I've wondered if that's why he married her. Good genes. And it worked. Bobby was cherished from day one. I was an accident — neither of them wanted another child, but my mother rationalized that if it were a boy, it might solidify their shaky relationship. Wouldn't two be better than one? When I was born, it all fell apart. A few years later, Robert Abbott left and took his son with him. Money can be a devastating tool. He got away with a lot by using it."

"Did you get to know your brother?" Izzy asked.

"He was eight or so when they left, and I was six. I adored him. And then he deserted me, left me with a mother who didn't like me and was pretty sure that I was responsible for everything bad that ever happened to her. I hated him for that.

"For a while my mother had the legal right to see Bobby sporadically, so I saw him on those wretched weekends. He had already bought into his father's distaste for me, but I clung to him. Begged him to make things better. Of course he didn't. And finally Robert Abbott managed to sever all connections between Bobby and his mother. Bobby was relieved, happy. He hated being forced to come to our humble home."

"What power parents can have over children," Nell said.

"I had a decent grandmother." She smiled at Birdie. "That helped some, but she died early."

"Your mother remarried?"

Tess nodded. "And I eventually got a scholarship to Salem State. I loved school, but when I came home for break my freshman year — mostly because I didn't have any other place to go — there was a For Sale sign on my mother's house. They were gone. Just like that. I never saw her again until she got sick."

Nell's eyes rested on a large photo that Sam had taken of Izzy and Abby. It hung near the fireplace. Izzy was holding Abby and they were standing on Good Harbor Beach, with the ocean in the background. Izzy's face was in profile, Abby's nearly so, with her curly blond head thrown back, her laughter almost audible. Izzy's face was filled with such raw love it almost hurt to look at it.

She looked over at Tess Bean and her

heart swelled. A young woman who had suffered — and survived. And with her heart intact. Tess could still love and be loved. Survival at its core. Gabby was right. Tess was remarkable.

"Why did you come to Sea Harbor?" Cass asked. "Was it because of Bobby?"

"Oh no. I didn't come for Bobby — I didn't know he was here. I was pretty much dead to him. And he to me. Besides, my coming here was not planned. When my mother died, she left me something. A total shock. It was a scrap that had been tossed to her from Robert Abbott to finalize the divorce. Some worthless property he owned."

"The little cottage on the Beech Tree Woods shore," Nell said, smiling.

Tess smiled, too. "I think she left it to me because she thought it was worthless, which was what she thought of me. But I'm not worthless. And neither is the cottage. I love it. It's my home."

The women listened, their hearts wide open, and each of them wishing a different childhood for Tess. But none of them felt sorry for her. Tess wouldn't allow it.

Nell looked over at Birdie, who at that moment was sending up a note of thanks for sending Gabrielle Marietti such a fine role model.

"It must have been a surprise to find Bobby here," Izzy said.

Tess smiled down at Red, who seemed to open one eye to make sure Tess was still there and then closed it again.

"Sure was. The day I started at Sea Harbor Community Day School there was an article in the town paper about the Harbor Club. It included a picture of its handsome, personable owner. Bobby Abbott. I had five minutes of feeling sick. And then I walked along the shore and I felt better.

"Bobby and my father had determined too many aspects of my life. I refused to let him have any more power over me. I refused to leave a place that was my own, just because he happened to be in the same town.

"I knew we would run into each other some day, and that was okay. I could handle it. And, of course, we did. From an environmental perspective Bobby was doing terrible things to the ocean, and I told him so. But what I didn't realize was that my feelings went way beyond what damage he was doing to the ocean. I thought the years had lightened my resentment. Not forgiveness — I wasn't there yet. But maybe that I had buried the feelings, rendered them ineffectual. But I hadn't. And I'm sure that was part of the episode at the cove that Gabby witnessed.

"He deserted me when I was just a kid who needed an older brother. The resentment and pain were still there. That day at the cove he made fun of me. It still hurt, and I needed to somehow get rid of that feeling. I didn't like it controlling me. Maybe pushing him into the water that day was a part of my own process. An exorcism? Or maybe a baptism? It was my turn to toss something aside. So I did, both Bobby and my resentment."

"Do you know what happened that night?" Izzy asked.

No one asked what night Izzy meant.

Tess saw Red wince and she began to massage his hind legs. Around and around, gentle, then firm, then gentle. "No, I don't. All I know is what I did that night, not what ended Bobby's life. I've gone over it a million times." She looked at Izzy and Cass. "Remember that night? I saw you both. My emotions were raw that night, it was my birthday."

"Your birthday?" Izzy said.

"Yes, but it's silly, isn't it? I've never paid attention to birthdays before, but that night I was fragile, not a usual state for me. And maybe that's why I was distressed when we saw the small things those rude thugs had done with the compost bins. I stayed out on Gracie's deck for a long time after that, sorting through my life. Calming myself down. Finally, when I was nearly frozen, I started to leave, walking down past the bins. Bobby must have seen me, and he came out the kitchen door of his place and stopped me."

Izzy and Cass exchanged a look, but Tess was looking at Red, as if he were somehow giving her permission to go on.

"I stopped. And he walked over. It was dark, and really cold." She paused, and for a minute they were not sure she was going to continue. Finally she did.

"He handed me a piece of lemon cake, all wrapped up. And then he wished me a happy birthday. *Happy birthday.*" She shook her head. "Our birthdays were close together, so maybe that was how he knew. He said he had another gift for me that we could talk about some other time. Something about a will, he said. He kind of laughed and I assumed the will thing was a joke, so I ignored it, but I was having trouble with the birthday wishes and the cake and all. I was emotional, anyway, and to have this galoot — my only living family member — express something in a way that wasn't mean or nasty or dismissive, was beginning to get to me.

"So I murmured something to him, I don't remember what, and I walked away. I don't handle emotional moments well. He called after me once, so I stopped and turned around. I stood there freezing and was about to leave again when he lifted one hand. A wave? Or to stop me?

"And then he said, 'I love you, Tess.' "

CHAPTER 30

They huddled around Izzy's fireplace, skeins of yarn and half-knit sweaters and hats in their laps, and their emotions a mess.

Cass had taken over the couch, curling up and claiming exhaustion.

Tess Bean had left them all in a state. She said that she had to leave for a party — the one Gabby and Daisy were planning. She and Margaret Garozzo were the token adults.

"The gang," she said with a smile, seeming lighter in spirit and step as she hurried out into the cold.

Tess had stirred their emotions early on, even before she began to talk about her life. It began as they watched her mesmerizing touch and whispered words to Red. But by the end of her story, they were puddles inside, but holding it together because anything else might have disturbed Tess.

"It all fits," Cass said, her fingers moving

fast as she decreased each row, nearing the crown of her third beanie. "It explains things that didn't connect before. It ties everything together," Cass said. "He was her brother. *Geesh.*"

Izzy thought back to the day shortly after Bobby died when they had seen her on the wharf. "We thought she looked sad. Not frightened or relieved or any of those things. She was sad. One person's story — and it answers so many questions."

"Except one," Nell said. "Who murdered Tess's brother?"

Tess's brother.

It was as if Nell's single statement rallied them. They kept the knitting needles moving — a sweater, hats, a cowl — but the focus was not on parties or plans or gifts. Even plans for a holiday *hygge* knitting gathering were set aside.

The focus was on answering that one question: *Who murdered Bobby Abbott?* On laying out what they knew. And alongside it, what they didn't.

They would layer suspicions and intuitions and emotions around the facts.

"Much of what Birdie and I were looking into was Bobby's life. And that's been helpful. It explains what bothered all of us and where he came from, some understanding of the man who grew out of that child, that upbringing. We know what Tess was holding back from the police — and from all of us."

"I understand why she didn't talk about it with the police. It was difficult enough for her to bare her life with us. In her mind it wasn't relevant to Bobby's murder, so she told them the things that were," Birdie said.

"The police will need to know about the relationship," Nell said. "But hopefully they won't push it any further."

Izzy wasn't so sure. "I think the best thing we can do for Tess is find out who really killed her brother. And do it quickly. We were heading in the wrong direction trying to pull things out of Bobby's past. We need to find a new direction. I think we need to concentrate on Bobby's life here in Sea Harbor and walk around in those shoes for a while."

"But as we do that, we need to keep in mind what we have learned. Bobby Abbott was a terribly spoiled man, one who probably had a thimble-sized conscience, if that," Nell said. "That's where we look. Who did he hurt right here in Sea Harbor? A part of me thinks we already know. It's right here. We just don't know that we know."

"The fire in the woods is a place to start. It's not a coincidence that it happened so soon after Bobby's murder," Birdie said.

"We talked to Alex Arcado last night." Nell refreshed them all on what the fire chief had told them.

But what seemed more relevant was what his wife, M.J., had said.

"Someone was using that cabin for meeting women," Birdie said. "M.J. was sure of it. It had been fixed up to be comfortable."

"To be a comfortable *bedroom,*" Izzy corrected. "I think that's a given. Margaret Garozzo walks in the woods, too, and even she was aware of activity there."

Nell thought back to seeing the clearing, the cabin. First with Ben, then with Izzy. And then the encounter with Margaret. She had clearly seen things going on down that path. "It was a wreck of a cabin when Ben and I found it. Clearly used by vagrants. Windows were broken and there was trash around it." Nell thought back to that day.

And then she remembered something. She had picked up some trash that day.

She walked through Izzy's kitchen to the mudroom, then rummaged around in the pocket of her parka. It was still there.

"This doesn't say much for my cleanliness," she said, returning to the family room. "But I picked this up when Izzy and I were walking around out there. I shoved it in my pocket to throw away later." She dropped the crushed and smelly cigarette package on the table. Bright green, with a Canadian flag on it.

It wasn't much. But they knew Bobby Abbott smoked. And Nell had seen him before, on the wharf, holding a green pack of cigarettes, with a Canadian flag on the front.

Izzy took over. "So Bobby Abbott had a liaison — maybe more — but I think we only care about one. Who was he with recently? Who would have wanted to erase any sign of being there? And why?"

"Margaret told me Bobby Abbott was a bad man. Somehow I think she knows something about this," Nell said. "She definitely didn't want us taking Abby near the cabin."

"True," Izzy said. "It was almost as if it would contaminate her."

Birdie lowered her head, looking at the cuff on Gabby's sweater. "Maybe," she said. But she looked concerned.

Nell could see Birdie was reluctant to pursue that path. She tucked the thought aside to talk to her later, wondering if she had talked to either of the Garozzos.

The image of Penny sitting near the cabin refused to leave the room. Finally Izzy, feeling she was betraying doctor-patient privilege — although she was neither the doctor nor the patient — told them about the file in Dr. Virgilio's office.

They listened carefully.

"So Penny Abbott was pregnant?" Birdie asked.

Somehow it wasn't what anyone expected. And a small amount of shame, along with self-recriminations, accompanied the feeling. Mothers came in all shapes and sizes. And temperaments. Who were they to judge, after all?

"She was clearly distraught when she wasn't pregnant any longer. At least if the scene in the woods was any indication. I am almost sure that must have been what was going on there," Nell said.

Izzy agreed. "The clinic receptionist also talked about how upset she was. It was almost as if she was giving Clark this amazing gift. I think the reason Clark was so happy the day I took Purl in was because he knew they were pregnant. He was happy, she was happy. And then in one day it was stolen from them."

It was a sobering thought.

One they took with them into the rest of the day, turning it every way they could.

Cass began stuffing her yarn into a backpack, checking her watch. It was Sunday, church was out, and that meant a visit to her mother. As she headed for her coat, she said, "Mary Halloran doesn't suffer lateness gladly. Although she does make the most amazing Irish stew in town. Danny and I are going to get ourselves some."

The break came at a good time. Izzy had to get to the store to help Mae with the Sunday knitting group. It was a small group, Mae had said, easy peasy, but Izzy insisted on being there. And with Sam and Abby gone, she'd be sitting around the house trying to figure out why people killed each other. Knitting was far more appealing.

Birdie and Izzy quickly cleaned up stray pieces of yarn and a few forgotten napkins, while Nell checked in with Ben.

"Ben is headed to the yacht club for Sunday football," she told Birdie as they climbed into the car. "It's a little early, but I think I'd like to stop in at Garozzo's Deli for a salad or soup. Maybe take some home for dinner."

Birdie agreed, although neither was hungry. Harry and Margaret had both been on their minds.

The deli was already crowded when they arrived, the specials printed on a large sign out front. Most of the people were waiting in line for take-out lasagna and Margaret's minestrone soup.

Birdie rubbed her cold hands together until they turned pink. She looked around, waving to a few people, then spotted Harry coming out of the kitchen.

He spotted her and grinned, wiping the damp heat from the kitchen stoves off his forehead. "To what do I owe this honor? You two don't usually show up on Sundays."

Nell looked into the back. "A table for two somewhere, Harry?"

Instead of waiting for the hostess, Harry waved for them to follow and ushered them back to the Harbor Road side of the dining room, seating them next to the window. "I'll send someone over," he said, looking slightly harassed.

"Is everything all right?" Birdie asked. "You're looking tired, Harry."

Harry looked around the dining room, then planted his hands on the table, fingers splayed. "It's Margaret. It's all these things she's doing."

They nodded, listening. Silence was the best enticement for getting Harry talking.

"I don't want the police talking to her. Don't want her upset."

"Of course not. Why would the police

want to talk to her?"

"You asked me once if she knew Bobby Abbott."

"I remember," Nell said.

"She mentions him, talks about him sometimes in her sleep."

"What does she say?" Birdie asked.

Harry took a long breath. "She says he was a bad man. Though in her dreams he may be still alive, I dunno. Or haunting her, maybe. Why? Why would she be troubled by a man she never met? He was Penny Turner's friend, you know. I wanted to ask Penny about it, see if I could figure it out. Why Margaret has the nightmares."

"Did you?"

"Yeah, I did. In a clumsy way. I mean, the guy is dead, and rumors around this place say Penny knew him pretty well, if you know what I mean. So, what did I say? *Was he a bad guy? Why does my Margaret have nightmares about this guy? Did you have an affair with him? How can I get rid of him?* No, I said, 'Hey, Penny, this Abbott guy. Was he a good guy?' "

"What did she say?"

"She kind of chuckled and said that she knew nothin' about the guy. Except that he was dead. 'So, why worry about him?' Her words, not mine."

"Well, that's her answer, then, I guess," Birdie said.

Nell hesitated. Would it ease his mind to tell him Margaret may have seen Abbott in the woods with a woman? Headed to a cabin for the night. Maybe even with Penny Turner — no, *probably* with Penny Turner. Margaret thought Penny was bad, too. But maybe Harry should stop thinking about it as good or bad. Margaret might think it bad, others might not.

She looked over at Birdie, and they both were sad for Harry. But to say anything to him would probably only do one thing: Harry would make Margaret promise never to go into Beech Tree Woods, her special, private place, ever again.

"The photo in the paper might have disturbed her," Nell offered. But more likely, almost assuredly, it wasn't the woods or the photo in the paper. It was that Margaret may have come across a dead man before anyone else had seen his body.

And that, perhaps, was something they maybe should share with Margaret. Harry needed to help keep Margaret safe.

Harry was visibly distraught when they told him their suspicion. "She loves going out and helping with those cleanups," he said, his hands worrying his apron into knots.

"And they watch out for her. The girls love her," Birdie said. "She's kind and motherly and works as hard as they do. But sometimes she takes the wrong path down to the water. And one of those may well have created nightmares."

"Margaret loves that little Tess," Harry said, trying to get his thoughts around the possibility of his wife seeing a dead body. "Some folks around here think Tess is the one who killed him. I want to kick them in the you-know-where."

"Well, they're wrong. You and I both know she didn't murder anyone," Birdie said, dismissing the idea entirely. "But we will know very soon who did kill Bobby Abbott. Perhaps that will give Margaret a good night's rest."

"I'm counting on it." Harry seemed somewhat relieved.

Birdie placed her small veined hand on top of his and squeezed it tight. "Harry, my darling man. You and I have been friends almost from the beginning of time. I love you dearly, and I love Margaret, too, and I'm saying this out of that love."

Harry looked down, leaving his hand beneath her small palm and feeling its heat. He nodded. "Yeah. I know what you're going to say. We need to go see Doc Mackenzie," he said softly. "Take Margaret in for a little checkup."

Birdie nodded. "And your village is here, right behind you. All around you. Don't you forget that for a single moment."

Harry nodded, and then he wiped his forehead, or maybe his eyes, and stepped aside as two bowls of minestrone soup were delivered to the table.

But he wasn't himself, the two women thought. Not bragging about how incredible the soup was, or exchanging jokes or gossip and sweet compliments. Harry wasn't Harry today. Concern can do that. Love can do that.

Birdie and Nell ate their soup in the comfortable silence of friendship, watching the shoppers walk by outside the windows, Santas ringing bells, and carols pouring out from a loudspeaker somewhere. It was festive but subdued, even though the activity was the same that went on every December.

A familiar voice pulled them away from watching the world go by and they looked up into the smiling face of M.J. Arcado. "That soup is beyond wonderful," she said, holding up a container. "Dinner."

Birdie and Nell smiled, agreeing completely.

"And people watching is, too," Birdie said.

"Sitting here is like being at a dinner theater."

M.J. nodded, but it was clear there was something else on her mind. She moved closer to the table, leaning in, and lowered her voice. "We talked about the fire last night, and your being in the cabin that day, Nell. Alex got news today and he said to share it with you if I saw you."

"My fingerprints?"

M.J. smiled. "No, but they were able to confirm what Alex had said last night. Everything hadn't burned to the ground. It wasn't an accomplished arsonist who did this."

"Did they find anything?"

"Not that will necessarily point to the arsonist. But they found something else. A crocodile leather belt that had fallen behind a metal bucket. It was fancy, Italian, and expensive."

M.J. paused, like a culinary judge on a TV show, waiting for the silence to grow heavy. Then she said, "It was Bobby Abbott's."

Nell and Birdie managed to look surprised.

Well, the belt was a surprise, Nell supposed.

"There was one more thing. I don't think

it's significant, but they found some medication."

"*Medication?* What was it for?" Nell asked.

"For allergies. It's one of those nonprescription sprays. FLONASE I think. My grandson uses one because of their cat. The kitty makes him sneeze."

Chapter 31

Nell and Birdie had bundled back up, warm scarves looped around their necks, coats buttoned from top to bottom, and headed up and down Harbor Road, making a sizable dent in holiday shopping. But the real motivation, they both agreed, was distraction. One that didn't come easily and only worked at all because the wind had picked up and keeping warm took momentary precedence over figuring out a murder.

Finally, exhausted, they headed for Izzy's yarn shop for warmth, a chair, and, a cup of cider left over from a knitting session. They were walking past the hardware store, about to cross the street, when Lucky Bianchi, head down and thumb flipping messages on his phone, walked out the door and straight into Birdie, scattering her packages to the ground.

He looked up in horror. "Oh geesh, Birdie. I'm sorry." He bent over and scooped up the packages. "I don't know where my head was. Australia, maybe? Iceland? Geesh, Bianchi," he scolded himself. "Get a grip. This is Birdie Favazza you're plowing into."

His cheeks were bright red, from the cold or embarrassment, the women couldn't tell. But he was making them smile. And smiles were worth their weight in gold today.

"Lucky, you're just like your father. Anthony would be thinking of some big deal he was about to land, or sometimes just what kind of Scotch he'd drink that night, and everything else would simply turn into fog. Beautiful gray fog protecting him from the world beyond his mind."

"Yeah, that's a good description. Fog." Lucky laughed. "So, where are you two headed on this beautiful, freezing, windy day? May I be of assistance?" He attempted a bow, but dropped another one of Birdie's packages with the dip. "Okay, this is crazy. I'm going to deliver both of you and these freakin' packages wherever you're headed. Your wish is my command. Throw it at me."

"How about Izzy's yarn shop across the street," Birdie said.

Lucky made a show of stopping traffic, dropping only one additional bag in the process, and in minutes they were in the warm confines of Izzy's shop.

The main room was empty, but at the sound of the bell, Izzy loped up the three steps from the back room. Her face brightened.

"I'm so glad to see you guys. The perfect threesome. I need some help."

"Help?" Lucky said. "I've already rescued these ladies from the perils of Harbor Road, and you want more from me?"

Izzy grinned and began walking toward the alcove, motioning for them to follow. "Spiced cider awaits."

They walked down and shrugged out of their coats and jackets, throwing them over the fireplace chairs. Birdie retreated to her favorite, settling in and warmed by the remaining glowing embers in the fireplace. Dozens of candles were still scattered around, but they had been extinguished and Izzy had clearly been working. Her computer was out on the coffee table, her new reading glasses beside it. She poured them each a mug of cider and sat down.

"Lucky, this is like you're our deus ex machina. Dropped right down in our midst to help us out."

"Uh-oh," Lucky said. "But I guess I've been called worse." He glanced over at her computer and read the name in the search engine. *"Penny Turner?"*

"Yes."

Nell and Birdie leaned forward. They had given themselves a diversion, but it hadn't completely worked. Penny Turner was very much on their minds, too. Along with a dead man lying on the shore, a fire, and a town in need of closure.

"Why are you interested in Penny?"

"Because Gracie and Tess Bean aren't murderers. Nor are you. And until we find out who is, lives are being screwed up and toyed with. You're included."

"It's okay, Iz. I talked to the police, and, sure, they have to ask what they have to ask. But I didn't kill Bobby."

"But someone did, Lucky. And maybe you're not worried. But I am. I don't like walking along Harbor Road or running along the shore, or leaving Abby at a babysitter's house and knowing that a murderer might be living in the same neighborhoods or running along those same streets."

There was passion in Izzy's voice and weariness in her eyes.

"The police are still looking at a couple of workers he was having some trouble with. And a guy from one of the fishing crews who caused some trouble one night and Bobby got him fired. And don't forget that Bobby liked women a lot. Some weren't happy with him. He could be a jerk. I know the chief is aware of all this."

Nell listened and wondered why Lucky couldn't think further than he was seeing. But before she could ask, he began talking again, more thoughtfully this time.

"Okay, sure. I do get what you're saying. I don't mean to be blasé. I agree that it's wearing on people. And I know that the weight of suspicion is an awful thing. I see it having an effect on Tess Bean, especially. She's good at pretending she's okay. But people aren't as comfortable with her as they are with me because she's still considered a newcomer, so they don't give her much leeway. It's not fair."

Birdie reached over and patted his arm in approval. "Yes, the police are doing a good job, but it doesn't hurt to keep on the lookout ourselves," she said. "Sometimes it's easier to get closer to people when you don't have to wear a uniform and announce yourself." She smiled, tugging one out of Lucky, too.

Nell looked over at Lucky. "I think the concern with Penny is that she is somehow in the middle of all this, and we know so little about her." Nell repeated what they'd learned about the fire. "It seems pretty clear Bobby and Penny were the last two people in the cabin before it burned."

"I can believe that," Lucky said. "Kind of an unfortunate choice of place for an affair, but each to his own."

"I'm convinced she really loves Clark Turner," Izzy said. "So, why?"

"Adams," Lucky said suddenly. "I just remembered. That's her name. I met her once before she married Clark. But you have a point, Iz. I wondered about that. Penny was a controlling lady. Planned things out. All that flirting? Calculated. I liked to watch her work the bar, the room. She had fun. And it was innocent fun, really. But — and I admit, I'm not an expert on these things — I think she does love Doc Turner."

"Did Bobby have a problem with the flirting, the way she was in the bar?" Izzy asked.

"No. He liked her. I was surprised sometimes. Penny somehow had his number in a way not many people did. And I could tell that she got him, well, excited sometimes."

"Did you find anything else about her in your search?" Nell asked.

Izzy shook her head. "Only that she was from Danvers. I found that in some obituary of a relative."

Lucky nodded. "That sounds right. That's where the Hooters was that she worked at.

An old college buddy bartended there and he introduced us once."

"Do you know why she left?" Birdie asked.

"She was fired. But from what I hear, it wasn't entirely her fault."

"What happened?" Nell asked.

Lucky wrinkled his forehead, thinking back. "There was some kind of a ruckus in the bar. The girls were all pretty well trained to handle things, and Penny especially so. Karate, boxing, martial arts — she'd done it all. Probably to protect herself. One night a customer had had a couple too many and came on too strong to one of the girls. When she called for help, Penny went to the rescue. 'Wonder Woman,' they called her. She flipped the guy over and threw him against the wall."

Izzy let out a breath, and Nell downed the rest of her cider in one swig.

"Penny? That little thing?" Birdie said.

Lucky shook his head. "And the guy broke an arm. Penny Turner is one strong lady."

CHAPTER 32

Lucky got up to leave shortly afterward and offered Birdie a ride on his way. To make amends for dropped packages, he told her with a grin.

Nell stayed behind, helping Izzy check the fire, and clean up the remains of the afternoon knitting *hygge.*

Izzy concentrated on the afternoon's knitting *hygge.* "It was small, intimate, and wonderful, really," she said. She rattled off a few names, ones that included all ages: Daisy Danvers's mom, Laura, a few of her friends, a stylist from MJ's Salon. "Oh, and Tess came. I was especially happy to see her. Lucky's right. She really needs times of quiet and peace and soft music. Margaret came, too. The knitting relaxes her in a way I hadn't noticed before. She sat by herself and didn't say much, but I could see her body loosen, her face relax."

"Birdie talked to Harry today. It's so difficult for him to see the changes in someone he loves so dearly, the lapses in memory." They had all seen it happening, though few, if any of them, had talked about it. Words would make it real. Now facing it was another story. It would take a village. And the villagers would all be there.

Izzy's face grew pensive. "In the middle of all this mess, there are moments of grace," she said.

Nell looked up, unsure of where she was going, but touched by the tone in her voice.

Izzy stopped for a minute, a forgotten afghan in her hand. "There was a moment today when someone mentioned the bar over on the wharf reopening and I saw a subtle change in Margaret. Her face grew tight and that soft smile she has faded into nothing. Tess saw it, too, and she moved onto the window seat beside her. And then, well, you know that thing she does with Red? She did it with Margaret. Just very subtly and gently rubbing her neck and her arms and a hand. Margaret's face changed, softening again. Her shoulders relaxed, and she picked her knitting back up."

Izzy walked over to the bookcase and turned off the music. Her head was down. "It was touching," she said softly.

Nell's cell phone rang, breaking into the

moment, but not erasing it. Nell tucked it away and answered Ben's call.

Pizza, he said. He and Sam were sitting on the floor playing with Abby's new *Paw Patrol* characters — oh, and Abby was playing also — but they were now headed to Papa Diego's for cheese pizza. Abby wanted them to come, too.

Papa Diego's Pizza and Karaoke Lounge was crowded, but Ben and Sam had found a place in a corner and the women spotted them right away. Abby was standing on the booth seat watching a group of girls at the microphone, singing along with Neil Diamond as he belted out "Cherry Cherry Christmas."

Izzy hurried over to cover Abby with kisses. Nell squeezed in next to Ben and gave him one of her own.

"Long day?" he asked, looping an arm around her shoulder.

"They all seem to be these days."

Ben nodded. He turned slightly away from the Perrys as Sam and Izzy caught up with Abby's antics and day. "Jerry says they have leads. A serious one, although proof seems to be in short supply, or, at the least, difficult. A couple of pieces aren't sliding into place."

Nell listened carefully. She and Izzy had almost hesitated about coming to dinner, feeling they were so close to exactly that. Pieces sliding into place. Tangled clues right out in front of them that just needed some unwinding. Something was about to come to them, Izzy said. Another deus ex machina. Ready to fall in their laps. All they needed was to be open for it, be ready.

But there wasn't much one could do on a Sunday night. And passing up Abby's pizza invitation was definitely not an option. Even for a deus ex machina.

"Laura Danvers is right, this is the best pizza around," Nell said as a double-tiered stand was placed in front of them and plates and napkins passed around.

Sam pointed to the sign on the table near the pile of napkins. "Made from one hundred percent recycled paper. Looks like Tess has been here."

They laughed. "She's making her mark on the environment," Ben said.

And on people, too, Nell thought.

Sam looked over at a group of women, about his and Izzy's age, heading for the microphone to belt out Mariah Carey's original rendition of "Always Be My Baby."

"Hey, Izzy, isn't that your old college friend? Jill something or other?"

Izzy strained to see around weaving bodies and finally spotted her in the quartet, arms around one another, singing their hearts out. "Beer karaoke," Pete Halloran had nicknamed it. Singing energized by a brewski or two. "You're right, it is. Jill Carpenter."

"Clark's cousin?" Nell asked.

"That's the one. She's here for a while, taking care of a sick aunt." Izzy continued to watch them as those in her own booth focused back on cleaning up spilled apple juice.

Clark's cousin who talks fast — and a lot. Izzy thought back to the confusing conversation at the Ocean's Edge. *What did Jill say about Clark and Penny?*

The group finally relinquished the microphone to a waiting couple and headed back to the bar.

"Be back in a sec. Just want to say hello." Izzy slipped out of the booth and followed them.

"You guys were terrific," she said, walking up to the group. "Mariah Carey is in big trouble."

Jill spun around, beer dribbling down her shirt, and laughed. Her cheeks were flushed from singing and beer. "Goofy, aren't we? Good to see you, Izzy. I love that about Sea

Harbor, running into friends at every turn."

"Me too. Hey, Jill, do you have a minute? I want to ask you something."

"Oh sure, of course," she said, grabbing her beer and following Izzy to a quiet corner.

"You said something at the Ocean's Edge that I didn't quite catch. Or maybe didn't hear right."

"Hmm. Okay. Was it about my cousin Clark?"

Izzy nodded. "We were talking about Penny, actually. The two of them getting married. And you mentioned how Clark was committed to *not* getting married. You said something about 'when everything happened.' A bad relationship? I wasn't sure I understood what you were saying."

"Oh sure, I remember now," Jill said, draining her beer. "We were talking about the amazing Penny. His angel from heaven. Here's the thing . . ."

Clark Turner's cousin leaned in so close that Izzy could smell the beer on her breath, and she explained, several times, in fact, exactly why Penny Turner was truly Clark's angel from heaven.

CHAPTER 33

Izzy found Cass easy to convince. It was her day off, anyway. But Cass insisted they meet at Coffee's, where the java was real, not Izzy's watered-down shop coffee.

Birdie had been for a walk and seen Gabby off to school. She'd have Harold drop her off momentarily, provided Cass reserved a chocolate croissant for her before Coffee's ran out.

Nell knew the get-together was important. She and Izzy had torn apart her conversation with Jill Carpenter until it made sense, understandable to anyone. She arrived at the coffee shop even before Cass, and staked out a back table, away from inquiring ears.

Izzy hung her coat on the back of the chair and pulled her iPad from her bag. "I took some notes last night," she explained. "Besides, one never knows when you'll need the *World Book* at your fingertips."

Quickly and logically, something Izzy was

an expert at, she told Birdie and Cass what Nell already knew. First, about their talk with Lucky.

But far more important, all about Izzy's conversation with Jill Carpenter. And her oversized praise of Penny Turner, about how Penny was the best thing that had ever happened to her cousin. An angel from heaven.

And why.

"Cass, close your mouth," she said when she was finished and the pieces had come together for each one of them with a resounding thud. The surprise that she and Nell had slept with was clear on the faces of Birdie and Cass.

"Ben said the police are making progress, and that they needed a couple pieces to slide in place."

"I'd say they're sliding nicely," Birdie said.

"Almost," Izzy said.

Getting close, having some confirmation about what they *felt* to be true, was exciting. But coming to grips with the fact that lives of people they knew would be disrupted forever was sobering. And sad.

Izzy opened her bag and rummaged around for her phone to check in with Mae. And then she remembered.

She had stashed it on the bookshelf during yesterday's knitting session and then gone off for pizza without it. Sam had said it was a good thing. Separation for one night from a phone. Everyone should try it. And he had guilted Izzy into leaving it in the shop overnight.

"Here," Cass said, handing her phone across the table.

Izzy punched in Mae's cell and asked if maybe someone could run it down to Coffee's. Mae was back in a second. "No phone, Iz. I looked all around, the floor, behind books. You sure it's not in that huge bag you carry?"

Izzy looked in her bag again. But, yes, she was sure she had left it at the store. She had put it down on top of a pattern book Laura Danvers had ordered. And when she handed Laura the book later, she checked her phone for messages, then set it back on the shelf.

"Weird," she said, looking at the others.

They all commiserated, then chastised themselves and each other for being so dependent on cell phones.

Izzy turned on her iPad, clicking on the *Find My iphone* app. "It probably slipped behind something at the shop," she said.

The map appeared, the red dot telling her exactly where her phone was. But it wasn't at home. Or at the shop.

"That's impossible. That can't be." She

nibbled on her lip, thinking, then looked at the others. "I think the app is screwy, but I need to check," Izzy said. She stood and began to gather up her belongings.

"Not alone, you're not," Cass said, and the others echoed the same as they followed her out to Nell's car and piled in.

"Treasure hunt!" Cass cheered, trying to lift Izzy's frown.

Nell parked in the small, narrow parking lot near Beech Tree Woods.

"This makes no sense at all," Izzy mumbled as they began walking down the path.

"Siri makes mistakes now and then. Perhaps that app does, too," Birdie said. "But we'll find your phone, one way or another." She walked ahead with Izzy, breathing in the smells of the trees, the dappled sunlight guiding them closer to the water.

Izzy checked her iPad when the path split in two, turning down the narrower path. The one that led directly to Tess Bean's cottage by the sea.

They could see Tess's bike tracks as they walked through the trees, the water soon becoming visible ahead.

"It's so beautiful down here," Nell said. "I can see why Tess loves it."

The trees finally gave way to a small clearing with a cottage tucked back against the trees. There were curtains on the windows and what had probably been a thriving summer garden off to the side.

Izzy looked around. "The app tells you where, but not *exactly* where." They started scouting around the ground, realizing the closer they got to the water, the less chance they'd have of finding it.

Nell looked up at the cottage. "If Tess is home, she's going to think she's being attacked." She headed toward the door, just as it opened.

Tess stepped out on the stoop. "Hi. What's going on? Are you clamming? Season's over, I'm afraid."

Izzy looked up and laughed. "So sorry, Tess." And then she explained about a wayward app that had brought them to her house.

Tess looked dumbfounded. "Here? That's crazy," she said, although she hesitated slightly when she said it. Then she frowned, looking around the yard.

"Let's check my place," she finally said.

"That's even crazier," Izzy said. "How would my phone get in your house?" But she followed her inside the cozy, neat cabin. It smelled of soap and pine and a slightly floral scent from a dried bouquet of wildflowers that Tess had arranged in an old glass bottle. Everywhere Izzy looked were touches of nature, a worn woolen rug, the fish yarn display that Mae had given her, bowls of acorns and walnuts looking like art.

"It's beautiful, Tess," Izzy said, her voice in awe.

"Thanks, but, honestly, Iz, I don't think the phone is here. The place is so small I would have already tripped over —" And then she stopped midsentence. She walked to the window and looked out at a small shed, tucked into the woods a few yards from where they stood.

"Oh, Margaret, no," Tess whispered to herself. She walked back outside and headed toward the lean-to.

Izzy watched from the window, then came outside just as Tess opened a small creaking door, crouched down, and disappeared into darkness.

Izzy and the others started to walk over, but Tess emerged and walked back toward them. "I need to explain something," she said. She took a deep breath, then began.

"Sometimes people with early dementia have personality changes — the changes may come and go. Some accuse others of stealing. And then there are a few who may do the stealing — the borrowing — themselves. It took me a while to realize that Margaret Garozzo was taking things, but when I did, if I saw her with them, I would try to return them. I knew she hid them somewhere, but she wouldn't tell me where. And I didn't want to frustrate her. She feels safe with me and that's important to her. But I think I've found her stash." She looked at Izzy. "And I suspect your phone is right on the top."

Izzy smiled. "Oh my. Oh, dear Margaret."

"She walks out here often. I just didn't know she was bringing me all these gifts."

"How do you know how to accommodate Margaret, how to help her?" Nell asked.

Tess's answer was simple. And utterly compassionate.

"I discovered my mother had early dementia. I took care of her until she died, and I learned lots of things in the process." She smiled. "She still hated me, and I wasn't crazy about her. But at least I could help her along the journey. Margaret is different. She is a lovely lady." Tess went inside her house, then came out in a second, holding an empty box and a flashlight. "Let's get your phone out of there before the woodland creatures eat it."

They walked to the shed door and watched in amazement as Tess carefully pulled things out of a pile in the dark building. Izzy's phone, Birdie's knitting set, books and nails, and Gracie's ceramic salt and pepper shakers. Mayor Scaglia's Tiffany compact. And then she kept going. Even remnants of Mae's ancient ham sandwich were visible.

Each piece was a piece of Harbor Road, the stores Margaret loved. The people she loved. The street where she worked nearly every day of her adult life.

"They're little pieces of her life," Tess said. "It's touching." Tess peered back inside, looking around the ground to be sure she wasn't missing anything.

Izzy clicked on her phone flashlight to help, bending low and moving the light around the dirt floor.

It was Cass, leaning over Izzy's shoulder, who spotted it, just as the beam of light turned the dull artifact into a shiny piece of silver.

And it was Izzy who cried out.

The missing piece.

Izzy and Cass recognized it instantly. They had seen a man wear that same silver slide with the turquoise stone. The slide that had held the leather strands of his bolo tie neatly together.

The slide that probably came off in another man's hand as he desperately grasped onto the tie to save himself from falling to his death.

The slide that Margaret Garozzo found in a dead man's hand when, early the next morning, she walked down the wrong path on her way to pick up plastic trash.

A bad man in Margaret's mind.

But Clark Turner's shiny slide was beautiful.

CHAPTER 34

It was what the police needed, the two pieces that tied up the case.

Ben poured drinks as they gathered at the Endicotts' house early that evening. The kitchen island was already filled with pickup food, anything Nell could find in the refrigerator or cupboard and a few things that had magically appeared as friends gathered.

The days had been long. And this one seemed to be the longest of all. Police cars. Sirens. And a man they knew in jail.

But it was finally over.

Cass leaned over the island and grabbed a hunk of cheese. "It almost makes me think we were walking around with dark glasses on. This is all so clear now, so . . ."

". . . so in front of us," Gracie filled in. "And it's been in front of us all along. That day near the rocks when Margaret stood staring at Bobby Abbott, except Bobby Abbott wasn't there anymore. But she still saw him, like she had that awful Sunday morning when she'd walked down the wrong path."

"But went away with a treasure. Clark Turner's bolo slide."

The mention of Clark's name brought a sadness to the room. They had all known him. And liked him.

"It's a mystery why good people sometimes give in to that dark part of themselves," Birdie said. "It seems Clark did it for love."

"But he had love," Tess said.

Much to their pleasure Tess had joined them at Ben and Nell's that evening. It was bittersweet, and Nell worried it would be difficult for her. On the one hand, her brother's murderer was in jail. But on the other? On the other, it brought a difficult history into the light of day — and put to rest.

Tess told them that she needed the company of the four women who had traveled this recent journey with her. She certainly understood people's feelings about her brother. Her own feelings were layered and complicated and would probably take her a long time to sort through.

"When did someone suspect Clark Turner?" Tess asked, seeming to find comfort in standing between Birdie and Izzy. "I liked Clark."

"A lot of people did," Ben said. "But Penny's relationship with your brother always brought Clark into the picture, as far as the police were concerned. They knew about Penny's affair with him from Harbor Club staff Bobby had bragged to. That put Clark into the jealous-husband frame immediately," Ben said.

"But the irony is that wasn't why Clark killed him," Nell said. "It was Izzy who solved that part of the puzzle, something we'd been grappling with."

"No, it was my talkative friend Jill. I mean, who tells someone in a bar that her relative had testicular cancer when he was in college and the chemo made him sterile?"

"Apparently, Jill," Cass said, pouring herself a glass of fizzy water.

"Right," Izzy said. "According to Jill, the doctors told Clark he'd never have kids, not ever. So he decided he wouldn't get married. He'd been taught that having children was essential to marriage, the main reason for it. Clark didn't mind too much because he liked cats and dogs better than most people. But then he met Penny, and he fell hard."

"Did Penny know Clark was sterile?" Sam

asked. "You would think that might have come up."

"No," Ben said. "At least that's what he told the police. He was crazy about her and couldn't chance anything that might take her away from him."

"And then there was Penny — who really wanted the marriage to work, had her own vision of the perfect family, the perfect wife, and a perfect child. Even ordering meals from Harry's deli so Clark would think she was an amazing cook. The sad thing is she didn't need to do any of those things. All he wanted was her," Nell said. "Such sadness."

"But Penny got pregnant?" Tess asked. "How does that fit in?"

"Bobby had been after her for a long time," Gracie said. "Lucky Bianchi said it played itself out in the bar. Bobby liked the way Penny was so self-assured, didn't really care about him one way or the other. A challenge."

"The police talked to Penny this afternoon, but briefly," Ben said. "She'd been trying to get pregnant, to have the perfect, normal family. But when it didn't seem to be working with Clark, she gave it a go with Bobby, thinking she had nothing to lose. Maybe she'd get pregnant and Clark would think it was his baby. And, voila, it worked.

She was well on her way to having the perfect family."

"But of course Clark knew," Danny said.

"Sure," said Nell. "He knew he couldn't father children. But he only cared about Penny, so he went along with it."

"Chief Thompson said Clark completely broke down and confessed everything. Every single thing he did was for Penny. He wanted the baby, the new house he was planning for them, and, more than anything, he wanted Penny. But that Saturday night —"

"The night of the bolo tie," Cass clarified.

"Apparently, Bobby had found out she was pregnant and was joking about it. Penny read him the riot act that night, but Clark overheard, and his fear that Bobby might try to interfere pushed him off the deep end."

"I can't imagine Bobby would have done a thing. He certainly wouldn't have wanted a child," Gracie said.

"But Clark couldn't be sure. He knew Penny had met Bobby in the cabin, so he couldn't be sure of that, either. He went over that night and set it on fire thinking any traces of Bobby and Penny being together would be erased," Cass said. "His fingerprints will be there right alongside

Penny and Bobby's."

"And Izzy's, Abby's, and Nell's!" Ben laughed.

No one had asked before, and Nell hadn't thought about it. But she did now, a sadness coming with the thought. And an image of a young woman suffering a great loss. Alone. Sitting on a cold, hard boulder.

"What happened with Penny? Where is she?"

Ben hesitated, then realized that although it might not make the first page, it would certainly make the second. "Penny knew Clark had gone back to the bar that night. And she knew he had overheard Bobby joking about her being pregnant. She put it together, knew Clark had killed Abbott.

But she also knew she was partly responsible for it all, and decided to let it be. They would have their baby. Their perfect life. Until she had the miscarriage. For reasons only she knows — probably reasons of the heart — she packed up her things and she left Sea Harbor, left Clark. The police know where she is and they've talked to her today. She's told them everything she knows and it all fits. And that's all we know."

The group was silent for a moment. Outside, night was falling and a pot of Garozzo's soup, heating up on Nell's stove, was creating magical aromas. Nell walked over to the kitchen window and looked out. At first, she thought she was seeing a hazy reflection of the lamplights dotting the backyard pathway. But a second look revealed a soft white blanket of snow gently falling and covering the path.

It's perfect, she thought. *Cleansing.*

She turned back to see Birdie holding a glass in the air. Her other arm held Tess Bean close. And it was to Tess that she looked when she gave her toast.

"To friends. To family. Forever grateful."

Chapter 35

It was Gabby's idea, with help from her friend Daisy, and it touched Birdie deeply.

The holiday knitting *hygge* would be held at the Favazza estate, in the family room that spanned the back of the magnificent home, but was as intimate and cozy as a small den.

"It's perfect," Gabby said. "It screams *hygge.*"

She was right. The room *was* perfect. Eight-foot windows that looked out over the ocean in one direction, the harbor in the other, but it was the fireplace that Gabby knew would make it memorable. The enormous structure that Sonny Favazza had commissioned men from the quarry to build rose all the way up to the twelve-foot ceiling, the hearth itself big enough for Gabby to lie in.

"But you and your friends can suggest things, too," Gabby assured her grandmother, not wanting Birdie to feel left out.

But Birdie didn't feel left out, not in the slightest, not when she had the great pleasure of watching her own granddaughter bring to life the room that she and Sonny Favazza had danced in and had loved in and had lived in through the great joys and great sorrows of their life together. It was a holiday miracle.

The evening weather turned out to be a perfect one for the fire that Harold had laid for the event — cold skies with moisture in the air. Wintry air. A full moon shining down on the ocean below, dancing sparkles like tiny skaters twirling on water.

Long cedar ropes hung from the ends of wooden beams that stretched across the ceiling, looping along the sides of the room. Cushioned love seats and chairs were close enough to feel the warmth of the blazing fire and covered with fleecy throws, just in case guests' comfort clothes needed a layer.

Gabby and Daisy had collected thick, wooly socks and woven them into a wreath that Harold hung above the mantel. Near each chair and couch were baskets of yarn, containers of needles. And all around the room were platters of cookies, cakes, and small sandwiches, and a pot of thick soup was kept warm on the sideboard.

Just inside the terrace doors stood the tallest tree Gabby had ever seen, filled with silver balls and tiny lights. In between the lights were hand-knit sheep and sleds and reindeer, and knit socks and beanies for children's charities in every color of the rainbow.

Birdie stood at the door with Gabby and Daisy as the cars began coming up the drive. Women, carrying knitting bags and dressed comfortably in festive pajamas and robes and thick fuzzy slippers, walked up to the door.

Izzy, Cass, and Nell arrived first, ready to help with last-minute details. But they weren't needed at all. All they needed to do was help welcome the stream of knitters who had come to be warmed, to be content.

"This is magical," Tess said in a hushed tone. She walked slowly into the family room with Margaret on her arm.

"A *hyggelig* room," Gabby corrected with a laugh as she walked by.

"Danish magic," Margaret said, musing that she must have a bit of Danish blood in her somewhere. Her smile was soft, peaceful.

Tess chuckled and walked with her around the room, over to a grand piano in the corner, its lid covered with candles, tall and short, fat and skinny. Margaret sat on the bench and hummed an old tune, then played a few notes. Then a few more.

The doctors had prescribed diet and exercise and medication for Margaret, but her memory was fragile, they said. It would be a journey with deserts and mountains, and sometimes a sweet, soothing peace. But what fed Margaret's spirit right now were people. And walking. Knitting and caring. And Tess Bean's soothing, comforting massages. And Harry's love, now calmer, softer, and understanding.

Gabby, in her red-and-green-checked long johns, walked beside Birdie, helping people settle in, their knitting in their laps and their voices softer than usual, some friends not talking at all. "We're creating a *hyggelig* memory," she said, tossing out the word she'd mastered and was throwing around as if she had invented it.

Birdie laughed. "We're creating joy and peace and comfort. Or encouraging our friends to find it in themselves."

Izzy sat on the arm of Nell's chair, watching her aunt's fingers moving in graceful rhythm. As old as time.

Cass was curled up on the love seat next to them, a plaid afghan over her pajama bottoms, her feet cozy in pink rabbit slippers.

An intimate kind of smile on her face, as if she were speaking to someone they couldn't see.

She looked sleepy.

Birdie looked over at her, too. A look of love and delight. The knitters had had their own *hygge* the evening before, and Cass, a *hyggelig* naysayer not that many days before, had ended up being the unlikely center of it. Sharing with them how her life was about to change. And how each of them was to have an integral role to play in helping a lobsterwoman take on a whole new project.

Birdie settled a soft afghan over Cass's knees, then sat, picking up her knitting. Gabby's orange sweater was growing as fast as her amazing granddaughter herself.

Izzy moved to the couch and sat down next to Cass. She watched as her friend reached for her knitting bag, thinking about the ties that bind a friendship together. Was it true that you might feel a friend's emotion before she, herself, did? Or hold her thoughts and her emotions so tight they became a part of you?

Nell's eyes were on Cass, too, and her heart full. Cass and Izzy. Birdie. What gifts these women were. And the gifts continued to come.

To a few others in the room, Cass's smile

seemed softer tonight. And secretive. But Cass didn't handle secrets well, and the smile soon gave way to simple happiness as she pulled out her newest project and spread it across her lap.

Others in the room glanced over and then smiles grew all around the room.

Next to Cass, Izzy was quiet and peaceful, and filled with a new kind of joy as her dearest friend in the world pulled a ball of baby-soft yellow cashmere yarn from her bag, and began picking up stitches on a tiny newborn blanket.

Cass held it up for all to see, then grinned happily as shouts and cheers filled the room and eyes dropped to the tiny bump just visible beneath her pajama tops. Cass patted it gently.

Nell, Izzy, and Birdie wiped away their tears and joined the happy congratulations.

New life. Perhaps the nicest Christmas gift of all.

ACKNOWLEDGMENTS

My warmest thanks to Dr. Jerry Wyckoff, who has shared many insights with me into parenting and children, their emotions, and their world.

And to a reader and new friend, Kristen Frederickson, who has generously given me permission to reprint a recipe from her own cookbook (written with her daughter Avery Curran), *Tonight at 7:30: One Family's Life at the Table.* Kristen is also the author of a delightful blog, *Kristen in London.*

My thanks to Linda Dawkins, my South African reader and friend and talented artist, who has granted permission to reprint her original pattern for the forest glade cowl.

As always, my warmest thanks to the Kensington family, to my Jane Rotrosen family, to my 'idea friends' who tackle my stories with verve, suggestions, and always encouragement, and to my readers, who keep me inspired to write about these four

Sea Harbor women.

And to my family and friends, whose patience knows no bounds.

Thank you.

SLOW-BRAISED CHICKEN THIGHS WITH OLIVES, CAPERS, AND BAY LEAVES

From *Tonight at 7:30: One Family's Life at the Table*
By Kristen Frederickson and Avery Curran
Reprinted with permission of the authors

Serves 4
Turn oven to 300°F/150°C

8 chicken thighs, skin-on, bone-in
6 cloves garlic, minced
1 white onion, cut in half and sliced thickly
1/2 cup/100g oil-cured black olives, pitted and cut in half
4 Tbs capers (rinsed, if cured in salt)
6 fresh bay leaves
1/2 cup olive oil
1/2 cup chicken stock
1/2 cup white wine
1 lemon, juiced
Fresh black pepper

Lay the thighs skin-side up in a large baking dish. Sprinkle over them the garlic, onion, olives, and capers. Tuck the bay leaves in among the thighs. Pour the olive oil, chicken stock, white wine, and lemon juice over the chicken. Grind fresh pepper over the thighs and cover the dish tightly with foil.

Bake at 300°F/150°C for two hours, then remove the foil and raise the heat to 425°F/220°C and cook for a further 30 minutes. Serve with steamed basmati rice or warmed sourdough bread, to appreciate the cooking juices. If you want to make more of a fuss, strain the cooking juices through a sieve into a frying pan and sprinkle over a tablespoon of flour. Whisk over low heat to make beautiful gravy.

You can find this recipe and many more in Kristen and her daughter Avery's beautiful cookbook, *Tonight at 7:30: One Family's Life at the Table.*

Kristen's blog about her life in London can be found at www.kristeninlondon.com.

FOREST GLADE COWL©

Designed by Linda Dawkins
Reprinted with permission from the designer

From the designer: *I'm happy with the stitch technique that developed from a yarn over and a knit 2 together. These simple stitches have manifested into a slanting pattern forming a cowl. The cowl is designed in multiples of 2, so it's easy to make it larger or smaller by reducing or increasing the stitches by 2.*

Measurement: 58 inches around and can be wrapped two or three times

Materials
8 (5mm) circular needles
100 grams of DK yarn
Sewing needle for the ends
Stitch marker

Abbreviations

yo: yarn over (wrap the yarn under the needle and over to the back). This creates a hole.

Pattern Instructions

Cast on 220 stitches and join for knitting in the round, place a stitch marker at the start of the round.

Round 1: Knit

Round 2: (yo, knit 2 together) Repeat across the round.

Rounds 3–5: Repeat round 2.

Round 6: Knit

Round 7: Purl

Rounds 2–7 are the rounds that make up the pattern. If you want a thicker cowl, just continue with the pattern repeats (and add another skein of yarn). When you are finished with your last pattern repeat, just finish with a knit round and not a purl for the border.

Bind off loosely (use a larger needle size if you prefer).

(Reminder: If you would like to shorten or lengthen this cowl, just use multiples of 2.)

Visit Linda's blog for more notes on this pattern, pictures of the finished cowl, and additional patterns: www.naturalsuburbia.com/2013/01/the-forest-glade-cowl-pattern.html

ABOUT THE AUTHOR

Sally Goldenbaum is the author of over forty novels, most recently the Seaside Knitters Mystery Series set in the fictional town of Sea Harbor, Massachusetts. Born in Manitowoc, Wisconsin, Sally now lives in Gloucester, Massachusetts, with her husband, Don. In addition to writing mysteries, Sally has taught philosophy, Latin, and creative writing, edited bioethics and veterinary healthcare journals, and worked in public television at WQED Pittsburgh (then home to *Mr. Rogers' Neighborhood*).

The employees of Thorndike Press hope you have enjoyed this Large Print book. All our Thorndike, Wheeler, and Kennebec Large Print titles are designed for easy reading, and all our books are made to last. Other Thorndike Press Large Print books are available at your library, through selected bookstores, or directly from us.

For information about titles, please call:
(800) 223-1244

or visit our website at:
gale.com/thorndike

To share your comments, please write:
Publisher
Thorndike Press
10 Water St., Suite 310
Waterville, ME 04901